Storm of Silence

Also by Geoffrey Mehl...

Fiction (Tommy Kane/Mandy Owens)
STRAY CATS
NINE LIVES
GO PHISH

Landscaping/Sustainable Design
PENNYSLVANIA NATURALLY

PERENNIALS: HABITAT AND CULTURE

A GARDENER'S GUIDE TO NATIVE PLANTS
OF NORTHEASTERN PENNSYLVANIA

Learn more at www.geoffmehl.com

ISBN-13: 978-0-9862766-8-2
ISBN-10: 0-9862766-8-5
Printed in the United States of America

Storm of Silence

by Geoffrey Mehl

Chapter One

The bus swerved right. Andrea Delvento's concentration on a ragged paperback book evaporated.

The driver leaned hard on the horn as he veered sharply left. Andi looked out the window. Some poor guy changing a tire. Ford pickup, white, late model, couldn't catch the plate. Barely on the shoulder, tight against a guide rail. Close call. She exhaled. Tough break. At least she didn't have to worry about breaking down somewhere in rural Pennsylvania, probably miles from the nearest exit.

Instead, she could stagger through a gooey romance novel found abandoned in the terminal waiting room many miles ago, where her dreams had soured into lousy memories. She could ride a half-empty bus filled with air that seemed musty and stale. In a cramped seat. Across the aisle from a snoring guy. Two rows back from a couple with a baby that finally stopped crying. After four hours. And who knows how long before that, at a stop that served terrible sandwiches and awful coffee. With fetid restrooms. The stop where the baby couple boarded the bus to join a mini-community of people who did their best to ignore each other.

* * *

Clay Garrison squatted next to a shuddering wheel cover, inverted to form makeshift prep tray for six lug nuts. He glared at the tattered tire. Blown. Shredded. Demolished. Couldn't hang in long enough, a victim of carelessness.

Whooshes of air from passing cars were one thing, rushes of air in the wake of passing traffic pushing hard, sometimes too hard, against his back. The gust from the bus and the blare of the horn had to be the crowning touch on a day, a week, a month at rock bottom. "Thanks, pal, I really needed that," he said, mostly to the lug wrench in his hand.

He struggled for balance in a crouch grown weary. In a simple act of defiance, he rearranged the lug nuts back into a perfect line in the wheel cover. *Get your chin off your chest, buddy. Shake it off.*

Everybody said he'd done the right thing, making a stand. Then they didn't just stab him in the back. They denied they were even in the room. It had been a while since it all went sour, and the taste was still rotten in his mouth. Only tomorrow kept him going.

The blown tire leaned against the door further to his right. The old truck was more rusty than trusty, just transportation. He sighed. No sense in being angry or disappointed about the tire. The warning came twelve hundred miles ago. A grizzled mechanic named Frank wore a grease-stained jump suit, had a stubble beard and a mouthful of bad teeth. Frank had wiped his hands on a gray rag when he explained a slightly out of alignment front end caused the tire wear on the inside. Clay said no thanks to the cost of repair and hoped the tire would reach his destination. Frank had shrugged and said maybe, but don't hit no potholes.

Which, of course, he did. Pulling left to the middle seam of two eastbound lanes to avoid a nasty-looking pothole on the shoulder edge, he clipped the crater of a big one. The bang jolted the truck and coffee in the cup holder sloshed over the edge. Then came the pull as the tire went *whoomp-whoomp-whoomp* on a sad trek to gravel, miles from the nearest exit.

Coulda, shoulda, woulda. Lately, it had been the story of Clay's life, not a great place to be at the age of twenty-six, already second-guessing too many not-so-great decisions.

One by one, the nuts returned to the wheel. New tires would be another pinch on a thin wallet, and no way could he ask Mitch for a little help. Being out of work and having a tougher than expected time finding a new uniform and badge had worn thin. He sighed, pursed his lips and reached for the last lug nut. Tough it out, get it done, maybe catch a break tomorrow.

* * *

Andi yawned and stretched to ease stiffness in her shoulder. The romance novel had all the appeal of late-night incident report forms. She shifted her weight to reassure her butt that it wouldn't be much further. But knees ached and the rocking motion of the bus discouraged a notion to stand to flush circulation into her calves.

The trusty watch on her wrist had stalled again. A dying battery, for sure. *Coulda, woulda, shoulda*. But ten bucks was a lot to ask at this time in her life. Maybe her luck would improve soon, but for now she could only guess the time as after four o'clock.

She returned to the novel and the dreary fortune of poor Lynette, whose torrid affair with Vincent had gone down in flames when the evil Caroline ratted them out to Vincent's wife, unexpectedly revived from some sort of coma. Vincent was a real sleazeball, typical of too many men she'd known. Andi closed her eyes and envied people who could sleep on a moving bus. The infant further forward stirred for a moment, but quieted, a lucky break. Yes. It had to be after four. Probably on her way home from work, Mer would change and then be back in time to greet Andi with the effusive smile she'd offered ever since they met in tricycle days.

Everybody else knew Meredith Barnes as Mer, but to Andi, *Mer-Bear,* the one person in the whole world who understood Andi, and the one person Andi trusted completely. They would laugh and tease and giggle and finish each other's sentences. The thought brought a smile to Andi's face, giving her a sense of calm and patience after a long day, a long week, a long couple of months.

Mer-Bear had been there when the work and effort and promise and dreams evaporated. Like those of the insipid Lynette, who should have known better way back in Chapter Ten when Vincent started hitting on her.

Andi sighed. A least Lynette didn't lose her job, her dignity, four years of work in college and months of arduous training. Just a creepy boyfriend, and a fictional one at that. Maybe Andi would hurry through the last few chapters to find out if Lynette got her life back on track or went off to some sort of monastery. Perhaps in Tibet. Where they keep deranged twin brothers and sisters that fly out to haunt fictional heroes and heroines.

Enough. She closed the book and put it aside. Lynette would have to remain an enigma, except to the author and publisher and bored secretaries in Dubuque, Iowa. Andi would focus on tomorrow. A recruiter of some sort, maybe a slot on a decent force where talent mattered and upward mobility came from merit, not who did the groping.

Mer-Bear would not approve of the business outfit in her bag. Mer went for bright and flounce and daring necklines, which probably worked well in commercial real estate. Law enforcement was very different and conservative seemed best for a federal position.

Mer would want Andi to wear her hair down, tumbling across her shoulders. But this time the better choice would be up, like classy assistant prosecutors did.

While it appeared to be a welcome chance in an awful job market where ugly words in the grapevine took their toll, there was no way she'd succumb to some perv. She'd flip burgers in fast food before going anywhere near that situation again.

The bus braked, paused, and lumbered into the terminal. Andi sat up, leaning toward the window as it pulled into a long platform, where bags would roll right out of the bay and onto smooth concrete. Mer-Bear, waved, wearing a gaudy pink t-shirt with huge block letters that said, "Andi's Pal," with a big arrow pointing up to her grinning face. She unfurled a matching shirt that simply said, "Andi."

Andi beamed and waved back. Gosh, what a perfect friend.

* * *

Clay braked to a stop behind a paused Greyhound Bus. Turn signals proclaimed the driver planned a right turn, probably into a narrow space because the big vehicle went wide left for the turn.

It gave Clay a chance to check the address on a scrap of paper. Yeah, three blocks up, one over and then a slight left at a Y-inter-section, the one he could never remember the name of, the one that bore to the right.

Four twenty-five. Probably home from work, Mitch maybe had a couple of cold ones in the fridge. Clay yawned and arched his shoulders. A few minutes to go.

The bus driver must have been waiting for some sort of traffic to clear, but finally it crept forward and into the station. Clay took his foot off the brake. The pickup gently rolled forward, picking up speed once the bus left the street and a couple of pedestrians scampered to the curb.

Downtown remained a mixed bag of storefronts, couple of bars, a few restaurants. His dad's old place had been carved up into a Chinese takeout, some sort of jewelry boutique, and a shop that sold cupcakes. A big "going out of business" sale sign hung in the window of the cupcake company.

All the action had moved to the edge of town, a strip of big-box stores and chain restaurants. Not much of a memory, Big Bill Garrison's Steakhouse had slid into bankruptcy when trendy names opened up a buffet of shopping centers.

Which is why Clay never went into the restaurant business. His dad, a broken man by then, had pushed and prodded Clay to go into law enforcement, calling upon long-time drinking buddy Herb Conley to apply encouragement. After his dad succumbed to smoking, drinking and too much rich food, the retired police chief opened some doors, got a scholarship going, moved to Florida and died of liver failure six months later.

A glance at what used to be Big Bill's gave Clay a reality check and focus on making the next turn. Nothing like coming home, tail between legs, but of the guys, Mitch Whelan would be cool with it. Together, they had the best — and the worst — season in high school football. They shared a dorm room and then an apartment at college. They split many a pitcher at many a bar. Criminal justice and journalism got along fine.

Times were tough for Mitch, too. Dumped by that wacky, well, whatever her name, he'd been taking it out reporting on the politicians at the courthouse. Maybe he was finally getting it back together. An open parking space right in front of Mitch's place. First lucky break of the day, week, heck, month.

* * *

Unabashed squeals, open arms, an embrace that made everything better. And then a step back to admire the shirt.

"Oh, my gosh, that is so, so..."

Meredith laughed. "Yes. Exactly."

The guy from across the aisle on the bus, who'd snored for

hours, stared as he passed.

Andi beamed and pointed to herself. "I'm the pal, okay?"

He looked away and hurried on.

Meredith continued to chuckle. "C'mon, Kit-Kit, let's get your things."

"Oh, wow. I haven't heard that since —"

"I know, about fourth grade."

"Fifth. You were calling me that when I went ga-ga over some boy and insisted you stop."

"That boy was Nathan English and he is still a loser."

The driver tugged Andi's bag from the luggage bay and parked it at her feet.

Meredith cocked an eyebrow. "This is it? One lonely carry-on? You're planning on staying for what, twenty minutes?"

Andi rolled her eyes. She had two dollars in her hand but gave the driver only one. "Long story. First I want to see if I can still walk. Then I want to get out of these shoes and... And thank you so much for sharing your place." She tugged the handle high and tested how easily the suitcase rolled on the pavement. "I promise not to be a bother."

Meredith laughed. "Oh, right. The two of us under the same roof? The neighborhood will never be the same. Hungry?"

"Starved. Steer me to the nearest fast-food place and I'll be fine."

"Not a chance. We're eating in."

"Mer-Bear, no! You took up, like, actual cooking?"

"More like picked it up at the supermarket on the way home. The miracle of microwaves, Andi. One of these days I'll be able to guess the times."

They reached Meredith's car and popped the trunk. "So what's on the menu?"

Mer dropped her sunglasses back down onto her nose. "I don't know exactly. Some sort of brown meat and green things, you know, like vegetables? I was in a hurry, Andi. It looked kind of healthy, okay?"

* * *

Mitch Whelan ran his fingers through his hair and scratched the back of his head. "Yeah, well, bro, no problem. I mean, the sofa's not the most comfortable place to sleep, but, hey —"

Clay grinned. "Sure beats the cab of a pickup truck. Sorry about... what's her name?"

Mitch passed a cold bottle of beer. "Don't remember, don't want to remember, don't care." He popped the cap and hoisted the beer in a toast. "Here's to old times, dude."

Clay chuckled and echoed the gesture. In the center of a cramped and disorganized living room of a second-floor apartment, the lager went down smooth and easy.

"Oh, hey, yeah. You want to eat? Probably got the growlies, big time, being on the road all day. I got some stuff, but we could order out for a couple of pies, whatever." He looked up. "Or not. Look, there's a couple of decent places to eat down the block and I still got a little on the cards. I mean, not in your league, but —"

Clay smiled and waved him off. "You're putting me up, man. Least I can do is cook. What's in the fridge?"

Mitch stepped sideways to block Clay's path. "I dunno. Food and whatever. Stuff you pick up at the convenience store when you're in the mood to be righteous."

Clay took a step forward and Mitch adjusted his block on the path.

"So, Mitch, let's have a look and —"

"You don't want to go in there, bro."

Clay scowled and pushed past, but paused inside the portal. "Dude. This is not a kitchen. This is a disaster."

Mitch winced. "Yeah, well, y'know, been busy and stuff."

Clay began to roll up the sleeves of his shirt. "Uh-huh. Okay, first, we clean. *Then* we cook."

Chapter Two

Meredith had only a quarter bottle of white wine in her apartment. Her solution to the shortage proved marvelous.

She had gently worn down Andi's reluctance to go anywhere after a non-descript meal, catching up and relaxing laughter. She had politely ignored difficulties and the mystery of the recruiting note that arrived in the mail the week before. And had suggested they go out for wine.

"It'll take the edge off your interview anxiety," Mer had promised. "No pressure, just people who come mostly for the music, couples mostly." As Andi raised an eyebrow, Meredith confessed. "Well, okay, a few guys. But decent."

"Oh, Mer, I don't know. I'm not exactly in the mood and I want to get focused on this meeting tomorrow."

Meredith had replied with a look of impatient disapproval, put her hands on Andi's shoulders and leaned in. "Listen to your Mer-Bear, okay? You need to unwind. Remember that jazz place we used to go to, near campus? You loved it. Dragged me there every Friday night. Pete's is better."

Andi nodded. The campus town pub was cozy but sophisticated, the alternative to rock concerts and techno-bars, where people drank domestic wine and upscale beer from glasses instead of tossing shots and doing whatever drugs were fashionable at the moment. "Hm. Better? That's hard to believe."

Andi nodded while Mer gathered her phone and began tapping out a message.

After a moment, Mer smiled. "Well, let me prove it then. Besides, once we split the last of the chardonnay, all we have is water. Thursdays they have this great trio — piano, standup, drums — a group that does mostly old standards."

Andi sighed.

"Your kind of music, Kit-Kit."

"Not interested in picking up any men."

Meredith's tone mixed reassurance with encouragement. "We'll dress down, real casual. I've got a t-shirt that says 'Get Lost', but gosh, Andi, it's impossible to make you unattractive. We'll have to make do with discouraging vibes, maybe hinting we're lesbians. C'mon. It'll be fun."

"Okay, okay."

A smallish bar, Pete's was intimate, busy and partway down what must have been the usual Main Street of town. Bar stools were full, but a few open tables on the opposite side gave Andi hope. Mer ignored them and led Andi to empty seats at the piano bar, toward the back.

Andi settled onto a tall stool in front of a little card that said reserved. She nodded as the guy with the mic introduced the trio. "Oh, wow, this *is* nice."

Meredith shrugged. "So I know the bartender — *professionally* —and he owes me a couple of spots. Least I can do for my best friend, right?"

"You're amazing."

The trio waved to polite applause and started the set with "Pick Yourself Up." The bar guy arrived with glasses of wine and nibbles. Music bathed Andi's mind, washed away anxiety and shampooed her brain with comfort.

* * *

Mitch Whelan displayed a pair of tall-necked brown bottles. "Last of the lager, buddy. If we want to get wasted, we're gonna have to go out."

Clay chuckled. "Not tonight, pal. Gotta see this guy tomorrow, maybe a new spot somewhere. Recruiters don't usually rep small departments, so I'm hoping for mid-size and up, civil service, good track to major crime."

"Yeah, I hear ya. Not like this dump. The department is pure politics, where you gotta know the right people, kiss the right butt, keep your mouth shut."

Clay lifted the fresh bottle in a toast. "You got that right."

Mitch shuffled around trying to decide what to say.

"Go ahead, buddy, say what's on your mind."

Mitch glanced back toward the kitchen. "I don't know anyone else who cleans a kitchen top to bottom *after* a meal. And what you did with that stuff in the fridge, wow, amazing."

"No big deal."

"Yeah, well, I'm sitting here feeling like crap for not having anything to offer in return."

"Trust me, the sofa's fine."

"Nah. It's a junker from some second-hand place run by a church." He brightened. "Hey! You're still into jazz, right?"

The question caught Clay off guard. It'd been a long time since he'd paid any attention to it and longer since he'd been to a club. Mitch probably had some old recordings.

"I know this spot, new, on the main drag where there used to be an appliance store. Called Pete's. Dude got a license from someplace, opened a little jazz club. Bar, a few tables, live groups four nights a week." Mitch rolled on as recollection sharpened. "Pretty good. I did a fluff piece for the weekend-entertainment section a couple of months ago."

After hundreds of miles of driving, any bar lacked appeal. "Thought you were a country-western guy."

"I am, man. But this place has some decent stuff. None of that weird modern junk or that lounge goo. I remember, bro, from when we did the bars off campus, what you went for."

Clay applauded the thoughtful memory. Plus Mitch seemed hopeful, his pride and dignity on the line for a kitchen rescue and a meal out of assorted leftovers that worked out okay.

"C'mon, Clay, let me buy you a round. Who knows, maybe we'll find a couple of chicks, have a few laughs."

Clay laughed. "Hey, I thought you swore off women, after whats-her-name, that wacky redhead —"

"Yeah, well, turned out she swung both ways and wound up getting the hots for some yoga instructor. I couldn't deal with it, bro. I mean, probably doing it wrapped up like a pair of pretzels. Whew. Gives me the willies thinking about it."

Clay nodded. "And now?"

Mitch shrugged. "Well, I gotta get back in the saddle sooner or later, right." After a moment of silence, Mitch took a hit from the bottle and sighed. "That came out, like, *wrong*, man. I meant —"

Clay raised a hand. "Okay, buddy, let's go get a beer, hear what this club's got. But I don't plan to make a late night of it."

* * *

Andi struggled to remember the last time she'd been out with fun friends, not having to chatter but rather just savor smooth sounds. Meredith correctly called it: calming, relaxing, pushing tension away.

A talented woman named Tricia Sherman, whom everyone evidently called Trish, played piano, with Jerry Something on bass and Evan Smiles on drums. They played half-hour sets, with fifteen minute breaks in between. Singles and fives halfway filled a giant brandy snifter on the piano. It hurt that she could not bring herself to spare anything of the last twenty to her name.

Mer must have sensed it. She tossed ten dollars into the tip glass, saying it came from both. Trish looked at Andi's eyes and nodded appreciation.

Andi sighed. Tomorrow absolutely had to be better. Either that, or she'd have to enlist Mer-Bear to bail her out from a mistake. Again. Maybe with her connections, she knew somebody who could find a down-and-out, ex-police officer, a job. But no rent-a-cop work. Security seemed a career dead end. Better to learn, say, real estate than do that.

Andi took the last sip of wine in the glass. Meredith would stand another round, but it would be wrong to accept. Time to lift the chin, smile, make some sort of excuse about staying sharp for the interview, have some fun, enjoy the music.

Trish smiled and looked into Andi's eyes while she laid her fingers on the keys. That wonderful signature standard of Frank Sinatra, from *Guys and Dolls*.

Oh, yes, Andi thought. The lyrics danced through her mind. "And so the best that I can do is pray... Luck be lady tonight!"

* * *

Country would have been okay. Mitch listened to it constantly in the dorm and it was hard to avoid in Oklahoma. But the moment they drifted into Pete's, time raced back to happier moments.

A solid trio laid out a bright and happy and hopeful sound and the lyrics to a great song popped up into Clay's mind. "...Stick with me baby, I'm the guy that you came in with. Luck be lady tonight."

He smiled and basked in the melody.

They snagged a pair of open stools at the bar, ordered Yuengling draft, grabbed a handful of peanuts and tuned into the music.

Mitch said, "So did I tell you or what?"

"You did. Thanks, buddy."

Mitch looked around. "Not a bad crowd for a Thursday, eh?"

"Not bad." Mitch wasn't conducting a marketing study, searching instead for solo women in a room full of couples and single guys doing the same thing. Some things never changed. But Mitch was probably right. Can't be permanently on the job. Time to lighten up and enjoy the moment. Didn't matter if bar peanuts were on the stale side, maybe by twelve to eighteen hours, and the brand too salty. Typical of many bars, they went cheap on the freebie snacks.

But crisp beer and fine music helped put thoughts of tomorrow on hold and speculation about meeting with whoever sent the letter a week ago was fading fast.

Mitch lightly jabbed Clay with an elbow. "Hey, there you go. Check out the pair at the piano bar. Oh, wow. Now *that* is one foxy chick."

Clay leaned out to look past a flock of shoulders and arms blocking his view. No luck. But then two people in the way separated. Long brown hair, tumbling over shoulders, easy smile, big brown eyes. "Yep. Very attractive."

Mitch continued to stare. "Dude. Attractive is not the word. Gorgeous is what she is. That blue sweater was made for that body."

She tossed her head when she laughed and the hair swirled with it. Despite the distance, he could see the sparkle in her eyes. But she wasn't wearing a blue sweater. Some sort of a light tan or beige turtleneck and a darker brown jacket. Classy, real classy.

The song ended with a flourish and a round of applause as the trio gently segued into a softer, slower tune with a silky, romantic air. Now Clay saw the woman in the blue sweater. Short hair, blonde, cute in a corporate sort of way. He took a long, steady sip from the beer. "Yeah, Mitch. Gorgeous. Definitely gorgeous."

* * *

Meredith looked toward the bar, probably hoping to catch the eye of the bartender for another round of wine. She chuckled and said, "Don't make a thing of it, but there's a couple of guys at the bar and one of them is staring at us, probably you. Hm. Seems kind of cute."

The trio played "I Only Have Eyes For You." Andi forced herself to look straight at Mer, feeling warmth in her cheeks that wasn't coming from the wine. "You're joking, right?"

"Nope. Not at all. Bet you can't avoid looking back. Betcha, betcha, betcha... Hah, you lose."

Andi returned her attention to Meredith. "Okay, not bad. In a puppy-dog sort of way."

"Puppy dog? You're kidding. I *really* go for guys with that bad-boy look and blond hair on the longish side, the kind that's made for my —"

"Mer-Bear! Gosh, cut it out. I'm beginning to get embarrassed. Besides. The guy has short dark hair and, okay, he's not bad looking. Besides, I said —"

"I know, I know. No more guys."

Which sounded final, absolute, arbitrary. "At least, not now. My career is a mess, my bank account is dust, my credit card is screaming. I've got to stay focused, get back on track."

"And this mystery recruiter? Doesn't sound terribly promising, if you ask me."

Defensiveness swept through Andi and she focused on her empty glass before she felt Mer's hand on the back of her own.

"I'm sorry, Andi. I was out of place. Let's enjoy the music for a while and then you can get a good night's sleep and be fresh for what will probably be another one of your stunning successes tomorrow."

Andi nodded. "Thanks, Mer-Bear. No offense taken. I'll be okay. Either way. Honest. But first, I need to make a stop in the ladies' room."

Meredith smiled appreciation at her friend's forgiveness. "That little hallway right at the end of the bar. It's on the left. If you bump into that blond guy...."

When the trio shifted into an arrangement of "A Fine Romance," Andi laughed. "You're incorrigible, Mer. Absolutely incorrigible. Back in a sec."

* * *

Mitch ordered another round, which Clay decided would be the last. "So, what do you think? Should we do the gallant thing and buy the ladies another glass of whatever they're drinking?"

"Not for me, buddy. I'm going to be in town for a day or two and I'm out of here. No offense, but there's no future for me in this kind of town."

Mitch nodded. "You're probably right. I sometimes get the feeling that I'm just killing time here myself. Maybe I ought to try for a bit more, you know, challenging."

The bartender delivered fresh glasses. He made no attempt to refill the dish of peanuts that Mitch had been munching.

Clay said, "You should, man. You're a good writer and could probably make it in the big time."

"You think?"

The beer had become old, heavy, filling. "Yeah, I think. Besides, now that you've unloaded whats-her-name, the wacky redhead, you're free to go for it."

"I dunno, bro. Pretty tough business. Like on national, I mean. Lotta guys trying to make it."

Clay softened his tone into a tease. "Yeah. Crowded field. Or you could play it safe in the smaller market, not much competition." He glanced toward the piano bar. The brunette with the brown eyes had gone. "And go for that blonde. She looks like she'd be fun."

Mitch slumped back in the stool to think about it.

Clay stood and suppressed a yawn. "Okay. Meantime, I gotta make a pit stop. Where's the —"

"End of the bar, narrow hallway. On the right."

Chapter Three

Clay slithered and apologized through a collection of bodies along the bar. The crowd had doubled in size and people sounds were making it difficult to hear the music at the opposite end.

That, plus a couple of beers and a long day on the road, carved the edge off the evening. Time to call it a night.

Two women, holding matching Manhattans and facing each other, twisted to allow passage. Seductive smiles, lubricated with alcohol. Close enough to make body contact.

Clay sucked in his body for the thinnest possible profile. "Sorry, excuse me."

The woman facing him pulled her shoulders back and leered. "Not a problem, big guy."

Clear of one obstacle, he focused on the next and ignored giggles behind him. Yeah. Time to collapse on Mitch's junker sofa. He looked up for bearings. At last. Directly in line with the restrooms sign. Half a dozen guys milled around, but this time he more assertively cleared a path.

He found a line at a hallway wide enough for one, but not two. Those huddled around the portal had to step back whenever someone of either gender finished, muffling the music. He estimated two men were ahead of him.

Then he recognized the brown jacket in front of him. Long brown hair, in loose curls cascading down and across her shoulders, half onto her back. About five-eight or five-nine, a little taller than he'd estimated from his perch at the bar.

She took half a step back to allow a departing patron to pass, the scent of her hair intoxicating. Her shoulder bumped into his chest. As she turned further, his eyes followed the line of her neck upward, into a soft and easy smile and on to her dark eyes, dark as coffee and sparkling.

She said, "Oh, gosh, I'm so sorry."

* * *

She'd collided with the guy at the bar, the one with the puppy-dog look, the one with the man Meredith had visually fondled. Well, not so puppy-dog up close. Taller than he looked from a distance, broader in the shoulders. Patient eyes, a calm, placid smile.

He raised his hands, palms out. "It's okay. No harm done. Kind of tight quarters."

"Popular bar, I guess."

"Come here often?"

She shook her head but stayed focused on his eyes. Nothing reticent or bashful. Confident, but not cocky. "No, my first time. I came with a friend."

"Ah, yes. I think you were at the piano bar."

"Yup." He wore a pale blue dress shirt, open collar, navy blue blazer and it worked well together. "And I think you were over there, with another guy?"

"Yeah, Mitch. Good friend, nice fellow."

"And how about you? Are you a regular?"

He chuckled. A cute little bashful chuckle, never losing eye contact. "No. Same as you, first time. Mitch recommended it, knowing I'm a jazz buff from way back when."

She'd been staring at him and fought embarrassment by looking away. "Me, too. But nothing too noisy or strange for me. This is a nice group, just my style. Love the old standards." She said to him, "So. Are you from around here?"

"No. Well, originally, but I've been away."

"And now you're back."

"For a couple of days."

A heavy guy, five-ten, two-twenty-five or thirty maybe, pressed in tight. He perspired profusely from his forehead and scowled. "Hey, you two gonna yak all night? You're blocking the way to the can."

Her new companion evidently didn't enjoy the proximity and attitude. He raised his left hand, palm out. "Okay, sir, I need you to take a step back..."

The heavy guy grunted. "What are you some kind of bouncer?"

"No sir. I'm a —" He paused.

Andi felt her eyebrows jump. *A what?*

"— I'm tired, had a couple of beers too many. Tell you what, sir, why don't you go ahead of me? The way you're walking, I'm betting you might not make it in time otherwise."

The heavy man looked stunned and withered on the spot. "Yeah, well, okay, buddy." He squeezed past behind and tried to scamper toward the restroom door.

Andi said, "Nice."

"Think he'll get there in time?"

"No. Not a chance. Even money says he'll wet his pants." She extended a hand. "Hi. I'm Andi."

* * *

A soft and gentle touch introduced a firm grip. She had an infectious smile and mischief danced in her eyes.

Okay, he told himself. Take a step back, find some sort of demeanor. "Clay. Clay Garrison. Nice to meet you."

"So, you're visiting — let me guess, your friend Mitch — for a couple of days?"

"That's correct. I'm in town for a meeting."

She crossed her arms, but her gaze would not let go, as if searching his face.

"Ah. And then?"

The easy answer would be to lie, mumble plans about returning to Oklahoma and some kind of life. Or he could be brutally honest and say he'd probably be living in the front seat of his pickup until he got a job flipping short-order burgers on a flat top and shoveling fries. "Not sure. Sort of in between. Depends, I guess. And how about you?"

She leaned in to speak confidentially, but had to raise her voice to be heard. "Well, I'm staying with my friend — the woman at the piano bar I came in with — and I'm here for some sort of job interview. And then we'll see."

"Some sort?"

"It's difficult to explain. Are you planning to relocate here?"

"Like I said —"

"Oh, right. *Depends.* Say, if you do and need a place, my friend is a real estate agent." She dug into her bag. "Let me see..."

Inwardly, Clay winced. Renting an apartment was about the last thing he wanted to do. "So your friend —"

Andi nodded and beamed as she produced a business card and presented it. "Meredith Barnes. She's a real estate agent, specializing in commercial properties, but she handles everything. She's excellent. Especially if you're looking to buy or open a business."

"Mind if I pass it along to Mitch? Mitchell Whelan. He's a reporter on the local newspaper. He was, ah, impressed."

She laughed.

"What's so funny?"

"Meredith said the same thing about your friend. Okay, honest. I'm definitely not vetting here. Have you known him long?"

"Sure you are. But the answer is, since high school. Nice guy, lot of fun. We were teammates."

"What sport?"

"Football."

"Any good?"

"Pretty lousy, as a matter of fact."

"What position did you play?"

"Quarterback."

She nodded. "I should have guessed."

"Why?"

Andi shrugged. "Oh, I don't know. You sort of seem like the quarterback type, I suppose." A woman exited the hallway and passed between them. "Ah, looks like it's my turn."

"Turn for what?"

She laughed and pointed. "The restroom."

"Oh." Heat filled his cheeks and ears. "Of course." He lunged for a total lie. "Sorry, it's been a long day and I'm totally foggy."

Her smile and eyes said she wasn't buying the lame excuse. "Here comes the heavy guy. And no, I don't plan to stare to see if he made it."

Too quickly, he grinned and fell into the game. "Want me to?"

"Um, no." She pulled away. "And yes, Clay, nice meeting you. Maybe we'll bump into each other sometime. Again."

"That would be good." He thought, impossible, improbable, not likely, nice while it lasted, nicer when she lingered for a moment.

"Oh, and I'm sorry about the shoulder thing. So crowded..."

Clay hugged the remnant of the conversation but knew it had tapered off. "I'm not."

She smiled and gave a little wave with the tips of her fingers. "G'night." He watched her for the few steps into the narrow hallway and then realized it must have looked kind of sleazy, staring at a woman en route to a toilet.

* * *

Meredith leaned against the frame of the bathroom door, her arms crossed. She wore a thick blue terrycloth robe, a little faded, a little baggy, perhaps a favorite she'd had for a while, that barely cleared the flip-flops on her feet. "...And so, you walked away? Seriously?"

Andi looked up into the mirror to evaluate the eyebrow situation. A toothbrush handle protruded from the right side of her mouth and paste foam oozed from her lips. Eyebrows looked okay, so she resumed brushing, mumbling, "Uh-huh."

Mer sighed. "You know I would have understood if you wanted to spend a little more time with him."

"Uh-huh."

"But instead you said good night. Probably did that little finger-tip bye-bye wave."

Andi paused, raised her left hand and illustrated the gesture.

Meredith shifted her weight and sighed. "Gosh. That's just, just...just so..."

"Uh-huh."

"He looked taller than you. With broad shoulders, like a football player."

Andi continued to brush and spat the spent toothpaste into a swirl of running water. She rinsed her mouth, wiped her lips with a tissue, and lingered at the reflection before turning toward Meredith. "He said he was a quarterback."

"In college?"

"No, high school."

Meredith shrugged. "Still counts. Wow, a quarterback. I can't imagine..."

Andi cleansed her face and picked a hairbrush from her toiletry bag. She chuckled. "But you'll try, right? Besides, he said he wasn't a very good quarterback."

"And the guy he was with?"

Andi nodded. "Mitch Something. Whelan, I think. Clay said they were teammates, but I don't think he mentioned the other guy's position."

"Probably a wide receiver. He looked like a wide receiver."

Andi laughed toward the image in the mirror, the one wearing a sports-gray nightshirt with the bold pink block letters across the chest exclaiming "Hot Babe." A gift from Mer-Bear last Christmas before being a Hot Babe abruptly became a terribly hurtful thing. After a couple of months at the bottom of a dresser drawer, it suddenly wasn't so bad. Well, not too bad. But it draped her body because Mer had given it as a present. She pulled her shoulders back and straightened her posture. She thought, so, okay, decent. One more issue to put behind her. Still in her early twenties, life could be rearranged.

She faced Meredith, wearing a contented and assured smile. "Oh, Mer, *all* the hot guys look like wide receivers to you."

Meredith spoke in a defensive tone. "So, I prefer them tall and lean and blond and kind of rugged looking. What's wrong with that?"

"Well, Clay said this Mitch guy's real nice, and a reporter on the local paper. And now you know where to set up a stakeout and whether it's worth it."

"Do you know if he's, like, unattached?"

The question caught Andi off guard. "Gosh. Well, I assume so. Why?" Meredith reacted with incredulity. "Okay, okay, dumb question. Sorry."

Meredith nodded forgiveness, with a hint of anxiety in her eyes. "They could have been two buddies just out for a couple of beers, right? I mean, the good ones seem to be taken. Unless, of course, they're, you know, gay."

"Yew! Hm. No, I don't think so." Andi packed up the little bag.

No way could she leave it on the too-small vanity for the couple of days she planned to be in town.

"Really? Why?"

Andi stepped toward the door. Meredith backed up and to the side to allow her to breeze past.

"Because, Mer-Bear, Clay said his friend Mitch was impressed with you."

Meredith's eyes widened. "Really? *Really?* And you didn't think to mention this because...? Oh, Kit-Kit, that's so mean and cruel!" She pursued Andi back into the living room, pulling up short when Andi whirled.

"Okay, Mer, please. I said I'm not into any sort of a relationship right now. I've got to get back on track, work-wise, and I just know this meeting tomorrow morning is a long shot. But I'm desperate. It's not money or a place to stay or little comforts. It's my self-esteem on the line."

Meredith's expression tumbled into shame. "Sorry. You're right. I know, I know. You've endured more than anyone should."

Andi sighed and laid her palms on Mer's shoulders. "Oh, Mer-Bear. You're a wonderful friend and I love you dearly. A wonderful night out, a great place to go, and we had a perfectly gorgeous time. But now I'm really, really tired, and I need sleep in the worst way."

"Of course. I was being selfish. And silly."

"No, no — your usual warm and bubbly self, which I need, too." She drew Mer into a hug. "You're the perfect friend, Mer-Bear. You really are."

Chapter Four

Mitch hoisted a purple coffee mug bearing a ridiculous saying on the side. It shrouded his grin but not the astonishment in his eyes and he took a sip.

Clay awaited reaction. "Well?"

Mitch shook his head. "Dude. That's the best coffee I have ever had. No lie, buddy. No lie."

"You're sure?"

"Hey, man. It could be total crap but it would still be fine. I mean, I can't remember the last time somebody made coffee in my own kitchen. In the morning, before work. But it's still good, miles better than the stuff I get on the way to the office."

"Well, somebody must have tried. I found it in the cupboard, next to the sink."

"Yeah? Wow. Hope it's not polluted. How'd you make that? It's exceptionally decent."

Clay nodded. Should have checked the expiration date beforehand. No sense in it now. Probably not a good idea to know. Instead, he held a French press aloft and tried to give an elemental explanation, but Mitch's mind seemed to be elsewhere.

It had been a long night on a sofa as advertised, a makeshift bed with a spare set of sheets, blanket and a pillow that carried the faint scent of marijuana, flabby springs and lumpy pillows. He sampled his own coffee to rinse away the memory. It would have to do. When he looked up, Mitch appeared to linger.

Clay said, "So? You look as though you've got a question."

He shifted his weight several times and took several small sips. "Well, you haven't said anything about the two chicks. I mean, you were doing the cordial thing with the brunette. And I don't blame you. I mean, she was, like, super foxy."

Clay grunted. "Not much to tell. We wound up waiting in line for the restrooms, said hello, chatted."

Mitch cocked an eyebrow. "Dude. Had to be more than that. I read the chick's body language and she was, like, into you."

"Andi."

"Andi what?"

"No idea. Just Andi."

"You didn't get a number or anything?"

"Nope."

"Wow, man. That's totally lame."

Clay put his hands on his hips. "Well, for the record, she's in town for a couple of days, some sort of interview, and since that's also what I'm here for, I don't see much of a future in it. Neither did she."

"Yeah, but you gotta admit, a real looker, right? I mean, drop-dead gorgeous."

"True."

Mitch nodded in a thoughtful way, trying to work into what Clay guessed would be the next question, but he could no longer keep him on the hook.

"So she's staying with the blonde that she was with. Old friends, I guess."

Mitch became alert. "Yeah?"

Clay masked a teasing smirk by digging into his duffel in search of a tie. "Yeah. She works in commercial real estate, a broker. Meredith something."

"You wouldn't happen to have caught a last —"

Clay faked a furrowed brow and held the tie up before a dusty mirror. Conservative gray and red stripe, no stains or spots. Not the same as police uniform black wool, but it would have to do. "Oh, yeah. Barnes, I think. Yeah, Meredith Barnes."

Mitch lunged for pen and paper, knocking over a stack of magazines in the process, muttering, "Meredith Barnes, Meredith Barnes."

Clay wanted to make a breakfast, but three foam takeout boxes and half a case of beer in the fridge didn't offer good options. "Yeah, and it seems she — the blonde — thought you were, well, you know, interesting."

Mitch looked up, eyes wide and jaw agape. "No lie? And you didn't think to mention this until just now?"

"No lie." But his casually serious expression faded to a grin.

Mitch scribbled on the note pad and, when he looked up, chuckled. "You are one mean dude, you know that?"

Clay chuckled and finished his coffee. Meeting at a restaurant of some sort, relatively early, meant a meal might be included. "Yeah, so it would seem."

Mitch smiled. "What the heck. We'll get'm next time, right, buddy?"

"Absolutely. You're good with no breakfast?"

"Yeah, man, totally okay. There's this babe in Classified who always comes in with a box of doughnuts, the fast food ones. She knows I go for the chocolate frosting ones, the kind with the sprinkles?"

"Yeah, I know which ones." The sort of breakfast that should be banned as toxic, or at least tasteless, pretty much the same difference.

"Yeah, so she comes around with the open box and leans real sexy-like against the side of my desk and sticks the goodies under my nose. She bats her eyes and lets me choose and then she always says I can take the other one too, she doesn't mind, and so I'm good to go. If I time it right, I've already got company coffee

in a paper cup, so, yeah, it's the breakfast of champions. Or whatever, you know?"

Clay shook his head. "No shame, eh?"

"No, none. Hey, she's ten years older than me and married to
a truck driver. And if she wants to pass out free doughnuts, who
am I to argue, right?" He parked the mug next to the sink. "Okay,
buddy, I gotta get going. Close the door behind you on the way
out. It'll lock. Good luck with your meeting with the guy."

Clay lifted his mug in a toast. "Thanks, pal. And good luck
with those doughnuts."

"Yeah, for sure. Ha. Y'know, this classified babe, she's got a
body like you can't —"

Clay raised a hand to interrupt. "Too much information,
man."

Mitch nodded. "Yeah, guess you're right. So. I'll catch up with
you later. Maybe we can go out, have a couple of frosties, burger,
whatever."

"Or I could stop and pick up some stuff, cook for you."

The idea seemed to take Mitch by surprise. "No kidding?"

"No prob."

"You mean, like a regular meal and stuff? Hm. I bet you can
do it, too. Learned pretty good from your old man, I bet."

"Learned enough." Enough to know to stay out of the restaurant business, but also enough to know his way around a kitchen.
Pop had a great crew back in the day, and while a dozen pals were
doing kid stuff, he'd learned just by hanging out and looking interested.

Mitch gave a wave on the way out. "Great. See ya."

* * *

Andi scurried through a labyrinth of narrow side streets. Her
watch had stopped again and could not be revived. She winced.

Coulda, woulda, shoulda.

Now the air chilled the first fine droplets of a faint drizzle struck her face. No hat, no umbrella. Not that it mattered. Meredith's trusty old hair dryer lost its warmth a minute before she would have been done. Despite a promise to replace it right away, it didn't help at the moment. Any sort of rain would make it worse.

She paused at a familiar intersection. She'd been on the opposite corner a few minutes earlier. Her shoulders slumped at the realization of hopelessly lost.

She tugged her phone from her bag. Battery oozing power, hugging twenty percent. Should have recharged last night, which would have been easy to remember if they hadn't gone out to the jazz bar. But it made no sense to be upset with Mer about it. Her own silly fault.

She could still make the meeting if Mer could take a distress call and give directions. If Mer knew where Andi stood. If the rain stopped. Drizzle intensified and she looked around for ideas while Mer's phone rang. A second, third, fourth, fifth time, about to go to message, which meant Andi would have to get lucky or call it a day.

A wire trash basket attached to a street light pole offered a discarded newspaper. A makeshift umbrella. The phone connection clicked in. *Yes,* she muttered to herself. *Thank you, thank you, thank you.*

"Hey, Andi, you okay?"

Calm, she told herself. *Calm.* "Sort of. I've managed to get confused and I'm, well, lost."

"Where are you?"

Andi read the street names from the sign above. "Southwest corner, I think."

"Ah. Okay. Not too bad. I'll walk you through it."

"Really? You're a lifesaver, Mer-Bear. Sure it's no trouble?"

"Nope. A guy who'd been interested in a property just left. Couldn't close it. No sale. I'm sitting here licking my wounds."

"It's starting to rain."

"Ouch. Really — you okay? I mean, after the hair dryer..."

Andi glanced at her wrist. "My watch died."

"Ooooh. You *are* having... Okay. Let me think for a sec."

Pedestrians had magically produced umbrellas, except for two guys in hard hats working on a store front and a man in a suit who didn't seem to mind. Well, maybe a little. He picked up his pace and ducked into a doorway, relaxing as he entered some sort of a small office building.

Folded in half, the newspaper worked, but in about five or ten minutes, rain would be dripping off a corner, not good.

Mer's voice brightened. "Okay. From where you are, make a left, go up one block, then a left..."

Andi winced and stepped away.

"Don't worry. I'll get you there. Got to do something after that hair dryer thing. I'm going out at lunchtime for a new one. Maybe I could pick one up for you?"

"If I don't make the appointment, it won't make any difference."

Meredith steered the conversation to assuring, casually talking about dinner plans and the club they were at the night before, and about Clay's reporter friend.

Andi wondered if Mitch had written anything in the paper above her head, a cloud of newsprint serving a useful purpose. For the person who should have paid attention to a weather forecast, should have borrowed an umbrella, should have been more familiar with the route. Maybe it portended any hope of getting a meaningful job in law enforcement.

She'd made the right after the left and, sure enough, a main street of some kind, wider, busier with traffic, and signals at the intersections. She spotted the restaurant.

Meredith sounded pleased and excited at the same time. "You're still a couple of minutes early, Kit-Kit. You can cross at the corner ahead, come back on the other side."

She gauged distance to the corner. Then the restaurant directly across the street. Then considered the rain. "I'm good, Mer. Thanks a bunch. I'll catch up later."

She disconnected. *No time to be a good and proper citizen. Cross here.* She winced and stepped between two parked cars. A glance to the left. *Good. Get across. Get inside. Get warm. Get dry.* She gripped the phone in her right hand, ignored the wet left sleeve, ducked her head and scampered across.

Blast of a horn. Tires, skidding on wet pavement. Turn to...

A crushing blow to her back. Staggering, tumbling, falling forward. Trying to deflect crashing into a parked car. Falling, falling to the curb. Huge weight on her back.

Someone on top of her.

* * *

Clay had no time to react to exactly where they landed. An elbow, hard into his chest, the air in his lungs shoved out, hard. Piercing pain, dead center, in the sternum.

Below, the woman snarled, an obscenity blurred into a growl, a bark. Her effective elbow forced him to abandon his grip. She pushed hard with her shoulder, rolling away, kicking with knees and feet. She went left.

He rolled right and struggled to a sitting position while she scrambled to her feet. Half a step back, into a profile, her hands reaching for her right hip. Automatically. Groping for something that wasn't there.

When she realized it, she glared at him.

"What are you...." Her eyes narrowed. "You're the subject from last night. In the bar."

Clay displayed a knowing smile and rubbed dirt from his hands. "And you're a cop."

She crossed her arms. "I am not."

Clay stood up and checked his clothes for damage. "You were reaching for a service weapon."

"I was not! I was reaching for my hip, which hit that pavement head-on and..."

In the street, the truck driver had rolled down the passenger side window. "Yo, lady, don't you know no better'n to walk out into traffic? Not payin' no attention? C'mon. Get off the lousy phone, would ya?"

Clay stepped in while brushing his hands at soiled clothes. "It's okay, buddy. I got it."

The truck driver scowled. "Yeah, well, you got yourself a real ding-dong girlfriend, pal." The window rolled up and he returned to his spot behind the wheel, making a gesture toward the guy leaning on the horn in the car behind him.

Andi snapped, "And I'm *not* your ding-dong girlfriend, sport. Oh, man.... My clothes are just...just...*ruined*." She looked forlornly at the brown jacket, now smeared with whatever they kept in the gutter.

Clay continued to check his own jacket and pants. He muttered, "Better than getting killed."

"Really? *Really?* Right now, I'm probably better off dead. I'm supposed to meet someone here. Right here. Right now."

Clay nodded. "Yeah, me too."

She threw up her arms in resignation. "Yeah, well, I hope they put you at a table far, far away, bud. The last thing I ever want to see again is you." She wheeled and stalked toward the door.

Passersby stared at Clay. He sighed, made a herding gesture with his arms and said aloud to no one in particular, "One of those days, folks. Yeah, yeah, move along, okay? Nothing more to see here."

Chapter Five

A waitress pointed at an older man, mid-seventies maybe, grinning and waving to Clay. He wore khaki, hanging loose from a bony frame, not law enforcement or a workman's uniform but more like... Yeah. A guy going fishing. The long-brimmed baseball cap had some sort of tattered embroidered logo in the middle of it and his hands belonged on a fly rod.

Clay strode forward, hands still moist from a dryer in the men's room that didn't run long enough after scrubbing mud and nearly black sticky stuff off his fingers. With any luck, the guy at the table would not notice the soiled trousers or an unknown stain on his jacket sleeve.

Still wearing a broad smile, the guy, stood as Clay extended his right arm to shake hands. "Mister Pike?"

"That'd be me, son, that'd be me. And you're Clay Garrison. Call me Gideon. Nothing fancy with me." He paused to wink and chuckle. "Although, there are some folks who'd toss out names that'd make the gals in this place blush something fierce." Pike stood three inches taller than Clay. Lean, fit, well-tanned, his grip assured and powerful. He gestured with a sweep of his arm. "Sit, sit. We're here to eat, son, here to eat."

A waitress with a carafe of coffee approached. She wore a snug tan dress and apron and a name tag identifying her as Adele. Her effusive smile suggested Pike to be old friend and a favorite customer. "Top that off for you, Mister Pike?"

Pike pushed his cup toward the table edge. "Thank you, Adele." He faced Clay and chuckled. "They make first-rate coffee here, Clay. First rate. The sort of spot every town should have. A good place to settle, I believe." Gideon took his coffee black and sipped with evident satisfaction. "Idiot doctors think I ought to cut back on caffeine, you see. Say it's not good for circulation or the old ticker. Or whatever. What do you say, Mister Garrison?"

Clay turned his own cup upright in the saucer and eased it in the direction of the waitress. "I'd say, Mister Pike, that you're the sort of man who gets what he wants."

Pike laughed, freely, the way a guy does when he doesn't have a care in the world. "Gideon, son. Call me Gideon."

"Yessir." He nodded to Adele and she filled his cup.

Five minutes late for the meeting, Clay discarded instinct to interrogate, not the best way for a desperate man to launch interview for whatever job Pike had in mind. He'd expected a recruiter, maybe a head hunter, possibly an H-R guy from a force someplace. But not an old fellow organizing a security team for a hunting trip in Canada or Africa or wherever. Clay reached for deference and apology.

"Sorry I'm late, sir. Had a bit of an incident outside."

Pike nodded, the twinkle in bright blue eyes offsetting weathered lines on a face conditioned to exposure to much more than office fluorescent or soft private club lighting. He nodded toward the large window to his left, looking out onto the street. "I saw that. Yessir, I did. Quick thinking. Man of action, takes a risk."

"Merely trying to do the right thing, sir."

Pike brushed off the modesty. "Saved that gal's life, I'd wager. She didn't seem too happy about it, though."

Deference evaporated. "Yeah, well, I guess to some people, a phone call is more important than getting run over by a truck."

Pike chuckled and looked up and past Clay's shoulder. "That so? And what do *you* think?"

Heat poured through Clay's cheeks and ears. Andi stood right behind him, her arms crossed, her expression one of utter disdain.

* * *

Clay scrambled to his feet. She took a defensive step to the side. He caught his chair as it tipped over and fumbled long enough for her to win the moment, his face bright pink and his expression sheepish embarrassment.

She cocked her head and softly said, "Nice one, Slick." Then she said to Gideon, who had stood and moved far enough to the edge of the table to gracefully shake her hand. "And you'd be Mister Pike?"

"That I would, Miss Delvento. I believe you and Mister Garrison have already met?"

Her gaze slowly shifted back and forth between the two men. Her jaw tightened. "I'm afraid we have. Once too often as far as I'm concerned. Look, Mister Pike, I'm sorry I'm late but I had to clean up as best as I could and —"

Gideon kept smiling and waved off the response. "Perfectly all right, Miss Delvento. No harm done. I believe the lad saved your life a few minutes ago."

She shot a glare toward Clay, looking hopeful, on the side. Yep. Puppy-dog eyes. The day had bottomed out. Time to write it off as a disaster, let it go. "Very well, then. Thank you for saving my life, Mister Garrison. I was careless. For perfectly good reasons, but still..." She faced Gideon. "Look, sir, this is probably not going to work out. There's clearly some sort of mix-up. I thought I had the time of our appointment correct, but you're meeting someone else. So, again, my apologies and now I think it's time for me togo. Have a nice day."

The men exchanged glances. Clay seemed puzzled. Gideon looked bemused as if playing some sort of a cruel, embarrassing, power game. She forced a smile to mask anger bubbling between her ears.

* * *

Clay felt intrigue as she ignored a gesture to be seated, a tremor in her right hand and a quiver on her jaw.

Pike's easy smile had taken a turn toward patronization. "I see. Well, Miss Delvento, I must have been misinformed. My sources tell me that you're not the type to cut and run at the first couple of hurdles."

"I... I... Look, Mister Pike. I don't know what sort of game you're playing, but I'm not a pawn on the board. And as far as I'm concerned, I think you should get better sources."

Her eyes had misted over, but she stood her ground for a long moment. *She's not hurt. She's angry, really furious.* He suspected stress of the incident had probably put her on edge, creating a distraction at a time when she needed focus.

Pike's appeared dismissive, trying to avoid a scene in a public place not as a courtesy to Andi, but to avoid resembling a first-class....

Clay interrupted the first syllable out of Pike's mouth. "Okay, sir, that's enough." He got to his feet and looked down at the host.

Andi sighed. "Clay, don't." She raised her hands, palms out. "Just...just don't. I can handle it."

Clay shook his head. "I'm sure. But I can't. Look, Mister Pike, I don't know what you're offering and right now, I don't care. Count me out."

Andi rubbed her nose with the back of her hand. "Sorry, Clay, it's been a crappy string of bad luck and I'm tired. And thanks for putting yourself at risk out there. I was dumb and stupid and

careless and I owe you one for having my back. I'd buy you breakfast, but...."

*She doesn't care what Pike thinks. She's treating him like a
piece of casual furniture. She's tough as nails.* Clay replied with a
smile. "It's okay. I've got seven bucks to my name and there's a
fast-food place a couple of blocks south. My treat."

Between them, a fistful of cash plopped onto the table.

Pike said, "Take it, kids. Divvy it up any way that seems fair.
Call it —"

Andi responded with the sort of satisfied smile that comes after making a good collar and nobody got hurt. She picked up the
money and offered it to Pike. "I think you dropped this, Mister
Pike. You should be more careful, sir. Flashing a wad in a restaurant can bring you serious difficulties."

Pike showed a paternal grin of approval. "Keep it, Andrea."

"Not for a moment, sir." She opened her hand and allowed the
bills to tumble to the table, with a fifty floating into a partially
empty coffee cup. No one moved to rescue it.

From somewhere on the periphery, Adele arrived, pad in
hand, her voice cheery. She at least pretended to be oblivious to
the cash scattered on the table. "Are you folks ready to order? Or
do you need a minute?"

Pike reached for one of the menus tucked in the rear of a tray
of table accessories that included napkins, catsup, sugar and al-
ternatives, an assortment of single servings of jams and jellies.
"I'll need a minute, Adele. Maybe these folks are ready to order."

Andi's jaw dropped and she stared at Pike, who immersed
himself in the listings of specials as if nothing had just happened.
Clay's attention went to the cash, all hundred-dollar bills except
for the one in his coffee cup. He plucked it out and parked it in a
tent shape.

Pike said, "O'course, I'm assuming these young people are going to let me buy them a meal. They're precisely the sort of people

I'd enjoy having for company."

Clay shook his head. "Mister Pike, I don't think you heard —"

Pike closed the menu. "Oh, I heard all right. My kind of people. Quick-thinking, heroic, courageous. Lot of pride. Integrity that you don't see much of anymore. You could have let her hang out to dry, Mister Garrison. But you saw exactly what I saw. And you partnered up, on the spot. Oh, come on. Sit down, have a first-class breakfast, hear what I have to say. Still not interested? No harm done. Interested? You'll be handsomely rewarded."

Clay looked into Andrea's eyes, seeking a cue. Faint shrug. Good enough. Without a word, they sat and opened menus.

Pike beamed. "Adele, put me down for the businessman's special, and don't spare the bacon. Then give these folks whatever they wish. It's on my check." He reached out to gather up the cash and stuffed it into his shirt pocket.

* * *

Andi faced the age-old dilemma. A grandiose offer from the host, a senior guy. Order whatever, anything. She peeked over the top of the menu at Clay. Furrowed brow, eyes shifting rapidly up and down, right and left. He had the same issue. Starving, but not daring to get carried away. She found Pike's choice on the left hand side. Eleven ninety-five. Okay, she thought. Starting point.

The businessman's special included three eggs, any style, with three pancakes, bacon or sausage, juice. He'd ordered the eggs up, probably so he could stab the yolks and make them bleed out on the platter.

The healthy options featured fruits and yogurts, a little more expensive. Simpler combinations were less, but, after chasing across town on foot and nearly being killed by a truck, seemed a bit scanty.

Calmer now, more in control, Andi for the second time today

had Clay to thank for it. The sting of a potentially major bruise on her right arm had settled into a dull, stiff ache and she flexed her fingers to work the muscles.

Yep. A serious evening of recuperation seemed probable.

Adele wore a placid smile while seconds of indecision ticked away. Clay seemed the type who'd go for a nice steak, half a carton of eggs and a sack of potatoes ground down into home fries. Eighteen bucks and a full belly.

The thought caused her stomach to twinge but the little voice in her head encouraged sin on a major scale. French toast. Ton of bacon. A half a gallon of syrup. Ten ninety-five.

Last night, she'd considered Clay to be another guy in a bar, a passing person going nowhere in her life. She'd never expected him to be a rival for the job, whatever the job was, but with his moves today and her stumbles, he'd become a shoo-in candidate. Probably won when he prepared to walk away from the old guy who toyed with a coffee cup while watching both of them squirm with the simple task of ordering breakfast.

She studied his face. The first guy who'd stuck up for her in, what, the last six or seven months, maybe longer. The kind of guy that she perhaps could take a gamble on, relatively safely because she could still walk away, think about doing something totally different with her life.

And Pike, who still exuded an aura of smug superiority. Time to take him down a peg or two.

Fresh fruit and yogurt combination rose to the top of the list.

Clay said, "You know, I think I'd like a couple of eggs, scrambled, rye toast."

Adele scribbled. "Side with that? Bacon? Sausage?"

"Sausage. Two. If it's on the lean side."

Andi's eyes skimmed up the left side of the menu. He went cheap. Five ninety-five. She mustered a smile. "And I'll have the same."

Chapter Six

Clay shifted his weight in the chair, a metal-framed stackable with firm, black vinyl seats. Each pedestal table hosted two or four of the same, neither cheap or fancy, but in the price range of an experienced owner eager to get a business up and running. The layout, on the loose side, hinted there were once booths on the street side and counter service on the interior.

The restaurant was not among storefronts he recalled from years past. Cozy, subdued décor, the usual darker woods topped by a muted green and featuring consignment paintings by a couple of local artists, each bearing a discreet price tag in the bottom right hand corner. Staffing and grooming hinted the restaurant prospered. At this hour, breakfast service waned and several waitstaff were enjoying a break near the cash register.

Andi, directly opposite, drew his attention like a magnet while she ladled charm on Gideon Pike, mostly banter about being a stranger in a small city, things they'd discovered, where they were from. Furious minutes earlier, she now behaved as if a momentary spat had fluttered away, like the passing rain shower, displaced by an effervescent glow from sunlight pouring through the window behind her. The same easy smile, the same easy heat, as the night before, a mesmerizing attraction.

Which was suddenly a problem. He needed to slide into a conversation that appeared to have Pike totally enchanted. Clay toyed with the drained coffee cup before him. Maybe she hadn't let it go, instead building interrogation simpatico, gently leading the old guy into a trap. Like a cop. A really good cop.

The way she broke free on the street. Got to her feet. Hands going straight to her right hip. Exactly the way it's supposed to be done. And it *was* an interview for some sort of police work, and she *was* also invited. No doubt about it. Law enforcement. Maybe too young to be a detective, but possibly federal. Whatever her status, she had mastered interviewing. If Pike was doing a comparison test, she likely had the inside track.

They were laughing, and he could sense no opening. She had shut him out of the action, pushed him outside the circle. Now the challenge became a graceful exit from a losing situation. She could have it. He'd get back to Mitch's place, figure out what to do next, maybe find something to cook. He'd lost.

Then Adele arrived with three platters. Eleven minute ticket time. Not too shabby. And Andi's spell dissipated.

* * *

Andi pulled away from the table to allow delivery. Adele had separated her from Pike with plates, cheery banter and a warning the platters were warm.

There were clearly more than "a couple" of scrambled eggs, overwhelming tiny sausages and rye toast. A man-sized portion, but inviting. Gideon shifted paternal charm to the waitress and won another cup of coffee.

Clay turned his plate to a point of satisfaction with the organization of things. His expression was indifferent, as if he was wishing to be somewhere else. Her eyes followed the line of his shoulders down across his arms and to his hands. The mound of eggs would be no problem for him. He'd been waiting quietly, patiently perhaps, for food to arrive, half a step back from her and Pike.

Observing.

His hands unfurled knife and fork from a rolled-up napkin and, in one soft motion, he smoothed the paper on the table and placed the utensils in a precise line.

He was one of those officers whose reports were perfect, whose uniform was always neatly pressed, whose shoes were always shined. Who never made a mistake. *Yes.* One of those taciturn men who were incredibly precise and organized, who would absorb every blabbered word from a subject, and then make his move.

Like, she thought, the way she blabbered on to Gideon Pike, desperately hunting for a way to shoot the old man right out of the saddle, but withering in his charm and deciding to let it go. Meanwhile, at just the right moment, Clay will probably say exactly the right thing and get the job. A career in real estate with Meredith might be okay.

The condiment tray offered orange marmalade and strawberry jam. She reached for marmalade, a good consolation prize for rye toast.

Adele interrupted. "And you, miss? More coffee?"

Andi looked up. "Huh? Oh. Yes, please."

Above the condiments, her fingertips collided with Clay's.

She recoiled. "Oh, sorry."

"No, it's okay. Go ahead." He waited for her, then also took a packet of marmalade.

Gideon Pike chuckled and reached for the tray. "I'll go for strawberry. I've always been a strawberry man. Best jam, hands down, you see."

Clay showed no reaction as he peeled paper from the tiny packet and scraped marmalade onto his toast. *We're both marmalade people. Pike isn't.* Perhaps neither of them was suited for whatever job Gideon Pike was about to discuss.

* * *

Clay feigned interest as optimism fluttered away. After driving halfway across the country with a wallet running on empty, prospects of getting a career back on track bottomed out.

Pike's eating habits matched his directness. He carved and stabbed, chewed ferociously, and poked at air with, gratefully, an empty fork to make a point. Instead of declaring a defined position flat-out, he backed into it, like a time share salesman pitching a gullible mark.

Andi gave courtesy to an elderly man who'd picked up the tab and believed it entitled him to a monologue, mostly about his career as a successful businessman. But her expression became stony and sparkle faded from her eyes. Perhaps she, too, yearned to check her watch and bail at the first opportune moment.

Gideon gathered the last of his meal into one heaping bite, chewed with vigor, and pushed the plate aside. "...And that, of course, is what brings us around to you people. Now, mind you, I'm already impressed. You've both displayed the qualities that caught my attention in the first place. Well, not mine exactly, o'-course. Trusted people I retain to do research for my own interests. But that needn't concern you."

Andi gave up on the last of her toast. "Well, sir, it does. I've been through background checks and generally know what's going on when their done. I get a little upset when people I don't know start digging around in my personal life."

Clay nodded. "I'd agree with that. Look, Mister Pike, I'm grateful for the meal and your time, but when I accepted your invitation, I believe I made it pretty clear that I was interested in law enforcement —"

Andi's smile went from patronizing to smug. "I *thought* so. You're on the job."

"Was. And you're...?"

She sighed. "Okay. Also past tense. I'm looking for another

opportunity."

Pike leaned back. "And you shall have it. Both of you. My offer is good for two, a team, partners, you see. To work on a special project. All legal, o'course, nothing shady."

Clay asked, "Private?"

"Well, yes. That's a good word."

"Sorry, not interested, sir. For many reasons, but mostly because I don't care for peeps and there's no way I'm going to be somebody's muscle."

Gideon nodded. "I see. Well, it's not a muscle job, but I'd be grateful for some first-rate investigative work on a matter of some importance."

Andi tilted her head and cocked an eyebrow. "How grateful?"

Clay said, "Now, hold on. First, I'm not licensed to be a private investigator and second, I'm barely out of the police academy and still on probation —"

Andi persisted. "*How* grateful, Mister Pike?"

She and Pike reconnected, and, again, a sense of being excluded tumbled down the length of Clay's mind, heart, body.

Pike said, "Why, I'm sure we can consider what's fair, just as soon as I give you a sense of the scale of the, well, problem."

Andi said to Clay, "We could at least hear him out. I'm, er, *was*, also a rookie, but who knows? Maybe he's lost a pet, a cat, a dog, or trying to beat a traffic misdemeanor. We could pick up bus fare for a couple of days' work."

"Without a license."

"Minor detail."

Gideon said, "Private investigator licenses in this state are relatively easy, you see. If you know the right people, have friends in the right places at the county offices. District attorney's office, clerk of courts. Slight obstacle. But, Andrea, it's not as trivial as a traffic ticket or a beloved missing pet. May we speak with an understanding of confidentiality?"

It sounded ominous and Andi's reaction showed she thought so, too.

She said, "Fine by me. Clay?"

Nothing to lose. Push back. "As long as the confidentiality goes both ways. I'm not interested in anything illegal. First, I want to know why us. There are numerous experienced investigators and, if there's a crime involved, any number of capable law enforcement agencies."

Andi smiled reassurance. "Not to mention defense attorneys. You didn't do anything illegal, did you, Mister Pike?"

Gideon seemed impressed with her directness. "No. In fact, the more I see you two, the more satisfied I am at my decision to retain both of you. You asked 'why us?' and the answer is simple. As a team, you'll be ideal for the task."

Clay waved off a coffee refill. "And why is that, sir?"

Andi nodded agreement, but now her arms were crossed and her expression had become serious.

"You'll be dealing with a cold case, twenty-five years old. And a group of people with whom certain personality traits may prove useful. The case concerns my daughter, Kimberly, found dead, an apparent drug overdose, in a rehab center where she had been undergoing treatment for her addiction."

Andi relaxed. "I'm sorry for your loss, Mister Pike. Was it —"

"Her own doing? Probably. No reason to believe otherwise. And no one seems to know how a sixteen-year-old got access to whatever caused her death."

Clay said, "And you want us to figure that out? After twenty-five years?"

"No. What's past is past. Of more interest to me is the fate of her twin daughters, my grandchildren."

Andi's eyes widened. "She had children?"

"Not entirely sure. You see, the reports indicated that she lost both of them late in pregnancy, stillborn."

Clay nodded. "Tragic. Because of the drug addiction?"

Pike shrugged. "Maybe. But I've always had my doubts. Now I'm an old man, living out his years in a sort of retirement. And before I go, I'd like to be certain. I'd prefer a fresh set of eyes, untainted, no predispositions, with no management from myself."

The exaggerated protest about age was wearing thin but she was drawn toward clarity. "I gather the family believes the twins were deceased?"

"Yes. And I'm certain they have their reasons."

Clay said, "It should be easy enough to check. You certainly don't need us for that. Your own lawyers could run it down without much difficulty."

Gideon smiled. "It's complicated, son. Complicated. I seem to be the only one haunted by the question, and I'm prepared to pay whatever it takes to be satisfied."

Andi asked, "And what if they were not, well, deceased...."

"Alive? Then I'd want to know what happened to them. Know where they are. Make amends."

Clay said, "Sometimes people don't want to be found. They want to be left alone, because they have a life."

"I'd respect that."

Andi cocked her head. "*Would* you?"

Her unabashed directness became a challenge. She sounded as wary as he about rummaging around in the closet of skeletons of some powerful clan.

"I would. You'd have my word on that."

Clay said, "You do realize that the odds favor the stillborn report. Records would certainly show —"

Gideon glared incredulity. "Trust me, Clay. Records can be altered, created, destroyed, rearranged. That's what makes this entire matter a bit more complex than — what had you said, Andrea? — oh, yes. A bit more complex than a lost pet and bus fare on to the next little incident in your life."

She winced. "Sorry. I was being flip."

"Yes. You were. Miss Delvento, you and Mister Garrison were picked for this opportunity because you bring fresh eyes and a fresh perspective, because you're both very bright and posted exceptional marks in your training, and because you're the sort of a pair that can possibly deal with the people involved in this matter. It's going to take some very special traits."

He stood and tossed the wad of cash back onto the table. From his shirt pocket, he produced a folded scrap of paper and allowed it to flutter down. "I'm certain that you'll want to discuss it between yourselves." He handed each a business card. "My private number's on the card. You can reach me there any day, any time. This is not an either-or. This is both. Or nothing. You'd be well rewarded."

Pike wiped his hands with the napkin and stood. "You two enjoy your day. Let me know if you're interested."

He strolled away, not a hint of age in his step.

Clay nodded toward the paper on the table and said to Andi, "Well, okay, then. Which of us is going for the note?"

Chapter Seven

Meredith inhaled a slab of pizza, chewed frantically, and mopped a trickle of grease from the corner of her mouth. She had curled up on a second-hand overstuffed chair opposite the sofa that served as Andi's makeshift bed.

Between them, on a coffee table wobbling under the weight of the delivery box, half of a large sausage with extra cheese pizza remained. The scent of the pie hung thick in the air, so pungent that, under any other circumstances, Andi would have opened a window as a prelude to a good night's sleep. Tonight, she didn't care.

"Mm," she declared with satisfaction. "This is *so* good. I love the pizza from Aces, just love it. This is such a treat." She partially folded the remnant of the slice in her left hand and used her right to catch drips.

Andi sipped wine and fought an urge to wince. Much too sweet, much too, well, something, but it came with a screw-cap bottle in the discount aisle of one of Pennsylvania's state stores, on sale.

Meredith didn't seem to mind, and said, "So. The old guy gets up, leaves you with this — what's his name?"

A mild sense of warmth fluttered through her cheeks. "Clay. Clay Garrison. He seemed like a decent guy."

"Even if he knocked you to the ground so you wouldn't get killed by a truck?"

Andi smiled. "Probably instinctive. He's an ex-cop, Mer."

She tilted her head to the right for another attack on the slice. "So are you, Kit-Kit. And then what happened?

Andi sighed. "Yeah, well... anyway. Pike tosses a wad of money on the table, didn't even thumb it or count it, like he knew exactly how much, and says —" She mimicked his voice. "— 'this'll cover it, and your time as well.' And he walks away. By now he's probably interviewing someone else."

Meredith nodded while she chewed.

"So Clay and I looked at each other. He picked up the cash. I half expected him to pull out evidence gloves, but he didn't. It came out to exactly one thousand and fifty dollars. Which we divided evenly, and left the fifty for the waitress. We each kept a business card —"

"The one with just his name and phone number?"

"Yes. And then I spent most of the day just walking around."

"Thinking."

"Yes. Oh, Mer, I've got to figure out what to do next."

"You mean, you're not going to take the old guy's offer? Gosh, Andi, you make a couple of calls, get copies of the death certificates, put in your bill. Charge some outrageous amount. And hope he pays."

A fourth slice seemed justified, even if it had cooled. She hesitated. "Oh, and Mister Pike also left a note when he left." After rummaging through her bag, she retrieved what she picked up and examined while Clay counted cash. She unfolded it and waited for Mer to wipe her hands before passing it.

"Okay, Andi, a list of five names. I have no idea who they are."

She slumped back into the softness of the sofa. "I'm guessing relatives. Suspects, at least in his own mind. That's what Clay thought, too. But I got the very strong impression that he wasn't at all interested in the proposal. Mister Pike made it very clear he wanted both of us or nothing."

Meredith finished her wine and returned the glass to the table, which wobbled in response. She gathered up Gideon's business card and offered it with an outstretched arm and a look of stern maternalism. "So you call him up, say you're interested, but you have no way to contact this Clay person, hope for the best. Gosh, Kit-Kit, it's easy money."

"Actually, I do. Have a way to contact Clay, I mean. He's staying with that Mitch guy. Just before we left, we decided to exchange phone numbers. You know, one of those Hollywood things, have your people call my people and all that."

"He did?"

"On the back of the card." *And my pen didn't work. He immediately loaned me his, the third time he rescued me.* "So. Anyway, maybe we could warm up the rest of this pizza and watch some silly old movie and get wasted on this awful wine? And then you could tell me about how I could get a job in your real estate office."

Meredith's smile seemed more rueful than amenable. "Yeah, well, good luck with that. It's been really slow lately. The market is soft, not many buyers and suddenly everyone is thinking about selling. I'm pretty sure my boss isn't doing any hiring. But yes. Something will turn up. And I think my microwave still works."

* * *

Clay's right hand hovered over the pizza, sifting shredded cheese in a pale yellow blizzard across the freshly-assembled landscape. It was the last of materials from Huey K's Restaurant Supply, in what they called a beggar's bag.

Huey Kreschmayer had been way too generous, the same kindness as the long-ago day Clay walked halfway across town for a handful of supplies to cook a surprise birthday dinner for his father.

Still holed up in an old warehouse in a former industrial district, Huey K's hadn't changed. Huey'd put on a couple of pounds and his hair thinned even more, but he still barked with authority at sales staff who probably didn't take him seriously, but pretended to. And so they talked old times, over pastrami hoagies Huey assembled himself from off-the-books stock, about when the steakhouse was the best place to eat in town and one of Huey's major customers. A half-dozen chefs arrived to stock for the weekend, prompting a cue to build the beggar's bag, which Huey said would be no charge for an old pal come back to visit. But a couple of twenties changed hands anyway.

Huey knew the restaurant where Clay, Andi and Gideon Pike had met. "Gal by the name of Christie Goff owns it. Been in business for a couple of years. Showed up with a divorce settlement and a dream. You know the drill, right? So I helped her over a coupla the start-up bumps, because y'know, what's good for the trade is good for Huey. She does okay, strong on breakfast and lunch service, might do better with supper. But lately, it's a crappy business to be in. Well, you know that, o'course. Your old man did pretty good for a long time, one of my best customers, until things started to sour. You getting into the game, Clay?"

"No way. I was only there to meet a guy."

Into the beggar's bag went a few pounds of restaurant-grade high gluten stone ground flour, some of the custom sauce for an upscale parlor downtown, fresh produce, pound of yeast, and enough pizza blend mozzarella to really load an eighteen incher. Ninety minutes later, Clay went with a fourteen-inch screen and pan, about the limit in Mitch's postage-stamp kitchen. Maybe the extra would stuff an omelet or top eggs, up, the next morning.

But first had been the matter of cleaning the oven and praying the thermostat would be halfway accurate. Mitch had no idea and didn't mind relocating stored cookware, now stacked on the end of a counter with barely working space for the pie.

Mitch arrived in the late afternoon, his shift complete, and happily popped the cap off a regional IPA, ice cold and very dry while Clay prepped pizza. "Y'know, bro, you're gonna have to write all this down. I saw you do this just once before. Remember the night we broke into the kitchen at college so you could make that pie to impress —what was her name? —"

"Ellen McClaskey."

"Yeah, Ellen. And you scored because of it." He took a long pull from the bottle. "Which is why you gotta teach me how to do this stuff, just so's I can do the same thing, man." He held a bottle aloft. "You want one of these?"

"Yeah, thanks." Clay stood erect and took a half step back to inspect a really loaded pie, probably twelve to thirteen minutes if the oven was actually four-fifty. He dusted scraps from the rim of the screen and returned to hovering low over the project. Fresh basil, coarsely chopped, a drizzle of virgin oil, and one last glance before it went into the oven and he accepted the beer from Mitch.

"How long, buddy?"

"Twenty minutes. Thirteen to bake, five to cool, then slice. I suppose you don't happen to have a pizza cutter?"

"Naw, man. I get my pies from Aces, downtown. Fourteen ninety-five and you eat and pass gas half the night. Theirs comes cut. Man, this is gonna be good. A Clay Garrison pie, and we don't even have any chicks to impress." Mitch saluted with his bottle. "So where'd you get the pizza goodies?"

"Huey's, over on South Forest."

"Cool. So how'd your meeting with the guy go?"

"Not great. The guy gave us some cash for our time, and that's about it."

"Our?"

"Yeah. The woman from the bar last night."

"The blonde?"

"No. The one with long brown hair. Andi Delvento."

"She was hot, man. Really hot."

Clay took a hit from the bottle and wiped his lips with the back of his hand. "Yeah, she is. And an ex-cop, like me."

Mitch winced and shook his head. "Aw, man, that's like... Wow. I never figured her for a cop."

"Pretty good at it, too. Had the guy who set up the meet eating out of the palm of her hand."

"Yeah, I bet. She looked the type, buddy. So, some kind of audition?"

"I'd been hoping he recruited for a regular police job, but he wanted a private investigator. Two, actually. He wanted both of us, package deal."

"Yeah? Oh, wait. You've got a thing for PI's, if I remember."

"Oh, yeah."

Mitch assembled a reminiscence and spoke it. "On account of that jerk over on Fourth. Storm or some... Glenn Storm. Major slime ball."

"That's the one."

Mitch scratched the back of his head. "Yeah. The guy died a few months ago. Everyone said booze, but the word was drugs, painkillers. From some local doc. The talk claims the coroner covered it up." He paused for a sip. "But, yeah, no big loss there."

Clay grunted. "Yeah, well... So, buddy, today I got had, but no harm done. We walked out of there with five hundred apiece, a little walking around money."

"Yeah? Like, what happened, man?"

Clay told the story, a casual play-by-play, beginning with the incident on the street with the truck and ending with a display of the business card. Meanwhile, the pie came out of the oven, looking better than expected. After all, a guy with no rotary cutter probably didn't have a timer, either. The scent of fresh pizza filled the room and they cracked their third beer. Clay patted his pocket and pulled out the business card. "But, lucky you, the phone number on the back belongs to the blonde you were drooling over. Andi's staying with her."

"No kidding?" Mitch studied the card. "So who is this old dude, anyway?" He flipped the card and his eyes widened. "Are you kidding me?"

Clay began to slice the pie with Mitch's cutlery, about as sharp as a butter knife. It would have to do. "Yeah, Gideon Pike."

"*The* Gideon Pike?"

"Is there more than one? Want to go six slices or eight?"

Mitch waved him off. "I want to check..." He reached for his shoulder bag and pulled out a notebook computer, took a look at the card and typed. Within moments, he had an image on the screen and displayed it. "This the guy?"

Clay glanced up from his task. Six slices would be fine in a fourteen-inch pie. "Yeah, that's him. Only he wore a baseball cap, long bill, like a fisherman."

Mitch focused on his computer, muttering, "Oh, wow."

"What?"

"This dude is like a billionaire. Got his fingers into all kinds of businesses, working out of some holding company. Holy..." He looked up. "You hooked into the big time, bro."

Clay sought a hot pad to put under the serving pan, finally opting for a folded hand towel. He shifted the pie to the table, already set for two. "Still don't want to do PI work. Plus, as far as I'm concerned, it's too strange. Guy is probably delusional, old age and all that."

Mitch settled into a chair and tugged a slice. "Yeah, well, if you don't want it, I'll put my name in the hat."

A twinge of guilt rippled through Clay's mind. Mitch would not qualify, and it would be polite if he portrayed it as a bad deal that Mitch should avoid it, kind of like sitting next to a guy sneezing and coughing. In the end, he went for being up front. "Sorry, buddy, he wanted for people with law enforcement experience.

Hey, I wanted to ask you if there were any reporting slots open on your paper. You know, just to tide me over?"

Mitch laughed and cut a hefty slice of pizza. "Bro, the last place you want to be is at my work. The conglomerate that bought out the conglomerate last time has been bought out by an even bigger conglomerate. The word is that they're about to do some serious cost-cutting. Which means guys like me."

"Nah. You're a good reporter, one of their best."

Mitch chuckled. "Yeah, and a major pain in the company butt. This, by the way, is the best pizza I ever had. No wonder you got laid back in college. Hey, if I was gay, I'd be — nah, never mind. The thought is just way too grotesque. But, hey, you ought to open a parlor here in town, give the dudes at Aces a run for their mon-ey."

It wasn't a bad pie, all things considered, but just for fun. "No restaurants. No PI work. I wanted law enforcement, a quality slot."

Mitch devoured the slice, burped and reached for a second. "Yeah, well, good luck with that, man."

Chapter Eight

Under bright, fluorescent light in a chain supermarket a short walk from Mitch's place, Clay thumbed through a stack of packaged boneless pork chops.

He hunted a pair rather than set of six, without luck. The top two neared freeze-by date and were deeply discounted. Tempting, but not yet that desperate. None won awards for appearance. Older patrons dominated thin early morning traffic, drifting past.

A bored-looking meat worker, on the heavy side and covered with an already-soiled apron, waited several steps away. When Clay re-stacked chops, she asked, "Can I help you?"

"Looking for a package of two."

She seemed late-shift tired. "I can custom wrap it if you want, but the price break applies to the larger packages."

"That's okay. I don't have a store card."

"Suit yourself. But you ought to get a card. You'll save oodles of money. See the customer service desk." She nodded toward the front of the store.

Clay smiled. "Thanks for the advice. But right now, I'll make do with a package of two."

The meat worker shrugged. "It'll be a couple of minutes. You can continue shopping, come back."

Clay considered the short mental shopping list and the light weight of the basket in his left hand. "No problem. I can wait."

She nodded and padded into the fresh meats sanctuary,

walled off by the standard high refrigerated display case running in a straight line toward the deli department.

He yawned and silently debated yams versus white potatoes, fresh vegetables easily sauteed, maybe some fruit. Depending on how fresh it was.

A soft voice behind him said, "Hey."

In a sweatshirt too large but jeans that looked custom-made, Andi wore the same radiant smile that melted Gideon Pike the day before.

She pushed a small cart, bearing six assorted frozen dinners and said, "So. Good morning."

He grappled with words to organize a sentence. "Morning. You're doing a little shopping?" Then he kicked himself for stupidly asking the obvious.

* * *

She looked at the frozen meals in her cart. Two chicken, two sort-of beef, two vegetarian. A trustworthy brand, with sauces that would melt in during the microwave experience, safe on the calorie side but not memorable. A variety, Mer's favorites.

She studied his face again. Nice guy, polite, pleasant. Looking pretty good in a denim shirt over worn jeans and some kind of boots. A cowboy without the hat, but a little on the soft-spoken bashful side, decidedly better than macho cocky and swaggering.

"Um, yes. You know, well, a variety. Shopping for my friend, the one I'm staying with. Trying to be a decent guest." And trying not to sound like a total idiot.

"Meredith."

"You remembered. Yes. We go way back. How about you?"

He nodded toward the meat lady, who'd finally wrapped a pair of chops on a table fifteen feet away. "Yep. Me too." He pointed to the dinners in her cart. "Staying for a couple of days?"

The meat lady arrived and passed the package to Clay. She looked at Andi.

"Oh, sorry. No, I'm not..." The meat lady nodded and shuffled along the counter toward a customer lingering over trays of fresh fish. Clay offered a soft smile, to which she said, "Yeah. You too?"

Clay examined the meat and dropped into his basket. "Not sure yet."

"So, who's the cook?"

He laughed, a gentle, disarming kind of chuckle that pointed to a guy who could poke fun at himself. "Well, certainly not Mitch. I don't think he knows which side of a saute pan is up."

"Are you, like, a chef?"

"No, not really. I get by, that's about it. Why do you ask?"

"Uh-huh. Well, you said 'saute pan.' Most guys would say 'frying pan' or maybe 'skillet.'

He nodded. "That's because they *are* different. A saute pan has straight sides. Skillets or frying pans have slanted, and they're good for fast-frying. But a nice saute is better for searing or slow, mostly with sauces."

Charming. Absolutely charming. "Ah, you *are* a chef, not a —" she lowered her voice to mimic a thick, South Philly blue-collar accent — "guy, yo, makin' the meat." She switched to one of a popular TV cooking show host. "Like, with six pounds of hot seasoning. Gotta kick 'er up a notch."

He smiled. "Nope. I mean, I enjoy cooking, but... It's like this. My dad owned a restaurant, here in town."

"Owned?"

"Past tense. It went bust, then he passed."

"I'm so sorry."

"It's okay. As you'd probably expect, you pick up a few things. But no formal training. Never went to school for it. And, mostly, a saute pan, because that's all Mitch has in his kitchen."

The meat lady drifted back into proximity, perhaps in case

Andi changed her mind or Clay decided to pick up one of the beef roasts on the other side of the glass next to them.

Andi said, "I think we should move on, before we get a citation for misdemeanor lingering. What else are you getting for a meal that's probably a whole lot better than the chicken or the beef, and that soy-thing that I should be eating, but probably not today?"

"I need some produce."

"Mind if I tag along? I could use a few pointers."

He laughed again. A reassuring laugh, the kind guys use when opening their circle to newcomers. "Here? I'm just hoping for reasonably fresh."

"Which is better than I ever do. I mean, that's why they invented cans or those microwave packets."

Display islands of cheeses and sausages punctuated the portal of the produce department. He said, "Well, okay, then. But you do realize that, at this sort of thing, there are guys much better than me."

They entered a field of greens and reds and yellows with more subdued lighting other than the hidden illumination above fruits and vegetables.

So cute. "Aw, Clay, now why do I doubt that? Besides. This is the third time we've bumped into each other, and you know what they say about that."

He sighed.

And the blush is cute, too. "Exactly. What sort of vegetables or whatever is on your menu tonight?"

* * *

At every stop, he felt increasing pressure. Summer squash, onion, tomato and green beans should have been easy, but supermarket produce had its limits and Andi had prodded his pride.

Definitely not the sort of thing that he'd watch his dad's crew fuss over at dock marketplaces where restaurant reputations could hang in the balance.

Andi peppered him with questions, eager to learn and attentive to evaluation techniques he'd learned back in the day, when all assumed he'd follow in his father's business. Before it fell apart —thanks to Glenn Storm — and his dad pushed him toward being a cop. An actual police officer, not Gideon Pike's private investigator.

She hung close at displays, the scent and glow of her intoxicating. Their shoulders nearly touched, constraining his customary long reaches and wide gestures, unnerving his concentration. He finally exercised less than normal patience and pronounced the task done.

In the checkout line, Andi accepted the courtesy of going ahead and declined his offer to pay for both orders. "I've got it, don't worry. You know, we ought to talk about —"

He unloaded his basket and chuckled. "You're working me, the same way you did with Gideon."

The clerk, a woman barely out of her teens, zipped through the scanning of her dinners and bagged them. Andi handed her a twenty-dollar bill. "I am not."

"Uh-huh."

"Well, okay, maybe a little."

"Uh-huh."

She gathered the two plastic bags and the clerk set to work on Clay's dinner materials. "You're not the least bit curious?"

"No." He informed the clerk that the potatoes were Yukon Gold and she nodded.

Andi's shoulders slumped. "C'mon, Clay. It's a murder and two missing persons. We could do this. Make some easy money." She realized the clerk, her jaw open, stared at them. Andi assured her, "It's a hypothetical, sort of a scavenger hunt." A pause. The clerk seemed unconvinced. "Don't worry. We're both police officers, and it's a training thing."

The clerk nodded and weighed potatoes. She held the pork chop package aloft. "You know, if you buy the family pack, you get a discount with your card."

Clay smiled. "Yes, they said. But we're in town for the day and I don't have a card."

"I can't give you the discount on the store card unless you get a family pack."

Andi rolled her eyes. "He's more interested in the murder and the missing persons. Children in fact. But hypothetically."

Clay chuckled. "I'm not."

The clerk said, "That's twenty-three fifty-six, sir. Um, are you people really cops?"

He said, "In the hypothetical sense." He glanced down to the right for her name tag. "Thanks very much, Allison. Have a nice day."

"You too, sir." She stole a glance at Andi and mustered a faint, semi-sweet smile.

Clay said to Andi, "C'mon. Let's get out of here before we get arrested."

On the long walk to the exit, Andi said, "I came on too strong, didn't I? Yeah, yeah. I *knew* it. I came on too strong. Tell me I came on too strong."

"You want me to tell you that you came on too strong?"

"Well, no. I'd much rather have you say, 'Gosh, Andi, you did a great job persuading me to get involved in this Gideon Pike business. I'm raring to go.' But you're not going to say that. You're going to say I came on too strong and you're still not interested. Not in the slightest."

They walked half a dozen steps in silence.

She continued, "I mean, if it was me, no question. I'd love to know whether this guy is the real Gideon Pike, and what this mystery is about and why he picks us out of the blue and makes this big thing about both or nothing. I wouldn't be thinking about warming up a frozen dinner after Mer-Bear reminded me to recharge my phone. I could at least learn that Gideon Pike is some sort of a reclusive billionaire..."

"Mer-Bear?"

"Pet name from childhood. Meredith and I have been best friends since I can't remember. She thinks we should at least have a look at the case at least to find out whether this guy is *the* Gideon Pike."

Clay nodded. "And what does Mer-Bear call you? Persistent?"

She scowled. "Let's not go there." She sidestepped into his path and pulled up, nearly causing them to collide. "Look, Clay, I need this. I'm sorry if I came on too strong back there among the cabbages and carrots. I'm sure if it were the other way around, you'd probably be arrested for harassment."

He grunted. "Misdemeanor innuendo if nothing else, second degree."

"Okay. I'm sorry. I am. Chalk it up to rookie mistake. I went through school, the application process, the academy, training swearing I'd never use sexuality as a means to an end. Although that didn't exactly go both ways."

"I thought you did pretty good. I mean, not in a cop way, but in a...." He fell silent.

"A what?"

"Not important."

She nodded. "So you think I did, in fact, come on too strong."

He chuckled. Her inquisitive eyes sparkled and taunted and teased him at same time. "Okay. If it makes you feel better, maybe a little. Like when I showed you how to tell that spot on the cucumber meant it had been stored colder than it should."

"I see."

"It's okay."

She frowned.

"Really, Andi. I thought it was kind of cute."

She shook her head and her hair flowed back and forth with it. "What would be okay would be if...."

He sighed. "...If I agreed to at least have a look into this case. I know."

Her eyes loaded up with hopeful. "Okay, here's the thing, Clay. I'm out of work for too long and up against it. Doing fine until my training officer thought I was perfect for sex on the side because his wife's mean and his lousy kids are driving him crazy. He wouldn't accept no, and I got to the point of dreading being alone with him. His hands were.... well, never mind. When I got angry enough and went to internal affairs, they thought it so hilarious that they shared it with the guys in the squad room. And then the joke stuff started. And got worse and worse until I'd find incredibly disgusting stuff, even in my locker. I went to the chief, he shook his head and said he didn't see how I'd clear probation. I may as well turn in my badge."

"Wow."

She looked at him, directly, unflinching. "And that, Clay, is no bull. No con. No game. I spent half the night and a whole bottle of wine talking it out with Mer, and now I'm getting past craving to be in law enforcement any more. I need this job. Okay?" She abruptly looked away. "And if not this, with you, then I'll find something else." She faced him. "But I'd rather...."

"You know we're probably out of our depth."

She nodded.

"And it could be a whole lot of nothing."

"I know."

"And we're uncertain we can trust this guy who claims to be Gideon Pike."

"True."

He said, "We could meet at the library. That's neutral ground, right? In, say, an hour, start doing research. Or I could drive you over to your friend's to drop off the food, and then to the library. But we could meet later, if you'd be more comfortable."

She looked into his eyes, and smiled. "Let's drive together."

Chapter Nine

Clay shifted attention from Andi to double glass doors of the city library. She reached out to block his path. "No. Let me do it."

His hand lingered on the door handle, snared in a practice in-grained since his earliest childhood, the manners of gentlemen, the gestures of service.

"Clay, just once, I'd like to turn the tables."

Her smile widened and the instant he saw the twinkle in her eyes he abandoned confusion about gender roles and tradition. To play the competitive game of social amusement, he released a nickel-plated vertical bar on one of a pair of doors that opened left and right. "Be my guest." As she reached for the same handle, he added, "But from where you're standing, you're on the wrong door."

"I am?" She studied the options.

"Yes. It'd work if you were to my left when you opened it, I'd have a clear path to pass. As it is, you're reaching across my body."

"Because I'm on the right. I'd be blocking your path." Her shoulders slumped and she sighed. "So, I'm using the wrong door."

She'd put him in a position where he struggled to contain a chuckle. "Yep. The right one's a better choice."

She switched handles and pulled the other door toward her. "They teach you that in guy school?"

"Doors are a big deal in *customer service* school. Guys are simple, straightforward."

"Uh-huh. Anyway, it was an impulsive decision. Did it bother you? The door, I mean?"

Displays promoting coming events and new titles punctuated a broad lobby with subdued lighting. "No, it didn't."

As they walked, her head turned back and forth, probably sponging visual information. "Oh, good. I was worried."

He clung to the game, but his position felt precarious. "About a guy allowing a woman to open a door for him or the impulse?"

She scanned the entry of a basic public library. "The door, of course. I never worry about impulsive decisions. Let's get information at the desk."

Stacks to the right, a large open space to the left, mostly carrels for computer users. Straight ahead, an imposing mahogany lobby centerpiece under an immense line of metallic letters that spelled out *Circulation*.

Clay noticed the woman staffing the desk and stopped.

"So where do we...?" A step ahead of him, she paused. "What's wrong?"

Some things never change, he thought. The old city library, stuck for years on a side street in a derelict Victorian building nobody wanted, had a new facility in a former office building close to the county complex near the downtown square. A sleek and modern look compared to the make-do eclectic of his youth. But Mrs. Tidwell remained at Circulation, directly in front of the manager's office. She might have been Miriam to everyone in the Friends of the Library crowd, but she would always be Mrs. Tidwell to guys like him. He said to Andi, "Someone I recognize."

Her head tilted left and her gaze tracked his line of sight.

"Terrific! Always helps to have someone you know handy. And I bet you're dying to say hello, reminisce and stuff." She marched forward and he fell in beside her.

"Not especially."

Andi ignored him and closed the distance in long, assured strides, a smile steadily widening into full sunshine force, turning heads as she progressed.

Mrs. Tidwell's attention clung to a stack of paper, talking to someone on the phone. She hung up as Andi reached the counter and stepped slightly to the side to allow Clay to take the lead.

Old then and older now, she still dressed like a well-groomed school principal with hair pulled tight into a bun, making her skin look like it was stretched taut. Around her neck, a sparkling light chain ended on the earpieces of her half-rim glasses, over which she glared at him when her task ended.

Clay murmured, "Uh, hi, Mrs. Tidwell."

Mrs. Tidwell's eyes narrowed.

Not like sifting memories. More like working a mental card catalog, the old-fashioned kind, with long, agile fingers, with claws.

Mrs. Tidwell held a lone finger aloft. "Wait. Hm. Yes. I remember you, *Mister Garrison*." Ice clung to every syllable. "How may I help you?"

Andi cocked an eyebrow.

"Uh, well, we were hoping to... Um, could you direct us to the reference section, business-type stuff?"

* * *

Andi studied Mrs. Tidwell. Every library has one. And Mrs. Tidwell looked at Clay like a bird of prey evaluating carrion. Unconsciously, Andi drifted half a step toward him to show support.

The librarian pointed. "You'll find the reference section up that flight of stairs, Mister Garrison. Business materials will be to the right, halfway down the side of the room. There are tables and chairs if you plan to work. *Work*, Mister Garrison. Not shenanigans. I *do* assume you've learned the difference in the past ten years?"

Ouch.

Clay straightened. Cop courage, cop courtesy. "Yes, ma'am. I believe so."

Mrs. Tidwell's attention returned to the paperwork.

Andi leaned in, wrapped her arm through his, and smiled. "Don't worry, Mrs. Tidwell, I'll keep an eye on him."

The librarian's chilly gaze came directly to her. "I hope so. And you must be the latest girlfriend?"

Andi released Clay's arm. "No ma'am. Partner."

Mrs. Tidwell's imperious gaze went to the arms, disconnected. "Of course." Again, her focus shifted to the papers. "Have a nice day."

Three quarters of the way up a broad, curving staircase, she could no longer contain herself and whispered. "Wow. *Shenanigans?* Latest girlfriend? Ho, ho, ho. You must have —"

"Don't want to talk about it."

She shrugged. "Well, you can if you wish. I mean, we're partners and it's okay."

At the top of the stairs he said, "We're not partners yet. But anyway, in high school, well, we all did dumb stuff, kid stuff."

She craved details, but let it go. "Okay, and?"

"And no, it didn't involve a girlfriend."

"Uh-huh. But you were pretty popular? I mean, nice guys usually are."

He chuckled. "Probably not half as popular as you must have been. And I bet the teachers and librarians adored you because you were the perfect girl."

Heat filled her cheeks and ears as they entered the reference area and made their way to the described location. "Well, I had friends, but hardly perfect. A library once banned us for an entire month. Mer and me. We were terrible. But it was a high school li-

brary, not in the same league as Mrs. Tidwell's little store, an actual downtown library. Ah. And here we are."

"Where do you want to start?"

He had allowed her control of the situation, a pleasant change
of pace. "From that end. I guess we're looking for anything involving Gideon Pike. Any pictures would be great."

As they separated in front of a collection of bound business
reference books, Clay said, "I already know they look the same.
Mitch pulled up a couple of photos last night on his phone."

"Yes," she muttered while thumbing though the materials. "I
did too. Well, once I got it recharged. I take it you don't use one?"

"A cell phone? Did. Had to give it up seven months out of
work. Choice of rent or technology. If we both know what Pike
looks like, then what are we —"

She tugged a promising-looking book from the shelf. "Older
pictures, ones showing families. My guess is that the reclusive
Mister Pike was probably less bashful when he was climbing the
ladder."

He thumbed pages. "There are always guys who avoid the
limelight, and there are guys who live for it. Here we go. I think
I've got something." He chose a space on the nearest empty table
in a room full of empty tables, pulling a chair out of the way and
standing back to give her access. With space.

She tugged a pen and a favorite small spiral notebook from
her bag, the last of a bundle she'd bought months ago, and flipped
through ink-lined pages of notes and reminders until she found
an empty sheet, a few from the end. "Were you a limelight avoider
or lover?"

"An avoider. Probably one of the reasons I wasn't a very good
quarterback."

She scribbled key points from a page that showed a grainy
family portrait of the Pike family from long ago. "Either that or
the string of girlfriends or the library incident. Look, this one has

to be the deceased daughter. She looks terribly young in this picture."

"Ten or eleven. What's the date?"

"Hm. Thirty years. Would have made her fifteen or sixteen
when... Gosh, that's sad, isn't it? Hard to picture her as a mom."

Clay nodded. "All the more tragic because the twin daughters
were not live birth. If she was a junkie and the babies survived,
they would have been addicted, too. Their infancy would have
been hell."

Andi's fingertips tapped on the caption identifying people in
the photo. "But Pike thinks they might have."

"Awful long shot. And if they went into adoption or foster
care, who knows where they are now? It also strikes me as odd a
family with these kinds of resources would offload an unwanted
baby, well, two, into the system. More likely, they would have
managed it with the sort of discretion that big bucks can afford.
And if Gideon is the big dog, he probably would know exactly
what happened. Why hire us?"

She reflexively chuckled as she picked up her phone and
tapped the screen to life. "Because he's desperate. Didn't you get...
no, of course not. No phone."

Andi settled into the empty chair and scrolled through a stack
of messages, content with knowing that without her favorite
watch she could still get the time from a fully-charged phone.
"Okay, here we go."

The message said, "Await affirmative reply, your terms. Have
option to purchase agency to meet your needs. GP."

She passed the phone to Clay.

As he read it, his expression became increasingly puzzled,
tinged with skepticism. He murmured phrases. "Await affirmative? Your terms? Option to purchase? What agency?"

She shrugged. "I don't know. Probably some local investigation firm, small shop perhaps. What? What's bothering you?"

* * *

Clay took one last look at the message, signed "GP," and returned it to Andi. Pike could be referring to the Storm agency, technically defunct. Made no difference. He wanted nothing to do with it, under any circumstances. The building and the files in it could burn to the ground and it would be a civic improvement.

He said, "Private investigations work is the last thing I want to get into. I made the trek hoping to meet with a recruiter from somewhere in the region, get back into a uniform, behind a badge and go catch bad guys."

She seemed dubious. "That's what you said all along. What's different now? C'mon, Clay, don't hand me a load of bull. I've had too much of that lately and I already have too much respect for you."

He craved time to think but all he had was an empty chair opposite her. They were two of a kind, out-of-work cops screwed over by the system they took an oath to uphold, promising careers, hopes and dreams, flushed down a drain with lousy aftertaste. They were broke, ready to take any kind of work. Storm, whatever, no matter. Besides, the guy was dead, the office shuttered. It wouldn't help repair a crappy legacy for his father. Glenn Storm had probably damaged many others.

Andi sat quietly, her hands in her lap, her inquisitive gaze steady, those big brown eyes blinking every few moments.

He nodded. "Okay, so here it is. There's some history involved, personal stuff, private, family business I'd rather not get into, okay?"

"Okay..."

"So my guess is that Gideon Pike is upping the ante and he's got some kind of tentative offer going on a local detective agency, Storm Investigations. Let's just say there's some bad memories involved, okay?"

Her voice softened and relaxed. "Okay. And...?"

He looked away for a moment, and shrugged. "And I've got to get over it. Past it. Move on."

She nodded, looked down and her voice withered to a whisper, accepting defeat. "I understand."

"Andi, look, we're rookie cops. Barely out of training. At a minimum, this is complicated detective work, at which we have zero field experience. None. It's more than a cold case. It's totally frozen. The people involved are heavy hitters, the kind of big-leaguers that eat little fish like us for lunch. And don't have to chew before swallowing."

"Probably all true." She abruptly looked up, direct and defiant.

"What?"

She cocked an eyebrow and shifted to an expression of casual indifference. "Well, since the entire deck is stacked so high against us, and since we're on the ropes, and since we have no chance, what do we have to lose? Our dignity? Self-respect? The next paragraph on a resume? What's the worst that can happen? A few days' work, enough money to get us to the next stop on our job searches, and you can bury the Storm agency, R-I-P, dust your hands off and walk away."

"That about it?"

"Well, it's the most I could come up with spur-of-the-moment."

"I liked the resume part."

She chuckled. "Good, because I was saving that up for special."

He sensed a poor decision, but plunged ahead. "We may be rookies, but we're a pair of bright people. With, well, attitude."

"*Bright?* Cut me a break. More like *brilliant*."

He scowled in mock protest at the evolving idea. "I dunno.

More time on Mitch's sofa doesn't work for me. I mean, I know holding cells that are more comfortable."

"Yeah, but you could be one of those old-fashioned shamus types who had a cot in the office supply storeroom."

Running with it now, abandoning common sense, he said, "Or curled up under the desk with an empty bottle of cheap bourbon."

Andi laughed. "Hey, hey, that's my spot. And it's with an upscale brandy, thank you very much."

His turn arrived to laugh aloud, easily, relaxed, like... He could not remember the last time. Beyond, the reference librarian scowled disapproval. *Yeah, she'll probably turn me in to Mrs. Tidwell. Like the last time.*

Andi desperately tried contain herself and quiet them. "Shhh. We're going to wear out our welcome. So. What do you think? Seriously?"

He released a deep breath, making it sound halfway between a groan and a sigh of resignation. "Let's call Gideon and see what he has to say. And think about what we're going to charge for our time. I may have no self-respect, but I don't do *pro bono*."

Chapter Ten

Meredith sliced what might have been beef, buried in a gray-ish-brown sauce. She looked up, eyes wide and brows high on her forehead. "Seriously? He *cooks* food? As in, from scratch?"

Although Andi had followed microwave directions exactly, barely warm dinner wasn't worth a second blast. Heat-n-serve, safely bland, ordinary food. "Yes. He had pork chops and was hunting the right kind of squash, one of those green things that looks like a cucumber."

Mer nodded. "Zucchini. I think."

"With onions and peppers and tomato and some sort of sea-soning."

Mer poked at her meal. "So, that's a major wow."

Andi shrugged. "Because his dad evidently ran a restaurant here, he kind of picked up on it."

Mer chewed a pair of green beans coated with the same goo and looked ruefully at her plate. "Think he'd be willing to invite some starving, malnourished people over? I mean, now that you've got this fish on the line, you've got to get him in the net."

"Let's not get carried away. I know he's not excited about the detective agency. Some sort of history. And for me, this is one of those little diversions to restock a wallet, pay off some bills, then get back to —"

"I know, I know. Badge, gun, uniform, one of those vests squashing your chest, having drunks puke all over you."

Andi sat back. The charm had long left the plate of the half consumed meal. "Yeah. You got that right. Kevlar's great for guys, but not women. Kind of like those bone corsets of medieval costumes, but worse."

Mer continued eating. "A rotten way to promote cleavage, I bet."

"I've also experienced an intoxicated subject throwing up on me, not to mention heaving out the last of his party in the rear seat of the patrol car. The training officer thought it hilarious and made me mop it up, mostly to watch my butt and not the passed-out drunk sprawled on the sidewalk."

"Oh, wow. You poor thing."

Andi studied her plate. Clay and his buddy, Mitch, were probably eating a fabulous meal with a bottle of some sort of correct wine. Maybe they had company. What had the imperious Mrs. Tidwell said? Oh, yes. Girlfriend of the week. Of course. They were being guys, showing off for old flames, rekindled. Being cool, charming, impressive. She struggled to tamp down an unexpected surge of jealousy, but could not bring herself to finish her meal.

"You're probably right, Mer. It's been so long and I guess there's more to life than law enforcement. I never wanted to be an ordinary patrol officer, doing traffic, routine patrols. I wanted to get into major crime, investigative stuff. Be a detective."

Mer pushed her plate of alleged beef away, washing down the aftertaste with ice water. "And this *detective* agency deal is a problem because...?"

"I'm not sure it's in Clay's plans. He's willing to go along, mostly because I've been shameless about persuading him, but I don't sense it's a permanent thing for him."

Mer rested her forearms on the table and leaned in, her usual posture of being the assured confidant. "So, if Mister Glamorous Chef wanders off with his frying pan under his arm —"

"Skillet. He called it a skillet."

"Whatever. But you'd be left with some sort of a business pos‑
sibility that you could nurture and grow."

"Maybe. Mister Pike said both of us or nothing. I don't know
what would happen when Clay left. Hoping to get a sense of that
tomorrow morning."

"Who knows, you could talk me into becoming your partner."

Andi toyed with an idea desirable and preposterous at the
same time. "That's very sweet of you, but I'm sure you're doing
much better in commercial real estate." When Meredith looked
away, her expression drooping, she added, "Oh, Mer... what's
wrong?"

Mer slumped back in her chair. "A lot of office gossip today,
rumors, things not going well, cutbacks and layoffs. That sort of
thing. The partners were huddled with lawyers most of the day.
It's not looking too great." After a dreary pause, she brightened.
"Say, maybe we both ought to get out. That jazz club. Have some
laughs. Lots of guys in there, you know."

Andi chuckled. "I'm sure. But not for me tonight. I've got to
do my hair, get organized for tomorrow. We're dealing with the
infamous Mister Pike first thing in the morning and this time I
plan to be ready."

The image of the Pike family returned again to haunt her. Pike
seemed hard, distant, indifferent, bored. The others were cocky,
arrogant. Except for the little girl, Kimberly. Who looked sad, for‑
lorn. Not knowing that in a couple of years, she'd be an addict.
And pregnant. And dead.

* * *

Mitch stabbed at remnants of squash and pork, loading his
fork, and chewed fast and hard. He wiped his lips with the back of
his hand and returned to the keyboard of a laptop computer.

Already done, Clay waited to bus the table. He took a sip of beer from the brown bottle and reviewed the material on the screen. Five frames of the same web browser were lined up and slightly overlapping. Search engine collections of the images of the five people on Pike's list formed two rows.

Mitch belched without shame. "Nice meal, buddy. I gotta have you over more often." Without waiting for a response, he ran his fingers through his hair and returned to the computer. "So, okay, here's the people on Pike's list of suspects. Yeah. When caught off guard by some paparazzi type, they still reek of Big Dog with major pull. Man, you can sure pick people to go after."

Clay looked at the screen. "Just one. Maybe. A real, big time maybe. We don't know if there's a crime, or who did what, to whom, or when. Or if there was, the status of the investigation."

"Yeah, but that chick's got you into it, right? I mean, if she's as smart as you've been saying, there's gotta be something, right?"

"Andi. And I don't know whether she's taking pity on Pike, me, or herself."

"Yeah, but this dude Pike, he's willing to lay some serious cash on the table for the satisfaction, right? And set you guys up in the ashes of an agency that you wouldn't mind burying once and for all. This Pike guy could connect you with people in his league looking for a little peeper work."

"True."

Mitch paused to finish his beer and add the bottle to empty plates at the end of the table. "So. You make the guy happy, he gives you a big, fat check, you get out of that downtown dump and kind of, you know, upscale, get yourself a nice rack of suits, good wheels, some of those tough-guy shades, tap into the Main Line crowd. Beats rousting some drunk in a dark alley in the rain in winter, man. Not to mention town-hall garbage cops have to put up with."

Clay nodded, "Or play along with."

"Exactly, my brother. *Exactly*. What's the deal, a fifty-fifty with this Andi chick?"

"Yeah, partners, even split. Pike's terms."

Mitch digested the remark. "Yeah, well, we can work with that. Hey, if this guy Pike is doing the blank-check stuff, hey, I could be one of your crew, a legman, picking up tips from bars and where ever."

Clay laughed. "Keep in mind that in those circumstances, Andi would be your boss."

Mitch retreated into reflection. "Oh. Yeah. Hm. You got a point."

Clay took a hit from the bottle. "Figured I might. Besides, you've got a great job doing what you like, nobody pulling *your* chain.

Mitch grunted. "Yeah, well, pretty obvious you don't know dink about the news business. For instance, one of the people on city council has a daughter who's opened some kind of flower shop and she wants me to do a big puff piece about it. Which would be okay, except she's been giving me a hard time about everything. Can't make her realize that when she shoots her mouth off about some stupid thing, it's gonna be on the front page. The whole family is a pain. So I tell her to have the kid send in some sort of press release to the community desk people. End of story, right?"

Clay chuckled. "Waiting for the other shoe here."

"Yeah, next day my boss — the managing editor — comes up and tells me to do a nice big puff piece on Little Miss Flower Pot. But I'm in the middle of another piece and hesitate for a sec. And the jerk leans in close and reminds me that the paper's cutting back and do I want to work there."

Clay nodded. "I get the drift."

"Yeah, right." He tapped a face on the screen. "You know what? I like this guy, right here, Leonard. I think he killed the Kimberly kid."

"The son? How come?"

"He's got beady eyes, man. It's always the dude with the beady eyes."

Clay sighed. "You've got to stop watching conspiracy flicks. We don't know for certain the girl was a homicide vic, much less gave birth to twins, who maybe got mysteriously whisked away and possibly put out for adoption. We don't even know why it's such a big deal to Gideon Pike, twenty-five years after the fact."

Mitch tapped the side of his nose and did a lousy impression of Humphrey Bogart. "I'm tellin' ya, pal, something smells rotten and we oughta crack this case. Lay it right out. Send the bums to the pen...or the morgue."

"I think you need another beer, buddy. Why Leonard, the son? Why not Austin Hart, stepson number two? Or the stepson, Conrad? Yeah, that one on the left. Or Carlene, the stepsister?"

"Hm. Or this cousin, Baxter McKnight. His eyes are kinda beady, too. Hard to be sure with the fancy tan."

Clay popped the cap off another bottle. "You're hopeless. You've got to learn to build a case."

Mitch studied the list of names Clay had scribbled down the night before. "Come to think of it, maybe there was no murder, but Gideon's trying to put the squeeze on all five. Big family fight kind of thing."

Clay shrugged. "Maybe."

A fresh bottle of beer appeared in Mitch's hand. "So this partner of yours. She's pretty sharp?"

"Oh, yeah."

"And a looker, too."

Clay smiled. "That she is, which is why it's easy to underestimate her mind. What she lacks in experience, she more than compensates in style. We're supposed to meet down at Storm's old place tomorrow morning, get the ball rolling." He paused for another sip, then faced Mitch directly. "I probably shouldn't have to ask, buddy, but for the time being the whole business has got to be, you know —"

Mitch nodded "Confidential. Got it. No worries."

"Thanks, man."

"Yeah sure. You want to go out tonight, have a few, maybe that jazz club, see if Andi and Meredith are hanging out?"

Clay grunted. "If I'm reading Andi halfway accurate, she's probably going for an early night, to be ready for Pike tomorrow. I probably ought to do the same. Don't mind saying I'm not looking forward to being in that office."

* * *

Andi paced in front of a brick building that dated at least to the 1950s, perhaps before. "A-1 Bail Bonds, The First to Call," occupied the ground floor, still shuttered at four minutes past nine.

A sign on a side door said the third floor housed the office of Freddie Robles, Attorney-at-Law, who specialized in personal injury lawsuits as well as, conveniently enough, criminal cases requiring the services of A-1 Bail Bonds. A guy who might have been Freddie scurried past, lugging a heavy brown briefcase, a paper cup of coffee and a worried expression. He ignored Andi.

In between, Storm Investigations made no pretense of hours. From across the street, the windows suggested space behind it was vacant.

This time she arrived early, on the safe side of the street, decently dressed and groomed, her phone fully charged and the watch on her wrist ticking in perfect accuracy.

From the south, Clay appeared out of nowhere, his stride relaxed and unhurried, and he carried a cardboard tray with three cups. Coffee from the shop down the block, a round to impress everyone. She smiled and waved, chastising herself for not thinking of it first.

Be nice. "Morning, Clay."

He hoisted the tray to display the goodies. "Got some coffee. From Grounds Crew, a few doors down."

"Wow, thanks. I'm still new in town, don't know the better places." The flat-out lie to cover herself sounded okay.

"I guessed cream and sugar. Hope that's okay."

"Perfect." Correct, because while she was busy working Gideon in the restaurant, he had observed what she put in her coffee. She was unable to guess Gideon's preference, because she hadn't paid attention.

From somewhere past a string of parked cars, a black sedan swept in to double park. No citation or warning today. The driver opened the right rear door and Gideon Pike stepped out. He wore a gray suit, double breasted, traditionally collared white shirt and a navy blue tie. Black shoes, polished but not spit shined. The driver handed him a black portfolio, retreated and drove away.

"Ah, coffee!" he boomed. "Splendid, just splendid. Cream only, I hope?"

"Yessir," Clay answered while passing a cup into Pike's outstretched hand.

Oh, my. He's good. I'd also bet the last coffee is black, Clay's other option in case he had the cream-only wrong. It left her standing there clutching her bag in one hand and the cup in the other, unable to shake hands.

She stole a glance at Clay. Had he been gloating, he didn't show it. But she would've understood if he did.

Chapter Eleven

Andi's low expectations descended with each step up to the second floor landing. Severely eroded, narrow stair treads, shuddered under foot, the handrail wobbled, and drab greenish paint peeled from uneven walls.

Gideon took the lead and Clay followed after she motioned for him to go ahead. She'd learned to keep subjects ahead rather than behind, but also male cops couldn't be trusted a couple of steps below.

Sure, Mer. Why work in a modern office building with bright light, taupe walls and all the safety features when you can have this be the front door to....

Yes. A cramped little open room, coated in thick gray dust. Light barely penetrated two grimy windows. What used to be some sort of a divider, to create the illusion of an inner office, sprawled across on the floor near an overturned folding table. Two battered and mismatched filing cabinets, the drawers open and empty, flanked the space where the good one probably once stood.

And dust, everywhere. Little clouds blossomed with each step, drifted into half light, and coated a field of cobwebs drooping from places spiders mistakenly viewed with optimism.

Clay gave her a glance that hinted understanding. She returned an expression declaring *don't dare suggest it has potential*. He nodded. Hope for a partnership brightened.

Meanwhile, Pike marched through inspection as if he'd stumbled into the primary chamber of an Egyptian king's tomb, launching clouds of dust with every step. But there wasn't any gold. Only the junk a repo company leaves behind. Light fixtures didn't work, because there were no bulbs in them.

Gideon gestured for assistance. "C'mon, Clay, give an old fellow a hand at getting our desk standing properly."

No please. Don't..... Too late. The guys returned it to an upright position and a grey cloud erupted into the last of the room's clean air. She rubbed her nose to suppress a sneeze.

Pike stepped back to admire and grin. "Ah. That's better. Now it resembles an office, don't you think?"

Clay dusted off his hands.

Sure. Add a little more to the air. Andi crossed her arms and rocked her right foot on the heel of her shoe. "I hate to be a spoilsport, Mister Pike —"

"Please," he said. "Gideon. Remember, we're partners."

Clay atoned for his sin. "Well, sir, I don't know I'd go that far. I am amenable to talking about it." He glanced at Andi. "But I suspect that meeting here is a bit premature."

Thank you. She eagerly nodded agreement. "I'm not entirely sure you made a shrewd investment Mister — uh, *Gideon*. The infrastructure doesn't seem to be worth it, plus there is a considerable amount of paperwork ahead if we're to legally operate as licensed investigators."

Gideon reached into his jacket pocket and displayed two thick envelopes. "All done. Your PI papers, business license, weapons permits, various tax materials, and of course partnership documents for the LLC, which you'd have to sign, o'course."

While Gideon offered the envelopes to each in turn, she hoped her jaw hadn't dropped as much as Clay's.

Clay said, "These are dated today. How did you —"

Gideon waved him off. "I'm still a man with some influence. I think you'll find everything is in good order. Up to snuff. Ship-shape."

Clay murmured, "That's an understatement."

Gideon ignored the remark. "Now, I'll concede that your office is in need of some tidying up —"

Andi chuckled. "There's a more spectacular understatement. I'll bet you've already arranged for cleaning and decorating."

Gideon displayed the most smug smile she'd ever seen.

Clay said. "You're joking, right? No, I guess not."

"Commercial cleaners should be here in, oh, twenty minutes, said it would take about an hour and a half. Painters are scheduled for soon after. You'll have your choice of colors, of course, but I'd recommend conservative, on the corporate side. While they're sprucing up the place, feel free to visit an office supply shop." He produced a card from his shirt pocket. "It's a reputable firm. Ask for Janice Something-Or-Other, she'll fix you up with whatever you need to be comfortable. I want you kids to get started on my case right away and —"

Clay raised a hand. "Hold it. Just hold it a moment."

Andi drew a breath. *Second thoughts?* She remained silent. If they were going to be partners, they had to have each others' backs.

Gideon looked around. "Something wrong?"

* * *

Clay set his jaw. His counsel to himself oozed through his brain like liquid mud. *Be nice. Don't rock the boat. Be polite, deferential to anyone and everyone who might lead to a job. For once, watch what you say.* The muck choked his mind, drowning his soul. He desperately needed air. *Enough.* "Yes, as a matter of fact. Let's put it this way. I don't know about Andi, but where I come from this sort of opportunity doesn't fall off a truck and into your lap. You're making many assumptions, Mister Pike. You'll understand if I fall back on that old adage, about if it looks too good to be true..."

He stood on uncertain ground, knowing way too little about a partner and far too early in a career to make a comfortable guess as to how to arrange an interrogation. The detectives he'd seen passed the baton back and forth so casually that the subject couldn't keep up. One would keep careful notes, the other seemed indifferent to marking things down. He glanced toward Andi. Neither held a pad of paper, much less a pen.

Andi faintly nodded, evidently encouragement and willingness to tag along, see where things went.

Gideon smiled, one of those "trust-me" things con artists use. Clay still sensed no real leverage and Gideon spoke to fill the void.

"Absolutely understand your position, son. Absolutely. I'd prefer you two would accept the fact that your proverbial ship's come in, but yes, I understand how you might be a bit dubious. But we have to, at least for the time being, keep the incorporated name, Storm Investigations. Merely a formality to facilitate speedy transfer of the LLC from Mister Storm's estate to us. Now, I recognize that it's possibly somewhat uncomfortable for you, but my people tell me that you're a man of some backbone, that you can take adversity and not lose focus."

Clay's eyes narrowed. "You still don't —"

Andi interrupted. "Oh, I'm certain Clay understands. But we had questions of our own."

Gideon showed an expression of surprise, then puzzlement, and finally recognition. "Ah. I should have expected as much. I bring in a pair of talented investigators, I should assume caution at the least and suspicion at the most."

Clay resisted an urge to add *accusation* to the list. Motives with the group he'd examined the night before could lead in many directions. Today, there were no chairs in the room, no recording devices or observation facilities. Gideon stood the opposite side of the table, with Andi to the right, arms crossed but otherwise trying to look friendly. It would have to do. "Well, sir, I appreciate that you'd prefer to get started quickly and efficiently. If you have a few minutes, before the cleaners get here, I want to fill in some of the blanks. You don't mind, do you?"

Gideon tilted his head back and narrowed his eyes. "You're not suggesting I'm hiring you to cover up —"

Andi said, "No sir, we certainly wouldn't want to think that. I believe Clay wants to eliminate you from any hint of suspicion, as quickly as possible. It's routine. I'm sure you understand."

A twinge of impatience coated Pike's words. "Well, of course I do. There are certain ramifications —"

Clay pounced. "Such as? Previously, you said you were acting in a grandfatherly way, wanting to be sure that if the twins were alive, that an old wound would be healed. To do the right thing by them. Isn't that correct?"

Andi's voice went sympathetic, soothing, calming. "I'm afraid Clay's right, Mister Pike. I heard it, too."

Gideon's gaze shifted back and forth, distracted and confused at first. A twinkle of approval surfaced in his eyes. "Well, yes. What do you two know about proxy fights?"

Clay said, "They can get nasty if the stakes are high enough. Are they, Mister Pike?"

"Well, now, I...." His voice trailed off.

Andi said, "It's okay. You're the client, no shortage of privilege. And we do understand confidentiality on sensitive matters. But we certainly can't take on a case without knowing the facts." She glanced at Clay.

He picked up the cue. "Absolutely. How about helping us out here, Gideon? C'mon. Up front. Clear the air."

Pike hoisted an eyebrow and no one spoke for several seconds. "Yes, Clay. Very high indeed. It's a complicated trust matter and we can certainly save the specifics for a later time. But there's the matter of who's controlling a substantial amount of proxies on behalf of Kimberly's estate. If, by some chance, there are heirs, then the balance of power in the family fortune would shift rather dramatically."

Andi nodded. "I don't know much about complicated finance and trusts, but I gather you have a vested interest in whether the twins are alive, and, if so, how they might vote?"

"Correct, Andi. Correct, you are."

Clay assembled pieces further. "And there's some sort of deadline — which is the reason this whole business is pressing?" He wanted to say *desperate* but thought better of it.

The question won a benevolent smile from Pike. "In a nutshell, there's a twenty-five year limit on the way things stand. Within a few weeks, the entire matter is moot. Kimberly's shares pass to others."

Andi held Gideon's note high in the air. "A faction within the five on this list that you'd rather not see in control?"

"That sums it up rather nicely, Andrea. Nicely indeed."

Clay glanced at his watch. The commercial cleaning crew would be arriving soon. "Okay. What I think we need to do is get a quick rundown of people on your list."

Pike chuckled. "Well, they're the five players in the proxy fight, besides myself o'course. The people I want you to start with."

Andi's smile had morphed into sweet encouragement and Clay fought the urge to look at her as anything other than a cop. He backed away to let her take the lead in questioning. "It's okay, Gideon. We'll handle the investigation as we think best, but we're trying to save a step here." She looked at the paper as if reading it for the first time. When finished, she said, "Austin Hart?"

Gideon straightened his jacket and adjusted his tie. He spoke in a matter-of-fact tone, without hesitation. "Stepson by my second marriage to the late Jeanne Hart. On the list because he's got voting shares. You'll find him at the nearest playground. He's never accomplished much in life."

She nodded and focused on the list. "Other than to be rich." She looked up "Baxter McKnight?"

"A cousin, by an earlier marriage. Black sheep of the family, always involved in some sort of scandal. He lived with the family for a time after his parents died in a car crash. I'd suspect him of causing the clouds on a rainy day."

Clay had memorized the list, too, and his attention sharpened when Andi said, "Conrad Spence?"

"Stepson by my third marriage and Kimberly's older brother. He's the CEO, all business, firmly in control. A low-life string puller."

Clay asked, "And the mother?"

"Certifiably insane. Locked up in a clinic for her own protection."

Andi said, "Sorry. Kimberly was a stepdaughter?"

"Yes."

"So how about, uh, Leonard, Leonard B. Pike?"

"The B stands for Braddon. My eldest son. Not much for business, mostly involved in New York theater. Lives with his mother, Martha. We're divorced."

"Okay, and, let's see…. Carlene Elliot?"

"My eldest natural daughter. Active in company management and an ally of Conrad. We don't get along that well."

Clay said, "Can I assume in earlier years, perhaps when relationships were a bit more positive, that the family lived under the same roof?"

Gideon had thrust his hands in his back pockets and his jaw forward, into the questioning in what resembled defiance. "We did. Big spread in upper Bucks County, one of those gentleman farms. Kids and wives were into horses, but not in a competitive way."

Clay said, "Okay, and staff?"

"What do you mean? It was a farm, for —"

"Personal staff, cooks, butlers, maids, that sort of thing. From the time Kimberly was alive?"

Gideon seemed to relax. "Well, o'course. A house that size doesn't run by itself."

Andi's tone remained gentle, patient. "Can you remember their names?"

Pike scratched his jaw and his eyes seemed distant, as if reliving another place and time. "Well, there was a nanny, name of Madge... Madge Whittaker. Driver, of course. That'd be Fred Boyd. We called him Freddie, but I don't think he liked it much. Cook was the Eaton woman, big gal. Dixie. Dixie Eaton. Fellow by the name of Leroy Steel was the head groundskeeper, but I didn't know the crew. And then there was old Alvin, Alvin Flowers, the butler, and Ruthie, Ruth Towler, the maid. And no, I have no idea of their whereabouts, or if they're still alive. Scattered, probably."

Clay concentrated to remember the names. No one took notes and, while he had a pen, he had no paper, the little spiral pocket notebook just a memory.

There were many more questions, but a timid knock on the door led to an invitation to five people in work overalls to enter and appraise the situation. They seemed impressed with the enormity of the task.

Pike, looking rattled, used the arrival as an excuse to make his farewells.

Andi stepped into his path in a subtle blocking gesture. "One more thing, um, Gideon. How are we supposed to pay for our expenses?" She nodded toward the cleaning crew, awaiting direction.

It caught Pike off guard. The guy probably never directly paid a bill in his life. He had people for that.

Gideon chuckled and reached into the other jacket pocket. "Oh, yes, o'course. Here's some petty cash, company credit cards, and the bank account should be up and running."

Andi accepted an envelope stuffed with cash and quickly found the cards on the front side. "Bank account? Which bank?"

Pike's smile went smug again. "Why, you're crack detectives, aren't you? I'm sure you'll figure it out. Keep me informed."

With that, he wheeled and strode out the door, leaving a trail of dust to linger in stale air.

Chapter Twelve

Janice Something-or-Other turned out to be Janice Benton, effusive manager of Benton's Office Supplies, almost a city block from Storm Investigations, beyond the Grounds Crew coffee shop.

To Clay, she looked about thirty and had grown up in the family business. Janice said with evident pride the shop celebrated four generations — "The fourth would be me" — of continuous service to merchants and professionals, clinging to independence in an age of big-box brands.

She expressed delight that Clay and Andi were the new owners of Storm Investigations. "It'll bring new life to the street," she cooed. "Glenn Storm had close friends in the neighborhood, and folks miss him. Such a wonderful guy. But times change, it's been a few years, and we must move on, mustn't we?"

Clay caught Andi's bemused glance. *Yeah, terrific guy, and a good tip about what not to say about Storm on the street.* "So, I understand arrangements have been made to refurbish the office? Furniture, supplies, that sort of thing?"

"Oh, yes, Mister Garrison. Your representative visited yesterday, opened your account and the check has already cleared."

Andi smiled. "Wonderful. You know, it's been such a flurry with corporate and estate details, and we're new in town... Um, could you remind me which of the banks that was drawn on?"

"Oh, PennFirst, the branch on Third, I suspect." She tapped on her keyboard and studied the monitor. "Yep, and your store account balance of twenty thousand dollars is good to go." He shared a glance of incredulity with Andi. "Let me get one of our store cards for you. It'll have premiere club account information embedded on it, save you from bothering with paperwork when you come in."

Clay cocked an eyebrow while Andi gushed appreciation. She seemed better at this than he, adapting to the unexpected, blithe-ly, as if routine. They needed some sort of office. No way could they work this case out of Mitch's apartment, a coffee shop or jazz bar, or wherever she camped out. He scanned the large show-room, past the huddle of office supplies and electronics near the front and toward a collection of chairs, tables, desks near the rear. It might be Gideon's dime, but prudence mattered.

He snagged a pocket-sized spiral-bound notepad from a rack. "May I?"

Janice cradled a legal-sized clipboard and a pad of order sheets. "Of course."

He made notes as he trailed two women chatting as old pals do when sharing reminiscences.

They paused in electronics. "So, Mister Garrison, I'm told you're interested in a smart phone, but I'm afraid I don't know your system preferences."

Andi picked up a popular brand being marketed with an equally popular service provider. "These are nice, don't you think?"

Clay nodded and repeatedly tossed out a casual line of sup-port while Andi stocked the business. Contemporary furniture caught her eye, especially a desk.

* * *

Andi ran her fingertips across cool, smooth glass, perfectly clean, new, fresh. It would be a marvelous centerpiece in the first office she could call her own.

But she couldn't. If they set off space for a reception area, space came up short. She would have to share with Clay. No idea if he preferred wall space or a window. He might go for a desk or maybe a table and chair that wouldn't work with what she openly admired.

Janice must have sensed indecision and ramped up the pitch. The soft, elegant chair beckoned, the kind an executive might have in her office, beyond what she ever dreamed.

Janice took a step back. "Go ahead. Try it."

Andi suspected she was giving them space to consider it. "So what do you think, Clay. Is there room for two of these?"

Clay seemed to be doing an amazing job of either suppressing his own preferences or being extraordinarily deferential. Proficient at taciturn, yet also one of those super-organized guys who probably wanted everything, including their office space, arranged in a specific way. He didn't appear to be indifferent, making deferential a real and unanticipated treat.

He smiled, that sly little smile when his mind had already gone four steps down the road and waited for everyone else to catch up. "Possibly. Let's see...."

From his pocket, he pulled a miniature tape measure and offered her the starting end. *Amazing. How many guys carry a tape measure in their pocket? Probably cops well prepared for crime scenes.* She held her end to the edge of the desk while he walked to the opposite side, stringing out a thin yellow line.

"Well?"

"It'll work."

"With a reception space?"

He nodded and gestured for her to reposition the tape for the other dimension. "If it's at least twelve feet off the long wall."

"You're sure? I mean, I love the desk, and I hope you're okay with it."

Clay looked up from the ruler, toward Janice. "Do you have two in stock?"

"I believe so. And I can give you a little discount on the second one if you're buying two. Say, ten percent? That would be twenty-two fifty and change plus tax. It comes with an option of three different kinds of chairs."

Andi's hand caressed the back of the executive model. "This one's fine for me. Clay, you're sure they'll fit okay?"

"Well, they'd have to face each other, the way old fashioned partners desks did."

"That's what we are, right?" She hoped her sudden and unexpected glow didn't show *too* much, but Janice evidently understood.

* * *

An hour later, they sat side by side in a pair of metal folding chairs, near the office door. Sandwiches from Grounds Crew above paper napkins spread out over their laps. He'd chosen a decent ham and Swiss melt, which normally came with a small sack of chips, which he declined. Janice offered to deliver the chairs immediately, which meant the picnic lunch would have to be restrained. No chips. No matter. He didn't need the calories. Andi had ordered chicken salad without hesitation and wolfed it down from paper wrapping.

Foam cups of coffee huddled along the frayed edge of a pair of canvas tarps laid out by the painters. The commercial van said they were "Kostenmayer and Sons, Commercial, Residential, Interiors and Exteriors, Satisfaction Guaranteed." Eddie Kostenmayer mixed a fresh sample. One of two sons brushed some onto the distant wall of a space now bright and clean, but some sort of an off-yellow color that appealed to neither of the partners.

"So?" Eddie asked her.

Andi tilted her head left. The sparkle of a big, round earring caught his eye and invited time to look at her neck. She said, "Hmm. Definitely closer. But I wonder if it shouldn't be perhaps a little, maybe, warmer? What do you think, Clay?"

She spun faster than he expected and he jerked his head away from the view of the neck and toward the pudgy painter in the center of the room. Eddie had a pleading look in his eyes.

Clay cleared his throat at yet another variation on light gray of too many swatches on the yellow wall to know for certain. "Uh, well, I'm..."

Andi persisted. "Do you think it'll hide imperfections in the walls?"

Clay ignored Eddie And Sons and said, "Long time ago, my dad had the restaurant repainted. One problem yellow wall, patched repeatedly over the years, drove Dad crazy. They spent a long time debating it before the painter, an old guy whose name I can't remember, said, 'Bruises heal, scars you learn to live with. Sometimes a fresh coat of paint helps.'" He studied the wall one more time. "That new color? Yeah, I'm good with it."

Eddie looked relieved.

Andi furrowed her brow as she finished chewing a bite of chicken salad. "You're sure? I mean it's *our* office, Clay."

Clay told the painter, "First office. You know how it goes, Ed."

"Oh, yeah, absolutely. This is a great shade, very popular with young professionals these days. Give you a first-class corporate look."

Clay said, "Furnishings are on the contemporary side."

"Well, there ya go, lady. This is perfect for that kind of style."

Andi's expression remained contemplative. "Hmm."

Eddie stood still, his smile frozen. The sons waited behind him. Clay's arm went on pause, halfway to another bite of the ham and Swiss.

"Well," she said at last. "Okay. Go with it." She reached for her coffee, sipped and sighed. "It's gone cold."

He chuckled. "Which happens if you spent more than half an hour trying to describe a paint color and then tweaking the precise shade."

She sighed. "So what's next? Besides having the room painted?"

Clay shrugged and finished the sandwich. "We could sit here and watch it dry."

Eddie looked uneasy and rubbed his chin.

"Or not. I think maybe we ought to get out of here, let the guys do their work. Tell you what, Andi. Why don't I buy you another coffee? We'll get a little work done, stay out of their hair, get organized."

Andi said to the painters, "You'll be okay?"

Eddie nodded. "I think we got it under control, ma'am."

She said to Clay, "Coffee. Plus a slice of that cake they had, the chocolate one. It looked gorgeous."

Clay stood and faced the painters, shrugging. "What are you gonna do?"

"Yeah, buddy. It's tough, sometimes."

* * *

At the coffee shop, Andi resolved to pace herself. The first bite of cake went fast. The second, smaller, slower, gently, incredibly sweet and smooth, perfect with coffee in a large ceramic mug instead of foam. With two hours to kill while Eddie's crew finished the office facelift, she'd have to limit herself to a single slice.

They had a smallish, round table, one of a short line along the window. Opposite the entry, a counter served as the focal point for what was mostly take-out, the usual exotic combinations to which pedestrians were addicted. Across from them, higher, square tables were surrounded by tall chairs, some occupied by patrons working with laptops, tablets, phones.

Adjacent to the beckoning cake, Andi unfolded a sheet of paper and pressed out creases.

Clay munched fruit from a small fork. Of course it would be fruit. Some sort of combination of colors and textures that included oranges, apple, pineapple, stuff she could not recognize. There were guys who did that kind of thing to make cake lovers feel guilty. But thinking negatively about him would be unfair. For once, she felt comfortable being with a guy who wasn't wearing handcuffs. She said, "For the record, thank you."

He looked up. "For what?"

"For being patient, not being pushy, giving me space and respect. It's been rare for me lately, so, yeah, I'm pleased."

He smiled, that gentle, easy smile, the kind that comes from guys with a tremendous amount of courtesy, manners... self esteem.

"Okay," she continued. "The list of names. How should we work this?"

He pulled the spiral notepad from his shirt pocket and flipped it open. He'd made notes while they shopped, which she assumed were reminders, a to-do or to-buy note. Now she read his printing upside down. It was a list of the names of the housekeeping staff that Pike mentioned earlier in the day.

He said, "The computer guys won't do their installs until tomorrow, afternoon I think, and now I've got a total of ten names. I get the sense that Pike isn't going to hold our hands on this, that we're expected to find them ourselves."

She nodded. "Anyone stand out to you? Someone you like for it?"

"No. But we don't know the specifics of the crime — if there was one. Or if the twins exist. Or ever existed."

Andi succumbed to another bite of cake. "That's a logical starting point. Without a crime, then it's hardly worth bothering these people."

"I agree. But maybe by tracking down the players, which shouldn't be too difficult, at least the family, we might save some steps. Doing preliminary interviews and getting the history straight at the same time."

"Works for me. I'm beginning to think you were right, Clay. This is not going to be easy."

"Cold cases never are. That's why they're cold. I once hung out with a couple of detectives who'd fit in pieces of work on half a dozen inactive cases, one little scrap at a time. For months. Until a break. It seems slow, tedious. And Pike may be short on time. That deadline for the trust business."

She chased the cake with coffee to dampen an urge to wolf the rest down in hefty, un-ladylike bites. "Which I'd want to know more about. Your detective friends. How do you think they'd approach it?"

He chewed the last of his fruit and reached for the coffee. "Right away, they'd recruit extra hands and eyes. Volunteers. Guys wanting off beat work, traffic, but not interested in administration."

She laughed. "That's funny. Last night, my friend, Mer, put out feelers for a job. I guess her real estate position is shaky, about the agency having financial troubles."

"She have any investigative work background?"

The cake invited assault. "Well, no. But neither do I."

Clay chuckled, captivating and intoxicating at once.

He said, "My buddy, Mitch, the reporter? Yeah, he's on the outs with his boss, too. Looking for a change. The guy is incredibly talented at research, running down leads. But he can be a real pain sometimes."

"Attitude?"

"A little. More disorganized zeal. He grabs onto a tip and pushes it, sometimes too hard. But he's the kind of guy who'd probably be right at home on a California beach. Board, beer, babes."

"Isn't he the one who —"

"Yeah, he was fairly excited."

"That could be dangerous. Mer is, well, pretty social."

Clay sipped coffee. "Mitch was there when I needed it, no questions. As I said, we go way back. He's got flaws, but we all do, and bottom line is that we're tight."

"That's cool. Mer and I are much the same. Well, not that much, if you know what I mean, but...." She reached for the cake to mask embarrassment. When she dared to look up again, it was to that same patient, enchanting smile.

Chapter Thirteen

Clay drove into the parking lot on a rising tide of satisfaction. It had taken two pots of coffee and half-dozen doughnuts to gel two pairs of friends into a working unit. Mitch and Mer were eager to prove themselves in new roles, and Andi seemed to have a magic touch in managing egos.

It opened a path for Clay to coordinate information sifting and what seemed to be the easiest-to-find target. He'd heeded his father's counsel from years long gone: *when building a menu, master the basics, then go for gourmet.* They'd flown economy class to Los Angeles, went low on rental cars and made it to the upscale suburbs. The expenses stake from Pike might have been without limit, but Clay saw no need to run the tab. Andi had tolerated the plan without complaint, but seemed itching for ambush.

Now they cruised a country club parking lot, sifting through a collection of sparkling sports cars, top-of-the-line trucks and luxury sedans hunting one special Ferrari.

They'd passed three already, but white, yellow, black. He said, "And here's another one. Wrong color, though. Sheesh. Any one of them would cost more than most police officers make in a couple of years."

Andi muttered, "Closer to five or six." Her voice brightened. "There. Your one o'clock. That looks right. The red one."

The official Ferrari red dazzled under bright southern California sunshine, the black horse logo unmistakable.

Clay's immediately began a search for an open parking space in the packed lot.

She muttered, "Not good."

"Patience, patience. Ah, here we go." A huge blue sport pickup backed out of a spot, and headed toward the twisting road leading to a massive gate and the highway beyond.

She displayed a thumbs-up. "Nice."

He backed in, sandwiched between an immaculately restored Shelby Cobra and a Mercedes, the big one, an S-Class Maybach. "Ever get the sense that we're not in their league?"

She shook her head. "Not sure I'd ever want to be. Okay, Austin Hart. How do you want to play it?"

Clay looked out into the field of gold-plated transportation. "Good-Bad? Cool Fed? Bounty Hunter? Bumbling Detective?"

She grinned. "I like Pushy Smart-aleck for this one. Any good at it?"

"Saw it done once. You?"

She drew a pair of sunglasses from her bag. "I'm why they invented aviators and chewing gum." She had already slipped into the role, fun to watch, and the shades made her incredibly sexy.

He admitted, "No gum, sorry."

She shook her head and offered a spare piece "Gosh, Clay. We've been partners for an entire week. You'd think that by now you'd carry a couple of packs as standard gear."

"Yeah, yeah. What's the key to working this?"

"You've got to go real loose, push hard, no blinking if they push back. Y'know, kinda you own them and don't care. I've got an edge because I'm a girl, especially if he's alone or with a couple of guys. You might have to step in, get in his face, if he pushes back too hard."

He wiped his sunglasses and held them up to the light to inspect. "So where'd you learn this, the academy?"

She laughed, halfway between a giggle and a chuckle. "Nope.

Mer taught me, sophomore year. We could be terrible some-times."

"How'd that go for you?"

She shrugged. "Teachers hated it. After a while, though, you get to kind of enjoy detention. Meet cool people and get home-work done." She opened the door, oblivious to the vehicle next to it. "Ready?"

* * *

"Ready."

Clay's grin reassured her. A surge of confidence blossomed into full-blown cocky indifference. Attitude, for some reason stored away after high school graduation and her freshman year of college, now back in full bloom. Bright sunshine helped, as did the breeze through her hair. Clay seemed into the mood of the moment, which smothered self-consciousness. Directly head, the red Ferrari hugged pavement and looked ferocious. The hood fad-ed into a point and the fenders were lower than she expected. Maybe they could lean on it, rather than sit stadium-style.

It was great to be working again, an actual case. A hundred, no, thousand times better than third-shift patrol on deserted streets with an FTO who couldn't stop suggesting by-the-hour motels or private alleys and frowned on brightly lit all-night din-ers featuring coffee, doughnuts and witnesses. None of the stiff shirts, clunky shoes, or a heavy belt bristling with weapons and defensive tools. She marched forward in a lavender blazer over a light sweater, with loose-legged slacks, all of which were perfect fits and one of the better labels in an upscale shop. A week ago, she could never dream of walking through the door, much less handing over a credit card with such indifference.

Clay had taken the advice of Mer and Mitch and loosened up spending reins for himself. Well, a little. The economy airline seats and the tiny car were forgivable. But Mitch had been cute, haranguing his pal about seizing the opportunity to blue-chip it, with Meredith nodding right behind his shoulder. He relented, if begrudgingly, probably still in a state of shock over good fortune.

Although money flowed unchecked, Gideon had briefly hesitated when they called to add to the payroll. Clay's reasoning prompted a green light. No problem with salaries. Mer took twenty seconds to clean off her desk. Mitch needed fewer to tell his boss where to go. Now they were four. The extra help sped the process of finding Austin Hart, faster than they had expected, impressing Gideon, keeping the goose laying the golden eggs happy.

Clay checked his notes while they stared at the red Ferrari. "It's a 488 GTB all right. Around $320,000. Mitch tracked it down day before yesterday." He paused to pay homage.

Andi shrugged and drifted to the driver's side, picking a spot ahead of the front tire. "It's a *car*. Four wheels, motor, two doors and zero room for groceries." She settled onto the fender, leaning more than sitting. "And not terribly comfortable." She patted a spot to her left. "C'mon. Take a load off."

Club members periodically passed, en route to vehicles throughout the lot. Andi waved at several. "Okay, your turn. Do one of those guy waves or finger points or whatever. Pretend you know them."

"Sort of like casting a fishing lure, waiting for a bite?"

"You got it."

But he had no luck.

"Okay, Clay, my turn." Her arm went up. The guy with a light sport bag rushed forward, dismay and confusion on his face. "Bingo."

When within earshot, Andi called out, "Hey, Austin, nice to see you!"

"What the... Who are..." He cursed as his eyes continued to widen in horror. "Get off my car!"

The couple responded with expressions of innocent surprise.

Andi pointed as she stood and Clay followed. "This your ride? Wow. I would have thought you would be a little more upscale."

He swore again. "It's a Ferrari! Who are you people?"

Andi looked at the car again. "A Ferrari? A real one? I would have guessed a knockoff."

Austin Hart pulled a phone from his trousers, muttering epithets. "I'm calling security, have you two arrested...."

Clay stepped forward. "For leaning on a car? You're joking."

Andi ratcheted up her smile and reached out to the wrist of the hand holding the phone. She laughed. "Easy, easy. No need for all that. We work for your uncle, Gideon Pike. I'm Andrea Delvento, and this is my assistant, Clay Garrison, who, among other things, carries a nasty looking gun."

Hart's jaw hung open. "What?"

Clay nodded and moved closer. "Absolutely true, my friend. Now, why not put that phone away? Have a nice chat with the little lady, and we'll be on our way. I don't see any damage to your car, and I don't think you'll need to have any sort of embarrassment when the local law enforcement people get here. Okay? You good with that?"

Hart nodded but eyed both with suspicion.

"Great." Clay took two steps back and pretended not to listen, acting, perimeter security.

Austin demanded, "What's this about?"

"Relax, Austin. I've got a couple of questions. I would have made an appointment with your secretary, but who needs those eyebrows being raised around the office, right?"

"I don't have a secretary. I don't have an office."

"What sort of work do you do?"

"I don't work, honey. I party. So... what questions?"

"Look. Here's how it is. Mister Pike has retained our services to look into the death of Kimberly Spence and some sort of rumors that she gave birth to twin daughters. We've got to ask around, see what's going on, kind of get a picture of... well, you know how it is."

Austin rubbed his nose with the back of his hand. "Oh, crap, not again."

"Mister Pike does this often?"

"With tedious regularity. Look, Miss, uh —"

"Delvento. But you can call me Andi."

"Kimberly was fifteen or sixteen, a drug addict. Some sort of rehab, but she managed to get access to some, well, whatever. And she died from an overdose."

"So I heard. Okay, help me out here. You're a stepson to Mister Pike, isn't that right?"

"That's correct. My mother was his second wife."

"And that would be...?"

"Jeanne Hart. She worked for Gideon at some point, and they developed a warm and loving relationship."

Andi went for deliberately incorrect. "And you and Kimberly were about the same age?"

"No. No, I was older. Six or seven years."

"Which would make you now...."

"Forty-eight."

She leaned back in mock astonishment. "Really? Wow, I never would have guessed. You look great. Very fit. Work out, do you?"

"Thank you. Now, I'm afraid I —"

Andi refused to disengage. "So, I'm curious, what happened to your mother? Is she —"

"Deceased. A number of years ago. Ovarian cancer, in case you're wondering."

The unexpected detail startled her, and she she fought to hide it. "It wasn't, but my sympathies on your loss. It must have been hard on you."

"It was. Now, if you don't mind —"

Andi looked him directly in the eyes. "Hard enough to cause

you to get involved with drugs, such as, what, cocaine perhaps?"

"Absolutely not. And, frankly, I resent the implication."

"None intended, Austin. So. One other point of curiosity. You have a stake in the Pike company, don't you?"

"Yes. A very small share."

"How small in, say, dollars?"

Austin switched to a withering smile. "None of your business. And I'm sure that Gideon knows the structure of the trust."

"You're right about that. Did you inherit your share from your mother or buy in or...?

"It was a gift, a generous one, from Conrad. He wanted to be comfortable after my mother passed. Look, I thought you were interested in Kimberly, not myself."

"True enough, thanks. What's this about Kimberly having twin daughters?"

"Lost them, late in pregnancy."

"So she was pregnant when she was in rehab?"

"I suppose so. I mean, that's the way it was. But that's not important."

"That she was pregnant, or the babies died, or she died?"

"Any of it. All of it a terrible tragedy, and we felt badly about it. But life moves on, you see."

Andi gestured toward the Ferrari. "Oh, yes, I can see that. So, When did you last see them alive?"

"Them? You mean, her."

"Well, I guess you might say that if she was alive, but pregnant, you sort of saw all of them."

"That's the most ridiculous... Look. I've told you what I know. And trust me, young lady, Gideon has you on some sort of a wild goose chase. The old man is delusional..."

"Unbalanced? He seemed —"

"Rational? Yeah, he does. But trust me on the fact that he's trying to stir up trouble."

"What kind of trouble?"

Austin seemed to regret the remark. "Never mind. I misspoke."

"No, you said trouble. Clay, you heard him say 'trouble,' right?"

Clay had been pretending to observe the perimeter to ensure privacy for the meeting. Without looking directly into it, he faintly nodded and said, "Yes. I did."

Andi beamed and said to Austin, "There. You see? We both heard it. What kind of —"

But the interview had run out of gas. Austin had recovered from the ambush and became curt. He glanced at his watch. "I've got nothing more to say. Next time, make an appointment, okay? Now, if you'll excuse me, I have another engagement. You and your thug should step aside, or you will find yourselves in more difficulty than you can imagine, okay?"

In resignation, Andi tossed her hands in the air. Clay pretended to chew gum and shrugged, waiting for the last possible second to allow Austin to pass during a classic male-to-male stare down.

She called out, "Thanks so much for your time, Austin!"

Austin paused, as if debating about letting it go or making a real mistake. He looked over his shoulder, an icy glare intended to freeze Andi into a solid block of ice in seconds. "Do me a favor, honey. You tell Gideon that he's wasting everyone's time. Pick up your paycheck, whatever ridiculous amount it might be, and go find something useful to do. Got it?"

She smiled. "Gimme a sec, I'll write that down so I remember."

He grunted. "Yeah, see that you do, baby."

The Ferrari roared to life and fled, tires screeching on the corners, the rear end wiggling on the final turn out onto the highway.

Clay shook his head. "Not a terribly skilled driver, is he?"

Andi unfolded her arms and put her hands on her hips. "Not a very good liar, either. Mitch had no problem running down the drug thing and how he beat jail time by going into country-club rehab."

They stood in a driving lane of the parking lot and, behind them, a car beeped a warning. Clay gave a little wave of acknowledgement and led them back to the rented sedan. Andi shifted her sunglasses to the top of her head and checked messages while she walked.

"Ah, well, our list is down by one."

"Who?"

"Mer says they learned the family cook — Dixie Eaton — died twelve years ago. Mitch found the obituary and Mer confirmed it. A couple of distant relatives."

"Too bad. I hoped somebody outside the inner circle might have known something." He unlocked the door. "Sorry it's not a Ferrari."

She opened hers. "It's okay. I'm not a Ferrari kind of girl."

"Yeah, well, that was a Ferrari kind of interrogation. Thanks for the lesson."

She beamed. The budding partnership hummed along nicely, shifting into higher gear.

Chapter Fourteen

Andi guided the luxury rental into a random space in a sparsely populated but immaculate lot. She looked left, ahead, right. "Okay, I'm impressed with Boca Raton. I'm also impressed with the car, but gotta tell you that black doesn't work for me. This should be silver or gray."

Clay chuckled. She wore her hair up, in a tight style with a few strands out of control, drooping toward the collar of a slightly imperfect navy blue suit. Their costume colors matched only coincidentally. In contrast to his conservative dark tie, she'd splurged on a blouse that had a subdued bow at the neckline. The same sunglasses that taunted Austin Hart now complemented the look of a federal agent.

She checked herself in the rear view mirror. "Hate to say it, Clay, but I think I look more on the wrong side of thirty."

"That's the idea. How many assistant U.S. attorneys are mid-twenties?"

She laughed. "Only the smart ones, like me. You *do* know that impersonating is a federal crime that could get you three years in jail and a ten-thousand-dollar fine, right?"

He grinned. "However, we're not impersonating. Instead, giving a suggestion that you *might* be. And then only to flush the subject."

She tapped her fingertips on the steering wheel. "You seem pretty confident that he'll rabbit."

"Just a hunch."

Her eyebrows rose. "A *hunch?* From Mister Perfectly Organized? Gosh, Clay, I'm stunned."

Clay folded blank sheets of paper and stuffed the wad into his jacket pocket. "If your friend Meredith is as good as she says she is on evaluating prospects, and if my pal Mitch is as good as he claims on researching business types, then, yeah, Baxter will rabbit. Way too many indictments in his history, and I doubt if he wants to spend any more time with a grand jury. Give me maybe five minutes to get to the back door."

"Which is where Mitch is parked?"

Clay skimmed through the scanty collection of messages on his phone and tucked it into his jacket. "Yep. Waiting as we speak. With the camera and long lens."

"And if Baxter doesn't run?"

Clay chuckled. "Cuff 'em and call for backup."

She sighed. "You're a big help. Okay, let's do this. Out you go."

* * *

After waiting two extra minutes, Andi took firm, assured strides across warm pavement, wishing her jacket fit better but resisting an urge to unbutton it.

Three guys, two with silver hair and one bald, wearing khaki trousers and polo shirts, exited the long, three-story building. One lingered to hold the door for her while others admired the passing view.

"Thank you, sir," she crisply told the gentleman. "Have a nice day, fellas," she said to the others. In the lobby, sunglasses migrated to the top of her head and the building directory led her to a suite of offices on the second floor.

Northern International Investments had a sophisticated logo in brushed steel adjacent to a matching string of letters on the reception area wall, above a counter wide enough for six or seven receptionists but hosting only one. She marched forward with authority in a jacket too snug in the waist. Lawyers got tailored suits. Cops got pot luck. She looked like a cop.

The receptionist looked up for a momentary flash of credentials before the wallet snapped shut and returned to Andi's bag. "Hi, yes. I'm sure you can help. I'm here to see Mister Baxter McKnight in regard to, well, an investigation he probably is already aware of."

The deferential receptionist, late twenties, probably tall, wearing a blazer over a skirt, nodded and reached for a phone. She pressed a button, listened for a moment and returned the handset to its cradle. She smiled apologetically. "I'm sorry. Mister McKnight is not available. I believe he is meeting with an important client elsewhere."

Andi faked astonishment. "Wow. I thought I saw his car parked out front."

The receptionist's expression shifted toward arrogant. "I'm sure you saw someone, but not Mister McKnight. He always parks in the rear lot."

Andi nodded and excused herself, struggling to contain chagrin because Clay was, as usual, correct. On impulse, she asked. "Oh. One more thing. How do I get to the back lot from here?"

The receptionist spoke with a plastic smile. "To your right, end of the hall, down the steps. There are doors on either end of the building."

* * *

Clay waved recognition to Mitch, who'd split the distance in the rear lot for a spot from which he could observe the entire office building profile.

Mitch rolled down the driver's side window and hoisted the

camera. A thin but long lens was certainly adequate for the plan. Mitch pointed toward a luxury white SUV in the nearly-empty lot.

Responding with a thumbs-up gesture, Clay hurried toward a large shrub and lamp post for temporary cover. At the far end of the building, a middle aged, slightly heavy man paused, dug into his trousers, probably for keys, before scurrying across the lot.

Clay sprang from his cover and flashed his open credentials wallet. With any luck from the rapidly closing distance between them, McKnight wouldn't recognize it as meaningless. An authoritative voice might help cover the ruse. "Mister McKnight? I've got some questions for you."

Surprise and panic filled McKnight's eyes and his body tensed in preparation for flight. To his left, Mitch's long lens protruded from the car window. And behind, Andi stepped into view.

"Hold it, sir. No sense in running."

McKnight whirled. Andi unbuttoned her jacket and reached for her right hip with both hands. He spun further, paused to study Mitch, and slowly returned to the starting position.

"That's better, sir. I'm not in the mood for a chase and you look like you're way too far out of shape. Wouldn't want to have to deal with an ambulance when we could just have a nice, quiet chat."

McKnight squinted. "Look, my friend, my lawyers are negotiating with your office as we speak. There's no —"

"That stock thing the United States Attorney is working on? No, that's already out of my hands. No sir, I'm investigating a cold case, a mysterious death long ago involving —"

McKnight waved his hands. "I didn't have anything to do with that. Nothing. I wasn't even there. Out of the country, in fact. I don't know anything about it."

By now Andi joined the group, her gun hand relaxed and at her side, but the jacket still unbuttoned. She asked, "About what, Baxter?"

Baxter gave her a once-over look. "Who're you?"

She responded with body language and expression that growled *I mean business, buddy,* and nodded toward Clay. "I'm with him. So, Baxter, I'll ask again. About what?"

"Why, Kimberly. Kimberly Spence." An expression of wary suspicion returned. "Say. Exactly who are you people? Are you —"

Clay interrupted. "We're people who might help you with your little federal beef. Or make it a whole lot worse." He pulled the sheaf of papers folded in a blue wrapper from his jacket pocket.

Baxter took half a step back and waved it off. "No, no. Not today, buddy. You're not serving me with anything."

Clay tapped the phony document on his hand. "Well, then, what can you do for me, to help me out? I didn't accuse you of anything. Just wanted to ask a couple of questions."

Baxter's attention remained focused on the papers in Clay's hand and followed the paper back into Clay's jacket. "Just a couple of questions?"

Andi replied in a reassuring tone. "That's right, Mister McKnight... Say, can I call you Baxter? I'm Andrea Delvento, but you can call me Andi if you prefer. And my partner here is Clay Garrison. Me? I'd be up front with Clay. He's all business, trust me, and the guy over there in the car is recording everything."

Baxter took a look. Mitch gave a little wave. When Baxter faced Clay, beads of sweat were forming above anxious eyes.

Clay remained stern. "So? How about it, uh, *Baxter?*"

"I'm not saying a word if a recording is being made. That's what my lawyers would say."

Clay nodded. "Good advice." He motioned to Mitch, who rolled up the window and slowly drove away. "Feel better?"

"Yeah. Yeah. So, as I said, I don't know anything, okay? It was a long time ago. The kid was always strung out on something, the family had a tough time with it, they put her in rehab and she managed to get more heroin. She could do that, you know. Everybody says, 'Poor little Kimberly' like she some kind of saint, a victim. She was anything but."

Andi asked, "And exactly what's your relationship with the family?"

"A cousin, by a previous marriage. When my mother and stepfather were killed in a car crash, the Spence family took me in for a little while. Then I moved out."

Clay asked, "Why?"

"They didn't welcome outsiders. Very clannish, if you know what I mean. And they weren't nice people, either. Whenever one of them messed up, they'd find a way to blame me. After a while, I couldn't take it any more and left."

"When was that?"

Baxter paused to do the math. "Sixteen, seventeen years ago, maybe. I tracked down some relatives, moved out."

"Before or after Kimberly died?"

"Soon after."

Andi said, "I see. Someone said Kimberly was pregnant at the time."

"Not when she died. She was, earlier, but lost them."

Andi raised her eyebrows and opened the notepad in her hand. "Them?"

"Yeah, twins. Real shame."

"Know their names?"

"You didn't hear me. I said, *lost them.*"

"Know when the, uh, pregnancy ended?"

"I dunno. Month or two earlier, I think."

Clay's went for a tone more crisp and cool. "You think?"

"Yeah, well, that's what they said."

"Who said?"

"Conrad. And Carlene. He's a stepson, she's a daughter to Gideon Pike. Yeah, *the* Gideon Pike." A cocky edge had returned to his tone and posture. "So, if I were you, I'd be careful. These are big-time players, okay?"

Andi smiled. "Gotcha. Help me out here. How do you know the babies were stillborn?"

"Look lady, that's what they said. An outsider in a tight clan. And I think I've already told you too much, okay? I don't know nothing, and wasn't involved in anything."

Clay smiled. "Involved?"

"Hey, sport, that's a figure of speech, okay? I've got some pull myself, you know?"

"He's correct Clay. He's got a plush layout in that office building. Probably owns the entire thing."

McKnight's posture straightened. "Well, yeah, as a matter of fact —"

"There, Clay, you see? Mister McKnight is successful, wealthy, himself. He had nothing to gain by, well, you know...."

Clay shrugged. "Well, the U.S. Attorney has his doubts."

"Bogus charges. All of them. We'll have our day in court, I assure you."

Clay hoped a dubious expression looked would keep Baxter off guard. "Maybe. I hear that prosecutor is a real terrier. As a matter of curiosity, how did you come by your stake in Pike's empire? Some sort of inheritance?"

"No, no. A gift, from Conrad, many years ago."

Andi looked surprised. "Wow. After all the bad blood, he *gave* you, what, a handful of shares?"

McKnight beamed with pride. "Two and a half percent, as a matter of fact."

"Wow. That's impressive. Isn't it Clay?"

Clay said, "An impressive gift. Wonder why he'd be that generous."

McKnight shrugged. "Who knows? Maybe he and Carlene felt guilty for the cruel way they treated me. It's not as if they were being charitable, what with the money they've got."

Andi said, "Some people might say that sounds jealous."

McKnight drifted toward his car. "Me? No way. Everything's okay with me." He paused, as though he had forgotten something.

Clay asked, "So where were you headed? It appeared as if you left your office in a hurry. Must be some sort of a big deal appointment, eh?"

McKnight glanced at his watch. "Uh, yeah, um, that's right. A big deal. But you know what? I left some materials in my office. I'd better go back and get them."

Andi nodded and stepped away from his exit path. "Absolutely. Never good to be caught unprepared, is it? Nice to meet you Mister McKnight. Have a nice day."

Baxter said to Clay, "Now, about that subpoena..."

Clay raised his arms in resignation. "No idea what you're talking about, sir. I'm sure I can find a shredder to handle it."

Baxter's found a thin, uneasy smile. "Yes. That would be good. The right thing to do." His pace quickened as he approached the long, blocky building, glancing once over his shoulder.

Andi smiled and waved. "He's lying through his teeth, you know."

Clay put on a smile, too, and nodded toward the fleeing Baxter. "Oh, absolutely. No wonder Gideon had him high on the suspect list."

She said, "Nice work. I wondered about that phony subpoena — oh, wait, you said 'warrant.'

He shrugged. "Same difference. They say it works ninety-five percent of the time."

Andi chuckled. "And the other five?"

"You don't want to know."

Chapter Fifteen

Andi's shoulders slumped. Enchanted Cole Porter fans stuffed Pete's to capacity. Trish Sherman held court, with Jerry the Bass Guy and drummer Evan Smiles totally lost in the music. Clay stretched on tiptoes to scan for an open seat.

She said, "High price for working late at the office, I guess. Had no idea the trio had such an enthusiastic following."

"Client comes first. Welcome to being self-employed, where there is no end of shift."

She leaned in close to be heard, their heads inches apart. "So what do you want to do?"

Clay rubbed his chin. "Got an idea. Can you manage following me through the bodies toward the end of the bar?"

"Sure."

"And limp a little. As if you've been walking on a stone in your shoe for the last couple of hours."

She chuckled. "Not hard to do. These were not made for long days. Lead on, Garrison."

Clay took the role of an offensive lineman clearing a path for a running back. Using excuse-me instead of forearms, he navigated layers of mostly men forming a complex barricade. All faced the stage, listening to Trish's driving arrangement of *What is This Thing Called Love*, smoothly shifting into *Easy to Love*. The fourth time they'd visited Pete's, they should have known better than to be late. Andi clung to Clay's wake and ignored eyes roaming her body as they progressed, concentrating instead on why they were late. While they ambushed suspects, Mitch and Mer had done a ton of research — particularly Mer. Their friends earned fun time together, so they sent them to dinner and agreed to meet later at Pete's to celebrate. Meanwhile, Andi had skimmed paperwork, paying closer attention to Mitch's neatly — well, sort of neatly — organized summaries. Mer would go over high points later at the apartment. But Clay had been his usual fastidious self and wanted to study reports with care and she eventually had to pry him loose. Uncertain of his plan in the bar, she hoped to be rewarded with a drink. Anything would do.

Clay reached the line of occupied bar stools. In his fingertips, he held aloft a one-hundred dollar bill. "Buying a seat here. Any takers? No. That's okay. How about you? No? It's all right. You sir?"

Charmed by his precious effort, she put more drama into a phony limp and winced with each step. Halfway, a woman with shoulder-length blonde hair and a nice maroon sweater jabbed her partner and ordered him to yield his seat.

Clay beamed relief. The woman smiled as she slid off her stool and offered it to Andi. And snatched the hundred from Clay's fingers.

Andi said to the volunteer, "I'll buy you a round, if that's okay."

The young woman waved it off. "Hon, I'm usually on my feet all day, so I know how you feel. I'm good. Take the stool." She gathered her drink and led her partner out into the crowd.

As Trish cruised into a gentle arrangement of *So in Love,* Andi looked into Clay's eyes and struggled to find the right words. He laid out that soft puppy-dog smile and motioned for the bartender. Exactly. No words needed.

* * *

Clay ignored the claustrophobic crush. He stared over the long neck of a beer bottle at the way she brought the wine glass to her lips. At how the light caught the tip of her nose. At the line of her cheeks. And the edges of her hair. Their seats weren't the best, but not bad for on-the-fly. Somebody picked up pocket money. And he could pay for the privilege casually, like a guy with some serious pull, without thinking twice.

Andi had given her attention to the jazz trio, playing well. When silhouettes shifted, he spotted Mitch and Mer at the piano bar, laughing. Front row seats for some good sounds. Appropriate for close friends, decent people, team players who accomplished serious work faster than expected. Andi overrode their earlier protestations and offers to stick around and cover the material they had. "Go have fun," she ordered. And they did.

Mixed with background materials on Baxter McKnight and Austin Hart were a stack of document photocopies, mostly related to three deaths — two fetal deaths and then Kimberly Spence. No surprises. Despite the certainty this was a wild-goose chase, it was disappointing. But, for once, they were ahead with research about the next name on the list. Gideon's eldest son, Leonard, ranked as the least likely as a suspect.

At the now-cramped office, they'd debated possibilities about what sort of suspect he might be, trying to stay open-minded but aware it was all speculation. Andi seemed to be growing more suspicious. Intuition, she'd said. A feeling. Also eagerness to get to Pete's, so he put the probe on pause.

From her perch at the bar, Andi leaned back and pointed. "Oh, look. There they are. Aw, it's so cute." She did a little half-hearted wave, but half-hearted, fruitless in that crowd and at that distance.

He shifted forward, close enough to catch the scent of her hair. "They're having a great time."

She unexpectedly turned and they were nose to nose. Her eyes sparkled and she patted his arm. "Me, too."

* * *

Mitch ignored the late-night hour, liberally spraying much of a bottle of all-surface cleaner on a couple of square feet of kitchen counter. He tried to mop it up with a wad of paper towels.

Clay lounged against the kitchen door frame, trying to look as casual as possible without laughter. "Got a stubborn spot there, Mitch?"

His friend looked up. "Nah, tidying up some. You know. Don't want roaches or other creepie-crawlies."

"Yeah, I'd bet they'd drown in that pond."

Mitch sighed and reached for more paper towels. "Probably. I'll admit it. I'm not as experienced as you at this sort of thing, okay?"

"That's the third time in the last twenty minute you've cleaned that same spot, buddy."

Mitch paused and studied his cleaning area. "Yeah? Yeah. I guess you're right."

"And it's after midnight, which is kind of an odd time to clean a kitchen."

Mitch dropped the towels into a trash can and parked the spray bottle. "Yeah, you're right about that, too."

"Uh-huh. So... there something you wanted to discuss, to talk about?"

"Nah, man. We're cool. I'm doing good with this detective gig, like the money, and, well, you know..."

Clay nodded. "Yeah, I know. Meredith. How's that working for you?"

Mitch grunted. "Let's say you did me major favors, dude. I owe ya."

"Nah. We're square. I'm crashing at your place, using your fridge, running the tab on hot water. Least I could do for you, man."

Mitch scratched the back of his head. "You want maybe a beer?"

"No. I'm good."

"I could use a beer. Or maybe something with a little kick."

"Hey, man, don't let me stop you. I planned to hit the sack, but you can.... Wait. You've got a problem with the living arrangement."

Mitch tugged a bottle from the refrigerator and twisted the cap free. "Well.... okay, buddy, I don't want to sound ungrateful..."

"But?"

Mitch took a long pull. "Aw, forget it. Not a big deal."

"You want me out, right?"

Mitch looked relieved and embarrassed at the same time. "Well, I don't know if I'd put it exactly that way, but, well, yeah. Kinda."

"Ah. Meredith."

Mitch studied the floor. "Yeah. The, uh, social agenda kind of thing."

Clay asked, "You mean, right now? I can..."

"No, man. It's the middle of the night and stuff. No way."

"But soon."

"You ain't gonna fire me or be mad or nothing, are ya?"

Clay laughed at what had to be the most ridiculous conclusion he'd heard in months. "No, man. We're good. And I'm kicking myself for not picking up on, well, you know."

"It's okay, bro."

"I can look into it tomorrow, if that's —"

"It's *okay*. Okay?"

"Got it."

Mitch looked hopeful. "You're sure you're not angry or anything? I mean, she's a great chick, but we're tight. Right?"

Clay took a step toward the fridge, giving Mitch a fist bump along the way. "Yeah, buddy. Tight. And maybe I'll have that beer, give you a hand."

* * *

Morning sunshine cast long shadows along the street. Andi trudged up the flight of stairs the office with a cardboard tray marginally gripping foam cups from Grounds Crew, debating an office coffee club.

The guys, naturally, would be eager and probably toss curren- cy toward the effort. Mer would enthusiastically support an end- less carafe, always hot. But Andi knew they'd avoid the task of cleaning the pot, which would inevitably fall to her. And for a pinching second, the memory of the task in the squad room re- turned. The coffee detail went to rookies unless female officers were handy for the top of the list. No, she decided. Never again.

She balanced the tray on the palm of her left hand while fum- bling with the door key with her right. Selfish thoughts fluttered in. Maybe get one cup for herself, let always-late Meredith run her own errand. She sighed and shooed the notion away.

The door was already unlocked.

Someone forgot last night. Or there had been a burglary. Or maybe a burglary in progress. *Stop. Hands where I can see them. Or I'll throw a caramel latte grande right at your head.*

She peered through the portal, relieved to see Clay, poring over paper on his desk. "G'morning," she said. "You're in early. If I had known I would have got you a..." Her eyes found the foam cup to his right. It would be potent espresso, right to the top, black, the closest he could get to cop coffee. "...but see you're al- ready okay." She settled into her chair.

Startled, he closed a newspaper, folding it half, then half

again. "Yeah, getting a head start." He reached for a packet of computer printouts.

"Clay, it's okay to read a newspaper with your coffee. I mean, everybody does." She tugged hers from her bag. "I've got one myself."

"Catching up on community events?"

"No. I'm investigating apartments. Seeing what's available."

After a sip of coffee that would make mere mortals wince, his paper returned to the original position and he opened it to the real estate classified page. "So am I."

She parked her coffee to the left and turned to the same page, folding the sheet sloppily, fully aware that it might make him cringe. Right now, asserting independence took priority. "How come? I mean, I thought you weren't planning on staying any longer than this case would take. Hope things are okay?"

"Mitch's sofa leaves much to be desired. And, uh, he needs his space." He paused over the coffee. "Well, it's that he *wants* his space."

"Oh, gosh, that is *so* funny. Mer and I were talking last night."

He smiled. "Let me guess. She sort of hinted around that while you're a good friend and delightful roommate, she'd prefer to have —"

"Exactly."

"So we're both being evicted."

"Yep. Mer and Mitch. Kind of sweet, don't you think?"

He sighed. "Kind of *complicated.*"

She guided the tip of a ballpoint pen across a string of rentals. Houses, multiple bedrooms, motels by the week were out. "How so?"

"For a job we both didn't want, but took on for traveling cash, we're now in a refurbished office —"

"— Which is kind of small —"

"— Because now we have not a receptionist, but two employees, associates, licenses, permits —"

She nodded. "— Plus an account at a stationery store, and now a coffee shop."

He cocked an eyebrow. "You got an account at Grounds Crew?"

Andi shrugged. "I never have the right amount of cash handy, and can't think of the proper tip for the baristas, and I'm usually in a hurry, so, yes. I have an account and charge it. I'll figure it out later."

He sipped his espresso without wincing. "Putting down some roots are you?"

"Maybe. You?"

"I'm not sure. I need a place to sleep and shower for the time being. A kitchen would be a plus."

She read the name of a neighborhood and a one-bedroom listing. "How about that one?"

"Part of town you don't want."

She read another. "That sounds nice, but pricey."

"Better neighborhood, but a long walk from here."

A car. Getting a car made it even more complicated. She looked up. "You do know we're not going to share, right?"

"Never crossed my mind. Try the second one from the top in the third column."

The place seemed nice. If she took it, he'd be out of what was the prime apartment in the list. If she passed, his gallantry would be rejected. "Okay, thanks."

He gave up on the newspaper. "We could enlist Meredith. She must know the market."

"Good plan. But first we've got to get through this Gideon Pike business. We pulled some chains and rattled some cages, but we're being blown off by these people. Who might not be guilty of anything more than rich, powerful and arrogant."

He returned his attention to the sheaf of printouts. "Maybe.

Besides a furnished apartment, the other thing nagging at me were these." He handed her the materials.

"Okay, the stuff Mitch got from the records people down in New Castle. Death certificates for Kimberly and the twins. Other related documents."

"Notice anything?"

She thumbed through the papers again, certain a hidden clue stared her right in the face. Again. "Photocopies of stuff from twenty-five years ago. Nice and neat."

"The fetal deaths were six weeks prior to the fatal overdose. Her death certificate is for the correct date. The inquest followed Kimberly's autopsy. But look at the forms. They're identical in terms of fonts, penmanship, the date stamps."

She studied them with greater care, hunting for the slightest difference beyond the structure of the forms themselves. Different signature names, but written by the same person. "Oh, wow."

"Yeah. I think they're fake."

Chapter Sixteen

The taxi double-parked between two lines of vehicles hugging the curb on the Upper East Side of Manhattan. Andi peered upward at the building and down at her notes.

"Mer says she'll take the commission on any sale within eight or nine blocks of here. I can't imagine why."

Clay opened the door on his side. "I can. I suppose I've got the fare?"

"Your turn. I did the tip at the airport."

He dug into his pocket for paper money, told the driver to keep the change and hurried around the back side before she could exit. He held the door for her and when she reached the sidewalk, extended a hand. "What, no tip?"

"Chivalry, Clay. Think chivalry."

"Ah, of course. I wasn't up on the latest boundaries of behavior and anxious about appearing sexist or misogynistic or patronizing or whatever."

She smiled. "Don't worry, Garrison. I'll let you know when you cross the line."

They strolled toward a discreet entry to a tiny foyer. "Which line? I see a pair, as in double standard."

"If it makes you feel better, I'll get the door."

"Do I get to go first?"

"No. You can wait for me."

"I'm becoming confused."

She mustered the most condescending sigh she could and pulled the door open. "Welcome to the realities of your gender."

He paused to allow her to pass. "So much for blissful ignorance."

They scanned a collection of mailboxes suggesting one residence per floor. In one of the city's most prestigious neighborhoods, that kind of subdivision hinted that Leonard Braddon Pike and his mother, Martha, led opulent lives. Mer wasn't kidding about commission potential.

Clay made notes of names and numbers from the boxes, a detail guy as usual. But he was being such a good sport about her teasing. Guilt settled around a banter she hadn't enjoyed since... well, since college, long ago.

Take a chance. "You know what, Clay?"

"Hm?"

"This partner thing is working out pretty well as far as I'm concerned."

"Yup, I'd agree."

"Clay, you should know... Never mind, not important."

"Probably is. Go ahead."

She shrugged and looked away from his patient eyes. "I, uh, still have to work through some trust issues."

"I'm not surprised. You had the makings of a good cop, maybe fast-track to major crime. Certainly impressed me. But you ran into a bunch of total jerks. I've seen it. It's the kind of thing that leaves wounds, even scars. But I'm cool with it. Take your time. I'll be patient. So, meanwhile, our guy is on the fifteenth floor. Mitch had him down as a big-timer in several causes, mostly the arts, philanthropy."

"So how do you want to work it?"

He looked thoughtful for several moments. "Maybe we ought to play it straight?"

"I agree. I sense this one's not a weasel. Plus he's Gideon's son. Who knows how touchy that might be. And Mer had no trouble making an actual appointment. Said he was cordial. So, yeah, go ahead and ring the bell." He reached for the call button, pausing when she put her hand on his forearm. "And, um, thanks."

"For?"

"Being the kind of guy I'd want to be partners with. Somebody who respects me."

"Trust me, Andi, you've earned it."

"I know I get kind of flirty at times."

He pressed the button. "That you do."

She let her shoulders slump. "It's that they were using sexual stuff against me. I thought it might be handy to turn it around, make it work for me. I didn't mean it a personal way."

"No offense taken."

"I mean, I don't think it's fair to use sex as a weapon."

A voice on the intercom said, "Yes? Hello? Pardon me?"

She leaned forward. "Hi, Mister Pike. It's Clay Garrison and Andrea Delvento, on behalf of your father. We had an appointment."

"What's this about sex and weapons?"

Andi looked at Clay's smirk and struggled to maintain composure. "We were discussing a case, Mister Pike."

"Ah, well, I'd love to hear more. One moment."

A faint buzzer preceded a distinctive click of the interior foyer exit, beyond which two elevator doors resembled bank vaults rather than a hospitality area.

Andi shook her head. "Guys. You are all the same."

Clay laughed and opened the door for her. "That's because women are so inspiring."

* * *

Which, Clay told himself, described her perfectly, serene in a plain, efficient, cool elevator car. Standing next to him on a ride fifteen floors to ultra-posh, she exuded a glowing heat. It wasn't surprising that she excited the guys in that lame force. Cops are cops, the younger ones wearing macho armor and proud of it, the worst of them wallowing in it like twelve-year-olds with their first beer, cigarettes and girly magazines.

Amazing that commanders didn't see the potential of someone clearly as bright and disarming as she could be. For a couple of floors, he recalled patrol incidents where her sheer presence could have calmed a tense situation on a fast track to scary.

Yeah. She's made for this kind of work.

She stood relaxed, calm, someone in control and knew it. The expression she had when Mer and Mitch arrived that morning, trying to look as though they barely knew each other and doing a lousy job of it. Of them, Mitch had been the most flustered with the documents issue, and became more embarrassed when Meredith rushed to his defense. But Andi cheerfully put the matter to rest and made everyone feel better. Police work? Heck no. She should go into politics.

The elevator slowed to a halt.

A tiny plain room with a little table and a large potted plastic plant on the floor awaited them when they stepped off the car. Before he could knock, Leonard Pike opened the apartment door.

He wore gray slacks, a light blue dress shirt with a conservative tie, and a chef's apron extending across most of his body. He bore a striking resemblance to Gideon Pike from the old photos, including the effusive smile.

"Hello. I'm Leonard Pike. And you must be Miss — I assume Miss — Delvento and you'd be Mister Garrison." He shook their hands in the same sequence. "Won't you come in?"

Astonishing. A guy who had an estimated net worth with nine zeros tagging along after a serious number. The kind of guy who didn't seem to worry about a thing, who could buy Andi and himself thousands of times over and not think twice about it. Opening the door to people who hadn't been vetted. Or maybe had.

The spacious apartment featured contemporary furnishings, a little on the sparse side, but, in the context of entertaining a medium-sized crowd, about right.

Leonard introduced his mother, Martha Elliot Pike, who Meredith described as 72 years old and the first in Gideon's three marriages. After dancing around in polite small talk, Leonard announced he planned to prepare a lunch and would they join the two for a light meal?

Leonard said, "I rather enjoy cooking, you see. Dabble, of course, not at the same level as staff at Tintorelli's or Thirty-Seven Park, but it amuses me. Tell me, Mister Garrison, do you cook?"

Those were big names in New York dining then and likely now, at least twenty rungs up the ladder from Garrison's in its heyday, but Andi caught the cue.

She said, "Why don't you fellows take charge of the kitchen, while Mrs. Pike and I find someplace quiet to chat?"

Martha beamed approval and invited Andi to have a look at her collectables in the library.

Leonard gestured direction toward a kitchen way beyond galley-style postage stamp space typical of apartments in Clay's league. It rivaled high-end commercial and would have been right at home in any three-star restaurant. Nothing homey about it. All brushed stainless, well kept and neatly organized. With a commercial-grade walk-in refrigerator.

Leonard took cooking seriously and basked in serving as a tour guide to a visitor who appreciated the space and equipment. They finished at a prep table where he'd organized produce that would have passed the muster of the most discriminating chef. He poured wine, a good label, and returned to his task while Clay accepted the role of observer.

After a sip, Leonard unfurled a Boldric canvas knife bag, wall-to-wall Wusthof on the inside. "So. Father is on his biennial missing twins investigation — but he must be slowing down in his old age because, I believe, it's been three years since he last made a run at it. A rather sad little scruffy fellow named Storm, I recall. And you're the fresh kid on the block. Paying you well, I trust?"

Clay nodded. "We've been asked to look into it."

He set to chopping vegetables. "Two of you. My, my. The old man must be becoming anxious."

"And why would he be anxious?"

"Terms of the trust, of course. After twenty-five years, the estate of poor Kimberly reverts to the remaining heirs. Not that it makes any difference in the business context because Conrad is the trustee in charge of such things. But who needs loose ends?" He held a carafe aloft. "Care for oil? This is a particularly nice virgin olive."

"Italian?"

"Why yes. Mimi' Coratina. How did you know?"

"The scent, the color. The twins are loose ends?"

"Well, the ghosts of them certainly are. Father refuses to accept reality, that they never were. I suppose that sounds terribly crass, but after two decades the debate becomes tedious."

Leonard continued to chop and assemble, building elaborate salads from a palette of colorful vegetables, fresh, firm, precisely ripened.

Clay said, "It sounds as if you've accepted that reality."

"I have indeed, many years ago. You should understand, Mister Garrison, that my father and I are estranged, have been for many years."

"Why is that?"

"Not of any consequence here and now. But, frankly, I've moved on and my mother as well. We're active in the arts, notably in philanthropy, and I cheerfully keep my proxies in Conrad's corner. Mostly to annoy the old man. One of our foundations, by the way, honors Kimberly, although by most standards she hardly deserved it. She was a troubled person in many ways."

"Such as?"

"Well, such as... No. I think it best not to go there. Poor form, speaking ill of the dead. Yet, reality is reality, Mister Garrison. Kimberly was a drug addict and it cost her own life, but also two babies and probably contributed greatly to the mental distress of her mother."

Clay nodded and spoke softly. "Heroin is laced with tragic fallout."

"I'm sure. But Kimberly's drug of choice was cocaine. Sometimes pills, but mostly cocaine."

"Perhaps she graduated to harder stuff?"

Leonard focused on arranging elements of the salads. "I doubt it. She was deathly afraid of needles, of any kind. And not a smoker, if you get my meaning."

"But the cause of death was listed as —"

Leonard shrugged and rearranged some lettuce. "They sometimes get things wrong, you know."

"I'm sure. So. Tell me about the babies. Know who the father might be?"

"No idea. With Kimberly, it could have been anyone, even a stranger. I'm afraid I don't have first-hand knowledge of the matter, having been abroad at the time."

"Business?"

"Personal preference. Ours is not the most model of families, Mister Garrison." He stood up straight and took half a step back. Four perfect salads, nicely presented. "There. That should suffice for luncheon, don't you agree?"

"Very nice."

"Thank you. Now, I would ask a favor of you. I hope I've been helpful in your research — trust me, there's nothing there. You can probably count on due reward and move forward — but I would request that you not discuss it at the table."

"I think I understand."

"My mother is advanced in years and doesn't need to be distressed."

"Of course. But I wonder if you might answer one more question."

"Certainly."

"You mentioned the last detective to investigate the missing twins..."

Leonard smiled. "The last two outings involved a fellow named Storm, Glenn Storm. One of those stereotypical small-time private eyes, a total incompetent."

Clay pictured the little sleazeball and struggled not to react. "Okay, and...?"

"Well, the fellow took father for a small fortune, which was fine with me. The old man deserved it. And, Mister Garrison, I assure you the twins are not missing. They are deceased."

* * *

Andi sunk her teeth into a straightforward fast-food burger near the departure gate at Kennedy, chased it with a pair of barely-warm but salty french fries and a shot of a soft drink from a paper cup.

She said, "You're sure you don't want one of these? They're not too bad."

"I'm sure."

"I feel guilty eating in front of you."

"You should feel guilty, eating that thing."

"Sorry. The salad didn't do it for me. And since we have half an hour to kill before our flight back to Pennsylvania, I couldn't resist."

"It's okay."

She munched two more fries, biting off bits until they were nubs to be tossed into her mouth. "I bet you don't approve."

He said nothing.

"Yep. You don't approve."

"Eat whatever you want."

"So that salad. Could you make that kind of salad?"

"Yes."

"With all kinds of fancy veggies?"

"Absolutely."

"So you guys hit it off okay in the kitchen?"

"Uh-huh."

"The mother avoided the topic. Danced around and around it, as if pretending nothing was ever there. I mean, denial with a capital 'D'."

"Yup. And Leonard said that because Kimberly was afraid of needles, he doubted heroin would be the cause of death."

"Yet it was, Clay. But I can tell you don't approve of this burger, fries. Should I pitch it?"

"No, no. Feel free to poison yourself."

She inhaled the remainder of the burger and drew a massive amount of soda through the straw. "You don't approve. Did Leonard lie or is he out there in la-la land, too?"

"Not sure. But two things are true."

"Such as?"

"Many secrets are being covered up in this family."

She raced through the rest of the packet of fries. "Absolutely. And the other?"

"Your diet is terrible."

Chapter Seventeen

Andi stirred extra cream into coffee that Clay would certainly dislike. She had a table window in one the of low red brick buildings lining Lancaster Avenue, a subtle but stylish Bryn Mawr shop with a menu leaning toward pastry for the well-heeled of Philadelphia's Main Line.

In her earbud, Meredith's voice provided friendly relief from the stuffy pretentiousness of the entire Pike clan, whose reach extended all the way into Upper Bucks County. Mer reported in, another solid day of research, none of it optimistic, but comforting anyway.

"So, Andi, bottom line is that we're probably running into the same stone walls and dead ends that Storm did, the last time he went to bat for Mister Pike."

"It figures. The perfect accompaniment to coffee that's eleven ninety-five a cup and not anywhere near the quality from Grounds Crew."

Mer gasped. "That's terrible."

"You should taste it."

"No thanks. So, poor Mitch went back to New Castle, tried to put the arm on records people, and practically got thrown out. He said he went for last resort, an F-O-I lawsuit?"

"Freedom of information. They're supposed to be public records."

"Yeah, well, they said photocopies were the best they were going to do and no way were they going to let Mitch into the actual files to see for himself. I guess it's a gray area. Maybe we ought to hire a couple of serious burglars?"

Andi sighed. "A felony is still a felony. We'll have to work out some sort of plan. Maybe Clay has some ideas."

Mer laughed. "So where is Mister Hot Stuff?"

"Mer... Oh, never mind. He's out scrounging directions to somewhere in Lower Merion Township. Shaky address, and people around here are not exactly eager for publicity and attention. I'm half expecting local cops to show up and usher us to the town line."

"Wow. Lower Merion. Once again, I'll take the commission on any listing. Did you know that it has the fifth highest per capita income in the country? And the twelfth highest household? I can barely imagine the asking on one of their little spreads."

"How do you know this stuff?"

"Work in real estate long enough, you know where the money is. You could have been a cop there."

"No, thanks. Old guard blue bloods are the same everywhere. Okay. So, let's go over this one more time for the sake of my notes. I finally found a working pen and Clay is a detail hound."

The waitress paused to offer to top off her cup. Andi declined, and repeated for the third time that her party would be along soon.

Mer said, "Okay, here we go. The housekeeper, Madge Whittaker, says she's sworn to secrecy and won't talk. I did my best friendly-sister thing and struck out. The butler, Alvin Flowers, is deceased, natural causes, seven years ago. Mitch has been trying everything he knows on the chauffeur, Freddie Boyd, even variations on the name. No luck. Should he keep trying?"

Andi paused. It would be nice to have someone other than blood relatives to fill in some blanks. A missing driver seemed hopeful. But Mitch had already devoted too much time to it. "No,

Mer. Let's let it go for now. Who's next?"

"Another toughie. Ruth Towler — the maid — is evidently near death in a hospice, somewhere near Altoona. Some sort of cancer. Both of us tried to sweet-talk the daughter into a few minutes. But the daughter, Rhonda, adamantly refuses and made sure staff there locked the gate to us."

"Really?"

"Well, Rhonda must have guessed I planned to bend the rules. I mean, you know, a teeny bit."

Andi winced through a sip of bitter coffee. "Don't worry about it. I'm not used to the shaggy ethics of private eye work yet."

"I suppose you're right. Okay, Carlene Elliot. Got my notes?"

"Yes, Mer, thanks. Fifty-three, eldest daughter of Gideon and married to one Franklin Elliot, who's a corporate V-P with the Pike empire."

"Carlene is on the board of directors and the word is that she's tight, business-wise, with Conrad. The mother, Martha, you already met. Gosh, Mister Pike went through a whole parade of wives, eh?"

"True. And they're incredibly civil about it, at least to us."

Meredith chuckled. "Trust me, Andi, these are the kind of people who put on chin-up, placid smiles to mask messy family business most people would never want to have."

"It *is* surreal. Okay, I see Clay coming. I'll let you get back to work. Thanks a bunch. You and Mitch are doing a wonderful job."

"Sorry we couldn't have struck gold or anything."

Andi waved Clay to the table. "Don't worry. It's still early."

* * *

Clay parked the humble rental they got at the airport and sat in awe.

Like him, Andi seemed to grapple to take it in. Set gently on turf that most golfers would drool to walk upon, the Tudor-style mansion sprawled in several directions. A manor, the kind in movies, where the gravel drive is groomed as carefully as the perfect shrubbery. The kind where the grass is not just precision mowed and edged, not merely raked, but probably combed, too. Twice a day.

She pointed. A helicopter descended from the tree line, hovered over the perfect lawn, and plopped onto it. A guy next to the pilot hopped out, opened the passenger door and there she was.

Carlene Elliot. The second to last name on Gideon's list. Another billionaire in the stable of Pike offspring. Shorter than he expected, slight. No, probably closer to *fit*. Swimming, tennis, that sort of thing. Not bowling or running. As if it were the residence of the week, she strolled toward her mansion, lingering on the edge of the drive to examine the rental car as if it were a blemish. Intimidation stampeded through his mind, and thoughts gathered, as summer thunderclouds, of telling Gideon, sorry, thank you for the money, but they'd gotten squashed.

Nevertheless, he wouldn't want to be a patrol officer here, although burglary investigations might be intriguing. He barely organized the thought when Andi said the same thing.

She added, "I can't imagine the pressure of dealing with that kind of pull."

"Been there, done that."

She studied his face. "Ah, so that's it. You were one of those outstanding rookies who got bagged in town politics?"

"Yeah."

"Want to talk about it?"

"Now?"

"Good a time as any. I want to make Mrs. Elliot wait a few seconds."

He tapped his fingertips on the steering wheel. "So, okay, it wasn't money. The local power base. We had a solid traffic stop.

The back of the vehicle, an SUV, completely stuffed with nar-cotics. Plain view."

"And?"

"I got the subject's ID, returned to the unit to check for wants and warrants, advised my training officer. We approached the ve-hicle on either side. Textbook. The subject makes a thing out of his relationship to the mayor. His brother. The FTO wants to dump it. But I've got a major case, one of those that makes a ca-reer, or at least jump starts it."

"Except it was the mayor's brother."

Clay shrugged. "The law's the law. We ran it through the sys-tem. The guy beats the rap because the district attorney won't press it. The mayor calls the chief, the chief calls me."

"And that was that?"

"Yep. With a nice black mark on my record for stuff that could lead to a big time civil case against the city."

"Sorry. What about Mrs. Elliot?"

"Let's make our inquiry, watch our step."

She stared at him for several seconds, then reached for he door handle. "Okay, then. I'm up?"

Mrs. Elliot looked impatient.

"Yeah. Go for it."

* * *

Andi snagged a placid smile and waited. Carlene Elliot was one of those women to focus first on the guy and then move up in ranking. Immaculately groomed and dressed, but not pretentious-ly so, Carlene Elliot evidently slipped graciously into middle age with confidence, a good tailor and an outstanding hairdresser. So her eyes measured Clay first, quickly dismissed him, and gave her attention to Andi.

A pleasant smile came easy. They'd called it right. Andi

lengthened her stride and extended a hand. "Hello. I'm Andrea Delvento, and I believe we have an appointment?"

Carlene responded cordially, neither reticent or effusive, with a firm handshake. "Yes, of course." Clay earned a momentary glance. "And you must be Mister Garrison. Some sort of assistant, I assume." She gestured toward a massive front door lurking in a stone alcove. "May I offer a refreshment?"

"Thank you so much for seeing us. My, what a lovely, impressive home."

Carlene's smile softened. "Yes. It is."

The foyer could house at least a dozen people from Andi's home town. A staff person appeared to serve as a human coat rack and tend Carlene's coat and bag.

"I think tea would be lovely, don't you, Miss Delvento? And I assume that would be all right with your associate?"

No sense in correcting a workable impression. Clay seemed to pick up the hint, hanging back, to one side, looking placid and calm.

Andi beamed. "Yes. I'm sure it would. I'm grateful you could spare some time, and I promise to be brief."

Carlene moved toward a doorway. "Fine. We'll take our tea in the library, then. Will Mister Garrison be joining us?"

"If that's okay."

"Of course. It's just this way."

If the foyer impressed, the library pulled the air from her lungs. It resembled one of those massive movie sets for dramas involving British royalty. Tasteful antique-looking décor and high ceilings. Carlene steered them to the nearest oasis of chairs.

As they settled on facing sofas, the staff person delivered a tray of cups, teapot, creamer, sugar and a platter of pastry. Clay remained standing behind Andi. It fluffed her confidence like a pillow resetting for another round of comfort. The staffer nodded when dismissed and silently vanished.

Carlene poured, more like an aunt than a billionaire, and offered dainty porcelain cups, first to Andi, then to Clay. It looked terribly fragile in hands designed to crush metal objects. He declined pastry.

As she filled her own cup, Carlene said, "Well, then, describe this latest investigation that father's launched. I hope it's not the same dreary conspiracy theory about Kimberly and the unfortunate granddaughters."

Andi leaned into the posture of a sympathetic niece. "I'm afraid so, Mrs. Elliot. I'm given to understand there's some sort of a deadline coming up about the estate, and it seems as though Mister Pike wants one last look."

"Of course. The endless pet project of Father, who can't let go of a few lurid whispers. I'm certain that you must realize he's well up in years, retired from an active role in business matters, and for some odd reason fixated on ancient history. There's nothing mysterious about it. One of those tragic thing families must bear. We had been hoping that Father could enjoy his golden years, roam around in his adventures without the pressures of financial matters, take it easy."

Andi nodded. "I'm sure. I know over time he's hired others to investigate, but now wants fresh eyes, just to be certain. We're doing our best to give him a sense of assurance."

"I understand that you've already met with Leonard, Baxter, and Austin. What have you learned thus far?"

Andi shrugged. "The whole matter is pretty much as you described. A most unfortunate addiction leading to the fetal deaths of twin girls and to Kimberly's own death from an overdose of cocaine."

Carlene cocked an eyebrow and returned her teacup to the coffee table. "Heroin. She died from an overdose of heroin."

"Oh, that's right. Of course. I got confused when Leonard mentioned that cocaine was her drug of choice, and highly unlikely she would have turned to heroin."

Carlene smiled. "Leonard, being absent most of the time, was not in a position to know."

"Absent?"

"Yes. He and that chauffeur, Freddie something or other. But I'm sure you know about that sordid little business, too. In any event, you must be aware that drug users often escalate into more dangerous options. And that was the case with Kimberly, I'm afraid."

Andi nodded. "Yet, she was in rehab, where there's nothing illicit available to addicts. I can't help but wonder how she obtained enough heroin to kill her and her unborn children as well." She needed a pause, a distraction. She said to her partner, "You were curious about that the other day, weren't you, Clay?"

Clay said, "Yes. It *was* puzzling. But I don't have any sort of a medical background. I've got to confess ignorance on how drugs are administered and work. I guess pharmaceuticals of any kind are tricky business."

Carlene straightened and her expression went to a blend of pride and smugness. "Mister Garrison, it's not complicated. Besides the fact that those with means can make discreet arrangements, lethal doses of any narcotic will quickly affect the patient and a fetus, if she's pregnant. But Kimberly's children were stillborn many weeks earlier. And it's not likely that they did any sort of toxicology tests. Fetal deaths can have many unexplained causes."

Andi said, "Oh, that's right. You've got some experience in healthcare, don't you?"

"Why, yes. Volunteer work in Africa, Nigeria in fact, for a couple of years after college."

Clay asked, "You're a doctor? A nurse?"

"No, a tech, an aide, I'm afraid. It was a time when many of us were passionate about helping the less fortunate in the world. I did my bit, became somewhat disillusioned, and left the project because of growing business obligations here."

Andi said, "I understand. It must have been terribly sad, health issues in the third world. And then, of course, your father..."

Wistfulness evaporated and Carlene cooled to corporate chill. "Gideon, of course, had become a bit erratic at that time. Conrad and I were compelled to take steps."

Clay cocked his head. "Specifically?"

"Why, assuming control of the business. With Father no longer fit, there were matters to attend to. We had the support of everyone."

Andi said, "Meaning Austin, Baxter, Leonard?"

"Correct. Conrad is also the trustee for his mother's affairs and Kimberly's estate."

Clay smiled. "Which would become complicated if Kimberly's children had survived."

Carlene fell silent for a moment, then stood. "But, of course, they did not. Never existed. Now, I'm afraid I have some other obligations to attend. It's been a pleasure meeting with you, Miss Delvento. I *do* urge you not to trouble Conrad with this matter. He's a busy man and doesn't need the distraction."

Clay said, "We'll see. I think we owe it to Mister Pike to demonstrate we've done a thorough job and that, as you say, there's a simple explanation to the entire matter."

Her eyes narrowed. "Be cautious, Mister Garrison."

"Is that a threat?"

Andi interceded. "I'm sure it's just advice, a request for discretion, Clay."

Chapter Eighteen

Clay took one last look at the palatial home of Carlene Elliot before he bucked his seatbelt and reached for the ignition. "You thinking what I'm thinking?"

Andi said, "Care to bet she's *not* on the phone with Conrad right now?"

Clay brought the rental, a comfortable but not extravagant sedan, to life. She was right, of course. The first three on the list were outliers, but the scent of collaboration between Carlene Elliot and Conrad Spence was strong.

He said, "No, I wouldn't take that bet. In fact, I'd wager that Meredith's sudden good luck in getting an appointment with Carlene was engineered by Conrad."

"We're going to have to do some prep work on this guy. He's the big dog in the kennel, and Mer says he's the personification of Alpha Male."

Clay put the car in gear. Light brown gravel crunched under the tires. "Does that mean he gets a cape and some sort of super-power?"

"I wouldn't take this too lightly. No cape, but he's got a big piece of the business. His superpower begins with a dollar sign and a long string of zeros."

"I'm trying not to be intimidated, right down to my socks."

"Is it working?"

"No."

She sighed. "Me neither." Her phone rang and said it was Meredith, probably offering news and a dose of encouragement.

Backtracking into increasingly intense traffic toward the southern end of Philadelphia, Clay tried to conjure any sort of image of Conrad Spence as a regular guy, but kept returning to the cold, expressionless eyes of a family portrait from many years ago. The kind of eyes sharks have. When they're about to shoot in out of nowhere and take a hunk of leg for a snack. Darn right it was intimidating. One of the power guys, who pull strings a fellow never knew existed. The kind that walk away and you felt a sense of relief, but be screwed right to the wall an hour later. Helpless. With everyone maybe sympathetic, but taking a wide berth anyhow, as if the little guy was pancaked roadkill a dozen times mashed under tires.

He toyed with the possibility of a genuine wild goose chase. The clan could be totally guilty, but a couple of green rookies, unable to prove squat, were going to be hung out to dry.

Andi listened to Mer and wrote stuff down, looking like she struggled for legibility on a road laced with shallow potholes, the kind of road demanding both hands on the wheel and close attention to impatient drivers in hurry to die.

He said, "Coming up on where we've got to turn to go to the airport."

She motioned to go straight ahead. As they zoomed past the exit, she disconnected. "It seems we're going to Wilmington."

"Conrad?"

"Yup. His office finally returned Mer's call and — surprise, surprise — he grants us an audience. I've got directions." She looked toward him and offered a comforting smile. "You're not excited about this, are you?"

"I'll be okay."

"Sure? You were pretty quiet back at Carlene's bungalow."

"Didn't want to get in the way. You did great."

"Thanks." She was silent for several seconds. "Look, Clay, the worst that's going to happen is another zip-zero-nada. We get paid regardless, and the more I learn by inference about Gideon Pike, the less I care. They're an entire clan of sleaze in my book."

"I'll be okay."

"Sure? I can try to run point on this one, but maybe guy to guy is better. I don't think being girly is going to work, not with this dude."

"What did Meredith say?"

"She was relaying notes from Mitch, who did some asking around to some buddies he's got in the press around Delaware. Conrad is forty-six, Kimberly's blood brother, stepson by third marriage. He's the CEO, of course, supposedly cold, stiff, pin-stripe guy. The welfare of the front office is his sole interest, a kind of Scrooge, but younger. Not a chummy pal-type of person. Got a hefty stake of his own, but runs a string of proxies and rules with an iron fist."

"Wonderful."

"Both Mer and Mitch say not to underestimate this guy. He plays rough, okay? Not in-your-face, but more behind-your-back. If you want, I can do the sophisticated lawyer thing —"

"I'll be okay."

She bit her lip. "Okay, then." She paused. "Oh. And the groundskeeper guy, Leroy Steele?"

"Yeah."

"Dead. Early forties, drugs. Heroin, in fact."

"Well, that just makes my day."

* * *

Andi decided "anonymous" would be the best way to describe the Pike castle. Just as Meredith described it on the phone, a modernistic twelve-story boxy building, primarily gray but mostly glass, held court in the corporate neighborhood of the city, where office buildings were bashful about logos and names.

Parking was easy. Tenants had their own nearly-empty parking garage. Clay found a spot near executive elevators that soon whispered straight to the top floor.

Furnishings were sparse. The color scheme was corporate gray, navy blue, hints of deep red here and there. Straight out of a lobby décor catalog for the industrial indifference look, a business without a soul.

Clay was being quiet and detached, a mood reflecting the style of Conrad Spence's lair. Where wolves hung out, and everyone was vicious. She wore a business suit with a better label, but felt as though she'd fallen off a clearance rack in a discount store.

A severe woman with thick glasses and a charcoal pantsuit looked up from an empty reception desk. She said, "Mister Garrison?"

"Yes. And this is my partner, Andrea Delvento."

The receptionist barely glanced in her direction as she rose to escort them. "Mister Spence is expecting you."

Except for an overhead light above the desk at the far end, the inner sanctum was dim. The desk was arranged at a forty-five degree angle and a generous distance from the corner. Two walls of glass were muted with thin drapes, blocking sunlight and converting it into a grayish gloom.

Spence was fit, as though he worked out but didn't push it. Trim, but not burly, about six feet and wearing a tailored gray suit, light blue shirt and navy tie with a thin band of red and white stripes. He gestured for the couple to approach his altar and completed a telephone call with someone named Fitch. Not a friend. Not an employee or business associate. Someone with whom he was probably working some sort of a deal, perhaps to buy Oregon.

When he rose to shake hands, his smile was cordial but not friendly. And as Clay had said, his eyes were dark and lifeless, spoiling what otherwise would have been a ruggedly-handsome face.

He directed them to a contemporary leather-and-steel group of chairs, settee and coffee table, and accepted Clay's appreciation for fitting them into his busy schedule. Kind of off-handed, like they were a passing annoyance.

Clay barely uttered a syllable before Conrad cut him off. "Look, Garrison, I'm terribly sorry you've had to travel a distance, but I can assure you of two things. First, you're investigating a matter long resolved. A private, sensitive, family matter. With the sort of inquiries that tend to open old wounds and create discomfort. Second, you're doing it on behalf of an old man who, I'm afraid, is unwell. Doesn't want to accept the truth. Tosses cash around, childlike, bringing in investigators who, I'm certain, are more than pleased to take advantage of an elderly person's anxieties."

"I wouldn't say —"

Conrad raised a hand to silence Clay. "Of course. That's how the game works, isn't it? Now, let me be the fifth — it is the fifth, isn't it? — to assure you that my late sister Kimberly was the victim of an unfortunate addiction to narcotics —"

Andi interrupted. "Was it heroin or cocaine? There seems to be some confusion."

"Excuse me? I'm sorry, your name was...?"

Clay leaned in. "Andrea Delvento. She's my partner, sir. We're both asking questions here."

Conrad exhaled a sigh of impatience and straightened his tie while he leaned back and gestured for them to continue.

"My partner's question was whether it was cocaine or heroin."

"What difference does it make?"

Clay bore down. "Trying to tie up some loose ends, sir. As I'm sure you do, we take a certain pride in doing our job as well as we can. I, for one, prefer to tie this off as quickly as possible and let you continue on with your lives. Such as they are."

Oops, she thought. "I think what Clay means is that you're prominent and important people, but we're kind of stuck with a contract with Mister Pike. The sooner we can clear things up, the sooner everything can, well, you know..."

Conrad paused to consider the remark, but it seemed like he was staring at her. At last he gave his attention back to Clay. "Very well, then. Kimberly's cause of death was an overdose of heroin. I assume that was what she had been using. Why?"

Clay said, "Someone mentioned cocaine, her aversion to needles. I'm trying to clear up inconsistencies for my report."

Conrad looked mildly annoyed, but stole another glance in her direction, lingering long enough to ignite unease. "Well, I have no idea."

"I suppose it's not important. And we understand that she gave birth to stillborn twin girls some time before she was found dead herself."

"Yes. Several weeks as I recall. But that was a long time ago."

"And her mother was hospitalized about the same time, for psychiatric care?"

"Yes. At a private clinic. She was deeply traumatized by the entire affair, and there seems to be no hope for any sort of recovery."

Clay nodded. "Sorry to hear that. The entire business enterprise, it's privately held?"

"Yes. There are no outside stakeholders. A family trust has existed for these many years, much to everyone's benefit."

"And I understand that you, personally, gave shares to Austin Hart and Baxter McKnight? Yes? And why would you do that, sir?"

"My stepfather is not a pleasant fellow, Mister Garrison. He wanted both of them kept out in the cold. I thought that to be unfair. I was willing to provide each with a stake."

Clay looked up from his notes. "And what's the current value of the holdings of each?"

Conrad stiffened. Caught looking at her again, he turned away and spoke abruptly. "I'm sorry, but that's none of your business. It's proprietary information and I'm sure outside the scope of your investigation."

Andi asked, "But it's safe to say it's substantial money right? Perhaps nine figures?"

"I'm not going to answer that."

Clay said, "I understand that you're the trustee for your mother's interest as well as Kimberly's estate, correct?"

Conrad's exasperation seemed to grow, but his eyes kept drifting her direction. "Yes, yes. I have the majority of the proxies, except, of course, for Gideon and Carlene."

Andi said, "Impressive. I mean, your achievements on behalf of the entire family are stunning. I'm sure they're grateful for what you've accomplished."

"Yes, yes, I suppose so."

Clay said, "Well, except for Gideon Pike, right?"

"Look, Garrison, you're making more out of this than there is. I think Gideon's concern is relatively minor, perhaps due to some guilt over how he's managed to neglect family for many years. He gets on these campaigns, but soon enough, they fade away."

Andi tried a supportive smile. "Merely an old man's whimsy."

It seemed to work. Conrad relaxed a bit. "I'd say madness." Again his gaze lingered and then drifted back to Clay. "So how much is the old man paying this time?"

"That's kind of proprietary, too."

"Oh, come on, Garrison. We're businessmen here. What is it this time, a hundred, two hundred thousand? I can see that you're young and energetic and probably want to move this little matter off your plate quickly. Why don't I offer you a half a million, you get a report off to Gideon, and everyone walks away happy. Does that work for you? Perhaps you should open a restaurant, like your father. A better alternative to police work, at which you obviously failed."

Once again Conrad's attention went to Andi. This time she stared back, offering an easy smile and a warm reaction to what appeared to be shameless flirting.

Clay watched the exchange of looks. "I think we're fine with the present arrangement, sir."

Andi took a chance. "Is everything okay, *Conrad?*"

The moment evaporated. "Oh. Sorry. I didn't mean to stare. It's that you bore a striking resemblance... never mind, not important. My apologies if I made you uncomfortable. You're certain I can't offer you a bonus to expedite this matter?"

She responded with as much charm as she could muster and reached out to gently pat his arm, lingering for a moment. "No, Conrad. We're fine. We truly are."

Chapter Nineteen

Meredith and Andi hovered nearby while Clay studied the empty room. Size was okay, the shape decent. About normal, he decided, for an apartment in this section of town. The carpet, not a bad color, recently cleaned, the single bedroom decent and kitchen workable. Parking good, convenient. Still...

Mer glanced at a sheet of paper in her hand, "So what do you think of the drapes? They come with it."

Andi said, "They seem nice. Kind of neutral, would go with anything."

Meredith said, "Clay?"

"Huh? Oh, yeah, decent."

"So what's wrong with it?"

"It's unfurnished."

"Ah. Here's the thing. Anything halfway decent in this town is not going to come furnished. Unless it's a short-term rental, a sublet." Mer's tone became more direct, insistent. "Is that what you want?"

A fair but tough question, pushing the larger issue of just how long he planned to stay into focus. The investigation had come to a string of stone walls with no apparent path leading anywhere. It didn't matter if Gideon's suspicions were on the mark. The case still twenty-five years cold, the wagons circled tight, and their experience as detectives limited. In terms of sticking around, he'd been in, out, in and now thinking out again, facing a yawning morass of career uncertainty. With her experience in local real estate, Meredith had volunteered to agent for them, but the indolence of the past week didn't require an assistant to save steps.

Together the team had sat over way too much coffee and he'd tolerated way to much takeout as they sifted notes, reports, again and again. Dismay with the quality of people throughout the Pike clan, he reminded himself, remained an insufficient reason to defiantly press on.

One of the better cooks at his dad's steakhouse, on a topic he could not recall, had said, "You can bang your head on a brick wall all day long hoping to knock it down. But odds are, you're just gonna need an aspirin."

Lots of windows gave the apartment a bright airy feel.

Meredith gave up. "So, Andi, what do you think?"

"I like it. It's quiet, there's a nice park across the parking lot, rent is okay for me. Unless you want it, Clay."

Clay said, "The one on Seventeenth Street wasn't half bad."

Meredith threw up her hands. "Okay. Dealing with one fussy client is one thing, but two is beyond me. I've narrowed it down to three —"

Andi shook her head. "I don't think either of us were impressed with that one bedroom on the other side of town."

Meredith sighed. "So, okay. Two. Should make it easy. Why don't you two draw straws, flip a coin, whatever. Each one gets an apartment, and I get back to work."

Clay said to Andi, "You like this one?"

"It's fine. But only if you —"

"It's yours."

Meredith exhaled relief. "So you're going to take the one on Seventeenth? I think it had the larger kitchen."

Not by much, but it had a decent stove. Unfurnished, it had two bedrooms, one of which would be okay for storage. It had a one-year lease, with a hefty security deposit.

Meredith's phone rang, and she held a finger aloft to put Clay's decision on pause. She mouthed the word "Mitch."

Andi cocked an eyebrow, but said nothing, standing to one side with her arms crossed, staring out a window.

"Okay, guys, Mitch says we ought to get over to Grounds Crew right away."

* * *

Andi pursed her lips. Once again, Clay managed to wriggle off the decision hook, literally saved by the bell. In a way, she could understand. The case had stalled and no one wanted to talk about it anymore. Which made the whole apartment-hunting thing a diversion from being stuffed in a cramped office.

And it would be darn nice if Clay committed one way or the other. Gideon Pike kept wiring cash into their operating account, totally indifferent to numbers becoming scary. They'd have to schedule a meeting with him sometime soon to throw in the towel and let Conrad, Carlene and the others run the victory flag up the corporate pole.

The moment Mer completed the call, a resurgence of hope swept through her mind. And Clay got off the commitment hook for at least a few more hours.

After a ten-minute drive in light traffic to Grounds Crew, Mer's luck held. A parking space, right in front. Mitch had staked out an entire table, seated directly opposite a plain, sad-looking woman, early thirties, who might have been attractive with make-up and a fraction of a smile.

Meredith said, "I'll get coffee. The usuals?"

Mitch pointed to a pair of cups in front of him. "We're good." He turned to Andi and Clay. "Guys, I'd like you to meet Rhonda Towler. Her mother was the housekeeper —"

Andi extended a hand. "Of course. Hello, I'm Andrea Delvento. Andi. And this is my partner, Clay Garrison."

Clay said, "Very pleased to meet you ma'am. What can we do for you?"

Rhonda's expression suggested anxiety and anger and her tone was flat, weary, without emotion. "Perhaps it's what I can do for you, Mister Garrison." She withered into reticence, looking around as she bit her lower lip.

Andi reached out and patted Rhonda's forearm. "It's okay. You can trust us. And your mother?"

Rhonda took a breath. "Mom passed away several days ago. The funeral was yesterday." She glanced at Mitch, who nodded encouragement.

"Oh, gosh. I'm so sorry. Is there anything we can do to help?"

Rhonda reached into a purse on her lap she had been clutching with both hands. "Perhaps. I have a letter, some papers." A large manilla envelope came into the light and she laid it on the table as if it were infected. "I spoke with your Mister Whelan recently. He asked if it would be all right if you spoke with my mother. She was terminally ill, near the end."

Clay softly said, "We didn't know, and apologize for intruding at a difficult time. Please accept our condolences."

"I've had enough of the Pikes, you understand."

Andi said, "We *do* understand. How can we help?"

Meredith returned with coffee, placed the cups on the table, and settled into the last open seat.

Rhonda remained impassive and stoic, as if in a dark place with no easy way out. "For all these years, I never knew... never understood..."

Clay asked, "Understood what?"

Defiance flickered across Rhonda's face as her voice lowered. "That my mother wasn't a bad person. That she was caught up in a situation that destroyed our relationship. And that she was helpless to do anything about it." She shoved the envelope toward

Andi, sat back in her chair and crossed her arms, unable to make eye contact. When Andi gently picked it up, she drew a long breath and sighed as if relieved that a terrible secret no longer was, as if the past had been laid to rest.

Andi paused to ask, "May I?"

Rhonda nodded.

Documents slipped into Andi's hand. A note addressed to Rhonda. Two snapshots, newborn infants, clearly twins. Two certificates of a live birth. Father, unknown. Mother, Kimberly Spence. A sealed glassine envelope with three locks of hair, two wisps of fine blonde and one larger and darker, each bound with a tiny ribbon.

Andi looked up. "Did you handle these at all?"

"No, why?"

Ensuring the envelope was still sealed, Andy replied, "Because they may be evidence." She passed the paper documents to Clay and held the note to Rhonda aloft. "May I?"

Rhonda, looking tired, nodded.

Andi unfolded the paper, revealing a cashier's check, payable to Ruth Towler. A hundred thousand dollars. Almost twenty-five years old. The note opened with an apology for a painful decision.

Rhonda said, "Mom worked as a housekeeper for the Pike family, and for whatever reason was close to Kimberly. One day, I was shipped off to live with an aunt for a while, the initial story being that it was not a healthy place for me to grow up, they didn't like the servants having children running round, blah, blah, blah. Later, my mom said that she'd become pregnant — didn't name the father — and that the Pikes were agreeable to letting her have the babies and giving them up for adoption. I was utterly crushed that my mom would do such a thing, and we became estranged."

"Except that your mother wasn't pregnant. Kimberly was."

Rhonda nodded. "About that time, Kimberly and some of the others were doing a lot of drugs, partying, that sort of thing. One night, just at the end of the school term, things got out of hand and there was some sort of assault."

"Rape?"

"Yes."

Clay interrupted. "She said the incident occurred just *after* school was out for the summer?"

"Yes."

"But the birth certificate says the twins were born in October, nearly full-term. She must have been four months pregnant at the time of the assault. And you went to live with your aunt in...?"

"Middle of May."

Mitch scribbled notes on a small pad. "I hate to be blunt, Rhonda, but your mom's relationship with Kimberly... Was she...?"

"No, not a supplier or dealer. More of a confidant, a big sister." Her voice trailed off. "And not a very good one, I guess."

Andi patted the back of Rhonda's hand. "I'm sure it must have been terribly difficult circumstances. I can't begin to imagine. There's just no way you can think poorly of her."

Clay said, "Okay. If the check was supposed to cover her expenses or keep it quiet, why, do you think, she never cashed it?"

Rhonda shrugged. "All I know is that after Kimberly died, mom was discharged and moved away. She spent the rest of her working life cleaning hotels. Got sick, died. End of story. We never spoke about what became of the twins."

Clay asked, "What do you know of Kimberly's death?"

"Not very much, other than she overdosed on drugs. Heroin, I think. I overheard my mom and Mrs. Whittaker — the other housekeeper, who had been Kimberly's nanny — talking about it before we moved away. I was ten at the time."

"And your mother was...?"

"Thirty-three. I barely remember Kimberly before all the drug stuff. She was a sweet kid. Mom said that, too, that she was really into horses, non-competitive riding. The family had a stable at the farm and we'd sometimes watch Kimberly having such a good time. I was so jealous. Then that all changed. Mom said it was sad to see her decline into the drug scene." Her voice trailed off. "I sometimes think she cared more about Kimberly than me."

Andi offered the check. "You should take this. It's part of your mom's estate."

Rhonda shook her head. "No. I don't want any part of those people. Besides, it's probably not any good, it's so old."

Meredith asked to see the check. "It's a cashier's check, drawn on a bank still in business, and there's no imprinted deadline on it. Sometimes they say it's got to be cashed in ninety days, but it looks like a good check."

Andi said, "Rhonda, I'm sure your mom intended for you to have it. Sort of an insurance policy. It was in an envelope with your name on it. Perhaps she's trying to make amends for something she could not discuss."

"I don't know..."

Clay said, "Take it. Make a life for yourself. If you have a problem with the check, give us a call. Our client will be able to make it good."

* * *

Clay waited for the others to bid Rhonda farewell. As he watched her leave, his mind shifted through a range of emotional gears, beginning with excitement and ending with a simmering rage. First the too-good-looking documents that Mitch obtained, now a witness walks in with evidence. Maybe they had been lucky when rebuffed by Rhonda Towler the first time around. Ruth might have still clung to a secret, maybe too far gone to provide coherent answers.

Meredith and Mitch lingered for several minutes before excusing themselves to return to the office, with Mitch agreeing to investigate regional adoption agencies for the proverbial needle in a haystack.

When they were alone, Andi asked, "Now what?"

"Looks like we have our work cut out for us. Nice interview with Rhonda. I would have blown it for sure."

"Nah. She *wanted* to talk, get it off her chest. I was simply convenient for her. But you helped, as did Mitch and Mer." She toyed with her empty coffee cup. "We make a good team, I think."

"Yes. We do."

"I think we need to have that hair DNA tested. I know, I know, agency labs can take forever, but privates will do it in a day. All we need to show is that the two blonde samples are identical and that the common mother is the one we have from Kimberly."

He said, "But we can't prove the third lock of hair is from Kimberly. The best we can do is prove the relationship of the samples."

She shrugged. "I don't think Gideon Pike is going to care. This is still a private investigation. The snapshot alone is going to excite him, maybe rattle some cages, break the logjam."

"We should talk to Gideon. We need to know more about his complicated financial arrangement, who's got what kind of pull."

Andi said, "I agree. If nothing else, I think it'll go to motive for why Pike takes so many runs at this. I don't buy the benevolent grandfather bit at all. He likes to come off with that folksy charm, but I don't see a paragon of family life."

He chuckled. "A description that seems to fit all of them."

She nodded. "You know, we don't have to do this. We could take the fee, walk away from this nest of vipers, wipe our hands, move on."

"Maybe so. But the thing about police work that attracted me is getting to the truth, no matter where the chips flew and fell."

"So. About the apartments?"

He shrugged. "Take whichever one you want. I'm okay with it."

"Mer worked so hard, trying to accommodate both of us."

And there, staring him in the face, the moment of commitment. All the objections to what had been a disappointing circumstance evaporated as trivialities. "I know. I'll take the other apartment."

Chapter Twenty

Clay paused to admire the size of the overhead bin. "There's something wrong about this. It's somehow..."

Andi laughed. "Yeah, luxury with a capital L. First class, no squashed legs, probably a nice drink and snack. I could get used to being a private eye."

"It just seems so —"

"Yep." She plopped into the window seat. "The way it was meant to be. You can take the aisle. You look like a guy who's perfect for passing a packet of peanuts."

He cocked an eyebrow. "Meredith's doing, isn't it?"

"She understands how expense accounts work. So get over it. Enjoy."

A flight attendant arrived. "Is there a problem, sir?"

"Yeah. I don't deserve this."

She peeked at his boarding pass. "It's your seat, sir. So I guess you do deserve it."

Andi said, "It's okay, ma'am. He was always an economy class kind of guy."

The attendant smiled. "Glad to see you're taking a step up in the world. Have a nice flight."

Andi patted the seat. "Told you Mer would take care of you. And we know Gideon won't care. *Especially* this time."

Which was probably an understatement. It might be an economy class duffel in the overhead bin, but it held an envelope that would probably shift the balance of power of a major financial institution.

If Gideon knew, he'd have dispatched a private jet to fetch it. But Andi wanted the pleasure of laying out in person, and for that she decided to travel first class to a rendezvous near Nassau, where Pike kept some sort of boat for deep-sea fishing.

As he buckled the seat harness, she leaned in and spoke softly. "There. Isn't that better for a guy your size? Look at the leg room. You earned this, Clay."

He chuckled. "We both did."

"Yes, but when you noticed the forms, it gave me new hope. I was about to throw in the towel and try to figure out what to do with a sad little detective agency."

"And now?"

"We're on our way to solving a major case. I've dreamed of this, like, forever."

He pressed the back of his head into leather that wasn't all that soft and luxurious, but probably better than seats a dozen rows back. "We're a long way from that. All we've been able to establish is probable cause, and it'll be up to Pike whether it goes any further."

"Ho, ho, ho. He's going to up the ante, I'll bet."

"Which means we'll have new problems to solve."

She sighed. "I know you're right, but for now I want to just mellow out and enjoy the ride. Do you think they have better snacks for first class?"

He grunted. "I doubt it."

* * *

Andi led Meredith's rolling overnight bag through the gauntlet of immigration, customs, and a parade of travelers shifting from one experience to the next. The terminal was open air, but the anticipated breeze was on pause and the humidity wilted everyone on the trek.

On the other side of his body, Clay bore the burden of his duffel with ease, using his height to advantage searching waiting drivers holding little signs with names.

But Andi's perspective was better. "There he is."

"You sure?"

"Gotta be. Okay, so my name is misspelled, but only by a couple of letters."

Clay followed her to the left edge of a loose line of drivers searching for clients. "He doesn't look like a driver to me."

"Is it the way he spelled my name or the vest he's wearing?"

"Yeah, the one reminiscent of ground personnel, the guys that service aircraft."

They greeted a lean man with a quick, eager smile, a couple of inches shorter than Clay.

"Miss Dulventa? Mistah Garris?"

She said, "*Delvento*, Andi. And this is Clay *Garrison.*"

"No matter. Please, you follow me. You have all your baggage? A good flight? Splendid. Just this way."

The transportation guy wheeled and was already six paces away before the couple was in motion. He didn't exactly stroll. It was more like a sprint to the end of the terminal and a guarded doorway. The transportation guy flashed his badge, the guard nodded, and the door opened.

To the tarmac.

The ground guy hopped aboard a golf cart, waited for the couple to get on, zoomed through a field of smaller private aircraft, and out into an open area and toward a bright, white helicopter.

The pilot disembarked, opened the passenger door and said, "Miss Delvento? Mister Garrison?" To the nods of affirmative, he accepted her bag first, then his, and directed them to take seats while he stowed their gear.

Clay cocked an eyebrow while buckling his seatbelt.

She said, "And you were anxious about a first class ticket on a commercial flight?"

Within minutes, an affable pilot named Phil had the chopper whining, thumping and shuddering, all while launching an enthusiastic monologue about sights they'd see en route to Gideon Pike. He opened with the inevitable question about whether they'd ever been to Nassau before, her confession to the negative and Clay's surprising "been a while." But her attention evaporated while watching two private jets land in quick succession and taxi into the part of the airport reserved for those for whom first-class commercial was just a silly joke.

Phil brought her back to reality. "Okay, folks, we've got clearance so here we go."

The chopper's jet engine cranked up and the rotor went into super-fast mode. The aircraft wobbled and lifted, floating now and picking up speed along the taxiway to an open patch of ground she presumed they set aside for such things.

In minutes, they'd swept out across the shoreline to follow a line of beaches, boats and a lot of bucks south.

She asked, "So how far do we have to go?"

"Just to the harbor. Couple of minutes."

All that. For a quick hop into town. Everyone else used a taxi or a hotel shuttle. "You know, Clay, I never want to hear about first-class tickets, ever again."

* * *

The trick to this sort of thing, he reminded himself, is to remain implacable, like it's routine, the sort of thing done at least once or twice before lunch. Aviator sunglasses aided the facade of calm, cool and indifferent to the passing view. Andi leaned forward, pumped, excited, eagerly sightseeing. The front seat, next to

Phil, would have been better for her.

Austin's car, Baxter's building, Leonard's apartment, Carlene's mansion. Not to mention the castle used by Conrad. He should have anticipated the lifestyle of the ultra-rich. Below, the houses and cars of ordinary people drifted past, a model diorama, distant, remote, impersonal. In the cocoon of a helicopter, despite all the gold-plated luxury, the Pikes were a pathetic clan. For being the patriarch, Gideon didn't seem to be carrying a lot of respect in his familial duffel. But then, neither did Big Bill Garrison, who'd gotten carried away with his own importance. Marital fidelity slipped away, into the waiting hands of Glenn Storm, harsh words and hurt feelings, a mother vanished in a mess that made the Pikes look like down-home church folk. Blame was everywhere, and all he'd wanted in the end was to be a cop, catch the bad guys, uphold the law.

The aircraft banked right, then left, over a pair of docked cruise ships and continued along a channel separating the islands. Dead ahead, an enormous yacht lounged between a string of marinas. The chopper settled into a slow, methodical descent.

Andi gasped and murmured, "Oh, wow."

Phil chuckled. "Yeah, that's Mister Pike's little toy. Cruises the world in it, but mostly hangs out in the Caribbean and the Mediterranean."

She asked, "Dare I ask just how big...?"

"Two hundred twenty five feet at the waterline."

It came with its own landing pad, toward the aft end of the vessel and marked with a giant H. What originally looked like a tiny rowboat turned out to be a twenty-five foot skiff, hanging from a pair of poles on the starboard side.

Clay said, "So you're on his staff?"

"Yessir. Mister Pike goes where he likes to go, whenever he wants. Okay, folks, we'll be aboard in just a minute or so."

A marshaller stepped onto the deck to signal instructions to

Phil, who didn't seem to need any. The aircraft hovered, rotor blade shadows fluttering on the deck, before it settled.

From a glass-enclosed area of the deck, Gideon Pike marched into sunshine, back in khaki and fishing cap, grinning and waving as the helicopter wound down into silence and passengers disembarked. It was hard not to like the guy, much less admire him.

* * *

If Carlene had her castle and Leonard his posh apartment, Gideon had his boat. He grandly presented a ship, perhaps hoping to impress a young woman like herself with an endless parade of astonishment. She struggled to remain casual throughout the tour, to mirror Gideon's casual understatement, but it all collapsed when he led them to an open-air deck.

A table large enough for eight, perhaps ten, was set for three. It rivaled the five-star dining room of a fancy resort where she and Mer worked on summer while in college. Her fingers could not resist caressing soft linen. No doubt the glassware was high-grade crystal, silverware actually silver, and plates a delicate porcelain. Pike's table had the view, the breeze, the atmosphere where all envy could gather and drool.

Clay tweaked the placement of forks to correct an imperfection in alignment. That hers were all on the same side of the plate seemed good enough. "It's amazing, Mister Pike. You do live very well."

He cooed, "It's Gideon, Andrea. And thank you."

"Andi is fine with me."

Pike raised a hand to gesture to a waiting steward. "I'm given to understand you enjoy seafood. Is that correct?"

Surprises never ended. "Yes, um, *Gideon*, very much."

"Very well, then. For you today we'll have sea bass, traditional peas and rice, fruit and a splendid coconut-guava duff. I've taken the liberty of selecting a rather pleasant chardonnay. California, o'course. I'm a patriot, you know. Clay will, I'm certain, tag along even though he's a meat-and-potatoes kind of guy."

Clay replied with the faint smile he used in gotcha moments, so perhaps he also found Pike's research thoughtful and unnerving at the same time. They sat on opposite sides of Gideon, were fed a superb meal untainted by business talk, focusing instead on Pike's restless love for the sea and roaming in style. When dishes were cleared and coffee served, Pike wiped his lips wore a smug expression.

Andi wasted no time with applause. "That was delicious, the best I've ever eaten. Wouldn't you agree, Clay?"

"Absolutely. My compliments to your chef."

"Clay's quite the gourmet, Gideon, so I'm sure you —"

Their host waved a hand. "Yes, yes, duly noted. Now. You kids have come to visit with a progress report, I believe. And I'll wager that it's nicely summarized in that envelope next to Clay's right hand, isn't it? Let's get down to it, eh?"

It was Clay's turn for sunshine, and she gestured for him to make the presentation.

He cleared his throat, clearly trying to sound calm, casual, cool. But not quite getting there.

"Yessir. No sense in being dramatic. We've obtained information that we think will be of value to you about the twins."

He offered the envelope.

"Ah, let's see what you've got." Gideon methodically opened the end flap tugged birth certificates, the photo, and Ruth Towler's letter into the light. For almost a minute, he studied each sheet several times and his thumb caressed the glassine envelope of hair lockets. All the booming exuberance left his voice and it lowered into a tone of firm resolve. "Ah. I love being right. Just love it."

Clay said, "Yessir. You were. All along."

Pike's attention remained fixed on the papers. "You know, you two have done me a remarkable service. Just remarkable."

Andi said, "Thank you, sir. We had a bit of luck —"

Pike looked up, the smile back on his jaw. "More than luck, young lady. More than luck. You've earned back all I've invested in you and much more. You know what this means?"

Clay sat forward, his forearms on the table and fingers entwined, a gesture he favored when he'd reached a conclusion and was comfortable with a sense of direction. "Yessir. It will have a substantial impact on the issues relating to the family trust. But I'm afraid all we've demonstrated is the twins were not stillborn, and were at some point placed for adoption. There's no evidence to suggest —"

Pike returned the papers to the envelope, closed it, and offered it to Clay. "But, of course, now you're going to find that evidence, locate the girls, prove what needs to be proven. You'll need these, o'course."

Andi said, "Gosh, Gideon, that's a terribly tall order and I'm sure time must be short..."

"What do you think it will take?"

Clay shrugged. "No idea, sir. We haven't a clue about even where to begin. I'd hate to make a promise I couldn't keep."

"Well spoken, Clay, well said. I'll ask again. What will it take to find them?"

Andi placed her hand on the back of Gideon's wrist. "Clay's trying not to get your hopes up, Gideon. We frankly don't know. It's such a formidable —"

Gideon responded by placing his other hand atop hers. "I have every confidence in you. There's no penalty for failure. I can grasp the quandary. However, there would be a substantial reward for success."

Clay leaned back, an expression of patience on his face. "But, sir —"

Gideon pulled away. "A million-dollar reward."

Andi's jaw dropped. "You're joking."

"Very well, a million apiece, plus any expenses you encounter. Blank check, Andi. Blank check."

Clay said, "It's that important?"

Pike smiled. "Son, a couple of million dollars would be a bargain. Your negotiation skills need help."

Clay's cheeks momentarily reddened. As he recovered, he leaned in again, the same gesture with his hands. She chose not to interrupt, stay back, observe.

Clay said, "Very well, then, Gideon. Let's start with a little candor on your part. Before I agree to the job, I want to know the details about this trust, what it's worth, what's at stake."

Gideon's confident grin evaporated and his jaw set in a chilly glare. "That's not the sort of information that we toss around, Clay, even if we are at each other's throats."

"Yessir. But you will. Because at this point in time, you just can't give it up, can you?"

Gideon glared at Clay, perhaps more at impertinence than a staff member needing prodding. He turned to her, softening his gaze, possibly hoping for an ally.

She shrugged. "I agree with Clay. Back on the day we met, you conceded that this wasn't just a friendly old grandpa kind of thing. You said the trust was complicated, with details for another time."

He nodded. "That's true. And those details —"

She leaned forward and smiled as sweetly as she could. "This is that other time, okay? And I think Clay's negotiation skills are just fine."

His gaze silently drifted back and forth between them for several uneasy seconds. At last he drew a breath and the grin returned. "Very well, then. I'm the principal shareholder, forty-five percent. In a moment of weakness with my second wife, I gave

Kimberly and Conrad fifteen percent each, which distressed my natural children, Leonard and Carlene, who hold ten percent stakes. My ex-wife, Martha, has five percent, part of the divorce settlement. For reasons you'd have to ask Conrad, he gave two and a half percent each to Austin and Baxter."

Clay asked, "So Kimberly's share would have gone to the twins?"

"Precisely. The trust specifies that the group manages the proxy in the interim, but after twenty-five years, it is to be divided equally among all the heirs."

Andi said, "So Conrad enlisted everyone to allow him to vote Kimberly's shares."

"Yes. In effect, making me a minority stockholder."

Clay drew a breath. "Which is how they gained control and —"

"Exactly, my boy. Put the old man out to pasture. Well, sea."

Andi said, "Just out of curiosity, how much is seven and a half percent worth?"

"Oh, I'd guess a billion-six, give or take a hundred million or so."

Clay smiled. "Which would buy a lot of appreciation from heiresses who may have no clue."

Gideon chuckled. "Well, Clay, let's just say I'm an optimistic fellow."

Chapter Twenty-One

Mitch stood in the center of the living room, a case of beer in his hands, and made a complete turn, his head nodding. "Looks good, bro. Sort of art gallery basic, without the art."

Clay wiped his hands with a dish towel. "You think?"

"Yeah. Cool. You got a sofa, couple of chairs, coffee table, lamps and stuff. Nice little rug in the center. The furniture match-es, so that's good. Looks like decent, too, like it'll last."

"Hope so, considering the prices. The guys delivered it a cou-ple of hours ago, set it up. Let me get that beer in the fridge."

Mitch extended his arms. "Yeah, y'know, like one of those housewarming gift things."

"You're a good man, Mitch." He accepted the carton from Mitch, who followed into the kitchen, painted the same white as the living room, but with gleaming counters and appliances.

"Dude. You did a new stove and fridge, too. Wow." He lifted his nose and sniffed. "Oh, yeah. Pizza. You planning to...?"

Clay unloaded brown bottles into the refrigerator. "No, Mitch. I'm planning on enjoying a good meal with good friends. And the old appliances that came with the place? Neither would stand to a health inspection, even for a guy on the take."

"Oh, man. And look. Like, an almost empty-fridge, too. Sparse, buddy, sparse."

"Just moved in, Mitch. Give me a day or so, okay? Want one of these?"

"Yeah, yeah. For sure." He accepted a bottle and popped the cap. "And your front door just, like, opened, no sticking. That's pretty good."

Clay echoed the beer move. "What can I say? High living. Clean personal habits. And a can of silicone spray."

Mitch hoisted his bottle in salute. "Yeah. Gotcha. Shrewd."

The doorbell rang and three tentative knocks followed.

Clay smiled. "Andi and Mer."

Mitch's expression shifted from awe to relaxed and hopeful. "Yeah, man. Time to get our manners on."

* * *

Half a step behind Meredith, Andi gripped grocery bags stretched to nearly bursting point, two in each hand.

Mer stepped back from the doorbell and her hands recaptured balance of a pastry box. "Andi, do you think they like chocolate cake? I mean, I could have —" She did her little hair flip thing, a habit whenever she was about to walk into a new situation, especially when guys were involved.

"Cake is good. They're guys, Mer. Chocolate always works."

"I could have gone with doughnuts."

"Nope. Cake's best. You picked perfectly."

"You think?"

"Trust me. They — Mitch — will be fine with it."

"You sure?"

"Absolutely." The door opened and smiles were everywhere. "Hi, Clay. Hey, Mitch."

Clay said, "C'mon in. Wow, you brought stuff."

"Yep." Andi held her bags aloft and Clay took possession. "Goodies, nibbles, some salsa, bottle of wine. And Mer —"

Meredith stepped forward, offering the box to Mitch. "I brought a cake, a sort of housewarming thing. I hope chocolate is okay."

Mitch laughed. "Are you kidding? We're guys. Chocolate is the right call."

He was rewarded with more than a light kiss on the cheek, causing Andi and Clay to shrug and shake their heads.

Andi said, "I'm smelling something gorgeous coming from the kitchen."

"Yeah, want to see?"

"Absolutely. If I hang in here any longer, it's going to be embarrassing. So, Mer, wine or beer for you?"

"Wine. The red would be good."

Clay examined the label. "Perfect choice for pizza."

Andi prodded him to turn and move. "You'd say that if it was a fifty-cent bottle of seltzer."

"No, no. It's true."

"Uh-huh. C'mon, partner, let's check out this pie."

And it was a heavenly pie. Clay opened the oven door and eased the top rack forward. Cheese bubbled, just beginning to brown. On a wave of heat, the scent of herbs and olive oil rolled over her.

"That's amazing. Really. How soon?"

"Another minute. Four or five to cool. Meanwhile, you can snag some wine glasses from that cabinet — yep, you got it — and I'll deal with the cork. This should breathe."

"Do you ever get tired of cooking, or run out of ideas?"

"No, why?"

"It's just that Mer and I manage on a steady diet of junk food and reheat, but, um, it's, uh, not, um, quite so..."

"What?"

"So, well, utterly charming." She paused. "Okay, that sounded dumb."

The cork gave a little pop when it left the bottle. Clay gathered a glass and cocked an eyebrow. "Taste? It's a perk of working in the kitchen."

"But I'm not working."

"So? We could lie."

"Ah. You're beginning to get the hang of being a private eye."

A modest amount of wine splashed into the glass, and their fingers touched, lingering for a moment, when possession passed. She swirled the wine and inhaled the scent of it. A very solid bur-gundy, imported. Considering the price, it was hopefully a decent brand.

He said, "Not doing very well at detection. It's been a long week of dead ends and false trails since our little cruise with Gideon. I keep coming back to the billions of dollars riding on the outcome of this case, trying to picture what it's like to be going along with an ordinary life and then have people like us walk up and change them so profoundly. I mean, we're being pampered a lot, but not on the scale these people live."

She sipped wine. Not too dry. The liquor store clerk had made a good suggestion. "I've been thinking the same thing. It's just so huge. It's like trying to put a yardstick to the universe. Did you ever figure out —"

"Yeah, I did some research on the value of the company, and then the percentages that Gideon laid out. The twins would divide fifteen percent of the trust. Based on recent market value, it's just a little under one billion, five hundred and seventy nine million. *Each.*"

"Wow. I think we're being underpaid at a paltry million dol-lars."

Clay leaned against a counter. "Which we have to share with Mer and Mitch..."

"...Who have certainly earned it. Good night to tell them?"

"Definitely."

"Think they'll be okay with the split?"

He smirked and cocked an eyebrow.

"Hm. Yeah. Okay, dumb question."

A buzzer sounded and Clay's hands slipped into oven mitts. "I think I'd better get the pie out of the oven."

"Good idea. Time to float down to Earth."

* * *

Clay did the math. One oblong table, four chairs, two candles, one pizza, a bottle of good wine. And the laughter and banter of four friends who'd drawn closer. Old relationships cemented, new ones added, a solid team that Clay hadn't expected the day of the flat tire or the first night at the bar. It was good to see Mitch happy, and Meredith seemed to reciprocate.

Kind of cute, Andi called it the other day, teasing that she felt like an older sister in a den of teenagers engaged in puppy love. Clay had replied that they were all the same age, just friends, and she gave him a stern look before punching him in the shoulder. He knew very well what she meant, she'd asserted, and was just giving her a hard time.

He'd tossed up his hands in submission and reminded her that they were totally stalled on even where to begin with finding the twins, who'd be twenty-five now and probably had no clue about their potential destiny.

Meredith was telling a hilarious story from her childhood about a horse with a mind of its own, an incident involving Andi, wandering off the assigned trail and...

Andi laughed, her eyes on the verge of tears. "It was just so totally funny. Oh, gosh, I was laughing so hard..."

Clay sat up. "Horses."

Meredith said, "Yep, that's what they were, Clay."

Andi sighed. "Were you paying attention at all?"

"Horses."

Mitch shook his head as if to clear away extraneous thoughts and too much alcohol. "Uh, you okay there, bro?"

Clay waved him off. "Horses. The key is *horses*."

Andi was the first to understand, tilting her head back and closing her eyes. "Of course. How could I have —"

Meredith and Mitch remained perplexed.

Clay explained. "Gideon said the various wives and children were into horses, although not in a competitive way. When he listed the various staff on the Bucks County farm — which, by the way, is where horses are common on gentleman farms — he didn't mention any people in connection to livestock, but I doubt that the women of the manor were out there slinging manure and caring for animals themselves."

Andi said, "So there had to be others, people Gideon didn't pay much attention to, because he was absent so much."

Mer returned her glass to the table so she could use her hands expressively. "But the housekeeping staff, the groundskeeper, they would have known them. And if Ruth Towler was enlisted to put infants up for adoption, then she might have sought someone trustworthy to help."

Mitch said, "Which brings us back to Madge Whittaker, who said she was sworn to secrecy and refused to talk about it."

Mer nodded. "She was very firm. I pulled out all the persuasive stops and she wouldn't... Because she was paid off? Because she and Ruth were very close? Because she's afraid?"

Andi's smile looked smug. "Or all of the above. Clay, we're going to have to take another run at her, only this time, not take no for an answer."

Clay shrugged. "There's no statute of limitations on murder."

Andi winced. "A little harsh, don't you think?"

"Good cop, bad cop. We just need to crack the shell, get some leverage to squeeze the others."

After exchanging glances with Andi, Mer drew a breath and counseled her lifelong friend. "I'd go with good cop if I were you.

Madge is a sweet, mature woman but firm about confidentiality. I sensed principled. You're the right person to persuade her to betray them."

Andi sighed and swirled the last of the wine in her glass. "Thanks a lot."

* * *

Andi inhaled air rich with the scent of moist soils and blooms, which gave the tiny floral shop a cozy, tropical feel. Glass cases filled with arrangements dripped humidity.

Clay had gone for a large and imposing look in a dark gray suit, which he had said was inspired by a hard-nosed detective he once saw working a crime scene. For her role, she'd chosen softer colors of a favorite knit with a decidedly feminine edge.

Madge Whittaker responded to the tinkling bell above the door by wiping her hands and offering an eager smile to what she might believe to be a nice, young couple about to share the joy of flowers with someone dear. Andi guessed may be early sixties, five-three, wearing a frock with the shop logo and her first name embroidered high on the left side. A pleasant, grandmotherly type, whose day was about to be ruined.

Madge glanced toward Clay and then to Andi. "Good morning. How can I be of assistance?"

"Ms. Whittaker? Yes? I'm so sorry, is it missus or miss?"

"Please, just Madge. And...?"

Clay produced an identification wallet, his face impassive, his gaze direct, looking ready to display handcuffs. "I'm Clay Garrison, from Storm Investigations, and this is my associate, Andrea Delvento."

Andi leaned in, made eye contact and beamed assurance. "Please call me Andi."

But suspicion seemed to linger. "I see. And what's this about?"

He said, "We're hoping you can assist us with an inquiry we're making concerning —"

"Oh, yes. Someone from your office called recently. I'm terribly sorry you've come all this way, but the answer is still the same. I've accepted a confidentiality agreement, you see."

He said, "I understand. However, we've gathered evidence suggesting Kimberly Spence did not die from an accidental drug overdose, but may have been murdered. Her twin daughters may have been born alive, probably placed for adoption, but records falsified. Some sort of conspiracy involving the housekeeping staff. It's a serious matter, and I'm sure the police will be looking into it."

Madge's expression withered into sadness, disappointment, anxiety.

Andi turned to her partner. "Clay, I warned you that Ms. Whittaker was just trying to do the right thing, got caught up in some terrible situation. I think you're —"

Clay remained aloof. "There's no statute of limitations on murder, or any accomplices involved in one, Miss Delvento."

She gave him a harsh glare of disapproval and said to Madge, "You have to forgive my *partner*. He sometimes gets carried away with his own importance. And he's under a great deal of stress lately. Clay, why don't you step outside, get a little air. You're making this poor woman very nervous. In her own shop. No need to make another scene."

Clay exhaled exasperation, pursed his lips, and showed a pretty good scowl. "Okay, have it your way. But our client —"

"I'll handle the client, okay. Just take a break, all right?"

When they were alone, Andi apologized in a soft, reassuring tone. "You're okay?"

Madge seemed to collect herself. "He's not a very nice man."

"No. But he's a very tenacious investigator, and he doesn't hesitate to call upon his cop buddies for pressure. I'm afraid I'm stuck with him, yet I want to be sure you're treated decently and fairly."

"Thank you. You're very kind."

"It would be very good of you to just help clear up a couple of teeny little points, nothing to keep you from your promise to whomever it was. Would that be all right?" Madge looked down to fidgeting hands and faintly nodded. "Yes? Oh, thank you so much."

Madge looked up, a touch of defiance in her eyes. "Well, it *does* depend on what you ask."

"I understand. Okay. Well, first, I understand that you were Kimberly's nanny?"

Madge nodded. "Well, initially. After she was twelve or so, it seemed rather silly. But the family kept me on as a housekeeper."

"With Ruth Towler?"

"Well, yes. Of course."

Andi continued the soothing tone. "We recently met with the daughter of Ruth Towler. Did you know she passed away? No? I guess it was some sort of cancer, but she left her daughter a letter explaining things, trying to make amends."

"I see."

"Did you know that Ruth was enlisted by Kimberly to pretend the twins were her own children, and then place them for adoption? I understand Ms. Towler was given a hundred thousand dollars at the time..."

Madge accepted a tissue from Andi to wipe misted eyes. "So you know, then."

"Twin girls. That were not stillborn." From her bag, Andi pulled copies of the birth certificates and a photo of the infants.

Madge studied the paper, her shoulders slumped in resignation.

Andi's voice softened even further. "And would it be correct to say you were also given some sort of a stipend, a reward for, well, sort of assisting Ruth Towler?"

Madge nodded again, looked up and gestured with her arm. "It was the seed money for my little shop, you see. For twenty-five years, I've lived with the fear that if it ever came out, the Pike family lawyers would descend like a plague of locusts, and I'd lose everything."

Andi's smile went to reassurance. "Trust me. That's not going to happen. It was between you, Ruth and Kimberly."

"And Carlene."

"I beg your pardon?"

Chapter Twenty-Two

Through his tiny pair of field glasses, Clay followed the flight of the ball. "Austin Hart has got the worst slice I have ever seen. Care fore a look?"

Andi shook her head. "I'm still amazed at the stuff you carry around, just in case. Anyway, here it comes. I can see it fine."

The ball took two hops and skipped into rough-cut grass outside the fringe of the fairway, twenty yards away.

He snickered. "Oh, bad luck. Must have hit some sort of a divot or something. I doubt he's going to get anywhere near par."

They marched toward the spot where the ball came to rest.

She said, "I don't know anything about golf. Don't want to know. Could care less. But I give you extra points for coming up with the most innovative ambush ever."

They stood for several minutes while the foursome made its way straight down the fairway and into the dogleg, a thicket of bunkers, and a narrow creek that looked artificial and meandered across a low spot in the fairway. Austin and his pals had to cross a foot bridge, their jovial tone dissipating at the sight of Clay and Andi.

Three of the four had placed shots correctly for the hole, well positioned for a decision on whether to lay up for a chip to the green or go for the flag and risk disaster if they missed. But Austin had to search for his ball. His expression soured as distance closed between them.

He growled, "You two again. I thought we were done with this ridiculous business about Gideon and his delusional thinking."

Clay smiled. "Nice to see you, too, Austin. Sure hope you don't handle that Ferrari as badly as you swing a driver. You might want to consider lessons or something to work on that slice."

"I don't need any of your crap today, pal. If I were you, I'd get out of here. This is a private club, you're trespassing, and security gets especially nasty with vermin like you."

Andi crossed her arms and hoisted eyebrows. "Vermin? Wow, Clay, I don't think he has a very high opinion of you."

Austin sneered. "Or you, honey. You might be conning the old man into being your next sugar daddy, but you're just second-class arm candy."

Andi sighed. "I liked vermin better, don't you think, Clay? I mean, Austin, if he can be vermin, why can't I? Don't you believe in equality for women? I bet not. But you should, sir, because —"

Austin used the blade end of a five iron to rummage through thick grass for his ball. "I don't want to hear it. I'm out here to en-joy a quiet round of golf with people who could buy and sell you for pocket change. We have nothing to discuss, period. I suggest you move on."

Clay stepped into his path. "I don't think so, Austin. I think you'd prefer to answer some new questions that have come up since we spoke last time."

"Get out of my way."

Andi put a sharp edge to her voice. "Madge Whittaker."

Austin paused and leaned on the iron. "Really? You're seri-ous? That old bat is still around? This is turning into some sort of pathetic joke."

Clay took a step closer and lowered his voice. "We had a chat with Miss Whittaker, sir. About the drug scene around the Bucks County farm twenty-five years ago. About you and Baxter and Conrad and Kimberly and two other girls and an awful lot of cocaine, pot, maybe some harder stuff. About parties that got, well, a little out of hand."

Austin glared, biting his lower lip.

Andi said. "We have birth certificates, a photograph."

"Proving nothing."

"And samples of hair. DNA tests prove they belong to the mother and two daughters. I'm wondering who the father might be."

Austin rubbed his nose with the back of his gloved hand, his demeanor withering fast. "So? The statute of limitations ran out."

Clay cocked an eyebrow. "Limitations? For statutory rape?"

"I didn't mean —"

Andi narrowed her eyes into an icy stare. "How about murder, Austin? You *do* know there's no clock on homicide, don't you?"

He stiffened. "I had nothing to do with her death. She over-dosed in rehab. No way any of us got her pregnant."

"You're saying she was pregnant before the party?"

He snapped, "At least two months. We all..." He paused and calmed his voice. "We all did the math."

Clay asked, "So everyone was doing drugs, you guys were messing around with underage girls, one of whom was pregnant?"

"Look, we didn't know... You know what? I think you're making some very dangerous allegations here. I have some very aggressive legal support, if you know what I mean. You people could be getting into some serious trouble."

Clay patted his jacket. "And I have a sworn deposition, DNA tests, and I'll bet many media people, especially those entertainment gossip shows, would have a lot of fun with this."

Andi nodded while the other golfers waved impatiently fifty yards away. "Tailor made for them, Austin. Tailor made."

He acknowledged his buddies. "You'll be sued."

She blended an expression of pity and sympathy. "But the scandal would be just terrible, wouldn't it? With all the passion about abuse and harassment, I doubt if you could get up a game of solitaire, much less golf."

"So, okay, how much is this gonna cost to go away?"

Clay said, "Hush money? I think there's been too much of that floating around already."

Austin pursed his lips. "Just think about it, okay?" The others called out, urging Austin to take a drop and play on. "Look, I've gotta find my crummy ball, get going."

Andi lifted her right foot to reveal a Titlist Pro V1 squashed into the turf. "This one? Gosh, I hope I didn't bust your ball."

* * *

Andi glanced at notes under the grip of an old-fashioned clipboard, chipped on the bottom right hand corner and marred with a smear of yellow paint on the right edge. It might have been around the block a few times, but it was a gift from Clay's magic box of useful stuff in the bed of the pickup.

"This has got to be it, Clay. One-twenty-two Wilson Road, exactly where Mer said."

She looked up, toward where he pointed. The building sign said "West Wind Adoptions, Licensed, Bonded, Confidentiality Assured." Her shoulders drooped. "Okay, Mister Smartypants. The directions you got from the convenience store guy, after we made the wrong turn, were good."

She took advantage of the mirror on the back of the visor to check appearance, made last minute adjustments, and reached for the door handle.

"The woman in charge is...?"

"Mary Jane Evans. She's got a masters in social work, a state university, apparently an old friend of Ruth Towler. And Madge Whittaker."

He asked, "So you want to take the lead?"

"Oh, yeah. And this time I'm going in as a good old-fashioned no-nonsense private eye."

He smirked. "A regular shamus. Gumshoe. A genuine sleuth."

"Right. We'll sweat it out of her, make her spill the beans, be a snitch."

"Uh-huh. Go for it, tiger."

She opened the door and stepped out into late morning sunshine. "Yup. C'mon, partner, let's not be a drag on the parade, okay?"

* * *

Clay looked into the warm eyes of Mary Jane Evans, the very image of what everyone wants a kindly and gracious grandmother to look like. She wore a conservative light print dress, had the requisite low-heeled black shoes and a chain dangling around her neck from glasses that had been out of fashion for twenty years.

And she immediately adopted Andi as a sort-of granddaughter, leaving Clay to tag along behind en route to her office and the promise of a nice cup of tea, probably one of those herbal concoctions. Andi's plan for a hard-nosed interrogation might be fun to watch.

They were directed to comfortable chairs opposite an old wooden desk, polished to a mirror shine, with all the papers, lamp, mementos organized to suggest precision and pride in professionalism.

"Please, make yourselves at home. I'll just ask Joan to fetch us tea. Does either of you take cream or sugar? No? Very well. I'll just be a moment."

Andi sat toward the front edge of the chair and folded her hands on her lap. She whispered through a forced smile, "Not one word, Clay. Not one."

"Yep. Got it."

When Mrs. Evans returned, she plopped into her chair with a soft sigh and a compassionate expression on her face. "Well, then. While we're waiting, why don't we get started? Thank you so very much for calling upon West Wind Adoptions, Miss Delvento. Your secretary spoke most kindly of you when she made the appointment." A pencil and notepad found their way into her hands and parked precisely in the center of the desk. "So. Perhaps you should begin with your due date?"

"I beg your pardon?"

"It's all right, my dear. When do you expect to give birth?"

Andi gasped. "Oh, no, no. I'm not pregnant."

Mrs. Evans cocked an eyebrow. "I'm sorry, I just assumed the two of you... Ah. Some sort of a misunderstanding. You're hoping to adopt a child, not place one."

Andi leaned back in the chair. "No, ma'am. I apologize if there's been confusion. My associate and I are hear to inquire about an adoption you may have handled, some years ago."

Mrs. Evans dropped the pen and raised her hands. "Oh, my dear, I'm very sorry, but these matters are in the strictest of confidence. I'm afraid I can't share anything with you."

An assistant tapped on the door, entered with a tray of teacups, a small brewing pot, and a creamer with sugar and two spoons, just in case the instructions changed. She parked it on the leading edge of the desk between Clay and Andi, poured and distributed cups and stepped back when finished.

"Thank you, Joan. That will be all."

Andi sipped from her cup, probably trying to regroup. When she returned the cup to the saucer, she leaned forward to place it on the desk separating her from the subject of the interview. And she gave Mrs. Evans the sort of smile a polite granddaughter offers up when receiving a token gift.

"I understand, completely, Mrs. Evans."

"I'm so pleased, my dear. These matters always have an uncomfortable aspect, so it's crucial that they be handled with discretion, you see."

"But if I could just ask one question..."

Mrs. Evans clung to the same expression, as if she'd been down this road a thousand times and knew exactly where she stood with the statutes of Pennsylvania. "No, Miss Delvento. You may not. If you wish, I can explain the various requirements and standards our agency must meet as part of licensure...."

"But, you see, there's a —"

"I said 'no,' Miss Delvento."

Andi pursed her lips, bit the lower one, and her eyes narrowed. Her tone took a harder edge. "I heard you, Mrs. Evans. Now perhaps it's time you heard me, okay?" Her tone abruptly softened and her eyes darted back and forth. "You see... I mean... Uh, that is..."

She turned to Clay, a look of helplessness and panic in her eyes.

Clay leaned forward and said, "I appreciate your rules and procedures, but I'm hoping you can help with a couple of details for our investigation. Could you do that?"

Mrs. Evans leaned back, clearly wary. "I can try but —"

Clay raised his hands in a gesture of understanding. "Twenty-five years ago, you were just getting this agency started. While working your way through school and into a master's degree in social work, you held a variety of jobs. Among them, you worked with the horses at Gideon Pike's farm."

The expression on Mrs. Evans' face went blank.

He pressed on, treading as carefully as he could. "You must have had a serious stack of bills from your education and getting this business off the ground. Now, we've come to learn that, one day, you got a request to place two infants, twin girls, for adoption. From an old friend."

Mrs. Evans sank in resignation and sighed. "Yes. That's true."

"Who was it?"

"Ruth. Ruth Towler. She'd managed to get herself into trouble and it was for her the only way out. Everything was done correctly and properly. No laws were violated. By the book, I assure you."

He said, "Are you quite certain it was all legal?"

"What are you implying, young man?"

"Suppose the babies weren't Ruth's. Suppose she was only an intermediary."

"Why, that's preposterous."

Andi reached into her bag. She looked as though she'd collected herself. Time to pass the ball back to her.

"Not at all, Mrs. Evans." Andi placed copies of documents on the desk. "These are the original birth certificates for the daughters of Kimberly Spence, for whom Ruth Towler worked. This is a photograph she kept of the two girls. A letter confessing her role in the matter. And this is a lab report showing hair samples in her possession were from Kimberly and two female offspring. There's no doubt, Mrs. Evans. You broke the law. Big time. But I'd bet you were well rewarded for discretion."

Dismay swept the eyes of the sad little old lady, probably seeing a career down in flames, the potential scandal, maybe even being led away in handcuffs by burly detectives.

"I...I...I don't quite know...what...to...say."

It was Andi's turn to smile. "Trust me, Mrs. Evans. I'm not here to create a problem, but solve one. We can forget this entire matter if —" She paused for effect, letting it hang in the air like a veteran detective would when he's got a suspect in a box.

Mrs. Evans choked. "If what?"

Andi softened her tone. "If you'd be so good as to take a peek at your old files and share with us the identity of the people who adopted the twins."

Mrs. Evans hesitated, probably considering options. She glumly nodded. "I understand."

Chapter Twenty-Three

Andi dropped her heels onto Mer's coffee table. A platter of snacks jumped and the wine bottle wobbled. She sprawled on a pillowy sofa and growled, "Argh!"

Meredith said, "If you squeeze that glass any harder, it'll shatter."

Words scattered and then felt fuzzy when she caught them, still wandering around as she tried to organize them into a slurred sentence. "Who cares? It's almost empty anyway."

"I could fill it for you."

Andi sighed and softened her grip. "I'm already way past flunking a Breathalyzer test. I couldn't walk a straight line in a cattle chute."

"Like the one to the restrooms at Pete's?"

Andi pursed her lips. "Exactly. I should pee." Her eyes narrowed. "How far is it to my bathroom?"

Meredith looked around. "Actually, I have no idea. Do you want help?"

"No. I might try to crawl, though. If you could point the... no, never mind. I think it would be just easier to..." She thrust the glass out into space. "Just easier to have another glass after all."

"Maybe you shouldn't."

"Mer-Bear, you offered."

"Yes, but before I realized that you might actually..."

"I wouldn't. I promise." She pulled the glass back and parked it on her belly. "I've had enough wine anyway."

"Okay..."

"Argh!"

"Exactly."

"I blew it, Mer. Absolutely choked. I planned to tough my way through an interrogation and she came across just so..."

"Exactly."

"And you know what the worst of it? Clay didn't say a ming. Um, fling. Um, *a thing*. He just let me make a complete..." She groped for a word and sighed. "A complete idiot of myself."

"Uh-huh."

"He *did*. He went heavy, like I wanted to do in the first place, and set himself up for an exit, leaving me to flop around by myself."

"Ah."

"And *then* he didn't say a thing about it. Didn't tease me or laugh at me or anything. Just folded it up neatly like one of his cute little notes and tucked it into his cute little pocket. With all the other... the other... He's saving it up, and someday he's going to pull it out and..."

"I don't think so."

Andi stared at the ceiling. "You're no help."

"I *know* he won't. Look, Andi, he's not that kind of guy."

"He's sneaky, you know. Very, very sneaky. Watches everything, misses nothing. Hides his emotions, never seems flustered." She sighed again. "He would have been a terrific cop."

"But now he's your partner, and almost as good as you."

"Argh! He's better and you know it. I have to decide if I'm going to have more wine, or pee."

"You could do both."

The possibility caught her off guard. "Really?"

"Yes. I could watch you crawl into the bathroom, like you did that one night..."

"Ugh. Don't remind me. Okay, okay. I know I'm being hard on myself."

Mer chuckled. "No. You're being too competitive. As usual."

"No, not —"

"Yes. You are. And if not?" Meredith's voice found a sharper edge. "Then don't you be all sulky, wallowing in self pity. C'mon. You adapted, your partner pitched in, you toughened it up, you worked the old lady, you got the information. We have a tremendous pair of leads on finding the twins, and you should be basking in a glow of success. It's not a competition, Kit-Kit. But, instead, you're sprawled out like —"

Andi waved her arm. "I got it, I got it."

"You should get off your self-pity and —"

"I know, I know. Focus."

"No, pee. I'd hate to think of you ruining fabric on a brand new sofa."

"Maybe I could just throw up or something? Okay, okay. I'll stumble into the john. And then you can make a pot. Of. Very. Strong. Coffee."

* * *

Mitch closed his fingers like heavy equipment and came away with a load of bite-size pretzel logs. He tossed several into his mouth to chase a sip of beer and stared at the huge TV screen.

They lounged on a soft leather sofa, feet indifferently resting on a coffee table, directly opposite a television Mitch had set up that afternoon. Sports channel commentators chattered about draft potential of college football stars.

Mitch snorted. "No way is that guy going in the first round, bro. I'd vote for third-round, maybe lower."

"Huh?"

"Aw, man, you're not paying attention at all. I get this slick tube set up and your head's elsewhere. Probably on the case. Dude, let it rest. You know, tomorrow?"

Clay sipped from the bottle. His attention drifted to the smoldering memory of the city hall meeting with the chief, the fire that could never quite be put out. When the chief asked the lieutenant to step out for a minute while the mayor and a couple of guys from the DA's office stepped in. They leaned hard, so hard that he choked, couldn't find the words. Easy to say he was blindsided, caught off guard. But he choked and he knew it. He said to Mitch, "Yeah, you're probably right."

"I *know* I'm right, man. You guys scored some major leads today, worked a source like no tomorrow, and we're set for a good run at, well, whatever."

Clay chuckled. It *had* worked out, and while Mitch ranked as his closest friend, she was his partner and Mitch now worked for them. "Actually, Andi pulled it off. I was on the bench, buddy, watching her work."

"You? Find that hard to believe."

"True. She wanted to lead and I figured, well, woman-woman thing. She went into the interview all hard-nosed, tough cop, and the subject turns out to be this sweet little old lady."

"Bummer. Hate when that happens."

Clay stared at the screen. "Yeah, but she changed gears, did the whole adoring granddaughter-type thing, all the way up to when the Evans woman clammed up. Then she tosses it me, to squeeze the subject, which I'm more than willing to do because I'm getting annoyed."

"So you beat up the old lady? Figuratively, I mean?"

Clay reached for pretzels. "That's the weird thing. She used me to turn the tone, then took back the lead and by the time she finished, she had the names of the people who adopted the twins. Andi had that woman scared to the bone, but managed to walk away all friendly and stuff."

Mitch nodded. "Women. They get all the breaks. But, hey, we got good leads, right? Who cares?"

They watched three video clips of wide receivers.

After a swig, Mitch belched. "But you care, right?"

"Not really." Which was probably true and why he'd said nothing afterward, like a busted play quickly forgotten.

"Yeah, right. Uh-huh. You're sitting there running it in your mind. You let her get in you head, man. Never a good thing."

"You think?"

Mitch lifted his bottle. "I know, buddy. I know."

"She's very good, Mitch. She would have been an incredible cop. I could see her working major crime, vice, rackets."

Mitch sighed. "Yeah. But she's your *partner* man. Lucky you. Lucky us. Besides, Meredith and I sure ain't keeping score. We're just digging all the money, the fresh starts. You giving any thought to when this is over, win or lose?"

"No. One case at a time."

"Yeah, well, remember, bro, three people got your back. You're not running solo any more."

Clay nodded, satisfied the tale had worked. "We gotta take another run at Baxter. And then the people in Kentucky. I got the sense from Andi's interview of the Evans woman they were first to adopt."

"Good plan. You'll get your game back on with that Baxter dude. Can't believe they busted a pair of identical twins to separate families, though."

"I guess it happens, Mitch."

"Yeah. But you're right about Andi. Meredith says she was always sharp, like, major league smart. Doesn't mess around. You know what I mean?"

Clay laughed. "Thanks for pumping up my ego, buddy."

"Just sayin'. You could do a whole lot worse, y'know. Look at it this way. She'll ramp up your game, push you."

"I gotta be pushed?"

"Never hurts, bro. Never hurts. Sharpens you."

Clay sighed and crunched through four pretzels while pundits droned on about a third division offensive tackle planning to enter the draft. "Oh, and that quarterback? He's going second round."

"You think?"

"I *know*, man. Based on his stats against —"

Mitch reloaded his pretzel hand. "Gotcha. I want you in my corner next time I get into a fantasy football, pool, though. Okay?"

"Okay. Tomorrow we're going to need —"

"Absolutely."

* * *

The receptionist under the stainless steel company name and logo seemed as indifferent and unhelpful as last time, when she had to scramble down two flights of stairs and race around the building to where Clay had everything nicely under control. But this time Baxter didn't get a lucky heads up and Clay spotted him making an end run.

A foot pursuit ended where Baxter had ducked into a doorway and Andi halted to read a sign identifying the men's room. Her shoulders dropped and her hands locked onto her waist. "Look, Clay, I know it's your turn, and I know I choked with Evans —"

He shrugged. "Nah. Just distracted for a second. It happens. No harm done. You want this?"

"Mind terribly?"

Clay grinned and approval. She barged in, and they wordlessly divided the task of pushing stall doors. Baxter hid in the middle one.

She called out. "Need to talk to you Mister McKnight."

"Hey! This is the men's room! Go away!"

"You think that matters? I'm waiting right here until you... Wait. Clay, kick the door in."

Baxter yelped. "What?"

"I'll count to five, Baxter. And you'd better have it zipped up by then."

"What? Hey, hey!"

"Three... four..."

"Okay, okay!" He yelped a curse. The stall door opened. "Who do you think you are?"

Andi stepped into his path, blocking exit from the stall. "Fun and games are done, Baxter. Today we're getting answers. No runaround. I'm not in the mood."

"This is a men's room!"

"Really? I bet the urinals gave it away."

"You've got no right —"

She stepped closer, stuffed fists into her waist and stood as tall as she could manage. "I've got every right, Baxter. Since you handed us all that crap in the parking lot, we've heard from a bunch of people. About some of the drug parties you and the other guys had with Kimberly. The stuff you stole from the family. And this garbage about stillborn twins? Just how long do you think you're going to keep your pathetic little business going when the press is screaming 'statutory rape?'"

He took a step back. Andi moved forward, into the stall.

"I want to talk to my lawyer."

"Those rules don't apply sport. Not here, not now. It's just you and me, and, brother, you haven't dealt with anything resembling hostile until right now, okay?"

Baxter leaned to look over her shoulder, an appeal to Clay for intervention. "Little help here, buddy?"

"Not your buddy, pal. Trust me, she knows all the moves. You don't come clean, you're gonna go for a swim in the toilet."

"What?"

Andi sighed to Clay. "I think he's hard of hearing."

Sweat erupted from Baxter's forehead and his skin began to flush.

She took a deep breath and lowered the intensity of her voice. "C'mon, Baxter. You've got a chance to make things right. I really don't care what you did, or why, or to whom. I just want to know the truth, okay? Help me out here, maybe get yourself off the hook." She took a step back and gave him space to breathe.

"You're being straight with me, right?"

"You've got my word."

Clay said, "And she's good for it, pal. I know."

"Okay, okay. Look, I gotta wash up, get my thoughts together."

She cocked an eyebrow and crossed her arms, leaning back on the heel of her right shoe. "Nothing cute, right?"

Clay stepped toward the door and Baxter must have noticed.

Baxter's voice dropped to a whisper. "Yeah. Nothing cute."

Andi stepped to the side to release him from the stall, then trailed him to the row of sinks, snagging a handful of paper towels to give him when he finished.

Baxter looked around, probably making sure they were alone, and said, "So, yeah, okay. Lotta drugs, mostly coke, some pills, a little weed. Coke mostly. Austin, Conrad, they were heavy into it. Kimberly was no innocent angel. She encouraged a lot of stuff. She was stoned a lot, usually just a running buzz, but sometimes she was totally zonked."

"Like the night when the maid caught you guys?"

"Yeah. I saw her. Madge Whittaker. Stuck her head in, jaw drops, and she vanishes."

"What did she see, Baxter?"

"We were all, well, you know, doing the, um, orgy thing. The other guys thought it funny, blowing the mind of the maid, and they said they'd take care of it, not to worry. But I was, like I said, an outsider, expendable, you know? So, yeah, I picked up a few things out of the house, just in case I needed road money."

"But then Conrad came through for you."

He accepted the paper towels from Andi. "Yeah, we were cool."

"So which one of you studs got Kimberly pregnant?"

"None of us. She was already knocked up. Probably the groundskeeper. He was doing Kimberly as well as one of the maids."

"Remember his name?"

"Leroy, I think. Don't know his last name."

"Which maid?"

"Ruthie. I heard she was pregnant, too, which is why she left the house around that time."

"What happened to Leroy?"

"No idea. Honest. I beat feet out of there, stayed clear of the whole family. Conrad surprised me with shares in the trust, so I just took it to be hush money, kept my mouth shut."

"Okay. Clay, do you have any questions?"

He said, "Just one. Was Carlene present?"

Baxter chuckled. "Nah. She was the fixer."

"How do you mean?"

He shrugged. "The one who always fixed things after the other guys made a mess."

"Did that include you?"

"Yeah, sometimes." Baxter placed his hands on his hips and shook his head. "That paper you had on me the other day. That was all phony, right?" Clay's replied with an enigmatic smile. "Yeah, thought so." He faced Andi. "So, look, we're good, we're all square?"

"Just as long as you've told me the whole truth, Baxter. I don't want to have to visit a third time, okay?"

Baxter nodded.

"Sure about that?"

"Yeah, yeah. I'm sure."

She smiled and stepped back. "All right, we're done. You can go."

After the door closed behind Baxter, Clay asked, "Got that out of your system, did you?"

She exhaled. "Yes."

"Feel better?"

"Definitely."

He paused and pulled the door open for her. "Well, okay, then."

Chapter Twenty-Four

Clay frowned and returned an unappetizing pastry to the plate. In the circle around a table at Grounds Crew, Mitch and Meredith were preoccupied with a collection of shared notes and each other.

But Andi had been watching and raised an eyebrow. "What's wrong?"

"Nothing."

She held an identical danish. "Yes there is. You made a face. When you put the sweet roll back on the plate, you pushed it away a little and you made a face."

Mer and Mitch looked up, their expressions curiosity lightly seasoned with puzzlement.

"It's okay, no big deal."

She sighed impatience. "Uh-huh. You didn't like it. You made a kind of scowly face and dropped it. Well, okay, not exactly dropped, but you put it down and it doesn't look like you want any more of it."

Mitch smirked. "Yeah, Clay. You definitely look unhappy with the sweet roll."

Meredith slumped back in her chair. "I don't believe this. We're supposed to be getting some work done, about these adoptive cowboys, and you guys are investigating a sweet roll?"

Clay gestured toward the plate. "Danish, actually."

Andi said, "Cherry danish, in fact. So what's wrong with it?"

Meredith crossed her arms. "C'mon, Clay. Just fill them in so we can get back to work. I've got a zillion calls to make and it's too noisy in here to concentrate with a cellphone."

Mitch shrugged. "Go for it, bro."

"It's a little stale, that's all."

Andi seemed to be faking an expression of concern, and over-doing it. "Well, of course it is. It's almost noon and this is a restaurant. Want to order something else?"

Meredith rolled her eyes.

Clay grabbed the danish. "Guys, I'm good. Watch me eat this danish, okay?" He took a hefty bite.

While Mitch rubbed his eyes with a thumb and forefinger, looking away, Andi watched intently. "You're very brave, Clay. Very brave."

Meredith drew a deep breath. "Okay, now getting back to the people who adopted the first baby...which might have been Kathleen?"

Mitch interrupted. "You know what's weird about this is that we've got two babies — now women — and nobody will ever know which one is which. Identical DNA."

Andi said, "Not necessarily. As the fetus develops, cell mutations can cause subtle differences. But you're correct that we'll never know which is which because we can't match hair samples to the specific certificates."

Meredith struggled with a stack of notes and half a dozen sheets of paper tumbled to the floor. "Sorry."

Andi said, "It's okay. Small table."

Mitch looked at Andi. "It's getting tougher and tougher, al-ways doing our work here."

She asked, "What do you mean?"

He glanced at Clay, looking nervous about saying something out of line.

"It's okay, buddy. We're a team, right?"

Meredith shuffled the retrieved papers and laid them on the stack in front of her. "Every time you guys are in town, you want to buy us a coffee and sweet roll. Even if it's a stale danish."

Andi said, "Well, yes. Kind of get you out of the office, treat you."

Mitch shook his head. "I used to think that. But maybe it's because you don't want to spend time there. We always go somewhere else. I dunno. Maybe it's bad memories for Clay. Whatever."

Andi fell silent for several moments. "Or maybe because it's just so crowded."

Meredith nodded. "Like, you were all excited, bought those big desks, which you never really use. So the space is very jammed tight, and.... Okay, when it's just Mitch and I, no big deal. But for all four?"

Andi spoke to Clay. "She's right. We're going to need more room, a bigger office. Offices plural, maybe?"

Her perfectly innocent question picked at scabs of old wounds, reviving the original resolve to continue his quest for a job with a genuine badge, sidearm and the authority to make an arrest. She was right, of course. The old Storm Agency office was as seedy as the guy who used to own it, and they'd merely put lipstick on a pig. Desperation had caused him to accept the job, just to gather traveling money. That, and an increasingly misguided thing about helping out hapless Andi, in dire straits. Who turned out to be enormously capable, way beyond need of his aid.

The apartment — another concession, going with the flow, a drunken fling on Gideon's dime. Just temporary, he'd told himself, again and again. The case moved along well and, the future temptingly optimistic. Bright possibilities for Andi, Meredith, Mitch, even himself — if he could avoid having Storm hanging around his neck, like an anvil on heavy chains.

Andi's fixed gaze encouraged commitment. Prepared to repeat

the question when he said, "Yes, we might have to consider that. Sometime."

He should have anticipated the tepid response, but knew as soon as he finished the line that Meredith and Mitch, in particular, were disappointed.

Andi bit her lower lip and barely above a whisper said, "Yes. I guess so." But her eyes were unchanged, pulling no punches. No wonder Baxter McKnight had so quickly wilted. Forty calibre bullets were cotton balls by comparison.

On the plate next to coffee gone cold, scattered crumbs were the only evidence of a stale danish, the precipitating pastry of predicament.

Glenn Storm was dead. Big Bill Garrison was dead. Herb Conley was dead. So were all the yesterdays, a few good, but then... The searing pain of being screwed over in small-city politics. The kitchen guys, raucous, carefree — and going nowhere. The sad, joyless nights of a family adrift and indifferent, just going through the motions. All grim memories.

Then there was the football season that began with hope in August and staggered through eight miserable games. Marginal coaching, indifferent players. And the night of cold drizzle in early November, trailing fourteen to ten with less than a minute to go.

Coach Sanderson — also dead — had sent in another stupid play from the sideline. Mitch had been angry, really fuming, filthy dirty and soaking wet and playing what he knew would be his last-ever game. He exploded with a string of obscenities that nearly cost them a delay-of-game, but ended with an idea and a whynot. He'd looked Clay in the eyes, weary, worn out, haggard.

Yeah. Why not? They had to pull it together, just one time, wall off the pocket, give the receivers time to run routes. Clay discarded instructions, called a new play. Long count, hoping to draw an offsides, but then the ball came. To the left, Mitch planted his feet and snarled like a wild animal, clobbering a linebacker, making time.

The ball in the air, taking forever, floating, floating, dropping, dropping, a dozen hands reaching.

Touchdown.

And Mitch in his face, biggest grin ever, unbridled joy, fists pounding on his pads, yelling, "Awright! Awright!" Over and over.

On the plate to his left, a scattering of crumbs from a stale danish that should have made no difference. Cold coffee, unfinished. A circle of people, good people, alive, saying "why not," because their backs were to the wall and they had nothing more than a pocketful of hope, talent, a dream.

Clay kept his focus on Andi. "You know, maybe we should. As fast as we can. Mitch and Mer deserve better and Gideon can afford it. He hasn't objected yet, but even if he does, well, so what?"

Andi didn't flinch. "You're sure?"

Clay turned to the others. "Yeah. I am."

Meredith smiled. Mitch nodded approval.

Andi said, "Well, all right, then. Meantime, we've got to organize another road trip. Mer, can you condense the research you guys did on these people in Kentucky?"

"Of course."

Mitch said, "It's thin, just a guy who knows a guy. The people in the horse world don't exactly leave a lot of footprints."

Mer laughed. "Hoof prints. Horses have hooves."

He sighed. "Okay, okay. If the shoe fits..."

The wisecrack suffocated under a chorus of groans.

* * *

Andi leaned on the top white rail of fence that seemed to run forever in both directions, circling a smooth dirt track. The scent of livestock and soil lounged in soft, humid air filled with distant thunder. Horses. Galloping along the backstretch, faster than it ever seemed on television, pounding earth at the turn.

Clay watched, too, through his favorite pocket field glasses, which he shared with her as four thoroughbreds entered the turn.

She asked, "What do you know about horses?"

"They're big, they're fast, and guys in Oklahoma used them on ranches and stuff."

"Mer says there's a whole little world wrapped around horses, from people who have them almost like pets to every level of competition."

"I wouldn't be surprised."

She laughed. "C'mon. Don't be so modest. Your reputation as a private eye is at stake here, coming up with that 'it's about horses' thing that really opened the door."

"Lots of horse people in Bucks County, Andi. Some of them have the pull to get serious about it. I just guessed at what Mer already knew. It's like any sport. Fans, players, people who make a living keeping both happy."

They fell silent, thunder overwhelming as horses struggled for position going into the final turn, trying for a spot at the rail.

"My gosh, they're huge. Ever ride one?"

"No, never did. You?"

"No. And I'm not volunteering today, either. It looks way too scary."

A voice behind them said, "That's because it is. You've got some of the most highly skilled riders atop one of the most powerful animals in the world. Pushing the limits hard, very hard. All for a few tenths of a second in a mile and a quarter, with millions of dollars at stake. Hello, I'm Willard Gentry."

They exchanged handshakes and introductions. He was maybe five-nine, five-ten, sixties or so, leathery skin, a guy that should have been in overalls but instead wore slacks and a pressed shirt.

Andi said, "Thanks for taking the time to talk with us, sir."

Gentry chuckled. "Sir? Now there's a word I haven't heard in a long time. Will's fine with me. I'm in charge of all the trainers here at Douglas Farms. We're exclusively into thoroughbreds, housing, training, stud services."

Clay said, "Well I'm impressed. It's quite a spread."

"Mister Douglas is, shall we say, an enthusiast. He's been in the winner's circle more than once at the Derby, Belmont, Preakness, a lot of others. How can I help you folks today?"

Andi said, "We're looking for a woman named Casey Evans. She'd be about twenty-five. I understand she lived here or worked her for a while?"

Gentry smiled. "She grew up here. Eats, drinks, thinks equine, and has since she could walk. For a gal who started out with a bale of tough breaks, she's done well. Real well."

Clay said, "Could you introduce her, point her out? We have what might be some very important personal information for her."

He lifted his hat and scratched the back of his head. "Well, now, that might be a bit difficult. She's not here, you see."

Clay nodded. "Know where we might find her?"

"This time of year? Wyoming most likely, maybe up into Canada. She's on the rodeo circuit. What's this about?"

"There's some influential people who would like to speak with her about an inheritance."

Gentry laughed. "I can't imagine what that might be. First off, a woman named Jeanne adopted her with some fellow I can't recall. Jeanne worked her for a few months, then took off with a drifter who didn't want a child. Y'know, we didn't even know her name, so we called her Casey, after a pretty little mare, name of Casey Delight."

Andi asked, "So who raised her?"

"That'd be me. Done the best I could. She turned out okay, considering."

Clay opened an envelope in his hand and produced the photograph of Kimberly Spence. "Does she look familiar?"

"Yep. Not the same person, but close enough. Hair's different and this looks like an older picture, if you know what I mean. So who would this be?"

"Her natural mother, Mister Gentry."

Gentry's eyes looked away, his jaw tensed, and he looked like he was stuck on a way to respond. "And she's just now getting around to looking for her own daughter?"

"No sir. She's deceased. But the family would like to get in touch, resolve an inheritance. Do you know if Casey has a sister?"

"No, I don't believe so. Wait. There was some kind of talk about it, long time ago, in connection with Jeanne. But frankly, I didn't pay much attention."

Andi asked, "Do you have a phone number or email or something where we can get in touch with her?"

Gentry smiled again. "Ma'am, I can tell you don't know much about rodeo life. They're off on a circuit, sleeping in trucks, trailers, sometimes a cheap motel that if you're real lucky might have a phone. I hear from her now and again, but no, sorry, got no way to get in touch. Last I heard, she was headed to Cody, Wyoming."

Clay said, "Great. Thanks."

Gentry paused. "You sure this is all on the up-and-up? I'd hate for Casey to get hurt. She's made a life for herself, done good, seems happy."

Andi patted his arm. "And we're most grateful to you for having been a person in her life who genuinely cared. Trust me, sir, she's about to have some really good luck."

They bid farewell and Gentry turned to walk away.

Andi said. "Oh, just one more question, Mister Gentry. Do you mind?"

Willard turned.

"By any chance, did Jeanne leave any sort of message for

Casey, like a note or something?"

"No, no, nothing."

"Uh-huh. And you're absolutely sure about that?"

"Yep. Now, if you folks don't mind, I've got some chores..."

Andi nodded. "Absolutely. Thanks again for your time."

Chapter Twenty-Five

Clay ignored the melting pot of New York City noise, echoing across concrete, and peered through the glass door. In the foyer of Leonard Pike's building, a short gray-haired woman concentrated on a mailbox, from which she drew several white envelopes. She took a furtive glance toward the street, frowned, turned away and scurried toward the interior portal, the tip of her cane jabbing at the floor while she struggled with keys.

Clay reached for the handle. Andi's hand arrived a fraction of a second later and parked on his wrist.

He paused. "We're not going through this door thing again, are we?"

She leaned in close. "Your four o'clock, white sedan, two occupants, probably male."

He pretended to respond to her hand while peeking over her shoulder. "You're sure?"

"Yes. I saw the one in the passenger seat at the airport, near the car rental desk."

"How can you be —"

"Wear a skirt long enough, you'll know."

Clay nodded. "Want me to —"

"No. Let's see if they're still there when we come out. If you don't mind, give me a hug or something. Sort of spin me around." She sighed. "C'mon, put a little enthusiasm into it."

Clay grinned and wrapped his arms around her.

"Okay, okay, you got the idea. Now, turn me."

She exaggerated a laugh as she swirled, the overdone toss of the head models use in commercials where everyone is supposed to be jolly and buoyant. "I think he took our picture."

He lingered in the embrace, reluctant to release her.

"I like your enthusiasm. Get a good look?"

Clay released her. "White males, medium build, late thirties, early forties maybe. We could offer to autograph the picture."

She chuckled and brushed down her jacket. "Not yet. But, hey, good performance. Now you can open the door."

He tugged the handle. "Feels like I've just been used."

She breezed past. "Welcome to the club, partner."

Between checks of his watch, eight minutes ticked away before the apartment door opened, this time by Martha Pike, her greeting as gracious as Leonard had been last time.

Martha said, "Your Miss Barnes was most courteous when she called, and it's lovely that you're prompt. Unnecessary, because we have no appointment calendar to speak of, but kind in any event. Please, make yourselves comfortable. Leonard will be along momentarily."

Andi and Martha lounged in small talk that gave every indication of having no consequence. Clay focused on a collection of modern art without any reference as to its significance and waited for Andi to steer conversation to a launch pad, ready for the moment Leonard strolled into the room.

Before him, wide, coarsely defined vertical lines, mostly shades of gray punctuated by red, filled a two-by-three foot canvas, like test swatches when choosing a paint color for the wall of a storage room.

Behind him, Leonard said, "Amazing, isn't it?"

"Yessir, I could agree with that."

Leonard stepped forward to join admiration of the painting. "Familiar with contemporary art?"

"No sir, afraid not. Ignorant, as a matter of fact."

"It's a Dustin Pearce, of course, relatively early, just as he was emerging from monochrome. This one is called *Fences*."

Clay suppressed an urge to suggest pickets had pointed tops. "So, his early work, as valuable as later in his career?"

"I was fortunate to acquire this one some years ago at a relatively modest price. Today? Probably not much more than one-fifty, two hundred or so."

"Ah. Of course. Uh, very impressive."

Leonard cocked his head. "Thousands, that is."

"Uh, oh, yes. Well. Very nice. Thanks again for agreeing to see us a second time. I promise to be brief."

Leonard gestured an invitation to join the ladies in a nest of pale blue sofas circling a glass coffee table in the center of the room, where every spot came with a view of either fine art or the Manhattan skyline. He took one across from his mother, while Clay followed Andi's preference for a chair.

Leonard leaned forward, showing a confident smile. "Well then. Your investigation goes well? You're making good progress?"

Andi and Clay exchanged glances. With her eyes, she faintly hinted he should take the lead.

* * *

Satisfied he picked up the cue, Andi leaned back in her chair, astonishingly comfortable for an ultra-modern style always equated with a variation on stadium seating.

The guys in the car hopefully had cramped quarters with lumpy cushions, and, with any luck, that extra cup of coffee they might have had would be taking an additional edge off their comfort. Never drink a lot before or during a stakeout, the instructor at the academy had said. Because sometimes it can be a long wait in the middle of nowhere. And then he chuckled and remarked that male officers had a distinct advantage over women in that circumstance, and the class tittered with laughter.

Martha Pike's smile seemed eager, her eyes hopeful, like a grandmother excited by a visit, not a matron in the stratosphere of wealth. "May I pour you a cup of tea?"

"That would be lovely. Thank you so much."

The tea trickled into a delicate bone china cup with a floral pattern that seemed Victorian, a style and manners of a time sadly long past.

Clay remained polite, deferential, soft-spoken, laying back like always, letting the subject wallow in a rising tub of self-confidence, perhaps stumbling into way too much cocky assurance, letting something slip.

Leonard probably didn't even see it as a game, complete with scorecard. Just a pleasant sort of guy who lived extraordinarily well, had connections the average person would die to get, thrived on a sort of understated prestige, and by-the-way hated his father and would do anything to put it to the old man. Martha listened attentively, almost serenely, as if the sleazy scandals of long ago were attached to someone else's family.

Clay finally got around to the birth certificates and reports that at least one of the twins had lived, grew up and roam the rodeo circuit.

Leonard accepted a copy of the document and studied it it with polite detachment, like a trivial clipping from the newspaper passed around over cocktails among old chums. He handed it to Martha, who showed the same indifferent reaction.

Clay said, "And so that brings us to a specific evening, during which there was something of a party that perhaps got a little out of hand. Austin, Baxter, Conrad, some others, plus Kimberly and evidently a liberal amount of narcotics."

"I'm not at all surprised. I'd heard some stories."

"May I ask from whom?"

"Oh, just the usual household gossip. Nothing specific. I was not there at the time, so my information is second hand, all hearsay, meaningless."

"Meaningless how?"

Leonard chuckled, a nervous edge to his tone. "Oh, I don't know. Just an expression. Certainly nothing that would, well, you know, stand up in court."

"Did you know Kimberly was four months pregnant at the time of the party?"

"That's a reasonable suggestion."

Andi sat up. "Leonard, I understand where you're coming from, but I think Clay's trying to get a sense of who the father of the twins might have been. As in, perhaps she might have had a relationship with one of the employees at the farm?"

Leonard shrugged. "With Kimberly, I'm sure anything was possible."

Clay said, "I was thinking about a driver..." He looked for Andi to take the cue.

She pretended to suddenly recall a name. "Freddie. Freddie Something. And he was a chauffeur, Clay."

A faint smile of recognition showed on Leonard's jaw. "Boyd. His name was Freddie Boyd."

Clay looked relieved. "Yeah, of course. Freddie Boyd. And there was another guy, a groundskeeper or gardener or something..."

Leonard said, "Yes. Leroy Steele. I'd think him the more likely of the two. In fact, of the two..." His voice trailed off. "But, again, I wasn't there at the time so —"

Clay leaned toward Leonard, his expression harder, his eyes direct. "Why would Freddie not be likely? And do you know where we might locate him to ask him the same questions?"

Leonard bit his lower lip. Martha looked to the ceiling and

slowly closed her eyes.

Andi spoke in a soft, reassuring tone. "It's okay, Leonard. We're just trying to be thorough, touch all the bases."

Clay took a deep breath and cocked an eyebrow. "You could spare us a lot of work if you'd just give us a little help here, sir."

Martha slowly nodded. "Leonard, dear, you know they'll find out sooner or later. You may as well clear the air right now. You've done nothing wrong."

Clay sat back. Leonard had taken the bait and Martha set the hook. From far below the window, the muffled sound of a car horn, from the next room, the gentle tick of a mantle clock. Even the carpet seemed to murmur while Leonard tapped his forefinger on his lips.

* * *

Within his mind, Clay craved noise. Pound a table. Bark a command, shove, push, prod, demand admission, confession, the open dike of a subject with nowhere to go. The sounds of chaos, of a half-dozen police radios blaring across pavement, sirens arriving. A stadium filled with pumped up fans, chanting, stamping feet, hooting and hollering and clamoring for a score.

And yet there was only infernal silence, not even a whisper, not even the sound of Leonard's forefinger meeting his lips, behind a fist that no longer had punch. A hush, a stillness, and he could only imagine the sound of his own heart, beating slower and slower, waiting. Patience fluttering away, out of control. Fighting the urge to shatter the moment or allow it to slip away by giving Leonard an extra two seconds to change his mind.

Leonard sighed. A rush of air, whooshing across the corner of the coffee table, bouncing across the walls, dying in the thick fabric of drapes framing a window of glass through which powerful guys, like him, could look down at all the little people, struggling to make their way.

Leonard sat erect, drawing a breath, his eyes fixed on the *Fences* painting. "Yes, it's time. Freddie Boyd could not have been the father of Kimberly's children. And I doubt very much if you'll ever find him. Heaven knows, I've been unsuccessful on that score for many years."

Clay gripped the leash on the tone of his own voice. "And why would that be, sir?"

A faint smile, a glance at his mother for encouragement. "Because, you see, Freddie was gay. And my lover."

"Okay..."

Leonard's expression faded from relief to melancholy. "Actually, it's not at all okay. We were extraordinarily fond of each other, and I make no excuses for it. I've long given up any desire to understand it. It was — it is — the way I am."

"There was some sort of falling out, then?"

Leonard said, "No. Not at all. My father learned of it, and did what he does best. Intervene, have his way, buy what he wants. He gave me assignments resulting in extended travel, mostly in Europe. And then he bought, pressured, managed, whatever, my dear Freddie. I'll never know precisely what occurred. But he destroyed my world, Mister Garrison. Utterly wrecked it. And then didn't care the slightest bit whether I accepted it or not. Gideon Pike was not about to be anything but in absolute control."

Martha nodded. "Gideon could be unbelievably cruel, Mister Garrison. I love my son. I've made my choice."

Andi cocked her head. "And your daughter?"

"She and Gideon are two of a kind. I shouldn't trust either of them, if I were you."

Clay looked toward Leonard, but saw the memory of garrulous Big Bill Garrison, surrounded by cronies at his favorite table in the steakhouse, holding court, telling tales, keeping them all laughing. But Big Bill got caught red-handed by a little sleazeball named Glenn Storm, his marriage instantly an afterthought, the mother of his son vanished, never to be seen or heard from again. Big Bill's world wouldn't last another eighteen months.

Leonard Pike, by contrast, had strange paintings of fences in a cocoon of comfort, a quiet life in philanthropic boardrooms, black tie theater, soft dinner parties. And his corporate proxy supported Conrad purely out of spite.

* * *

On the pavement, Andi paused to take in a full breath of regular New York City air, her hands thrust in her pockets, her focus on Clay. He seemed to be doing the same thing, getting mentally reset, sifting what they'd learned seven stories above them.

She sensed distance, as if his mind was elsewhere.

"You okay?"

He cracked a gentle smile. "Yeah, I'll be fine."

"It was pretty decent of you to let Leonard have his privacy, to promise confidentiality."

"I guess. But the others probably know anyway. They all know everything and they don't know anything. At the same time."

She chuckled. "You've got that right. Want to head out, get something to eat, go down to Fifth Avenue and buy a new tie or whatever?"

"I could use a walk. Like, around the block."

"Want company?"

"Sure."

They'd gone seventy-five feet when his cell rang. The white car loomed just ahead, two guys watching, their faces just coming into focus. Clay answered it and kept walking.

The guys in the car were grim-faced, determined looking, like they were not about to back down. Clay muttered something and disconnected. Only one parked car remained between them and the two surveillance guys.

"That was Mitch."

"And?"

"Change of plans. We're going back to Philadelphia."

"Let me guess. Carlene?"

"Yep. Mitch obtained Kimberly's records from the rehab place."

The distance to the white car was closing fast and the temptation to take a long, close look at the faces of the men strong. "I'm not entirely sure I want to know how Mitch did that."

"You don't."

"Still interested in the walk?"

Clay started to tuck the phone into his pocket. They were just a few feet from the men in the white car. He took two quick steps, lifted the phone, and aimed the camera toward the car. The two guys covered their faces and turned away.

Clay grunted, wheeled and said, "Okay, let's get going."

"Get that out of your system, did you?"

"Yeah."

She patted his shoulder and wrapped her arm into his. "Well, okay, then."

Chapter Twenty-Six

When they entered the terminal at JFK, she announced, "So, okay, I actually do want to know how he got it."

Joining a line for shuttle flight tickets, credit cards and identification in hand, Clay explained. "You have to remember Mitch is a very enterprising guy, an investigative reporter with, well, let's just say fluid morality. He bends rules a lot, always has, looking for an edge, an opening."

The line inched forward, mostly impatient, tired-looking guys in suits with shoulder-strap bags, the portable offices of company reps hopping from customer to customer.

"Fluid morality. I like that. So...?"

"So he got poking around with the custodial people at the Silverwood Clinic, probably spread a little cash around, got access to a storage room."

"Where they keep records."

"Yup."

"Which are supposed to be destroyed after seven or eight years or something?"

"But weren't."

"And they're on your phone?"

"Yes. One big attachment."

She said, "Hm. I want to see them. On paper."

"You're joking."

"No. Look, there's a business center over there. We can have them print it out."

"It's a thirty-page email attachment, and there's a line of waiting customers."

She cocked her head and her eyes sparkled. "Twenty dollars says we can make it on time."

Twelve minutes later, the line at the service desk painstaking crept forward. Boarding announcements for their flight became more frequent, more urgent.

She whispered, "Think could bribe a few people, like in the bar, to get us to the head of the line?"

"No way. I'm not putting out expense money to lose twenty bucks."

Another ten minutes crawled past on the clock above the service desk. Their flight was well along in boarding when she handed the clerk a fifty-dollar bill and urged speedy service.

After they sprinted to the plane, the last passengers to burst through the door before departure, he offered the twenty and settle into a seat for a nap.

Seventy five minutes later, the pre-landing announcements dissolved slumber. Next to him the sound of shuffling paper suggested Andi continued to study Mitch's report. He yawned but kept his eyes closed to embrace the remaining moments of a time out.

The jet descended and made a wide turn for final approach.

She whispered, "Are you asleep?"

"Not any more."

"You weren't really sleeping. I could tell. You were sitting there all kinds of smug, looking very proud of yourself. But not sleeping. Dozing, maybe."

"Then why did you ask?"

The landing gear under the fuselage whined as wheels unfurled and the landscape outside the window zoomed upward.

"Because I already knew you were awake. It would have sounded stupid to ask if you were awake."

"That makes sense."

Her voice was firm, her tone intense. "We have a lot of questions for Carlene. I want this one."

"Be my guest. She rubbed my fur the wrong way last time. I'll take secondary."

* * *

The cavernous ballroom at Goose Creek Country Club sprawled out before Andi like an arena between events, where darkly paneled walls and thick red carpet conspired to snuff any conversation into utter privacy. Despite the size, it felt cozy.

Tables for eight or ten oozed in formation from the far left halfway across the space, unadorned by linen and chairs. They looked rather sad, devoid of camouflage, the way heavily-used and worn tables are when naked.

Within the field, a group of women huddled. One side of a circle was well dressed. The committee, the people in charge, the organizers of an event. Opposite were others, in the uniforms of club staff, those who took the instructions with grace and made it happen. In the center, Carlene Elliot spoke with modest animation.

Many steps later, dialog grew into focus and as it did, heads began to turn. When attention clearly withered, Carlene herself glared at the intruders and marched from the circle to confrontation.

After whispered greetings, Carlene set her jaw and led them into a dim room where workers stacked chairs onto a cart. Andi's gaze swept the room. Piles of round and rectangular tables, chairs, even rolls of carpet huddled along the walls in muted whispers of shape and form.

Carlene's voice rose to command. "I need the room."

The two guys looked at each other, then to her. "Yes'm."

Behind Clay, a burly security guy in a maroon blazer appeared.

Carlene waved him off. "It's all right. Close the door on your way out."

"Yes ma'am."

She faced Andi, wearing an expression of curiosity tempered with impatience. "It *is* customary to make appointments. But then, that level of courtesy is probably not routine in your circle."

Clay hung back, taking a spot between Carlene and the door, his arms loose at his side, perfect posture to look relaxed but ready.

Andi took a shallow, fortifying breath and clutched the manila folder tight to her torso. "I do apologize for interrupting your meeting, Mrs. Elliot, and I promise to be brief."

Carlene brushed a stray hair from her forehead. "Very well, then, a few moments. But I believe I've already told you everything I know about this entire matter, I do have business to attend to, and important people are waiting for me."

"Just a couple of things to clear up some details, if you don't mind."

"But I *do* mind, Miss Delvento. You keep promising brevity, my dear. It's time for you to deliver, don't you think?"

"Yes'm. First, concerning the Silverwood Clinic. You and Conrad are on the board of directors, isn't that correct?"

"Miss Delvento, I serve on many boards. But yes, I believe so. Conrad thought it a good idea, to honor Kimberly's memory, so we are sustaining donors. Board memberships presumably are in recognition of our concern. And support."

"Of course. And patient records. It seems many of them are still kept in storage, well after they should be destroyed."

Carlene shrugged. "I have no knowledge of that. However,

thank you for calling it to my attention. I'll have someone look into it. These are sensitive documents, well secured, I'm sure."

Andi opened the folder. "There seems to be something amiss, then. These materials, concerning Kimberly's care and treatment, have raised a few questions."

Carlene's eyes widened, but only for a moment, then narrowed. "How did... Well. If, of course, they are genuine. Look, I have no knowledge of clinic records, how they were kept, the details."

"Kimberly was being treated for cocaine addiction, correct?"

"I don't recall. Now, if you could just get to the point —"

Andi took a sidestep. "Did you visit her often?"

"As often as possible. We were all very concerned about her well-being."

"Yes. I'm sure. What about Conrad, Austin, Baxter?"

"I believe I used the word 'all.'"

Another step to the side, with Clay now only in peripheral vision. "Of course. I just thought it a bit odd that your names didn't appear on any of the visitor logs."

"I have no idea why that might be, Miss Delvento. An oversight, perhaps. We visited often, concerned for Kimberly's well being. Where is this leading?"

"I just wondered if the visits might have been out of any sort of guilt?"

Carlene seemed wary, suspicious. "Whatever for?"

Another side step. Now Clay, and the door, were behind her. "Maybe in the aftermath of that party..."

"I don't know anything about any party. And frankly, I'm beginning to resent your tone, young lady."

A soft knock interrupted and a woman peeked in. "Is everything all right, Carlene?"

Carlene had to lean to the right to see, and took a step of her own. "Yes, yes. Give me a few moments, Jane."

Jane withdrew while Andi mirrored Carlene's movement, keeping herself between the subject and the door.

"Miss Delvento, as I said, I'm a very busy person, and there are important people —"

Andi took a step forward. "Yes, yes. Important people. I get it. Just a couple more questions."

Carlene sighed, impatience clearly rising fast.

"Did you have occasion to become familiar with Kimberly's doctors, nurses, staff?"

"That was a long time ago, Miss Delvento. I can't possibly —"

Andi turned pages in the records and casually moved closer. "Specifically, I was curious about, let's see... Oh, yes. Ellen Carson, R.N. She turns up late in Kimberly's period of care, several times a day, but outside of the usual notations for nursing rounds."

"If you say so."

"And she was the last person to check on medications before others discovered Kimberly dead, from an overdose of heroin. There were all kinds of observations, but no records of tests to prove anything."

Carlene crossed her arms and glared at Andi. "Miss Delvento, I caution you not to reach any ill-advised conclusions. You have in your possession documents illegally obtained, perhaps clever forgeries. Ours is a family that values privacy. Now I've been more than cordial and patient with inquiries certainly prompted by a confused, disagreeable old man, no longer capable of reasonable thinking. It's all rather shameful. You could very well be exposing you and your colleagues to very serious civil action."

Andi tidied the documents in the folder and closed it. "I understand."

Carlene took a step backward. "Do you? There's no evidence of wrong-doing, certainly nothing that will stand the test of the courts, especially after all this time. I think it's time for Gideon to simply let it go, accept reality."

"You're probably correct. These materials might not be helpful."

"Precisely. They prove nothing. After all, there's no signature by a licensed doctor on them."

Andi looked up and directly into Carlene Elliot's eyes. "And how would you know that?"

Carlene's expression went to ice. "This conversation is over. Get out."

* * *

Clay joined Mitch at a convenient spot along an empty wall to lean, watch, be amused. Sunlight poured across a line of newly-planted shrubs and through a string of windows, bouncing madly off pure white walls.

Fifteen feet away, Meredith extolled her discovery in commercial real estate mode, pitching the suite of offices to Andi. Who clearly needed no sell.

Mitch said, "You know it's a done deal, right, buddy?"

"Yup."

"And that they'll get first pick on the offices."

"Yup."

"I really don't want the one next to the restroom, bro."

"Don't worry about it."

"I worry about such things."

"You shouldn't."

"It's the flushing sound."

"Don't worry."

"You're sure?"

"Yup."

"They're probably going to pick out a bunch of art for the walls, drapes, chairs and stuff."

"Yup."

Mitch sighed. "And we're not going to have a vote."

"Nope."

"The thing with Carlene, it went well?"

Clay shifted his weight to the left foot. "Very well."

"Got her good, did you?"

"Andi did. Waltzed her right into the doctor-signature thing and *snap*, bagged her. She knew about it, all right. She'd seen the file. Your inside guy did great."

"Cost us fifteen grand. I was shocked when I saw all the boxes. That stuff should have been shredded or incinerated or whatever they do, years ago. Wonder why they never got around... wait a sec. The conspiracy freak in me says maybe somebody hung onto it for something like blackmail."

"Fifteen grand is peanuts to a guy like Gideon Pike. And, yeah, I had the same thought, but then, you'd go to a lot of work to prove anything. Although it might be worth it for those Conrad and probably Carlene are squeezing — if they are squeezing anybody. Maybe they were just sloppy. Out of sight, out of mind and like that."

Mitch said, "Yeah, I know. Carlene and Conrad are not our clients."

Andi and Mer disappeared into one of the vacant rooms toward the front. Laughter trickled out, the free and easy kind that good friends so easily share, a happy moment both of the women deserved for their effort.

Clay asked, "So what about this extra nurse, Carson?"

"No record of her anywhere. Leastways, not in Pennsylvania. I was able to run down licensure on everyone else except her. And I still haven't found where she went. So I'm thinking, maybe it was just some sort of human resources screwup. Hard to say just how tight Silverwood Clinic stuck to the law, but with blue-chippers for patients, I'd have thought they'd be careful."

"They sure weren't with patient records."

"Fifteen grand buys a lot of sloppy."

Clay grunted. "They were sloppy twenty-five years ago. You just proved it, that's all. How about our rodeo girl? Any luck with that yet?"

Mitch yawned. "Man, I shoulda gotten a coffee to go at Grounds Crew. We oughta set up an office pot, bro. Okay, so, nothing new on Casey, but I'm still confident. She's on the circuit in barrel racing, whatever that is, mostly northern states, Canada. There's a running string of rodeos they all seem to caravan to, but it gets complicated this time of year with events here and there, at the same time. I got calls out to the promoters."

"Sounds good."

"Yeah, well, it's taking a little while. I've got to step lightly. After all, I'm a guy wondering if they have a certain woman in the competition. Don't want to come off as a stalker."

"Okay. And Conrad?"

Mitch chuckled. "Oh, I'm sure you're going to hear from him pretty quick. Mer put out feelers while you were on the way back yesterday, but I'm ninety-nine percent sure ol' Carlene didn't waste any time checking in with the creep."

Clay nodded and gestured toward the space around them. "So what do think?"

"What can I say? Works for me. I've been poaching your desk while you're on the road and that ain't gonna work much longer. So, yeah, Mer's right that we need space. If we're gonna do this thing." He paused. "We are going to do this thing, aren't we?"

Clay sighed. "Yeah. I guess so."

"You didn't really want to be a cop anyway."

"Actually, I did."

"Still? I mean Andi, and Mer, and yours truly... It could be worse, man."

"Probably true."

The women returned from the tour, still laughing and inflating each other's expectations.

"More than true, buddy, more than true."

Andi's grin and sparkling eyes underscored Mitch's words. She asked, "What's true?"

"That we still have a lot of work to do, if we're going to earn our fee for this case. If we're going to afford new offices. If we're going to make our friends happy."

Andi said to Mer, "See, I told you he'd be good with it."

"I don't think that's what —"

"Sure he did. He adores the space. Didn't even have to look around. Knew it right away." She turned to pour a sunshine smile on him and batted her eyes. "Didn't you, Clay?"

Chapter Twenty-Seven

Andi placed her palms in the center of her desk, then spread them outward to fondle a gorgeous amount of space. The most she could ever recall as her own, the glass sprawled under her fingertips, silky smooth, perfectly clean, uncluttered.

Way out there, a four-line phone with only one of them working. An in-box, with just a few sheets of paper to carpet the bottom. A cute little green ceramic mug with a joke expression, for pens and pencils. The executive flavor of it all prompted a sigh of satisfaction. Several manilla folders bearing notes relating to the investigation, guarded the left edge.

Immediately beyond the border of her territory, Mer and Mitch huddled on metal folding chairs, comparing notes in folders they supported in their hands. Mitch gripped a ballpoint pen between his teeth. Mer's pencil impaled a messy bun above her right ear.

Clay's wry smile ladled guilt upon her and she swept her hands back together again. "What?"

"Nothing."

But, of course, it *was* something. He'd read her mind again, caught red-handed basking in a moment of luxury chased by nagging guilt. Behind her, to the right, the jammed work spaces of Mitch and Mer bore stacks of files, surrounding the single phone they had to share because desk space wouldn't allow for two.

Andi narrowed her eyes and glared at Clay. "Mer, how are we

doing on the new office?"

Mer looked up, startled. "Huh? Oh. Good. First of the month. Day or so to get the phones and wi-fi installed. Why?"

Clay's smile went smug and she hid out behind a hoisted coffee cup. "No problem, just looking forward to it."

Mitch muttered, "You got that right. I used to be a pack rat in a newsroom, but this... Anyway, no complaints. All I got today is Cody, Wyoming, something called the Cody Stampede. Big deal on the circuit, I guess. Barrel-racing entrants include Casey Evans."

Clay rubbed his hands together and flexed his fingers. "Nice, buddy. Real nice."

"Yeah, been chasing my tail for a week on that. Every burg in a thousand miles has some sort of little pony show and nobody keeps track of much. You've got pickups and horse trailers crisscrossing the plains and mountains chasing tiny purses in front of a couple of hundred fans. This one's a bit bigger, so they actually have a program going."

Clay turned to Andi. "Time to pack a bag again."

Her shoulders slumped.

Mer beamed a smile. "I saw that. Maybe I can help. You guys must have really pushed Carlene's buttons yesterday —"

"Andi did. It was elegant, really nice."

"Thank you, Clay. I got lucky."

"I liked the way you slowly shifted around her, getting between her and the door, just the way it's taught."

Mitch and Mer looked puzzled.

Clay explained. "Working a suspect in a closed space. You position the backup officer near the door, but the primary also wants to get between the subject and the door, not so much as a matter of safety as to intimidate the subject."

Mitch cocked an eyebrow. "No kidding?"

Clay shrugged. "Well, that's how one detective once described it to me one time over a couple of beers and a really bad sandwich."

Andi said, "I saw it done." Heads turned as she continued. "I was in an interview room with two guys from internal affairs. We'd just finished with a witness who'd been escorted out and I was getting the paperwork organized. The one blocked the door, the other worked his way around to close me in. Incredibly scary."

Compassion swept across Mer's face. "Oh, Andi, what happened?"

"Lucky for me, the captain needed the room. He knocked on the door."

Mitch and Mer murmured, "Wow."

Andi turned to Clay. "So, yeah, every once in a while I like to run my hands across this desk, which is way too big for this crummy little room, and feel not just the space, but the power."

Mer interrupted. "Can I get back to Carlene's buttons?"

Clay had gotten the message. "Definitely."

Tugging the pencil from her hair, Mer passed a phone message to Andi, then prepared to take notes. "Conrad's office called. He'd like to see you guys right away."

Andi smiled. "Oh, yeah. I *so* want to take a run at that guy, push some of his little buttons. How soon do you think we can get on his calendar?"

Mer's pencil went into action on a day planner.

Clay said, "No. I'd rather do the trip to Wyoming first. Make him wait."

Andi's jaw dropped. "You're joking. He and Carlene are our most likelies, they're running scared. We should push, *push hard,* right away."

"With what? That she and Conrad were both on the board of the Silverwood Clinic? That Conrad was involved in some hearsay drug party a long time ago? We already know he can't possibly be the father of the twins, and we still have to find the girls and prove a relationship."

"I just want to squeeze that creep and see what oozes out."

Clay shook his head. "That might be satisfying, but it's not what we were hired to do. Our job is to locate the missing twins, connect them with Gideon Pike. That's it."

She frowned. "Conrad is just so wrong. I like him an awful lot for Kimberly's murder and all the coverup after. I want to see him in cuffs."

Mer said, "Clay's right, you know."

"But —"

Mitch interrupted. "But I can also see Clay's game plan. He knows Conrad Pike is dirty, and he's got the two of them, Carlene and Conrad, running maybe not scared but certainly nervous. I bet Clay wants them to stew a little, let the tree shake, see what kind of apples fall out." Everyone stared at Mitch, who mumbled, "Well, okay, that came out kind of stupid."

Clay chuckled. "Nah. I kind of liked the apples part. But, yeah, let's pull Conrad's chain instead of him pulling ours. He's not going anywhere."

Andi slumped in her chair, crossed her arms and stared at the empty space in front of her. Everyone else had at least a couple of thick manilla folders. All she had was an open area she could rub with the palms of her hands.

Clay said, "Hey. You did *so* great with Carlene. You took the time to study, really study, the files from Mitch, and Mer, too. And you used your experience to cause the subject to make a mistake. A big one."

"They're dirty, Clay. I just know it."

"So do I. But Casey Evans is about to roll into Cody, Wyoming, to run a horse through an obstacle course. She has no clue how her life is going to change."

Andi's voice tumbled to a whisper. "I suppose you're right."

Clay smiled again, his patient smile, the one that could be so

exasperating. It could be considered patronizing. Like polite sympathy. Or amused brotherly. Or serene indifference, when taking
a step back to let someone else have the collar — and the credit —
and not be the slightest bit jealous. Because he knew he was better.

She scanned the faces around her and drew a breath. "Okay,
book us on a flight or whatever to Wyoming. But don't forget,
Conrad is mine."

* * *

With a furrowed brow, the front desk clerk at a nice hotel outside Cody, Wyoming, studied the computer monitor between
bursts of typing. After each pause, she faintly shook her head.

To Clay's right, Andi waited, her expression placid, benign.
But her patience fading fast, because she kept shifting her weight
from her left foot to her right and back again, the rate picking up
as the seconds on the big clock behind the desk marched relent-
lessly through another circle.

At last the clerk looked up, her expression one of compassion
and hopefulness. "I'm very sorry, but we have just the one room."

He exhaled. "I thought we had two reservations."

"Yessir. I'm sure you did. But evidently there was some sort of
mix-up. Perhaps the reservation service assumed that traveling as
a couple..."

Andi slipped into a forced smile. "Maybe there's another hotel
nearby?"

"Yes, ma'am, there is. But with the rodeo in town, everything
in Cody is booked. Anyway, I'm not sure you'd care for it."

Andi continued to fake a placid smile. "Because...?"

"It's popular with the rodeo people and all, because it's close
to the grounds and it's cheap. Showers, a bar and restaurant, and,
well, you know, a bit noisy and cramped."

Clay nodded. "So the one room you do have?"

The desk clerk studied the monitor. "Non-smoking. King bed."

"Maybe you could swap it for one with a pair of queens or doubles?"

"I'm sorry. We're fully booked. The buddies have them all."

"Buddies?"

"Rodeo people often travel in pairs to share expenses. Anything to save a dollar."

Clay looked to Andi for a decision.

She said, "Maybe you have a cot or a roll-away or something?"

"I can try, but..."

Andi's expression became intense and she leaned in. "I'm sure you can do more than try."

"Yes ma'am. But I just wanted to say the roll-aways are not terribly comfortable and —"

A smile grew on Andi's jaw. "Don't worry about that. He's at his meanest when he's all kinds of nasty from a lousy night's sleep. Me? I need that king, otherwise I turn into an absolute terror. Trust me, you don't want to know."

An anxious look filled the clerk's eyes, the kind that's half a moment away from calling nine-one-one. "Yes ma'am. Now, sir, if I could kind of trouble you for a credit card?"

* * *

Clay slowed to guide the rental through the portal of Stampede Park, the promised short distance down Yellowstone Avenue. Impossible to miss, because she saw nothing beyond it along a two-lane blacktop highway aimed at low, gray, treeless hills.

His usual calm and taciturn self, he probably filed every detail of the sprawling parking areas circling what looked rather like a smallish county fairground or perhaps a rural football stadium from somewhere in Ohio.

But with no trees, green fields, or all the other accessories of midwestern Americana. Only a field of dusty gravel.

Clay headed toward the back side of a grandstand, across which sprawled an enormous side proclaiming this to be the rodeo capital of the world, honoring the legacy of Buffalo Bill himself. A makeshift village of trucks, large and small, campers, stock trailers, portable corrals and a lot of faded denim under broad white hats.

She said, "So this was what Oklahoma was like?"

He chuckled. "Only without the hills."

"Can I be unimpressed?"

"Doesn't exactly live up to your expectations?"

"Not if you've ever been to Ohio Stadium in Columbus. That's a town that knows the real meaning of a horseshoe."

Clay drifted across the blacktop lot and eased into a spot near the ticket office. Four young women in wide-brimmed hats, calf-high boots, plaid shirts and jeans cut off provocatively near their buttocks strolled past, sipping from big foam mugs through straws and clearly excited about their prospects. He was working hard not to look, but most guys would have found it impossible.

He said, "Yeah, well the grandstand here is just about 100,000 seats smaller and the horseshoes around these parts go on hooves."

They approached what appeared to be an entry gate and two guys in western-cut suits.

"At least it's manageable in size. Here I thought we'd need an hour or so to find Casey Evans. Silly me." She said hello to the men and accepted the once-over that came with it. "Mind if we look around a bit? We're not here for the rodeo, just trying to find someone."

The taller of the two men rolled a toothpick from one side of his mouth to the other, then used the back of his hand to lift the brim of his hat. Receding hairline, but at least it looked groomed.

"You folks lawyers or something, maybe from Cheyenne? Laramie?"

Clay said, "No sir. Pennsylvania. And we're not lawyers."

"That right?"

"Yessir. We probably look out of place, being from the East Coast and all."

"That you do. Pennsylvania, eh? I got a cousin, in Philadelphia. Or somewhere near there."

Clay nodded and spoke with somber authority, the way guys do when gathered around the back of a pickup truck. But he overdid a facetious tone. "Probably Jenkintown. Lot of folks there."

"Yep, maybe so. What can I do for you?"

Andi said, "We're trying to get in touch with a rodeo competitor by the name of Casey Evans."

The second man, shorter and beer-bellied, asked, "Barrel racer, maybe?"

Clay said, "Yes. I believe so."

The first man nodded, "Well, you might want to make your way over yonder, just past the Buzzard's Roost, take yourself a look." He sneered. "Lot of folks there, too."

Clay's smile did a lousy job of masking embarrassment. After they exchanged a have-a-nice-day and a thank-you, she scampered to keep up with his long-legged pace. "Just had to get cute, didn't you?"

Chapter Twenty-Eight

Feeling increasingly out of place, Clay shared questions for directions with Andi. The gauntlet of mostly men, always in dusty boots and worn jeans and huge cowboy hats circled the main arena. It followed a line toward a string of blue gates below a covered grandstand that everyone seemed to know as the Buzzard's Roost.

Probably because in the center at the top was an enclosed booth area, similar to media boxes at stadiums everywhere.

Andi understandably had better luck in getting cordial replies than he. Calm and relaxed after the hotel front-desk showdown, she ladled out warm smiles and shamelessly captivated young cowboys along the way.

He was clearly not one of the community of professional rodeo competitors or even the more serious amateurs from around northwestern Wyoming. He wore a conservative suit, no hat, and ordinary dress shoes, and had already shed the lilting accent of Oklahoma.

A sense of pride and authority was one thing. But at the three-quarter mark of the trek to temporary corrals and a field of livestock trailers, it had become clear the wardrobe choice had been a poor decision. No matter. The path in a police uniform would have been the same.

Andi's streak ended with a group of seven women gathered in a loose circle. One was clearly distraught, the other six grim-faced and hanging tight out of support.

"Excuse me, but I wonder if you might..."

Heads turned and the glares could freeze a twenty-quart pasta cooker on full boil. A woman about thirty with a deeply tanned and weathered face, took a step forward. The apparent leader.

"Who're you?"

It wasn't a question. It was a demand, and it caused Andi to freeze.

Clay interceded. "Nothing to concern any of you ladies. My partner and I are trying to contact a Casey Evans, a barrel racer, who's supposed to be participating in the rodeo here."

The leader crossed her arms. "You people lawyers or cops or something?"

Clay retrieved a bit of Oklahoma twang. "No ma'am. We're with her family, and have some good news for her."

The distraught spoke up. "It's okay, Jen. Case could use a little good news right about now anyway."

Jen seemed suspicious, but gradually relented as friends eased into a loose line behind her.

Andi offered a disarming smile. "We've traveled here from Pennsylvania, on behalf of her family. Grandfather, in fact. It's a family matter, but I assure you —"

A voice from the group muttered, "Yeah, we've all heard that one before..."

Clay took a command posture. "My partner — Andi Delvento — and I, Clay Garrison, are actually here with some positive news. I understand your concern about outsiders. Look, tell you what. If you can direct us to where she might be, we'll be more than happy to be accompanied by whatever security people the grounds has, okay?"

Seconds of silence ticked away, with only the wind whispering.

The distraught woman, seeming to regain composure, said, "Case should be just beyond those trailers there. I can walk you over."

Andi said, "Thanks, but there's no —"

He interrupted. "That would actually be very kind of you — I'm sorry, I didn't catch your name."

"Suzanne."

"Thank you, Suzanne, we really appreciate it."

Jen's arms remained crossed. "Maybe I'll tag along."

"That would be fine. Wouldn't it, Andi?"

"Absolutely, Clay. Absolutely. Anyone else? No? Okay, then. Shall we?"

Clay couldn't resist a faint smile. Perfect. First and goal on half of a million-dollar contract. No time for a false start or off-sides. Piece of cake, if they could avoid a flag for a false start or offsides.

* * *

After a thicket of horse trailers, the pace unexpectedly slowed fifty feet from a large light brown horse with dark legs and tail. Two human legs hinted Casey Morgan was on the other side of the animal.

Andi's initially assumed barging in on a horse being tended was a bad idea, but a glance toward Suzanne, biting her lower lip, and Jen, her expression one of uncertainty, suggested otherwise. *Something's wrong. Suzanne and Casey have issues. Jen's the intermediary, and a reluctant one at that.*

Andi reflexively used her left arm to signal Jen to stop. Suzanne echoed the pause half a step later. Clay drifted away to the left, setting up a flank.

Jen said, "That'll be Casey. Want me to —"

As she stepped forward, Andi said, "No. It's okay. I've got it, thanks." Another twelve feet to the left, Clay made a wide path around the wary horse.

Clay gestured toward Suzanne and Jen to signal he had an eye on them. Andi nodded and called out, "Miss Evans?"

A slim, young woman leaned around the neck and head of the horse, a large oblong brush in her right hand. Clay saw it, too, and had stepped into a position where he was the point of a triangle with a clear view of everyone.

The resemblance to Kimberly was breathtaking. Thinner, five-eight, one-fifteen to one-twenty, dark brown hair, straight, a ponytail, brown eyes, no makeup. Wide brimmed hat, white. Plaid shirt, faded jeans, slim cut but not tight, brown boots, dusty from sandy soil.

And she pursed her lips into a scowl. "Who's asking?"

Andi stepped forward with authority at a measured pace, her hands visible and open. "Casey, we'd like to speak with you for a few minutes, if that's okay."

Casey's squinted as she looked past Andi's shoulder, toward the women on the perimeter. "Look, if you guys are cops or security or something, it was just a misunderstanding, no big deal. And if it's about that hotel bill in Billings, the manager said it was all settled."

Andi smiled, "No, no. We're not police or security. There's no problem."

Casey glanced toward Clay before her unflinching gaze locked onto Andi. "You people lawyers or something? You look like lawyers. I got no use for lawyers."

Seven feet from the animal seemed close enough. "No, not lawyers. Say, that's a very pretty horse. What's his name?"

Casey chuckled. "Well, I can tell right off that you don't know much about horses. He's a *she,* and *her* name is Whichaway." She stroked the horse's head and ear and cooed to the animal, "Isn't it, baby? But you like to be called Witchy, don'tcha now?"

Andi fought an urge to wince and masked embarrassment by pressing on. "Cute name, Witchy."

Casey continued to fondle the horse. "Yeah, that's because she's a buckskin mare, a grade horse. She's bigger than most, about fifteen-three, likely because she was probably sired by one of the thoroughbred stallions at the farm where I was raised. Because she's a grade horse, nobody had much use for her. And because she's a lot like me, we get along pretty well, even when she gets bratty and moody. Like me, sometimes." With her left hand firmly on the bridle, she turned her attention to Andi. "Anyway, you've caught me on a *really* bad day. I got no time for no bull. Our go-around has been moved up. Witchy doesn't like the local water and is a little off her feed. And my buddy — *yeah, that's you Suzanne* — got messing around with a couple of no-accounts and now we're just about broke. So if you're not a cop or a lawyer, and if you don't know nothin' about horses... Oh, crap. You're here to collect on a bill." She cursed to no one in particular. "Look, the vet knows me and knows I'm good for it, the feed will get paid for I promise, and I'm only thirty days on the truck. And if you're from the show, we'll have entry money on the table by the time the grandstands open. Lady, really, you can tell your boss it's gonna be all right."

Andi extended a hand across the front of the horse's head and hoped Witchy wouldn't bite. "No. We're definitely not bill collectors. Hi. I'm Andrea Delvento — call me Andi — and that's my partner, Clay Garrison."

Casey's handshake was tentative, but Witchy seemed nervous and Andi took half a step away. Clay remained on the perimeter and half waved.

"Casey, we're here on, well, family business, if you have a moment or two?"

A moment of panic filled Casey's eyes. "Uncle Willard. Is he okay?"

"He's fine. He told us you were on the circuit, and we've been working to find you. I wanted to speak with you about your mother."

Casey snorted. "Yeah, well, I sure don't. Got no use for Jeanne whatever-her-name is. If she's dead or something, I could care less. So you folks are just wasting my time and yours and maybe you ought to move along and let Witchy and I to get our heads together so we can earn a few dollars…" She went high on her toes to glare at Suzanne. "…So we can pay the doggone bills and maybe find new people to travel with. *Right, Suzanne?*"

* * *

Andi's glance to him was more than conversational punctuation. She seemed to be caught off-guard and her eyes were asking for reinforcements. He reached into his jacket pocket for the touch of soft leather and currency that didn't need to be folded.

"Tell you what, Miss Evans. About how much do you think you need to take care of things, right now?"

Casey's eyes followed his hands as he opened the wallet and a fan of hundred-dollar bills emerged. "You're joking, right? This is some kind of a come-on and —"

"No, ma'am. I'd very much like you to hear what Andi has to say, and if there's something I can do to help in the meantime, I'd be pleased to —"

Casey emitted a sigh and her shoulders drooped. "Right now, this very minute?"

"Yes. Right now."

"About twelve hundred. That's what Suzanne screwed us out of with those road boys last night."

Clay began to count it out.

"Plus another one-seventy five for, you know, incidentals."

"And the truck payment?"

"Three-eighty-nine fifty."

"Can I round that up to four?"

"Mister, you can round it as much as you'd like. But you know what? I'd rather be flat-out busted than to get into it with a couple of lawyer-types about my mother. She ran off with a no-account..." Again on her tiptoes and calling out toward Suzanne "...Just like someone who *used* to be a real good friend..."

Clay finished the count. "I've got nineteen hundred in cash, which should tide you over. This is not a loan. It's yours, no strings. That's it." He held it out toward her. The horse took a sniff but evidently decided it was not edible.

Casey stared at the wad of cash, then waved it off. "No. I can't accept it. I make my own way, have for about all of my twenty-five years, and don't want to be beholden to nobody."

Andi cocked an eyebrow. "You're too proud to accept a gift?"

Casey grinned. "Ma'am, you don't know life on the rodeo circuit. There isn't such a thing as a gift. There's luck, sometimes, but there can be good luck and there can be bad luck, and most of the time you can't tell the difference." Witchy appeared to be getting restless and Casey tugged on the bridle to get the mare back under control. She turned to face him. "So, Mister — was it Garrison? — manners tell me to say thank you very kindly, but no, keep your money. Like usual, I'll figure something out, okay?"

Andi snatched the money from Clay's fingers and lowered her voice as she pressed it into Casey's palm. "Pride's a good thing, Miss Evans. But knowledge is better. Trust me on that. A couple of weeks ago, I was out of work, flat broke, no idea what I'd be doing next. Then a guy came along and did the exact same thing as Clay, just now. All I had to do was listen. Before you argue with me — and I'd truly understand if you did — just tuck this into your pocket, get your game head on, the horse's too, and do your thing in the ring. After, we can meet somewhere if you'd like to hear what we have to say, then make up your mind. No strings. No obligations. No lies. If you still don't really care, you go on with your life. I get paid either way, so it makes absolutely no difference to me. But, trust me. There is a *lot* of money involved."

Casey's fingers curled around the money. She looked at Clay. "Is your partner for real?"

Not a good time to ask what was going on, what Andi had planned. But a good time to lay back, let the play run. "Absolutely."

She studied the cash and offered to return it. "Mister, it's a real sweet thing, but I just can't take a gift like that."

Clay pointed to Casey's hip. "That a piece of baling twine?"

"Yessir. I don't like leaving stray line layin' around, with the stock and all."

"Tell you what. I'll buy that piece of rope. I figure nineteen hundred dollars is a fair price."

She chuckled. "Mister, you're crazier'n most of those steers they use in places like this." After a pause she pulled the twine from her pocket and handed it to Clay. "Nineteen hundred dollars. You sure about this?"

"Yes, Casey, I am."

Andi interrupted. "Well, okay, then. How about we meet up later at that place near the arena?"

"The Steakhouse? It's nice for supper. If you want music, dancing, a regular bar, you ought to try the Painted Pony, just a bit further up. They're open late."

Andi smiled. "Works for me. Now, you get focused on what you need to do, and I'm very sorry for interrupting your preparation. Is there anything I can do to help with Suzanne?"

Casey folded the cash and stuffed it into the right front pocket of her jeans. "No. It's my issue. I'll deal with it."

"Catch you later?"

"We'll see. Maybe."

Chapter Twenty-Nine

This time, Clay's bribe to buy chairs was only fifty bucks, despite the bar being twice as crowded, twice as loud and the draft beer only half as good. The music was first-class honky-tonk for a second-class audience, almost all of which looked under thirty-five.

She asked, "So you have some country-western experience?"

"Hard not to when you spend time in Oklahoma."

By ten-forty-five, beer and bourbon had lubricated the rodeo crowd, liberating denim guys in big hats from any sense of bashful propriety and rhinestone women in cute boots from any sense of modesty.

Andi longed for Pete's and music gentle on the ear. Most of a steak that could have fed a dozen people remained on her plate, her belly full with the sensation of a waistline losing control. In her mind, patience slipped away, like summer in late September, and a sense of helplessness drooped into despair.

Andi pursed her lips. "She's not going to show. I blew it. I pushed too hard."

"It's early."

"It was early at six-thirty. She didn't do well in the race, probably not even place money, and I bet she's halfway to Utah or someplace. With Suzanne, the horses, the nineteen hundred bucks. I pressed it, too hard. Blew the whole thing. Pike's going to be upset. We're not going to be paid and I'm beginning to believe

I'm not cut out for this."

He sipped beer. "Don't beat yourself up. I'm the one who counted out a wad of cash, maybe squirreling the deal. Not much experience greasing palms. My dad would have done it right."

She shrugged. "Maybe it was meant to be. I was starting to wonder about what we're going to tell her. I mean, she has utterly no clue. She's got a life, a path she's on, and we're going to totally demolish it."

Clay grunted. "Doesn't sound like much of a life to me. Up to her ears in debt, a mess with this buddy person, Suzanne, back against the wall, nomadic life on the rim of disaster."

Andi fondled the half-empty glass in her hand. "But it's *her* life, on *her* terms, Clay. And it's not just the money. If she thinks the people around her now aren't all that great, what's she going to think of Conrad, Carlene and the others? Not to mention Gideon himself?"

Clay finished his beer and looked like he was thinking about another. "Oh, I don't know. I bet pride comes a lot easier with a billion dollars. Besides, we have no real sense of what she'd want in life. Just what we saw, today."

"I think I'd want to know. I mean, know who my real family was."

"If it is her real family."

She sighed. "Tell you what. Why don't I sleep on the cot, you take the bed, get a good night's rest. We'll slink home tomorrow and try to find Sister Number Two."

* * *

Lukewarm beer, on top of an oversized ribeye about two minutes beyond medium well and a back-alley California Bordeaux, left a heavy, full sensation in Clay's belly. Another round wasn't going to help.

Andi looked tired, worn down. Long day, then being stood up by a no-show. *Yeah. First and goal. Easy score. Uh-huh. Didn't see the free safety in the end zone...*

Bar patrons seemed to enjoy routine honky-tonkin', the kind that might lead to a parking lot brawl and a couple of drunk-and-disorderlies later. Midnight or twelve-thirty, maybe, the highlight of an otherwise quiet third shift. Meantime, some clung to the bar while others had coupled up to fill a small dance floor, two-steppers drifting in a clockwise circle.

And then Casey appeared, just inside the hall. He stood, raised a hand and waved it like a flag. "She's here."

Andi whirled and echoed his signal. "If this works out, I get the bed."

"If this works out, you can have the whole room."

As Casey navigated the darkened room, punctuated by reddish and orange stage lights, she focused on the floor. Her wide-brimmed hat would have made her totally unrecognizable as the distance between them closed.

Andi's smile evaporated when Casey looked up, six feet away. "Oh, my... what happened?"

Clay peered at her face. Right cheek swollen, bruise forming around her eye, split lip on the lower left.

Casey shrugged. "Uh, just a little mishap. Um, fell off the stupid horse, is all. It's nothin', really."

Andi shook her head. "It's not nothing. And that doesn't look like the sort of injury that comes from falling off a horse. Here, sit. We'll get some ice or something."

Casey raised a hand to signal Clay to stay put, but accepted his chair. She winced on the way down.

"Like I said, took a fall. Just hit my head in some junk near the stall's all. Careless, I guess."

He said, "Can I get you something, a drink?"

She shook her head and reached into her shirt pocket. "I came to give you back the money. Well, most of it, anyway. I'll be good for the rest, I swear."

Andi leaned in to hold Casey's hand. "Okay. Now, you want to tell me what actually happened? I don't believe you fell off Witchy. Or any other horse for that matter."

Casey's eyes misted over, the tip of her tongue testing the split lip for discomfort. "It's not important. The important thing is that I've got to hit the road. Tonight. I'm all loaded up, ready to go."

He spoke as softly as he could to be heard in the noisy bar. "And Suzanne?"

"We're done. I'm going solo."

Time to back away, let Andi take the lead.

"It's okay, Casey. I want you to keep the money, cover your expenses. But you could help me out here, tell me what happened. It's all right. You're with friends."

"Mister Stiles, he said I had to return the money. Otherwise, there'll be the devil to pay."

"Why?"

She tried to chuckle but winced instead. "It's like this. Ellis Stiles is a big dog in WPRA — that's the governing body of women's rodeo — and what he says goes."

Clay nodded. "Or even getting into competition is difficult?"

"Impossible. So. I came by to give you the money. It's sixteen hundred. He kept three for himself."

Andi's jaw dropped. "He did?"

"Yeah. Sorry. Look, I'll get it to you as soon as I can, I swear."

Clay said, "Don't worry about it. Andi, I think it's about time."

Casey looked puzzled. "Time for what?"

Andi tightened her grip on Casey's hands. "That matter we talked about earlier. Look, I don't know any other way to explain this except to say that if we can prove who you really are, you're going to be wealthy beyond your wildest dreams."

"I don't understand."

Clay said, "You might be an heiress to a fortune. All we need to prove it is a DNA test."

Casey's eyes drooped. "Now I've heard everything."

Andi kept eye contact locked on Casey. "If you don't believe me, then let's do a blood test. No match, no harm. And I'm sure you'll be well rewarded for your inconvenience. But if you are a match —"

"How much money?"

"The reward or the fortune?"

"Pick one."

Clay said, "Over a billion dollars."

"I find a million dollars hard to believe, sir."

"He said *billion*, Casey. And it's true."

She scowled into a skeptical expression. "And if I just leave town, real quiet?"

Clay said, "You keep your life as it is. This all stays confidential. But If you'd like, we can stay connected. Maybe through your, um, Uncle Willard. If you'd like, we can get in touch with him, maybe —"

She firmly shook her head. "No. Leave him out of this."

Andi cocked her head. "Why? Is there a problem we don't know about?"

"No, not with Willard, who o'course isn't my real uncle. Just the guy who raised me after my lousy mother split."

Andi smiled. "Who wasn't really your mother. You were adopted. An under-the-table adoption." She tugged the photograph from her bag. "I think this is your real mother. Her name was Kimberly Spence."

Casey studied the image. "Is she still..."

"No. I'm afraid she's deceased. Soon after you were born."

Casey's thumb gently stroked the image. "I... I... Don't... She... looks..."

Andi nodded. "Yes. So very much like you. But there's more."

Casey looked up. A tear formed in the corner of her swollen eye and trickled down her cheek. "More?"

"You have a sister. An identical twin."

* * *

A shadowy movement to her left shattered Andi's concentration. Clay noticed it, too. Standing to her right and just behind, he turned and took a step, emerging on her left side.

Polished boots, western-cut tan suit, string tie, matching wide-brimmed hat. Six feet, six-one, one-ninety. Toothpick. The guy Clay annoyed at the rodeo arena.

Clay moving in between, hands up, palms outward. "I need you to take a step back, sir. This is a —"

The man scowled. "Step aside, City-Boy."

"I don't think so."

"Look, boy, I'm Ellis Stiles, and I'm paying a little visit here to make sure she returned your fancy New York money. And to give you some friendly advice. Real neighborly, now. We don't need no trouble here."

Casey crossed her arms and squared her shoulders. "I did just like you said, Mister Stiles. I gave them the money."

Andi stood to double the barricade between Casey and Stiles. "Only it was three hundred less than we gave her earlier."

Stiles showed a knowing grin. "Well, honey, that's because I got expenses, you see. So I get a sort of a fee for this kind of business."

Clay's eyes narrowed. "And what kind of business would that be, sir?"

"Why keeping the riff-raff, the low-life, out of town, boy."

"I see. So you'd be the big dog around here?"

"You betcha, pal. Now, I'm the top man with the rodeo, and my brother's the mayor and I got cousins up and down the city police force, county too. And trust me, buddy, we can make all kinds of trouble for people who, well, you know, step out of line."

"That right?"

"That's right. Now, I tell you what. You two city people just make your way out of here, real quiet-like, and I'll take charge of this little gal."

Andi's jaw tightened and she knew her eyes went cold. "And why would you take charge of her? Oh, yes. You're the guy who hit her, aren't you? I'm thinking felony assault, wouldn't you agree, Clay?"

The toothpick in Stiles' mouth shifted from left to right, but his eyes were expressionless and his hands drifted downward. "You'd best control your woman, boy."

Clay said, "I'd like you to keep your hands where I can see them, sir."

"What, you think I got a piece?"

"I know I do."

"That right? And maybe you got yourself a real fancy city permit to carry?"

"Yessir. I do."

"You talk like a cop."

"People say that. A lot."

In a pleading tone, Casey said, "Mister Stiles, *please*. These folks mean no harm. Just trying to help me out. We're about to leave anyway, no harm done. Would that be okay?"

Stiles remained focused on Andi and Clay. The toothpick rolled to the other side of his lips. "You just hush, gal. Mind your manners."

Clay raised his palms in a gesture of submission. "Now, let's take it easy. Like the ladies said, we're about to leave, we don't want any trouble, and certainly don't want to be a problem. I don't think we've broken any laws, I don't think you have a probable for anything, and I know that all your local people are going to see is our tail lights, heading out of town. Okay?"

For several seconds, Stiles glared, then nodded. "You just do what you said, boy. We'll let it go. This one time." He took a step backward, turned, and strolled away, the dancers on the floor separating to open a path toward the door.

* * *

Andi looked furious, Casey scared. But it was no time for heroics, or even justice. "Okay. Do exactly what I said. No fuss, no argument. I'll settle up while you two get the vehicles. Casey, where's your truck and trailer?"

"Left side of the lot. I was only planning to stop in, give you the money, leave."

Andi said, "We're on the right. We'll go to our car and I'll drive you to your truck. We'll both come back for Clay. Are you okay with that?"

Casey nodded and stood. As they moved away, a bar maid delivering pitchers on a big platter crossed their path.

Fifty ought to do it. "This is for our table. Are we good?"

"Yeah, sure, mister. You need change?"

"No."

She beamed and wished them a pleasant evening.

Mercury vapor light from low poles outlined vehicles in the lot, almost all pickups. The half dozen guys into the open area directly ahead were in silhouette.

One guy stepped forward. Ellis Stiles.

"We're leaving, just as we promised, Stiles. No trouble."

"You say. I say you got my woman." He took a wide stance a dozen feet away and tapped a fist with an open hand. "Now, I just want you to show your fancy city-boy piece, real easy, real slow. Then I want to see it on the ground."

Andi extended an arm in front of Casey to signal her to be

still.

Clay raised his hands, palms out. "We don't want any trouble, mister."

"Your kind's always trouble, boy."

"Okay, my friend. I'm pulling my weapon from a shoulder holster. Let's all stay cool."

None of the silhouettes moved, but their hands were in shadows. The toothpick moved across Stiles' mouth and his fists were on his waist. Clay gently eased his weapon from the holster, gripping the butt with two fingers. He displayed it and warily lowered it to the pavement, hoping Andi would recognize an odd move for anyone who'd been a cop. Stiles gestured for Clay to step to the left.

Andi said, "Take it easy, Clay. Just don't hurt him."

Stiles chuckled and smacked his fist again. He wore tight police-issue gloves and grinned when he advanced. "Time to teach you some manners, city boy."

* * *

The three-eighty, thirteen in the clip and one in the chamber, came to Andi's right hand, as reflexively as a hairbrush. By the time she had taken a shooter's stance, she'd already ordered Casey to drop to the ground.

The line behind Stiles stirred, but her bark carried all the authority of a S.W.A.T team leader. They momentarily shuffled, confused as her aim swept left, right and left again. They obeyed her commands, hands above their heads, kneeling, hitting the pavement, face first.

Stiles never had a chance to see. Clay took three quick steps and doubled him over, dropped an elbow on his neck and caught the right hand as Stiles tumbled to the ground. A shriek of pain ricocheted off pavement and metal.

From his back pocket, Clay produced the short piece of baling twine and spun it around the howling man's wrist. "I'd lay real still if I were you pal. I think you might have a busted shoulder, and if you struggle, it's gonna hurt."

Chapter Thirty

Steaming water poured from the big pot, faster than Andi expected. She struggled to balance force of gravity against muscles in her forearms.

Meredith staffed a colander over the kitchen sink, wriggling it as cooked spaghetti tumbled in. "Keep going. You're doing great."

Two wine glasses waited at a safe distance. The hands of Casey Evans cupped a third as she echoed encouragement.

Meredith exuded confidence. "Go for it, Kit-Kit. It's perfect."

Discarding caution, Andi released the remaining water and pasta in a gush. Mer expertly shook the last water and deftly transferred enough spaghetti to feed six or seven football players into an oversized ceramic bowl, the bright yellow one with a band of spring flowers painted all the way around.

Andi deposited the cook pot on a cold stove burner. "So. I guess that's about it."

Casey beamed. "It looks terrific. I am *so* starved. Where should I sit?"

Meredith led the parade to a table decorated with plates, flatware, the open bottle of wine, a bowl of a heat-and-serve sauce and a basket of warmed-up garlic bread.

Andi said, "Anywhere. Usually it's just me, sometimes Mer. Can I get anything else?"

"Nope. This is perfect."

Andi took a breath. "I sure hope so. I've never really made

pasta before. I'm afraid I'm not a very experienced cook."

Mer was quick to the rescue. "Which makes you a whole lot better than me, queen of microwave. Which even then I get wrong most of the time."

Andi laughed. "You don't!"

"I do."

Casey smiled. "That makes three of us. Life on the circuit is all diners and fast food. But, hey, who's any good at cooking these days?"

In unison, Andi and Meredith blurted, "Clay."

* * *

A pair of chicken leg quarters sizzled in a nest of heavy stainless, a favorite ten-inch skillet, on a thin virgin olive oil pond. Clay's tongs confirmed what he'd already guessed. He gently transferred the meat to a stock pot of simmering vegetables.

A sauce pan of seasoned roux had just come together, but he paused to sip beer that had already warmed to margins of palatable.

Six feet away, Mitch leaned against the counter, clutching his glass. "Oh, man, that's a sweet-smelling meal you got going. About how long?"

"Couple of minutes to let the chicken finish with the veggies and sauce. We'll be okay."

"Okay?"

"Yeah. Not used to the stove yet."

"Clay, you can't top this at any of those downtown places. You're about the only guy who's ever turned vegetables into something a lot more than the green stuff they use to decorate plates. For sure, buddy."

Clay pretended to ignore the compliment. Half a dozen guys in chef jackets he knew could do this a lot better than he. But it was all right for on-the-fly, and way ahead of road food. A few stirs with a long ladle and about right. He plated the meal, vegetables first, the quarters arranged nicely atop and slightly left of center, then some extra sauce.

"Okay, Mitch, let's eat."

"Need another brewski?"

"I'm good."

Nostrils flaring, Mitch eased into a chair, a napkin finding the open collar of his shirt. He gathered knife and fork, which hovered over the plate for the few seconds Clay needed to seat himself, then launched an assault. When he came up for air, he said, "So. Andi's hosting Twin Number One and you got out of Wyoming without getting busted, which was good, and the horse got back to Kentucky?"

"Yep." The smooth sauce might be better with a little tarragon. "We beat feet to just outside Jackson Hole, snagged one of those anonymous motels. Put in a call to the uncle who isn't —"

"— Willard Gentry?"

Clay nodded. "He flew in the next day, picked up the truck, trailer and horse to drive back to Kentucky. As soon as he left, Andi and Casey booked a flight to here."

"Casey's horse ought to be glad to get back to decent grass and racing pals. This is about the best chicken I ever ate, buddy. So. This horse farm. Pretty big spread?"

"Seemed like it. Willard mentioned that the place was up for sale, so he didn't know how long he'd be able to board the horse. A buckskin grade mare she called 'Witchy.'"

"Wow. All kinds of horse expertise, bro."

Clay chuckled. "Not really."

"Yeah. So you actually busted the guy's arm?"

"Shoulder. At first, I thought I might have just separated it, but they said in the paper it was broke."

Mitch stabbed at a patch of cut green beans. "Serves the dude right. You shoulda taken his whole arm off."

"Actually, it was almost accidental. I just wanted to get out of there. But you know how it goes."

Mitch chuckled. "Yeah, like that one time, when you clocked that doofus linebacker from West High..."

"The unnecessary roughness was a bad call."

"Uh-huh. But didn't see him doing any cheap shots after that."

Clay shrugged and carved a slice of chicken. "What have we got on the adoption of the second twin? The Wade woman."

"Marilyn Wade. The trail went cold in Sharon — you know, just east of Youngstown? — twenty-two years ago. All I could run down was a vice arrest and a bunch of charges from the Mercer County District Attorney."

Clay succumbed to a trip to the refrigerator and the last six-pack from the case. Enough for another round after dinner after Mitch agreed to another bottle. "So what happened?"

"One of their regular sweeps of truck stops and the rest area out there along I-80. Bagged the Wade woman and a bunch of others. The usual. Possession — cocaine, I think — soliciting, prostitution, blah-blah-blah. Released on bail two days later. The guy at the D-A's said it was more to get the trafficking out of the county than anything, so a low bail and nobody surprised when everyone skipped."

"And the baby?"

"That's the twist. Child Protective Services comes in, takes the kid. Usually it's a foster care situation and confidential, but the clerk I talked to screwed up."

Clay popped the cap on his bottle. "How so?"

"She mumbles something about Wade's sister, and I go like, 'Oh, yeah, the sister, what's-her-name,' and the clerk says 'Emily' and I say 'Right, right, thanks very much.'"

"So you believe Marilyn abandoned the baby."

"Yeah, I think so. I mean, the last thing a hooker needs is a kid, especially if it's not her own."

* * *

Meredith turned back the red-checked towel and lifted the basket, bearing the last slice of garlic bread, offering it to Casey.

"No, no. I'm good, thanks. Stuffed, in fact."

"Andi?"

"All yours, Mer-Bear."

"You're sure?"

"I'm sure. Casey?"

Casey shook her head. Her eyes focused on the nearly empty glass of wine in her hand. "Mer-Bear. That's really sweet."

Meredith blushed while Andi explained. "As in Care-bear, from the old cartoon show. Mer's been my best friend, since like forever."

"Nice. In rodeo, we often have buddies — people who are sort of friends, who travel together to save on expenses. Gas, motels, someone to kind of watch your back. But not really close, you know?"

Enough wine remained in the bottle to fill two glasses and half a third, which was okay because she didn't really need any more. Mer and Casey accepted refills. "So, Suzanne was a buddy, then?"

"Yeah, but not the best of friends. Like I said, she got all star-ry-eyed over a bronc buster who sweet-talked her out of the cash we had and then blew town. Men. It never changes." She paused as the glass reached her lips. "Well, except for your partners, I'm sure. They seem like stand-up guys. The job Clay did on Mister Stiles was just so... Wow. Imagine that. I still call the creep 'Mister'."

Andi leaned forward. "It's okay."

Casey's voice firmed. "Yes. That's all yesterdays. What do you guys think happened to my sister?"

Meredith had cleared the table and settled into her chair for the last glass of wine. "Mitch had tracked the infant, who was two years old by then, to the Sharon area. That's just on the western edge of Pennsylvania, and a little east of Youngstown. Cops out there prefer crime, all kinds, to stay in Ohio, so they evidently do a lot of raids, mostly for show. Mitch lucked out when he got the name of Marilyn's sister, Emily, and I did some property searching in Mercer County. Maybe have a lead."

Casey's eyes widened.

Andi said, "Meredith used to work in real estate and knows her way around a deed recorder's office."

"Ah, okay..."

Meredith folded her hands on the table. "It turns out there's a diner just off the interstate, owned by one Emily Wade Jacobs. She and her husband ran the restaurant for a while before he died, and she took it over. Apparently there were some silent investors, but when Fred Jacobs died, they dropped out of sight, leaving Emily with the business. Mound of debt, too, but her credit rating's been solid ever since."

Casey nodded. "And my sister?"

Andi's tapped her fingertips on the glass. "That's where we come in. Ever been to western Pennsylvania?"

* * *

Mitch patted his belly. "Dude, that's one of those best-ever meals. Man. If you opened a restaurant, everybody in town would gain, like, fifteen pounds. Anyway, you're probably all stoked up for a road trip to ol' Sharon, P-A."

Clay gathered plates and flatware. "That's great work, Mitch. I'm not all that stoked. All the travel's taking a toll. I don't think Andi likes it very much, either."

"She's doing good. Meredith says, anyway."

The phone came to life, and for a moment Clay couldn't recall its location.

Mitch laughed. "Behind you, bro. And speaking of Andi..."

Clay waved him off, struggling to tamp down the heat in his ears as he said, "Hello."

A man's voice, distant and tentative, responded. "Mister Garrison?"

Annoyance blended with suspicion. *Fraud one-oh-one. Never say yes to a cold call on a phone.* "Who's asking?"

"Mister Garrison, this is Chief Warren Daniels, Miami-Dade, Criminal Investigations Division. Do you have a moment?"

Clay shoved the dinner conversation and thoughts of Andi to the side, to grasp for recollection about an application to Miami-Dade Police Department, maybe many months ago. "I do, sir."

"Mister Garrison, I'm looking at an application for our department you made some time ago. We've kept it on file. At the present time, I have two openings in C-I-D, Homicide. I've got some good recommendations about you and wondered if you still might be available."

Understatement of the year. But little red flags popped up like targets on a combat range. Like how the guy had his current number, even where he had just moved. After all this time, the source of the recommendation. And why a division chief made the call instead of a human resources clerk.

Daniels fractured speculation. "Mister Garrison? Is there some day or time we could discuss it?"

"Yessir, I'm still here. If it's okay, sir, could I give you a return call tomorrow? I need to check my calendar."

"That would be fine." He gave Clay a phone number and closed with, "It's a good unit, Garrison. Hope to hear from you soon. Have a nice evening."

Clay disconnected, drummed his fingertips on the table and said. "Can you get me a number for the Miami-Dade Police Department?"

Mitch reached for his notebook computer. "Yeah, sure. Florida? Gotta be Baxter. Did he swear out a complaint on you?" He tapped keys. "Okay, here we go, the main number." And he recited slowly as Clay tapped it into the phone.

An instant voice. "Miami-Dade Police. Is this an emergency?"

"No, just a question."

"Yessir?"

"Do you have a Chief Warren uh, Danny, Daniel, something like that?"

"Chief Warren *Daniels*?"

"Of course, that's him."

"Criminal Investigation Division. Would you like me to transfer the call?"

"Is that extension twenty-one-fifteen?"

"Yessir. I can connect you —"

"No, that's okay, thanks." Again Clay hung up. "Okay, the name's legit, and the callback number matches."

"So what's going on, bro?"

"Job offer, a good one."

"No kidding?"

"No —" The phone rang again to interrupt. Andi's voice had an immediate calming effect.

She said, "Clay, you won't believe this, but I just got a call. Ohio BC-Double-I. Bureau of Criminal Identification and Investigation. Major crime. They want to set up an interview. It could be a huge career break."

The memory of Conrad flared up in his mind. Conrad, leaning back in his chair, looking down his nose, his hands clasped high on his belly. The guy who pulls strings.

He said. "That's great! So you said...?"

"I, uh, stayed non-committal."

"Because...?"

"Well, I..." She paused. "Oh, wow. You got a call, too. Didn't you?"

"Miami-Dade, Homicide."

"No! Actual *homicide?* And?"

Clay took a breath and took an emotional step back. "And I think I'm going to find a diner in Sharon, Pennsylvania."

Chapter Thirty-One

Andi gripped the steering wheel just the way it's taught in pursuit training and periodically glanced at the rear view mirror. "How far to the exit?"

Clay reviewed notes in his hand, then checked the mirror. "Five or six miles. And no, I don't see our tail." He considered the possibility of coincidence, like the kind common on long stretches of interstate highways, where the same vehicles could be seen again and again.

"Darn. I could have sworn..."

In the back seat, directly behind Andi, Casey watched the rear window. "Just the same three trucks and the left lane hogger, same's as the last ten miles. Almost feel sorry, Andi."

"It's okay. I just have this sensation...sounds silly, I guess."

Which it didn't. Great cops have a sixth sense, the one that says the other five might be wrong, the one that can't really be taught, the one that would have made her an outstanding officer. Reason number four hundred and seventy whatever that she was an amazing partner. The dark blue SUV, late model, Jersey plates, that had been tagging along behind them for at least eighty miles, seemed to have disappeared.

Andi first spotted it when it trailed them into the last rest stop. She had asked, "Who comes into a rest area, parks way down at the far end, and doesn't even open the door to let a dog out for exercise?"

Point made, and now it was time to say her instincts were still respected.

Casey called out. "There they are. Just pulling around that red truck."

Front seat attention went to the mirrors.

Clay said, "Got it, Andi. Stay with the road. At least two, probably male, couple of hundred yards, but not closing. Your plan is starting to look real good."

"You bet it is. You're sure they're hanging back?"

Casey said, "Absolutely. Just keeping pace. I guess those trucks were slowing on the grade."

"Okay, guys, we've got a curve at the crest of this rise. I'm going to get into the right lane whenever you say, Clay."

"A mile, maybe. You've got room."

"I don't want too much, but that white rig'll pick up pace as soon as we clear the hill."

"You're okay."

She said to Casey, "How we doing back there?"

"He's right behind the lane hogger, but not signaling he wants to pass."

Andi smiled. "Perfect." The vehicle picked up just a little more speed to ease further ahead of the white rig.

"Half a mile."

"Got it. Okay, hold on."

She hit the turn signal, accelerated and swerved into the exit lane. The white rig driver seemed unfazed. Andi slowed sharply as they approached a stop sign. Behind, several trucks roared past. To the cross traffic, she muttered, "C'mon, c'mon, c'mon." Abruptly, she punched it into a right turn.

The blue SUV zoomed down the exit ramp.

Clay said, "There's the diner, five hundred yards. Okay, Casey, when we get into the lot, you're going to get out with me, real fast, and we're going straight into the restaurant. Got it?"

"Yessir."

Andi waited until the last possible moment to stomp on the brakes and turn into a crowded asphalt lot, racing past a wall of tractor-trailers and a dozen passenger vehicles. She glanced at the mirror, muttering, "Too slow, too slow. *Argh!*"

The blue SUV appeared a hundred feet behind them.

Andi cursed. "Change of plans, Case. Clay's gonna beat feet, but I need you to drop down onto the seat, as if you weren't here."

Clay understood. "Andi, go around the side, yeah, yeah, there, use that pickup to block the view."

"Got it." She accelerated, swerved through a turn with a one-handed spin of the wheel, skidded to a halt. "Go, go!"

Clay sprinted to the side entrance. Behind him, the sound of spewing gravel told him she was away. Inside, he turned to look. The SUV stayed with Andi. Not even a hint of doubt in his mind. The jerk had just made a mistake. She'd lead him into a town she didn't know, run him through a maze, lose him and be back in thirty minutes.

A cheery voice snared his attention. "You can just seat yourself, hon. I'll fetch you coffee and the specials sheet."

Booths lined the window side, shining aluminum coat poles punctuating each block of standard seating for four. Pull-down shades for late afternoon sun, still high in the air. On the left, a string of round stools, matching maroon vinyl, strung along a medium gray counter with a shimmering metal face on the front edge. Behind, the kitchen, three or four guys, working on brushed stainless.

The most empty space was in the field of stools, so he took the third just as the server arrived with a china cup on a saucer and a bubble pot of black coffee.

"Afternoon, sir. Here's today's specials. The pot roast is pretty good, and the meatloaf is fresh made. Both come with two sides." She pointed to a chalkboard adjacent to the service window. "And there's your choices today."

Clay accepted the coffee and went for a pair of packets of creamer. "Thanks. You know, I wonder if Emily might be working today? I believe she's the owner."

The server's smile withered. "You selling, mister?"

Clay casually stirred his coffee. "No ma'am. But I am here on a business matter. No problems, just need a couple of minutes of her time."

The server took half a step back and reflexively wiped the counter while giving him the suspicious eye. "Uh-huh. Well, let me just see if she's in today, while you have yourself a look at the menu. I'd give the meatloaf serious consideration."

After conferring with the waitress, a stout woman, five-four, fifties maybe, wearing a server's smock over a dark blouse and loose-fitting pants, marched toward him from the right. "Mister, I definitely admire initiative, but I'm not buying anything today. I'm happy with my current suppliers."

Clay extended a hand, which she took with a tentative, light touch and quickly let go. "Not selling anything, ma'am. I'm looking for someone and I've got some important news."

She squinted and looked past him. "You from one of those contest prize patrol things? They always have cameras and balloons and stuff."

"No m'am. My name is Clay Garrison. I'm a private investigator. I'm looking for the daughter of Marilyn Wade."

Emily laughed. "Mister, you come to the wrong place, way too late to boot. Marilyn was my sister all right, but she's been dead for oh, ten, twelve years now."

Clay offered a somber nod. "I see. And I'm very sorry for your loss."

"Yeah, well don't be. She was a drug addict, a prostitute, just the lowest low-life scum. She came through here a whole bunch of years ago, all high and mighty — had come into a bunch of money,

I learned that after I loaned her about all I had and she ran off with some tanker driver."

"Help me out here. About when was that?"

"Twenty years ago, maybe. Why?"

"And you learned of her death later?"

"Yeah, some sheriff called up one day, wondered if we wanted to spring for a funeral. Told him no way, so they did it themselves on the public dole."

"And where was that?"

"Texas. Some town near Dallas or something. I don't recall. But you ought to know that she wound up dead of a bunch of diseases and drugs and such, God knows where. They found her body after a couple of days in a dumpster behind a truck stop."

"Sorry."

"Don't be. They say she went through a whole lot of money she came into, a settlement or some scam, drugs and booze. She was trash, plain and simple."

Clay flipped through several sheets in his spiral notebook. "Sure hate to bring up bad memories, ma'am, but I had — let's see here — ah, yes." He stared at the pad like a slightly nearsighted person trying to focus. "Oh, yes. I understand she had a daughter?"

Dishes clattered from a spilled busing tray. Emily looked for the source of the noise, scowled, and turned back to face him. "Don't know nothing about that. Look, mister, if you want my advice, just let things lie. No need to dig up all kinds of ugly, you know? Marilyn caused enough pain to last five lifetimes."

"But if she had a daughter, maybe she might have left some sort of note, message, anything like that?"

"No. She didn't"

"It really would help our investigation if she did."

Emily crossed her arms, looking away again, this time with an expression of exasperation. "I said, no."

"I hear you." Clay took a sip of coffee. It needed a lot more cream. "Maybe I can leave you my card, just in case you remember something? I'm not out to hurt anyone. Just looking for Marilyn's daughter to share some good news, okay?"

"Listen, mister..." Abruptly Emily looked past him as she accepted the business card, "Yeah, sure. I'll do that." The card went into the pocket of her smock.

Clay turned to see what caught her attention. Andi and Casey had entered the diner, the light behind them giving each a glow. "Very nice. Who are they? I mean, you seem to know them."

Emily stared, only half paying attention, but quickly broke the self-inflicted spell. "Oh, nothing. That's my niece. Don't know the other person."

"Your niece?"

"That's right." A maternal smile grew on her face. "Hi, Allison. Off early today?"

* * *

Andi instinctively looked around, but only Casey stood nearby. Clay had to be talking with Emily Wade. No family resemblance at all. But she had clearly recognized Casey, mistaking her for...*an identical twin.*

Three seconds and four footsteps later, Emily looked flustered and apologized. "I'm sorry, miss, I confused you with someone else. Light must be playing tricks on me today. Or I'm just getting way too old."

Andi said, "Hi, Clay, nice to see you've found a good spot to park."

"Everything work out all right?"

"Oh, yes." More than all right. Elegant, chasing down the main streets of Sharon, being pursued instead of pursuing, until she perfectly timed a traffic light and made it on the yellow. The guy in the blue van ran the red, right in front of a local unit, which needed only five seconds to light him up and pull him over. She turned to Emily. "Hi. I'm Andrea Delvento, and he's my partner. I'll bet you're Emily Wade. I'd like to introduce you to Casey Evans."

Emily's eyes remained fixed on Casey, who extended a hand.

"Hi. So very nice to meet you, Mrs. Wade."

Clay said, "We were just talking about Emily's niece, Allison. And the light's not playing tricks on you, Emily. People confuse identical twins all the time."

Emily's jaw was agape and her eyes misty. "I'll be... I... I never knew."

Casey stepped in close and patted her arm. "It's okay, Mrs. Wade. Until a couple of days ago, neither did I."

"You look just like my Allison. Different hair, but..."

Casey smiled. "I'd love to meet her. Would that be okay?"

* * *

Two miles out of town, Mercer Veterinary Services occupied a low brick building resembling a house instead of an office. A gravel drive crunched under tires, a pleasant waiting room featured several barking dogs and wary cats accompanied by owners, and a receptionist who made the same mistake as Emily.

"Allison! I love what you've done with your hair!" Then a puzzled look. "But wait... Oh, gosh, ma'am, I am so sorry. You look just like one of our techs. How can I help you folks?"

Clay's expression remained placid, as if he did this sort of thing every day. Casey looked amused, just a bit anxious. "Actually, we're looking for Allison, Allison Wade. You said she was a tech?"

"Yes," the young woman said as she stood. "She works mostly with our large-animal service. Cows, horses, that kind of... Yes. I'll get her right away. Excuse me."

Casey bit her lower lip and concentrated on the floor.

"It's okay, Case. Take a breath. It's why we came, right?"

Sixty long seconds ticked away on a large clock hanging above a line of tan file cabinets along a beige wall from the reception window to a white doorway beyond. No turning back now. People always said the right thing to do is to let a family reconnect, no matter what the circumstances. They could figure things out for themselves, but they had the right to know. Still, no question that life was about to take an incredible turn for two women who had until just now a world in which they made their way. Maybe not a good way. Maybe it should change. But change — so unpredictable. *I always wanted to be a police officer. Like the guys in my family who were role models for decent. Maybe it was, for the guys. But it might have been nice to decide for myself, not have a decision shoved down my throat.* This was not going to be one of those nice little happily-ever-after things. Dreams, the kind people like to have, weren't necessarily going to come true for the twins. Yet now it didn't matter. Destiny was in motion. But maybe justice could be, too.

She caught Clay's attention, wondering if he thought the same. thing. Outwardly, he looked detached, professional, like she needed to do, right now. She took a breath and squared her shoulders.

A young woman entered, still focused on tugging a blue exam glove from her left hand. She organized a smile and looked up. "Hi. I'm Allison... Wade... How..." Her voice trailed off and her jaw moved but made no sound.

Only Clay had the presence of mind to speak. "Miss Wade, I'd like to introduce you to your sister. Is there somewhere we can go to talk?"

Chapter Thirty-Two

Andi marched into the office. "So what do you think?"

She twirled twice as Meredith looked up, then did a third, slower, turn.

Meredith's jaw hung open and an expression of uncertainty flooded her face. "What did you do to your hair? And that outfit — it has to be... No, wait. It's the sort of thing my mother would have worn."

"Does it work?"

"It *does*. That is, if you want to be on a magazine cover twenty or thirty years ago."

Andi beamed and bounded away. "Perfect. Hey, Clay, looking for an opinion."

Meredith sighed. "That's a wasted effort, Kit-Kit."

Clay dismissed a thick report and tossed it into a stack while Andi twirled again. "Opinion. On how I look."

He shrugged.

Behind her, Meredith said, "Told you so."

"Clay, does this make me look, well, kind of old-fashioned?"

Again he shrugged. "I guess. If you say so. So what was wrong with before?"

Meredith explained. "She's trying for a retro look. Wait a sec." She lunged for her desk, two steps away, and her hands fluttered through a stack of folders. From the fourth one down, she pulled a copy of a photograph and held it aloft. "Kimberly Spence. You've got the same hairstyle, same kind of top."

Clay took a closer look. "She's right. What's going on?"

"We're going to meet with Conrad, right?"

"Yes, but —"

Andi plopped down into her chair. "So. Last time we were there, he kept looking at me, kind of staring. At first I thought he was just kind of creepy. Even called him on it. He said something about a striking resemblance. And then I got thinking about how Kimberly looked."

"So the idea is to see if you can't get under his skin?"

"Absolutely. I'm just itching really lean on that guy, and thought I could put him on edge with a little shift of hairstyle, maybe an outfit that belongs from a time he'd rather forget."

Meredith offered immediate support, but Clay seemed reticent.

"Okay, Clay, what's the problem?"

"My turn at bat. I mean, if you really want to do it —"

"No, no. It's okay. It's just that last time you were uncomfortable and — trust me on this — I want to pull his chain so bad I can... Well, you get the idea."

"If it's all that important..."

A sense of wariness slithered through her shoulders and up her neck. "You think I'm going to come on too hard, probably blow it. Look. I understand. I've got a tendency to press..."

Meredith crossed her arms. "You *can* be a little competitive at times."

Andi dryly said, "Thanks, Mer."

Meredith raised her hands in submission. "Okay. I'm going to get back to getting case files organized."

"Good plan. So, Clay, did I just hear a vote of no confidence?"

He laughed and put on his supportive smile. "Not at all. I think you'd probably really rattle his cage."

"But?"

"But it's time for me to take a turn."

She tugged hair back over her ear. The style was uncomfortable, probably ridiculous. "This is not about back-and-forth, is it? This is about getting even for Oklahoma, having your chain pulled by those idiots in city hall. It's about your sense of —"

"Yeah. It is."

Which of course, it was. She'd confronted her own yesterdays and felt really good about it, but all along Clay was sort of hanging back a bit, being cautious. Until the parking lot in Cody. He needed the shot at Conrad, even though it really made no difference to the case. With lab reports confirming the twins, it was just a matter of setting up a meeting with Gideon Pike to let the old man have a chance at dragging both of them into the quagmire of the Pike clan. But somehow, he wouldn't blow it, not in the way she most likely would, coming on like gangbusters in the bad-cop role. He'd come up with his own game plan and maybe lay one of his subtle traps to boot. His gaze was steady, unflinching, but more hopeful than hostile.

She said, "Well, okay, then. You have a plan?"

"Yep."

She gasped. "You're going for Mister Milquetoast! You're going to go in all kinds of soft and deferential and lead him into a trap. Gosh, that's elegant. Can I be a prop?"

"Absolutely."

She kept her gaze on Clay. "Meredith?"

"Yeah, Andi."

"When's our appointment?"

"If you leave in the next twenty minutes, you'll be right on time. Take the turnpike, though."

A faint smile from Clay. "So, shall we go have some fun?"

"Sounds good. Beats paperwork any day of the week."

* * *

When the aide ushered Clay into the gloomy cavern, Conrad was working his way through blue folders, each shrouding thin documents. He shifted them to a stack of three on his left.

Without looking up, Conrad softly said, "Take a seat, Garrison. I'll only be a couple of minutes."

"Yessir. Thank you."

Another folder migrated to the competed stack and the next one opened before him. Except for the folders and an old-fashioned pen holder, the empty desk shone like glass in the half-light. His eyes scanned a document and briefly on a paragraph near the end. Pursing his lips, he signed it with a flourish and added it to the done pile.

He asked. "Good trip? You seem to be right on time."

"Yessir. No trouble with traffic."

Conrad opened the last folder. "Good, good. I hate traffic." This one had multiple pages, clipped to the top of the folder, and he lifted the sheets one at a time until he was satisfied, found the end, and applied the pen, which returned to the holder before him.

The aide had been waiting to the right, behind Clay, and silently approached to accept the documents. Conrad tightened his tie and ran a finger around the inside of his collar before leaning back in his chair.

"Thank you for coming, Garrison. I was beginning to worry we might not see you again. Where's your assistant, that pretty girl you had with you last time?"

Clay sat forward in his seat, hands folded in his lap. "Andi. My partner should be along in a minute or so. Freshening up and all that after the drive."

"Of course. Women have to do whatever they do, don't they? Well, Garrison, I'm on a little bit of a time crunch here, so let's get to it."

"Yessir. Suits me."

"As I said, we weren't expecting to see you again. We thought you might have come to your senses, moved on to some sort of personal injury trash or something."

"Excuse me, sir. Who's 'we'?"

"Well, the family, of course. I assure you that everyone's eager to put this entire sordid matter behind us, once and for all."

"And why would that be, sir?"

"Come on, Garrison. I'm sure the old man admitted he's running out of time with his periodic and pathetic efforts to prove a myth. A *myth*, Garrison. That's all it is. And I'm sure that by now, you realize it as well."

Clay forced a smile and allowed his eye contact to wander. "Just trying to earn my pay, sir. The right thing to do."

"Ah. Of course. The man of principle, the fellow who must do the honorable thing. It cost you a promising career, Garrison. A chance to atone for the sins of a weak, inept father, eh?"

"I do my best, sir."

The pinky finger of Conrad's right hand stopped stroking the edge of his desk and began to tap on it. "Tell me, Garrison, have you given any thought to your plans after you've failed on this foolish project?"

"Not sure, sir. Maybe look for police work again."

Conrad nodded and steepled his fingertips under his nose. "A noble goal. I often hear about opportunities of all kinds. Take, for example, the Miami-Dade Police Department. They have a first-class investigation unit. And, of course, it's Florida. I have a financial connection down there. You've met Baxter, of course. He's the kind of man who can be useful in the money sector."

"Interesting guy, Baxter."

"Well, yes. Not as strong as us, I'd say, but interesting."

"By 'us' do you mean —"

Conrad smiled. "Why, you and I, Garrison. And, of course,

Carlene. She's quite strong, wouldn't you agree?"

"Oh, yes. No matter what name she's using."

"I beg your pardon?"

"Carlene Elliot, Ellen Carson..."

For a moment, Conrad looked dumbfounded. He brightened and said, "Oh, yes, of course. She must have told you about the false name she used when she was a student, working in Africa. The family had, uh, been concerned about her safety, so there was a temporary identity."

"Oh, yessir, of course. I forgot she mentioned it."

Conrad sighed. "You really should pay more attention, Garrison. You're not much better than that clown Father hired before. Pathetic little fellow would wander around for a while, asking inane questions, clip the old man for a few thousand dollars and go back under whatever rock he came from."

* * *

Andi pretended to ignore a harsh glare from Conrad's well-groomed assistant, a woman in her mid-forties wearing a conservative tailored suit and shoes that looked Italian. After a light knock, the massive door swung wide to the right and the assistant instructed her to enter.

Andi smiled sweetly at an expression suggesting a homeless person had just wandered into an upscale restaurant. "Thanks, miss. You can go back to whatever you were doing."

At the opposite end of the room, Clay stood. Conrad did not, but his eyes tracked every step she made to the point where Clay invited her to take the empty chair next to his.

"Hi, Conrad. Nice to see you again."

"Likewise, miss... I'm sorry, I've forgotten your name."

"Delvento. It's Italian. It means 'of the wind.' Isn't that cool?"

In a tone of boredom, he replied, "I'm sure it does. Thank you for clarifying."

Clay shifted gears, going folksy. "Mister Spence — say, can I call you Conrad? — was just reminding me that Ellen Carson was the name Carlene used when she was a student, doing nursing work in Africa."

She flipped her hair, hoping it fell the same as in the photograph of Kimberly. "*Really?* Clay, you're confused again. Ellen Carson was the name of that nurse at the clinic, the one who signed the chart the night Kimberly died." She turned to Conrad, who had shifted in his chair. "You remember, right?"

Conrad waved a hand to gesture ignorance and said to Clay, "Look, Garrison, you've made a good game of it, causing a great deal of excitement and interest. But you know and I know that all the innuendo and whispers after all these years will remain, well, simply conjecture. You won't find any evidence to support these wild rumors."

But his eyes kept shifting back to her, and she replied with a serene smile, her head slightly cocked to the right, and an unflinching gaze.

Conrad shifted his weight again and sat forward. "But, as I said, not only are you in a hopeless position on finding any hint of, um, impropriety —" He again looked at Andi, wetting his lower lip with the tip of his tongue. "— and then, uh, you're also, well, time. I mean, *out of time.*"

Andi widened her smile. "Aw, Conrad, do you mean that deadline, the twenty-five year thing, the one where Kim's estate gets divvied up by all you guys, the billions and billions of dollars? You'd screw your own father like that?"

On Conrad's forehead, tiny beads of perspiration formed and his index finger tugged his collar away from his neck. He took a deep breath. "Miss... whatever your name is..."

Andi leaned forward. "Delvento. *Andrea Delvento.* Gosh, Conrad, are you all right? You look a little distracted."

Conrad moistened his lips again and looked away, first at his hands, then at Clay. "Look, Mister Garrison, I applaud your efforts. I'm willing to make it very much your worthwhile... that is, I'm willing to make it very worthwhile for you and Miss..."

She chirped, "Delvento. *Italian,* Conrad. Think Italian."

"Yes, Miss Delvento to drop this entire matter, sign a simple non-disclosure agreement."

Clay nodded. "How worthwhile, Conrad?"

"Let's say, what, ten million. Cash, wired to a bank of your choice. Offshore if you wish."

Clay continued to share a thoughtful expression. "That's awfully kind of you, Conrad. Worth thinking about, for sure. But you know what? Andi and I just wanted careers in law enforcement."

Conrad gasped his way through a laugh. "Cops. I could make you millionaires, and you just want to be cops."

Clay said, "Well, detectives, actually. I know, I know, we've got to put in our street time first, study hard for the exams, earn the grade. I come from a blue collar background, Conrad. Gotta earn it, buddy."

Conrad continued to take peeks toward Andi, averting his eyes every time she caught him and smiled. "I... I just don't understand."

Andi leaned forward, folded her hands on his desk and lowered her voice to intense softness. "It's really simple, Conrad. A lot of police officers like seeing a killer go to jail, like, for life. But me? I take special delight in bagging scumbags who rape their sister and then have her killed to cover it up."

Conrad jumped to his feet, his expression ice cold. "This conversation is over, Garrison. You get nothing, zero, zip. Get out of my office." He nodded toward Andi. "And take her with you. Neither of you have any idea how I can make life difficult for you."

While Clay stood and straightened his tie, Andi leaned back in her chair and tapped her fingers on the arm, staring at Conrad until she had enough, cocked an eyebrow and got up.

Clay grinned and went for a flippant tone. "Well now, Conrad, Andi and I sort of doubt that. But, hey, you're certainly welcome to try."

Chapter Thirty-Three

Close to him, Andi leaned on the yacht railing, soaking in sun-shine, gazing across a field of blue Caribbean, toward the horizon. Her hair billowed in a gentle breeze. The business meeting, chaired by Gideon's lawyer, Felix Underwood, was sixty feet be-hind them, out of earshot.

"You know what, Clay? The one thing I can never really get over is how quiet it is. I mean, you sometimes hear the breeze in your ears, but mostly it's just this endless space of quiet."

"I like your hair, back to the way you usually did it."

She turned to pour a warm smile all over him, like a refresh-ing shower to wash away sweat and dirt of labor.

"I sort of had to. I didn't want to freak out poor Gideon, give the guy a heart attack or a stroke or something. Then we wouldn't get paid." Her eyes twinkled. "Of course, I lie. But thank you any-way. It means a lot to me."

"You did great. Freaking out Conrad, I mean."

She returned to the view, her forearms resting on the gun-wale, hands folded together, her profile proud and enchanting. "Thanks for that, too. I so needed it, maybe as much as you."

"Yeah. It was good. First class partner work, as far as I'm con-cerned."

"Not many interrogation teams could have done it better, I bet."

He chuckled. "Yeah, like games where you're in the zone, you and your best receivers, and the ball is like on a wire, *zing*. Hard to understand, I guess."

She smiled. "Not really. Times like that are sweet, when it really clicks."

"We did good."

"You sound surprised."

Echoing her posture with the railing, he said, "Well, that first day, in the restaurant, with Gideon, it looked a little, you know, shaky."

She wore an expression of mock astonishment. "It did? Really? I sure didn't think so. Nah. I had every confidence that you'd shape up, pull your weight, get the job done. And you see? It all worked out."

A surge of heat in his cheeks and forehead came from more than the midday sunshine. A hat wouldn't have made any difference masking the embarrassment of how easily she could get to him. "So here we are, on the outside again. You know that expression, 'a boatload of lawyers'?"

"Yep. And, of course, Gideon has to be world class. Gideon, the twins — looking like deer in headlights — and what, eight, ten guys in suits?"

"Nine. Does it bother you?"

"The hapless twins or being on the outside?"

He rubbed his jaw. "Either. Both. Whatever."

She sighed. "Oh, I don't know. I guess... Yeah, a little. I was feeling... Well, with Casey, sort of like a big sister, which is silly because we're about the same age. But with Allison... Okay, don't laugh, promise?"

"Promise."

"Almost maternal. I mean, they're the same in so many ways, but I got the sense that while she didn't get herself into a fix like Casey sometimes did, she was just one of those young people who have already figured out there's not a lot of hope. So they plod along, head down, stay out of trouble."

He nodded. "Maybe. I can't imagine learning you've got a sibling — a twin to boot — about to be rich beyond anyone's wildest dream, and stumbling into a family disaster like the Pikes, all at the same time. Not sure I'd want to know. Safety in obscurity, all that."

* * *

Clay was probably right. It had to be an overwhelming barrage of impossible information, lives spinning out of control toward unknown directions. It would have been nice to sit with the twins, to help out, keep the guys in suits — and Gideon, the smooth-talking Gideon — at bay. Running interference. Yet, not her place. Today, it wasn't serve-and-protect. They were the hired help, and she had to let go. Glancing over her shoulder, she said. "They've been meeting for a very long time."

"I could find somebody, get some food or something."

"No. It's okay."

A steward approached, his steps tentative as he neared conversation among the boss's guests.

She turned to Clay. "Do you do wands or spells or something?"

He grinned, that cute puppy-dog look with the dimples and twinkle in his eye. "I'm a magical guy."

"That you are, partner. Yeah, that you are." She spoke to the steward. "Hi. Can we get a couple of sandwiches or something?"

"Yes ma'am. And perhaps a beverage?"

"Hm. I know. How about one of those pretty drinks with ice and a little umbrella? Doesn't matter what."

Clay displayed two fingers. As the steward turned to depart, he called out. "Oh, hey, the meeting. Are they still..."

"Yessir. They're having lunch just now."

Mer must have felt this way every time she'd show a property and then have to step aside to let the buyers discuss the showing between themselves. Involved, important. But just the hired help.

She told the steward, "Okay," and watched him cross the deck at an unhurried, kind of indifferent, pace and disappeared into the second deck of the yacht. "Clay?"

"Yeah?"

"It's not enough."

He shook his head, his smile looking rueful but accepting. "It's what it is. We did our job, which was to verify the twins existed and then to find them. We fulfilled our contract."

"And what comes next?"

He shrugged. "We get paid, move on. Hey, if you like the peace and quiet, we could maybe..." He looked around. "I guess we're somewhere in the southern Bahamas..."

"It's not enough. In fact, I'd bet our pay wouldn't be enough for the real estate, either."

He pursed his lips and his jaw tightened, ever so slightly. Probably wondering where he'd go next, which is what she'd been thinking all morning anyway. *Done. Dismissed. Hired help.* He took a deep breath. "It's all we're going to get, Andi. We're not law enforcement. Conrad was right. There's no way we can prove anything more than we already have. There's going to be a court fight between Gideon, his kids and a whole bunch of big league lawyers, to settle things."

"A boatload."

"You got that right. I'm sorry. That's the way it is."

She exhaled. "It's not enough."

The steward arrived with a tray of little sandwiches and two reddish-pink drinks in sweating glasses. Pale green umbrellas. Yellow straws. Kind of like a gratuity. A scrap of meat that comes with a pat on the head by a pleased master.

"I don't disagree, Andi, but —"

The sandwich featured some sort of fried fish, tomato, lettuce, mayonnaise. He probably thought it needed a dash of pepper or cayenne, but this time he didn't comment. "We missed something. We overlooked a crucial piece of evidence somewhere. We didn't put it together properly."

"We got the job done, Andi. Game over. Our team did good. C'mon. This is private investigator stuff. You do the work, you get paid. Justice isn't part of the contract. Trust me. I've seen it happen."

"Your dad?"

He sighed and took a hefty bite of sandwich.

She paused. "I want another run at it. We missed something."

"There's no time. They've got to get all this sorted out in, what, less than a week —"

She returned the half-eaten sandwich to her plate. "Then we have a few more days. Clay, I still say it's not enough." She looked up. "Are you with me on this?"

He paused, his sandwich frozen a foot from his mouth, his expression one of astonishment at a stupid question. "Yes, of course."

* * *

Clay found Emily Wade seated at the second booth from the end of the line, changing specials pages on a stack of menus, the thick plastic kind with stitched vinyl edges.

He slid onto the bench opposite her. "Can I give you a hand? My dad owned a restaurant and I used to earn pocket money setting up specials for the off days."

"Then you know how much fun this is. You sure, Mister Garrison?"

"Yes ma'am. And it's *Clay*."

"Sorry I was so short with you last time, Clay."

"It's okay. Hard days happen."

"How's Allison?"

Clay took a third of the unfinished stack and started pulling a sheet promoting pork and turkey platters. "Doing well. Connecting with Casey. Met her grandfather yesterday, along with a whole pack lawyers."

"Allison hates all that legal stuff. She's an animal person. I can take cats and dogs or leave them alone, but she always wanted to be a large animal vet. Never worked out, though."

He passed the empties to the stack she had started. "Why was that? She seems bright, dedicated."

"College is just so expensive. And with the diner and all, it just didn't work out."

Clay nodded and continued to pull sheets from folders. "Well, she might get a second chance. She's probably going to come into a lot of money. The DNA tests came back, proved she and Casey are siblings, that they had the same mother. An heiress to a fortune."

Emily nodded but kept her eyes on the work. "That's good. The restaurant business *is* tough. But I guess you'd know that."

"Oh, for sure. My dad went bankrupt, lost it all. He'd built a little place into an upscale steakhouse, but times change."

"Jacob and I nearly lost this place, too, a long time ago. But we, uh... We..." Her voice trailed off, fading into a sad memory, revived. She pulled herself together. "We did what we needed, to survive, to provide for Allison."

Clay placed the last of the empties on the stack, set old sheets to the side and pulled replacements toward him. "You know, the other day when we were in here, I asked you if Marilyn might have left a note, a message, anything, and you said 'no'."

"That's right. No sense in dredging up bad stuff from the past." She paused to take a closer look at the new sheets. "Aw, man... They spelled 'barbecue' wrong." She growled a pair of expletives and looked around as if the printer was still within cursing earshot. But evidently wasn't.

"That's too bad. Should I stop inserting the new sheet?"

"No. Go on. Nobody around these parts'll notice anyway."

Clay continued the task. "We were just following up on a couple of details, you see, and I wanted to double check."

"What kind of details?"

"The lawyers told me to say 'just routine' verification. But I got the sense that while the DNA tests were pretty good, it might not be enough. There's likely gonna be a big fight over the inheritance with the others — can you imagine rich people not wanting to share a few crumbs?" *As if a billion dollars was pocket change.* "I'd sure hate to see Allison lose out." He looked directly into her eyes. "Again."

Emily's jaw quivered and her eyes misted.

Clay kept his voice as soft and gentle as he could. "I'm guessing there's something that you didn't mention. Can you help me — *and Allison* — out here, Mrs. Wade?"

* * *

Andi found Willard Gentry in a metal storage building, halfway down a row of pallets stacked with immense white sacks. The printing on the side identified a popular brand of premium horse feed, a hundred pounds to the bag. Checking off items on paper affixed to a clipboard, he dismissed the helper as she approached.

"Well, hello, uh, Miss Delvento, wasn't it?"

Andi extended a hand. "Yessir. Nice to see you again. Busy day?"

Gentry waved his arm to identify the latest delivery. "Horses like to eat, and thoroughbreds eat a lot. Glad you found Casey. Nick of time, too. The circuit, it can get tough."

"Apparently. Thanks again for your help."

His eyes reviewed the delivery sheet and he tucked the pencil into his shirt pocket. "You're welcome. How's she doing?"

"Good. Met her natural grandfather and now there's just a whole army of lawyers. She's got to prove who she is."

Gentry chuckled. "I'll bet she don't much care for that. She never did like lawyers. C'mon, let me buy you a cup of coffee."

They strolled toward a sheet of white light at the end of the building.

Andi offhandedly said, "And, of course, she's getting to know her sister."

"Sister? I'll be..." He slowly shook his head. "Never knew of a sister."

She gestured at the supplies. "The overhead on a farm like this must be huge."

"Oh, yeah. It's a rich man's game on this level. Real players don't care much about bottom line. It's all about pride, winning, being the big dog. But it makes paychecks for fellas like myself, keeps us out of trouble. But the corporate types, that's another matter."

They reached the portal of the building and stepped to one side as a forklift truck, driven by the assistant, eased past and down the ramp. The impressions of truck tires lingered in the dirt, and she suspected a tractor trailer had unloaded within the past hour.

She shook her head in admiration. "I bet you've worked your way up to head honcho with a lot of work and dedication. What kind of trouble?"

"Yeah, trouble." Gentry smiled and his gaze turned to pastures and corrals. "And second chances. I used to be deep into gambling, long time ago. Got lucky. One of those second chances, a new life. I owe it all to the owners of this farm. But, you know, times change. They've got investors and committees running the show. There's been some talk they're gonna sell this place."

"That'd be a shame."

He shrugged. "Hopefully, someone will come along, step up, keep things the same." He paused to reflect on something. "So Casey's doing okay?"

"Yessir. They did some DNA testing and proved she and the other woman we located, Allison Wade, are in fact twins. Allison's a horse person, too. Works for a large animal vet. Second chances for both of them, I suppose."

"That's good. So how can I help you out today? I don't believe you're just here to let me know she's doing all right."

"Well, sir, as a matter of fact... Let me be right up front. There might be a catch. The other heirs are those same corporate types you probably encountered here. You know, kind of ruthless?"

He nodded. "That's a shame."

"Well, this is Casey's big chance, Mister Gentry. It sure would help if you could think again about whether Jeanne left any kind of a message, a note, a memento, something, anything that might help prove Casey's identity."

Gentry looked up, away, his jaw tensing as he bit his lower lip.

Andi waited for several seconds, stepped close and patted his shoulder, letting her hand linger on his arm. She lowered her voice. "Casey deserves a second chance, don't you think? Can you can help her, Willard?"

Chapter Thirty-Four

Uniformed officers and defendants in orange jumpsuits never saw this part of the courthouse. Clay studied the space. Half a dozen floors up from regular street crime. Plush. Wide, stone-tiled corridors, a lot of glass on one side and luxury paneling accented with brushed steel hardware on the other.

Next to him, Andi stared straight ahead, her jaw set firm. They shared a tufted bench, more like an oversized ottoman, probably quality leather intended to resemble vinyl, not the other way around. Probably intended more for decoration than comfort.

People in fifteen-hundred-dollar suits floated in little hushed packs, whispered exchanges blurred in echoes and overwhelmed by the clatter of four-hundred dollar shoes on some sort of marble.

He said, "Not a chair in sight. You'd think that for this crowd, there'd be some nice chairs. You okay?"

"Doesn't bother me a bit."

"We could go into the courtroom, get a good seat, maybe in the back?"

"Not interested."

"You sure, Andi? I mean, we've come all this way..."

She shrugged. "You can, if you want. I'm good right here."

"Well, okay, then. Let's get it started." He crossed his arms for a moment but it seemed silly. He relaxed and folded his hands in his lap while she reached into her bag for just a moment.

Straight across the hallway, an enormous clock formed a minimalist display on the wood. Hour hand, minute hand, a dozen round dots. To the right, a pair of doors, with a reserved black plaque, nearly illegible at this distance. Courtroom Four.

The minute hand had rolled past the second dot when Austin Hart showed, accompanied by a slightly shorter woman in a corporate pinstripe suit, mid-forties, graying hair in an efficient up style, looking very much like a no-nonsense attorney. Nothing casual this time for Austin. Dark gray suit, tight in the midsection. His stride forced the woman, lugging a thin briefcase, to scamper in shoes sounding like an uptempo drumbeat.

Andi stirred, as if she was going to wave. Austin ignored them today, stomped to the door, and conferred conferred in whispers for several seconds before the woman opened it for him and they entered the courtroom.

Baxter arrived five minutes later, just ahead of four guys, all of whom resembled the kind of lawyers a guy would hire to fend off a federal grand jury. And probably had.

Again Andi was about to wave. Baxter glared as he passed and looked away.

Clay said, "Wow. Chilly day."

She muttered, "Glad it's not just me. I was beginning to feel like a bowl of fetid potato salad at a church picnic."

"Terrible when people don't recognize quality investigative work."

* * *

The bench was uncomfortable beneath her, and her back muscles ached. Clay's offer for a seat, probably soft and cushionlike, even for the gallery, was tempting. But not today. Today, she'd stay on the bench.

Leonard Pike, who clearly had good taste in fashion, kept his

long pace in check adjacent to a dark wheelchair pushed by an attendant. Martha smiled and nodded to Andi, raising her arm to
direct their entourage, which included a florid man with a silver
mane and piercing eyes. He'd be the kind of lawyer she'd want if
she was ever in a jam. Most prosecutors would wither when he
stared at them. The attendant wheeled Martha to proximity and
Leonard extended a hand as Clay stood.

"So good to see you, Andrea. You look lovely today."

"Thank you, ma'am."

"It seems you've created quite a stir with the family. Good for
you."

Leonard nodded. "I'm sure Father will come up short in whatever charade he's presenting today, but I'm certain we'll all be
quite amused. Won't we, Mother?"

Martha smirked but gazed at Andi. "Amused? Oh, Leonard,
I'm certain of that. But never underestimate your father."

Leonard cleared his throat. "Yes. Well, we can't keep the judge
waiting now, can we. Are you joining us, Mister Garrison?"

"We'll see."

Leonard's smiled looked polite but anxious, and Clay sat
down as Martha's entourage departed for Courtroom Four.

Looking vaguely uncomfortable in the gray double-breasted
he wore on the day they met at the Storm Agency office, Gideon
Pike strode into view and marched to the bench. Clay rose with
her, but hopes to stretch evaporated when he grinned and motioned them to sit.

He spread his legs and stuffed fists into his waist. "You folks
doing all right? Of course you are. You've done great work, a fine
thing. I'd hoped to find you here. Not for moral support, o'course,
but just to say hello. I've already had my people wire you the
promised fee, and some extra for whatever lingering expenses you
might have. Yessir, a fine job, first rate. You've made an old man
very happy."

Oh, I just bet we have. Nothing like shoving your own chil-dren out of the corporate front office. She ordered up the most pleasant smile she could muster. "Thank you Mister Pike. It was a privilege to be of assistance."

Pike laughed and jabbed at Clay with an elbow. "You'd better hang on to this gal, Mister Garrison. She's first-rate, as good as I've seen. Knew it right off, o'course. The moment she kicked your butt on the sidewalk, out there in the rain. I may be a lot of things, Clay, but being a shrewd judge of character tops the list."

Clay's smile seemed as polite and phony as her own. "Thank you, sir. We're glad we were useful."

Pike reached into a jacket pocket and produced a card. "You keep this, son. Got my private number on it. Any day, any time of day. You need a little help, you just give me a call, okay?"

"Yessir." Clay tucked the card into his shirt pocket without looking at it. "I'll do just that."

He returned his attention to her. "You know, it's been grand getting acquainted with the twins. They're strong, handsome women. Take after their grandfather, you see. Good bloodline. I'm grateful that you not only found them, but took them in, gave them a, well, sister and role model."

Andi chuckled. "I'm tempted to tease you by again asking 'How grateful, Gideon?' But I'll leave it at 'my pleasure, sir.'"

Gideon laughed, but then took a long look at her. "You know, some people might say that if you wore your hair just a little dif-ferently... Nah. Never mind. Just an old man talking."

"Yessir."

He began to turn away. "Well now, Andrea. I've got to head on in, watch the fireworks. The others'll be along directly. You join-ing us? Ought to be first-rate fun."

Which might or might not be true. Andi extended a hand, which he grasped and firmly shook. "We'll see, sir. In the mean-time, good luck. And take care."

* * *

The door had barely closed before a noisy entourage interrupted Clay's moment of reflection and stormed across the stone floor, indifferent to volume of speech. He didn't need to look to recognize Carlene Elliot and Conrad Spence, barking orders, making demands.

Half a dozen attorneys were in the swarm, affirming what the two declared, probably to keep their jobs. Conrad didn't seem as tall as Clay remembered, but still stood a head above Carlene. Both wore navy suits. All they needed was a chest full of ribbons and epaulets loaded with stars to look like every third-world tinpot dictator.

At the sight of Andi and Clay, Carlene slowed and the group obeyed. She stared, hard, back and forth between them for several eternal seconds.

"Gentlemen, give us a moment, won't you?"

Two of the lawyers, looking anxious, murmured something. The others had cold, harsh expressions, the kind defensive linemen loved to lay on the offensive unit just before the snap of the ball.

Carlene raised her voice but looked only at Andi. "I said, *give us a moment, won't you?*"

Everyone froze.

Carlene allowed a half second to pass. "That would be *now*, people."

The flock obediently slunk toward the door to huddle up. Carlene and Conrad stalked across the open space.

"Well, well, well, if it isn't little Miss Troublemaker and her pathetic assistant."

Andi responded with a pleasant smile. "Hey, Carlene. Nice to see you could make it to the hearing. I was worried you might be off doing a some nursing work somewhere. Was it under just the one false name, or were there others?"

"Don't get cute with me, young lady. I could make your life totally miserable. Do you realize how much trouble you've caused?"

Andi shrugged. "You know, Carlene, I never really put a ruler to it. Hey, Conrad, you behaving yourself today?"

Conrad stepped toward Clay. "Garrison, can't you keep this... this... this *bitch* on a leash?"

"No need to get nasty, sir. She's just doing her job. And she's a lot better at hers than you seem to be doing. I advise you to take a step back, mind your manners, calm down. Or I can find a bailiff or deputy to haul you out of here in handcuffs after I file a bunch of charges."

Conrad looked to his shoes and set his jaw, struggling for composure. Carlene began to speak, but he raised a hand to silence her and rubbed his nose with the back of it.

"Tempers are a bit frayed, Garrison. And I'm sure you can understand why. You've managed to annoy some very powerful people. The sort of people who can be a great help — or a great hindrance — to what might be, shall we say, long and successful careers."

Clay nodded. "I'm sure. Thanks for letting us know."

"You're quite welcome. Now, I have no idea what stunt you and Gideon are trying to pull but I want to reiterate that Carlene and I would be, well, quite grateful for any accommodation you might make. Ours is a structure of confidentiality, agreements respected, rewards freely shared. I'm sure you understand."

Andi kept her focus on Carlene, but said, "How grateful, Conrad?"

"A ten million-dollar offer is still on the table. We've got a talented legal team with us and could sign agreements right now if you'd like. It would spare the family a great deal of difficulty, Miss Delvento."

Andi smiled again. "I am *so* glad you remembered my name, Conrad."

Carlene patted her arm. "Your colleague is a wise young man, Andrea. We could be good friends, you know. I could introduce you to the right people..."

"In exchange for what, Carlene?"

"Why your silence, my dear. A wonderful thing, silence. I'm sure your energetic little investigation has led you to perhaps some materials, some conjecture, even some conclusions."

Andi crossed her arms and studied her shoes. "I see. Help me out, here, Carlene. About what, *exactly*?"

The most icy glare she'd ever seen caused a shudder to race up and down her spine and she hoped it didn't show.

Carlene waggled a bony finger under her nose, hissing, "Now you listen to me, young lady —"

Conrad interrupted. "Carlene..."

"Shut up, Conrad! She's got nothing. *Nothing.* She can't. We've made sure of that. She can't prove I killed Kimberly any more than she can prove you assaulted her."

Conrad winced and turned away to take a deep breath, the sound of which rushed like an ocean wave across the conversation.

Andi's gaze remained locked onto Carlene's face, contorted with fury. "I know you didn't kill Kimberly. Ellen Carson did."

Conrad's voice fell to a whisper. "Fifteen million dollars, Garrison. Twenty. Carlene's correct, you know. We're very cautious, very *helpful* people. There's just no way —"

Andi ignored him. "There's no statute of limitations on homicide, Carlene. Ellen Carson could be located at any time."

Conrad said, "Twenty-five, Garrison. It's a good deal, considering you've got nothing left in your bluff."

Clay grinned. "Sorry, Conrad. Gotta pass. Say, have you ever met Kimberly's twin daughters? Here they come now."

* * *

Eyes widened and jaws dropped and Andi used the moment to slip her hand into her bag and end the recording. Conrad and Carlene scurried away to their lawyers and vanished into the courtroom. A burst of sunshine after a passing thunderstorm, Casey Evans and Allison Wade looked polished and confident in matching tailored suits.

A portly man mopped his brow with a handkerchief and shoved shaggy gray hair straight back. He struggled to keep the pace in a suit as rumpled as it was when they last met at the insistence of his client, Gideon Pike. Poor Felix Underwood. Forever frazzled. But he'd explained the trust, and how just the proxy of Kimberly's estate would tip the balance and allow Pike to regain control.

Casey and Allison held hands while Andi admired their appearance. "Wow. Look at you guys. I'm really impressed."

Casey laughed. "Poor Felix has been running with us all week, desperately trying to keep his credit card from screaming until ours arrive."

Clay smiled. "Looks like you're fairly confident."

Allison giggled. "Oh, absolutely. I don't think I've spent as much on clothes in my entire life as in the past three days."

"Good for you."

Andi's delight bordered on overwhelming. "I'm just so excited for you. Ready for this?"

They both nodded, but Allison said, "I think Case is going to be better than I. I'm still, well, kinda nervous?"

Casey patted her shoulder. "You'll be fine. Win or lose, we've made a deal with Gideon." Pride swelled in her voice. "He's going to buy Douglas Farms, and we're going to run it. We're going to call it Kimberly Farms."

Clay said, "Great choice. So. Leaving the rodeo business?"

"No. If we're lucky today, I think we'll be getting involved in WPRA, clean soiled hay from all the stalls."

"Good plan."

"Yep." She turned to Andi. "And no matter what happens, I wanted to thank you from the bottom of my heart. You really made a difference, Andi. I'll always be grateful." She drew a breath. "Now. You *are* coming to the hearing, right?"

"We'll see."

Felix stepped in to marshal his charges toward whatever destiny lay beyond the doors to Courtroom Four. After a few steps, he paused and said, "Oh, and by the way, you folks did exactly the right thing with the sealed envelopes from Mister Gentry and Mrs. Wade. I got a ruling just this morning that they're still sealed, so whatever is inside will be admissible evidence at the hearing to rule on the identity of Miss Evans and Miss Wade."

Clay nodded. "Rules of evidence. We did our best to protect them."

"You did well. Who knows what we'll find, eh?"

Everyone exchanged glances.

Allison broke the silence. "They're from our mom, our real mom, aren't they?"

Andi said, "I hope so. The handwriting on the outside looked like the penmanship of a teenage girl, not a more mature woman. Hopefully, you'll find the answers you seek."

Clay glanced at the huge clock on the wall. "Hey, you better get going. You don't want to keep the judge waiting."

They lingered for a round of handshakes.

Casey said, "C'mon. Don't you want to see how it all plays out?"

Andi sighed. "You know what? You go ahead. I'm good, right here. With my partner."

Chapter Thirty-Five

Andi blew a wisp of stray hair from her face, prepared to tackle the last of the boxes on her desk. The best of the bunch. Personal things, mementos and baubles from years past.

Meredith leaned against the door frame. "I can't believe you kept that. All these years."

"Gosh, Mer, you make me sound antique." She fondled a small, cheap trophy. "So, okay, ten years maybe."

"Eleven. I remember when you won it. You were jumping up and down like it was from the Super Bowl or something."

"The first trophy I ever really won. I mean, there were all those things you got for just showing up, participating. This was an actual competition."

Mer sighed. "I remember. I didn't even place. I was so jealous."

"Really? You never said..."

"No. I never did. It was your moment. You deserved it, too."

Andi looked with fondness at her best friend, ever, the urge to share a hug overwhelming. Like the parting hugs she got from Allison and Casey, before they separated in the courthouse. Now the stuff from storage, from her Ohio apartment, had a new home.

Mer asked, "So... how come you guys decided to keep the business name? I thought Clay hated it."

Andi held a little stuffed bear aloft and Mer rolled her eyes. "We couldn't think of anything better. I didn't really care and Clay found it rather ironic."

Mer said, "Uh-huh. I also can't believe you didn't go into the hearing, not knowing what was in those envelopes. I'd have about died to see it happen."

Andi drew a coffee mug with a silly saying out of the box. From her mom, just before she and Mer went off to college, excited and optimistic. Like Casey and Allison — who weren't Casey Evans and Allison Wade after all, but Karen and Kathleen Spence.

"It wasn't that important. I knew the truth. When Willard Gentry took me to his office and unlocked his desk drawer, handed me the envelope, I knew."

"Amazing you didn't open it, right then. I would have."

"Most people would. I believe Gideon's people had a pretty solid case that Casey and Allison are Kimberly's daughters, just the DNA and the birth certificates and the photos alone. Afterward, Felix said the letter from Kimberly to her daughter came with a lock of her hair. In her handwriting. The judge didn't even order a DNA test, but they probably will if the others appeal."

"Willard could have destroyed it. Anytime."

Andi tugged a framed photograph of her parents from the box and place it in a prime spot. Time to discard the empty carton, move on. "Guilt does strange things. Jeanne, via the adoption agency, had been paid off, too. Fifty thousand for herself and fifty for the baby. Which she gave to Gentry on her way to wherever. She kept her end of the bargain."

Meredith nodded. "You want some coffee? I made fresh."

"No. I'm good." She dropped into her chair and swung back and forth. The space was marvelous. "You did great, finding these offices. I feel like a professional for the first time, ever."

"So Willard...?"

"He said he was up to his ears in gambling debts, said he planned to just borrow it and put it back later, but never did."

"Scumball."

"No, I don't think so. The guy wept when he admitted it, un-loading twenty-four years of guilt and shame. He cared for Casey as if she were his own, did pretty good job as a surrogate father, I think."

"Amazing. And Allison?"

Andi smiled and caressed a souvenir. "*That* was brilliant work by Clay."

* * *

Mitch watched as Clay dumped a fistful of pens and pencils into a souvenir mug, just an oversized coffee cup with the west-ern-style lettering bold and a little faded. *Garrison's Steaks and Chops, Best in Town.*

"So you're gonna stick around?"

"Unpacking a box here."

"Yeah, but it's a small box. A box that size could get lost in my desk drawer. But your new office looks good. Kind of Retro-Swedish-Barren. You need more clutter, bro. Nice mug. I remem-ber it."

Clay nodded. "As far as I know, all that's left of Big Bill's. Dad bought these when I was maybe eight, nine, some sort of promo-tion. He was always doing that sort of stuff, a natural-born hus-tler." He studied the mug, rubbing his thumb over the words. "Anyway, I never drank from it. After high school, I wondered why I even kept it. Works pretty good for pens and pencils."

"Hard to let go sometimes."

"Yeah, Mitch. It is."

"So. For real, you guys are sticking around? Meredith and I sort of wondered."

Clay parked the mug and straightened the half dozen personal items on his desk in an arrangement locked in his memory. "For a while, anyway. Andi says you guys need responsible people in charge, so, somebody's got to do it."

Mitch chuckled. "She said that, did she?"

"She's got a set, pal. Smack you right upside the head, if you get out of line."

"Yeah, like, that was a brassy thing to do, just sitting outside that courtroom. Very cool. Right out of those old detective movies, the rough and tough gumshoe who doesn't care about nothin'."

Clay looked up. "Times change, buddy. I mean, look at this suite of offices. An accountant or a lawyer would love it."

"True. And at least you got the room by the can, not me."

Clay chuckled. "Life's tough man. For some people."

"Yeah, like that jerk Conrad and snotty Carlene. Who's plan was that, anyway? I bet ten bucks it was Andi. Kind of thing she'd do."

"You'd lose, pal."

"No lie?"

"Yeah, but don't tell her that. We'd been pushing their buttons pretty good, but Andi was hot to make a run at them for a criminal case. Only we really didn't have any hard evidence, most the witnesses were dead or who-knows-where. So we thought if she pulled hard one more time..."

"With Carlene."

"Yep. Andi had been all kinds of polite and deferential to her all along, but about drove Conrad nuts in the last interview. So the plan was to let her get all kinds of snotty in the courthouse, hope for a break."

"Which Carlene was more than willing to do..."

"Yup."

"So it's a pretty good idea never to tick off Andi."

"Yup."

"I'll make a note of that, man. So, Allison Wade...?"

Clay tested his chair, trying a swing left and right to make sure he didn't crash into anything. Lots of space, no worries. "When I interviewed the alleged mother, Emily Wade, I saw an incredible amount of anger, like a terrible memory she didn't want to relive. Almost too much, after all these years. So I went back, just one-on-one, and we talked about the restaurant business and how Allison was doing."

Mitch had abandoned the door frame and eased into one of the new leather chairs on the other side of the desk. "And?"

"Apparently Marilyn Wade was paid hush money, just like all the others, a hundred thousand dollars. Half of which was supposed to go to Allison."

"The veterinarian-wannabe who could never get to college because she couldn't afford it."

"Yeah. Because Emily took the money to cover business debts. But she kept the letter, probably out of guilt, maybe hoping to make amends sometime. When she handed it to me, I guessed from the handwriting that it wasn't Marilyn, but maybe Kimberly."

"So you never opened it. Man, I know I would have."

"Evidence. It has to be protected all the way through the chain. Andi ran into the same situation with Willard Gentry. Pike's lawyers got it ruled admissible, and that's all the judge needed."

"Cool move. Well, at least Emily Wade did the right thing in the end."

Clay evaluated the arrangement on his desk. Nothing ever changed, maybe a good thing, maybe not. "Oh, I don't know. The last thing she asked was, because she'd coughed up the truth for Allison — well, actually Kathleen Spence — did I think Allison might share some of her new-found fortune?"

"Wow. Like that's gonna happen."

"Who knows?"

Mitch lifted his coffee cup. "Oh, hey, I originally came in here to ask if you wanted some coffee. Meredith made it."

"Meredith? You're putting me on."

"No, man. For real. And it's not half bad." He stood. "C'mon, Clay. You could make her day."

* * *

In the small, odd corner of the suite destined for use as storage for office supplies, Clay reached for a foam cup from a stack of six.

Andi approached. "Decided to take the plunge, did you?"

"Oh, hey. Mitch said I should. Get all your stuff unpacked okay?" Stuck together, the foam cups would need two hands to separate them.

"For starters. Here. Try this." She offered a man-sized white ceramic mug with a hefty handle. "And be nice."

Clay turned the mug in his hand. The dark blue words said, *"Storm Investigations / Delvento & Garrison."* He looked up, into her sparkling eyes.

She shrugged. "We voted for alphabetical order. You weren't there, so you lost. If you don't want to use it for coffee, it'll be good for pens and pencils, on your desk."

"No worries." He turned to the pot and tugged the handle, coffee flowing into the cup.

Meredith appeared from the reception area. "Ah, good, you're both here."

Clay took a sip, nodded, and said, "This is really a great cup of coffee, Meredith. Willing to share your secret?"

Mer laughed. "No, Clay, not ever. So, okay guys, a couple of messages. Felix Underwood says the police down there thank you for the recording you made of the conversation with Conrad and Carlene, but don't do it again in the courthouse or you could be arrested. Gideon Pike transferred your fee to your bank, along with some extra to cover incidental wrap-up expenses — can you believe two hundred and fifty *thousand* dollars? — and thanks you again. Conrad is evidently out and Gideon has all the proxies except Leonard."

Andi shook her head. "Poor Leonard."

Meredith shuffled pink slips of paper. "The Spence twins invited you to a bash at Kimberly Farms. It seems Willard Gentry is going to be the new general manager, they're formalizing the name, that kind of thing."

Clay nodded. "Nice. But we should probably pass."

Andi stepped toward the coffee urn for a refill. Clay blocked her path, his arm extended. When he pulled it back, it held a small gift-wrapped package.

"What's this?"

"Something to open."

She tore away the ribbon and shiny paper, opened the box and withdrew an oversized white mug. Lettering on the side said, *"Storm Investigations / Garrison & Delvento."*

Her eyebrows rose. "Really?"

He shrugged. "Yeah, well, when we bought it, we voted to organize it by age over beauty."

"October fifteenth."

"September third. You lost. Get over it."

Meredith rolled her eyes. "I hate to interrupt, but there's a woman in reception..." She paused to decipher her own scribble. "Um, a Mrs. Noreen Hammond. She says she was referred by Gideon, some sort of matter to discuss."

Andi caressed the mug and smiled at Clay. "Well, okay, then."

THE END